Shifted War
By A. M. Simmons

P. O. Box 4043
Apache Junction, AZ 85178

ISBN: (Paper Back): 979-8-218-66850-1

Library of Congress Control Number: 2025908207

Front cover image by Ariel Marie Simmons
Book Design by Ariel Marie Simmons
Edited by Lauren Wise at Midnight Publishing LLC

If you are unwilling to defend your right to your own lives,
then you are merely like mice trying to argue with owls.
You think their ways are wrong. They think you are dinner.

—Terry Goodkind

Prologue

Nadi could feel the wind tearing at his clothes as he fell through the air. His heart raced as he looked at the golden sandy desert below. In the distance was the caravan of the Púca, his tribe. Their tents dotted the flat areas between the mounds of sand. The afternoon sun was beating down upon the dunes, causing the wind that hit him to feel searing hot. His turban unraveled in his quick descent toward the ground.

Above him came a fierce roar that cut through the air, reverberating in his chest. A smile broke across his face as he rolled to see the golden dragon watching him, blocking the sun. His brother, Zec, was on the dragon's back, dressed in the most delicate blue robes their mother could find. He was shouting something, pointing to Nadi's flowing white turban—but Nadi couldn't hear with the wind roaring in his ears. He knew it was something like, "Mother said not to get that dirty!"

Breathing a frustrated sigh, Nadi looked to the silence in his mind. The world became dark as he found himself in the familiar black sands. Looking to the sky in his inner world, he watched the stars and searched for the right constellation; Nadi needed the feathered wings of a burrowing owl. Those wings would help him to fly, and claws to hold the fabric. He made his trade, finding where the stars perfectly aligned into that form. His body shifted, the tan skin on his arms tingling as feathers grew. With his feet shrinking in his boots, he changed to have four clawed talons instead of five toes.

This form came from an owl, a companion for a traveling group of adventurers. The owl had been quite friendly and seemed to like head scratches. He was used with a druid to be their eyes as they searched for food, water, or dangerous paths to avoid. The druid didn't need to have a deep connection to animals that shapeshifters needed. Nadi's ability relied solely on the animals' trust, while a druid could use magic to tame, speak with, and transform. That stranger had taught Nadi how to gain the owl's trust by giving him a lizard. He told Nadi that to gain the confidence of any animal, all he needed to do was feed them.

Opening his blue eyes, he stretched out his brown feathered wings, catching the eddying breeze that lifted him. Nadi watched as his clothes tumbled toward the ground. The white turban was rolling through the air as it fell past him, the wind shifting toward where his parents stood. They spoke with Daron, one of the two Dragon Kings of the Quintania Mountains, the mountains separating the Gamada Desert from the ocean.

The dragons' keep, carved into the mountainside, was a massive structure that loomed over the desert.

Whitestone steps rose out of the sand to the entrance. Marble dragons stood guard at the top of the stairs and peered over the dunes. Behind them, large columns lined the wall, giving it a more civilized look.

With his blonde hair and golden-yellow eyes, Daron looked up at Nadi but kept his conversation going. The dragons in this land were similar to the shifters because they also had a human form. Still, they showed signs of being far more than mere mortals with their golden-yellow scales on their hands and around their eyes. Their pupils were slitted, giving their appearance a fiercely wild nature. Unlike the tan skin of the shapeshifters, theirs was a pale white.

With the turban tumbling closer to the ground, Nadi pulled in his wings and dove toward it. At the last second, he flung them open again and outstretched his taloned feet, snatching the white cloth from the air. Pulling up, he soared closer to his parents as his boots fell and hit the steps of the dragons' keep behind him. He glided behind his mother as she turned to see what had hit the ground.

"Your eldest son would make a great hunter," Dragon King Daron smiled as Nadi landed on his mother's shoulder, startling her. There were several kinds of dragons around the world. He knew of the four among the desert and heard stories of wild ones who rampaged and destroyed villages. Tiny ones could find their way into anyone's home, and ancient ones roamed the forests.

Still, his favorites were in this keep.

Spinning her head around to meet his gaze, his mother glared, eyes flashing red with her distaste for him being so careless with his clothing. Just as quickly, they settled into the light blue of her pride she could not hide. She tried to be angry, but her eyes gave her away. The eyes of a shapeshifter were what separated them from humans, giving away their emotions. They changed their mood, just like some jewelry changed color with heat.

His mother's dark brown hair was tied back in a long braid with a few strands had fallen loose, clinging to her sweat-dampened forehead. She tucked those behind her ear. "Get dressed before you embarrass your father."

Nadi jumped off his mother's shoulder and landed behind her. Switching back to his human form, he grabbed his clothes and rushed inside. Gems studded the ceiling and created a scene of four dragons fighting over the desert. In the center, a cluster of glowing stones hung down, lighting the hall. The walls held carvings of dragons in white stone. A dais sat at one end of the room with a golden throne planted upon it, and guards lined the entrances to hallways and entryways. To the right was a white-clothed table holding an abundance of food.

Nadi rushed for the table, going under to hide from prying eyes. A few of the guards laughed at his technique to stay hidden. Getting dressed, he heard his parents enter the main entrance hall.

"So our route is settled as it is every year," his father's rough voice echoed off the stone walls. "The migration time will soon be upon us, giving us a few extra days here."

"Sova," Daron's voice was filled with amusement. "Are you saying that you and Modra will take up my offer —that you pass up every year—and agree to a festival to celebrate our alliance?"

"Daron, I will never understand why you like these human festivities." Nadi peeked out from the side of the tablecloth and saw his father shake his head. "We are animals, if not beasts. Yet, with these almost human negotiations, we both benefit."

Nadi finished slipping his boots on and saw his mother glance at him. Her eyes flashed a few colors, and he understood he needed to get over there. Rushing to his mother's side, he stood at attention.

"Even as dragons, we do the one thing we can as humans and negotiate. Promise safe passage to humans and other creatures on airships, so long as they do not seek to explore the mountains. We barter with the supply of unfertilized dragon eggs and scales. Man's coin for our trash, so we may buy land or bargain for our safety when we cross the ocean. We know how to be civilized and can attend galas or balls." He handed him a goblet of wine. "Sova, we don't have to be animals or beasts. We can be kings."

Sova stroked his beard, staring at the cup of red liquid. "Our people have lived as nomads for so long that maybe we can leave it up to them to decide if they want to live as humans. We are a growing group, and some may choose their way. As Chief, I should open up that possibility to my people and let them understand how the rest of the world works. The Púca tribe may yet thrive from this. We have those who will stay with our traditions, but maybe we can fit some change into our lives."

Daron turned to Nadi. "What about you, young one? What would you want to be?"

Nadi thought about it and smiled, "I want to be a dragon, like you and Uncle Grumloc." Even though they were not related, the dragons were the closest thing to actual uncles, and so Nadi was permitted to address them as such. It always made Daron happy to be called uncle.

His parents both looked at him, concerned. Daron knelt at eye level as an uncomfortable silence filled the room. "You remember the story of 'Elias, the Dragon'? The beauty of your kind is that you can be almost anything you want. Yet, as a dragon, I am too powerful. I can only be a dragon or a human, and even then, born as a twin, I have to be a human because my brother chooses to be a dragon. We can switch, but it becomes more challenging as we age. So I decided to remain a human so he could be a dragon.

"I would like it very much if you could be a dragon too, but I would miss seeing all the other things you can become. You see, once you become a dragon, you can never change into anything else." His eyes held sadness as his slitted pupils became rounded. "You can be a Pirate or a Prince, but I'll be your dragon of an uncle any day."

Nadi knew the tale of Elias all too well. The story was told to remind them their powers had limits. Elias was a shifter who got so greedy with his abilities that he tried to become a dragon. Once he succeeded, he soon realized he was stuck in that form forever. Legend says that shifters who were greedy enough to try the dragon form became wild, non-shifting dragons.

"Why can't you two be a dragon at the same time?" He was curious about what he might learn.

The Dragon King was silent momentarily as he tried to find the right words. "A long time ago, we did not have human forms. A creature of wishes came to us and granted us this human form in exchange for a truth we kept hidden."

Just as Nadi was about to ask another question, Daron held up a hand to silence him.

"All in due time." He continued. "Before that time, if a twin were born in the same egg, they would become the same dragon—that is where two-headed dragons come from. Since the wish had been granted, we have not had any more two-headed dragons. However, Grumloc and I can only share the same dragon form and are considered the same dragon."

"Oh," Nadi tried to picture it. "You would look funny with two heads."

Daron laughed. "That is true. I'm glad I do not have two heads." He turned his attention back to the chief, "We must talk about Vadnera, though. Recent changes on the mainland are causing intruders near the mountains. Their new king has established a slave trade, and humans are wandering here to enslave any creature they can get their hands on. Two attempted to take a young dragon on a flight, damaging her wing. I think your tribe should hire someone to guard your people while we discuss laws with this King Lucin." His eyes fell on Nadi again. "I also hear there is a Princess of Vadnera who is just a year shy of Nadi's age. She could make a good bride and help make bringing peace to our kinds easier."

"You know the Oldens are stuck in their traditions." The Oldens were the oldest people of the tribe who held tradition as law and fussed if anything was not being followed to their instructions. "They would refuse to let the Eldest son of the tribe wed a human for the sake of peace. The world could be burning, and they would still screech about how we must follow tradition. Though, I agree it would be an idea if we can't get things done with a simple discussion of laws." Turning his attention back to his son, his eyes flickered with a moment of recollection. "Oh— Daron," Sova reached into his robes and pulled out a folded-up black cloak peppered with intricate gold designs. "On the subject of Nadi, he completed his first trade today and was given this cloak for some wool, but it seems to be of far greater taste than I would have preferred for myself."

The Dragon King stood up and studied the material. "It looks fine, indeed. The gold designs match my scales perfectly." He threw it on. "Such a grand material; I love how it feels." He pulled the hood up over his smooth blond hair. "I have to bring this when I travel to Vadnera. The Queen would enjoy it."

Nadi's eyes trailed down the robe, and he looked at Daron's bare feet peeking out from under the cloak's edge. Then, his eyes traveled to the ground, and he noticed the white marble floor was not reflecting the room in certain places. As he studied it, he realized he was looking at a design with circles and strange writing emanating from around Daron; the Dragon King was right in the center of it. "Uncle Daron, what is that design?"

Daron looked at Nadi, then down at the floor, "Oh, this is a symbol of protection. A sorceress painted it upon the floor, stating my enemies will be shown to me should they ever step inside this circle." He gave a twirl as he smiled. Once his back was to them, Nadi noticed the changes. A shadow bubbled out of the cloak and quickly dispersed across the floor. The bare feet of the Dragon King were gone, replaced by boots. Daron had also gotten a little shorter.

His father let out a low growl just as a grey light bathed the room, and everything suddenly froze. The figure turned around slowly, revealing it was no longer Daron. A man stood in his place. Blonde curls poked out from under the hood, and the brown-eyed gaze of a man Nadi had never seen before met his eyes. Nadi tried to speak or move, but it seemed time had stopped.

A glowing grey orb was in one of the man's hands. Slowly, he approached Sova. Nadi tried to yell, scream, or even will himself to fight, but all he could do was stand there.

He watched in horror as the man took the cup from his father's hand and swirled the wine in the goblet before raising it to toast. "To the dark angels: May they forever rot and never return." He drank the wine, put the empty cup back in his Sova's hand, and returned to the room's center. Suddenly, he spun around, and the cloak hit the floor.

Time started again.

Nadi fell to his knees. He caught his breath and realized the man wanted them to see what he had done. The sounds of guards shuffling caused his attention to the room around them. All readied their spears and pointed them toward the circle's center; a few even raised their weapons at Nadi and his parents.

The symbol on the floor suddenly burst into flames, burning brightly, taking the cloak with it. The cup dropped from Sova's hand and clattered against the floor. "No," he uttered as he stared at the cloth burning on the ground. "What have I done?"

An angry roar echoed off the stone hall's great white pillars just then. King Grumloc—Daron's brother, the other Dragon King—landed outside the keep, Zec still on his back, and swept into the hall. His golden eyes glared at Nadi and his parents, now huddled together. Smoke billowed out of the edges of his mouth. "How dare you!" Grumloc's deep voice shook in Nadi's chest, deafening his ears.

Zec covered his head, tumbling down from Grumloc's back. Their mother stepped toward him, then stopped; Nadi knew she'd realized it was too dangerous to approach the Dragon King right now.

"How dare you enter our home and steal away our kind! We show you kindness and hospitality. You bring in magic and lies!" A growl shook the room as he opened his wings and circled the family within the hall.

Zec scrambled and hid behind a pillar. Their father stepped forward, and Grumloc roared again.

"Grumloc—please. We did not know the cloak held magic or that there were marks on the floor. I thought it a good gift," he pleaded as he held out his hands to him.

"SILENCE!" Nadi had to cover his ears again. "I cannot feel my brother's presence, nor can I shift. He is still alive, but you have committed treason against our kind. For that, there is only war. I will take your oldest since you have taken my elder brother!" Grumloc looked at Nadi and let loose a roaring fire.

Nadi knew there was no escape; he could not move fast enough to get out of the way. He closed his eyes and threw up his hands, trying to shield himself from the blast.

Fabric touched his fingers as he felt the heat of the flames reaching toward him on either side. He only heard the screams of his mother. Just as the fire ended, he looked up to see ashes fall to the floor. The only thing he recognized was the brown braid still burned.

In an instant, his mother was gone. He looked to his father, who fell to his knees as his sorrowful eyes held the orange of fear. Cupping a hand over his mouth, he turned away from the scene. When Nadi's gaze found Zec, he was met with a red-eyed stare. His brother pointed his finger at him. "This is all your fault!"

The room seemed to vanish, leaving them alone in the darkness. Nadi backed away from him. "No, I didn't do anything!"

"It's all your fault!" The words echoed through the now silent hall, sinking into his heart.

Chapter 1

Blinking away the tears, his eyes opened to the world around him. He was no longer in the dragons' keep or the darkness. Nadi was back in his tent ten years from that dreadful day. His heart raced; even though he was relieved to be awake, he hated the guilt the nightmare had left behind.

Rolling over, he wiped at his tear-stained face and ignored the light of day. His head still ached from the spirits he had drunk the night before. An angry rumbling in his stomach told him he would regret waking up this early. He wanted to drift back off to sleep, wishing to forget everything.

Unable to sleep, drenched in sweat, Nadi rose to greet the unfortunate day, even though his body protested. The memory of his childhood faded as he groggily sat up from the pile of blankets on the ground. Sunlight spilled in through the tent flap. The sound of the shuffling encampment outside told him it was past dawn. He knew he was late.

Nadi tried to remember last night to no avail; the events seemed lost in the fog that clouded his mind. He looked around; his tent was barren except for a chest, a waterskin, and a rug under the blankets.

He grabbed the drink next to the makeshift bed, took a swig, and coughed. Nadi grimaced, realizing it was the ale he had stolen from passing traders. If his thieving hands weren't careful, it could spell trouble for the camp, but forgetting about life was his main priority. He didn't want to think about the past—how they left without his mother and fled—or the look on his brother's face as he blamed Nadi for what transpired.

Since her death, Nadi has resorted to stealing anything that was not tied down. It didn't matter who he stole from, either. People in their tribe often approached him when items went missing, and most would discover it was somewhere in his tent. Usually, traders were his victims. Bags on camels or pouches hung at the waist were what he was interested in. He wanted to find any magical item that would help him forget, but ale was what he had to settle for.

The tent flap opened, and his father stepped in. Sova wore his usual chieftain robes and turban, his brown hair now threaded with shades of gray. Nadi tried not to look him in the eye because he knew those eyes would be red.

"You were supposed to rise with the dawn!" He sniffed around the tent and then covered his nose. "Have you been trading for spirits again? You know we do not need that stuff in our tribe."

Nadi went to retrieve his stolen goods for another drink, but his father snatched it from him and poured the remaining liquid onto the rug. Nadi hung his head, realizing he had nothing to keep him preoccupied.

"This is the last chance! Your fate hangs by a thread, and you want to sit around and be a drunkard. The rules you break are serious, and with that, you face exile. Your brother will take his coming-of-age trial today, and you will escort him! Upon returning, you can wander the desert for eternity if anything is off about him!" His father pulled a set of gray traveling clothes from his robes and threw them at Nadi. "Get washed up and meet us at the east side of the camp. I assure you the food stores will be heavily guarded—so don't try to talk him into cheating his way out of this!"

This late in the day, Nadi didn't want to remember he had failed the trial by hiding in the food stores as a mouse until it was his time to return. His father knew because everyone who left usually returned darker from spending more time in the sun. Nadi, however, looked almost a shade lighter, if possible, from spending a month hiding inside. Less food was needed to sustain him, but it took him a while to stop trying to clean his whiskers after returning to his human form.

Seeing Nadi still sitting on the floor, his father grabbed the water bucket beside the tent flap and poured it over him. It was warm from the desert heat and not as cold as he would have liked. His father's rage had also soaked his traveling clothes. "Get up!" he yelled as he turned and stormed out of the tent.

It had grown quiet outside. Tent walls were so thin Nadi knew whoever was nearby had heard everything. He waited until everyone started moving again before getting into the wet clothes. There were perks to wearing damp clothing in the desert, such as keeping the body cool in the heat, even if it was short-lived, since the heat dries it fast. Yet, sand also tends to stick to wet surfaces, and if you think it only stays on while wet, you're wrong. Sand sticks to anything moist and stays long after it has dried, yet another layer when you're already sweating from the heat of the unforgiving sun. Pray your body never touches the sand when drenched in sweat.

Nadi stepped out of the tent and into the blistering heat. He shielded his eyes from the sun and found it was almost noon, the worst possible time to start a journey into the desert. He walked toward the east side of the camp, regretting the ale he drank for breakfast. Nadi grabbed a loaf of bread from a passing child.

"Hey, that was mine!" The boy cried out.

"Just go get another," Nadi mumbled as he bit into the loaf.

With the dragons running loose, Nadi knew food was scarce, but he wasted enough time and couldn't get his supplies in order. They had potted crops and ovens built from mud. Water was not much of a problem since an inventor had given them a gadget that could pull water from the air with a mesh material. The man had claimed it was not magic but science. Most of them were not convinced and chose other methods to retrieve water. Digging holes, using wells, and filling barrels at the oasis were all ways they found water.

Shapeshifters did not like the use of magic. Only the chief, his father, was permitted to use magic, but it was minimal compared to the sorcerers, wizards, and mages who traversed the desert searching for the creature of wishes. It was a legend linked to the disappearance of the other three dragon races of the desert. The black dragons gave up their physical forms to be shadows, while the red dragons wished to be the strongest and grew too large for their home. The gold dragons wanted a human form and traded their secret for it, while the silver dragon king had everything he desired and refused to part with anything to get the one thing he needed—an heir. The creature of wishes was cast out only to return and visit the queen, who traded her coveted fertile egg to free her people from his tyranny. They all vanished after she realized her trade was worthless. It was one of his mother's favorite stories.

Different from the story, their people were vanishing due to the gold dragons, and there were fewer travelers to trade with. Quite a few considered making a corner of the desert their permanent home. There was talk of taking over one of the abandoned dragons' keeps. On the other hand, the gold dragons went out of their way to locate traveling shifters and execute them by flame. Fewer and fewer travelers came to the desert for fear of being mistaken for a shifter. But shifters didn't need mounts since they could change shape. Eventually, it was learned the dragons don't seem to attack humans with camels or mounts. Some traders still risked the desert to barter with them, but less than usual. Almost ten years into a one-sided war, the shifter caravan was less than half the size it used to be.

Pushing the last of the bread into his mouth, Nadi thought about the fact there were no graves for their fallen. Their corpses did not litter the desert. Specific graves were like landmarks for the tribe to follow along their path. All the dragons left were ashes upon the dunes.

Nadi had just arrived at the east side of the camp to see his brother glaring at him. Since the incident at the keep, Zec had looked at him that way. Nadi thought he would look at himself like that if he could. It was his fault their mother died. Zec blamed him and would pass before letting Nadi forget that. Neither of them was pleased with having to spend the next month alone together in the desert. If Nadi had an option to go into exile right now, he would. But their father stood in the way of that, bending the rules as far as he could to keep his sons around. Zec would probably tell him to leave when they got out of sight.

His father motioned for them to stand next to each other. "We send you out into the world to learn from your animal forms and survive with them just as they survive in the wild. May you learn how they live, gain strength in the smallest forms, and understand the potential of all you can do." His father wrapped a collar around his neck, just as a caravan Olden, Edna, did the same to Zec. Together, may you both survive this trial."

As he pulled away, Nadi noticed a red cord linking the collars. A smile crossed his face as he realized he could remove it after they left, and he almost laughed because his father thought a leash would keep them tethered.

Seeing the smile on his face, Sova began to laugh. "Did you think it's going to be that easy? Go on—try to remove it."

Nadi reached up for the clasp at the back of his neck. To his dismay, it was no longer there. Understanding he could not escape, his smile vanished. His father had thought of every route Nadi would have taken to cheat his way out of this.

"These collars are designed to keep you two together but will not stop you from changing forms. They are used in the slave trades in other countries and came in with the last trades we did. Since you were more focused on stealing ale, you failed to see when it passed into my hands. Cutting the cord will not change anything since it will only reconnect." He stared at Nadi in amusement. "I'll see you both in a month."

Nadi looked at Zec, who was glaring at him with even more anger than earlier. "Your face will get stuck like that if you keep giving me the evil eye," he said.

Zec turned away, picked up his pack, and started into the desert, yanking Nadi along. Mother used to say, "If you don't have anything nice to say, don't say anything at all." It seemed Zec lived by those words. He rarely spoke to anyone, but realistically, Nadi didn't think highly of anyone either. The ones who have survived hid in their tents or spent most of their time as animals. One of the villagers spent all his time as a goat, which made everyone uncomfortable.

Looking back, Nadi saw the village was getting farther away. He faced forward and stared at the back of his brother's head. Zec went on in silence through the sand, not once turning back. While Nadi chose to face the desert barefoot, his brother was wearing sandals. It was odd for a shapeshifter to put on any form of footwear unless they met with other caravans or formal greetings with village heads. But they didn't have formal meetings anymore.

"Those sandals look nice." Nadi tried to break the silence.

Zec just glanced over his shoulder and kept walking. Nadi noticed his eyes were always red when he looked at him. It is hard to hide your emotions when your eyes tune to your mood, but Zec's thoughts were more challenging to read because his eyes rarely changed.

He tried to think of a time when they were a different color and thought back to the joyful expression

Zec wore while on Grumloc's back. Images of the disaster flooded his mind, making him wish to drown it with ale or spirits. He wouldn't care if dwarves didn't make it.

Looking back one last time, Nadi could no longer see the tents. Lost to the sands, just like their footprints would be once the wind picked up. He studied the waving lines of dunes' sand. Travelers often compared it to the sea, but Nadi wouldn't know—he'd never even glimpsed a lake. They saw ponds at the oasis, but travelers insisted those were puddles compared to the ones from their homelands. Nadi wondered how the ocean would be.

In the distance, he spotted a camel on a dune. Nadi forgot even the essentials, but he could hope for ale or to steal meat when they were distracted. He began waving his arms and calling to the rider, "Hey! Do you want to trade?"

Zec spun around and reached for Nadi's hands, "What are you doing? We have slave collars on! They'll think we escaped. We could be captured and sold, you idiot!"

The rider looked in their direction and started coming off the dune. It was a single rider, which meant nothing but a traveler or a single trader. Nadi knew there was nothing to worry about; slave traders worked in packs. Shifters were on the list now that their numbers had dwindled, but changelings were worth more.

Traders had stories of places outside the desert where changelings could change into anything living, as long as it was of the highest population in the room, town, or city. Stick a changeling in a place with a harem; you get another beautiful woman of that room's most populated species. Wealthy lords enjoyed them since they could only bear children with another changeling.

On the other hand, if many changelings are confined together, they would look like a mass of shadows with red eyes. It's easier to tell how many are in the same room if cages separate them. The horrifying thought sent a chill up his spine.

The camel kicked up sand as it came to a halt, the rider eyeing their collars. "You have something to trade?" She said behind the cloth covering her face.

Zec's eyes widened as he stared at the rider. His gaze turned blue, and Nadi wondered what could have changed. He had been angry about everything until now, and his eyes showed contentment even though his expression showed shock.

Nadi shook his head and asked, "Do you have ale or spirits?"

She eyed them more closely. "Shifters who desire ale or spirits? I heard about it but never thought I would see it." Reaching down at her side, she rummaged through a tan sack on her camel. A moment later, she pulled out a brown glass bottle that portrayed a long-bearded dwarf with a hammer imprinted on it.

It was Nadi's turn to look shocked. Dwarven Onyx Ale was an expensive brand that travelers often mentioned but never seemed to have. One sip can put a man out for a day and a half, if not a week. The only problem was that Nadi had nothing to trade for it.

"You don't have anything to trade?" Her tone was disappointed.

"We have sandals," Nadi almost shouted. "We have clothes or—"

"Save it, shifter. You have one thing I might be interested in, which must wait until after dark. Where are you traveling to?"

Zec seemed to come back to reality, "What do you mean . . . after dark?"

She looked at him, and the blue in his eyes suddenly turned orange with fear. "I'm not normally a day person, but even with a bloodstone, the desert sun can be brutal."

"You don't normally see a vampire in the desert," Zec said in a shaky tone as he looked away. A smile tugged at the edge of his mouth.

Turning to her, Nadi could see the red in her eyes. Very few creatures have red eyes, vampires among them. Travelers mentioned the characteristic, but Nadi was unsure if a vampire's eyes were always red or if a particular emotion caused the color. He guessed she certainly would get along nicely with his brother.

"You don't normally see two shifters chained together like slaves." Her retort sounded amused.

Nadi laughed. "We're heading to an oasis. It takes about a day and a half to get there."

Behind him, he could feel Zec's eyes glaring at the back of his head. Nadi did not want to turn around but noticed the vampire was looking at his brother, her clothes covering everything but her eyes. Wrapped from head to toe in black fabric, Nadi wondered if she was hot in all those layers.

"Do you not approve?" she asked Zec.

"This is a journey we are supposed to take to ensure we can survive on our own, but one last day with a companion couldn't hurt," his brother said with a frustrated sigh.

Nadi nearly jumped for joy. Quickly, he switched forms into a fennec fox and leaped onto the vampire's lap. His clothes lay in the sand.

"Why should I carry your clothes?" Zec demanded.

Nadi happily chittered at him, but nothing he said could be understood. The line was just long enough for Zec to pick up his clothes at an awkward angle. Being tied together was going to take a lot of work.

For Nadi, there was no better place to nap than on the cold lap of a vampire. Even under the sun, she was ice cold to the touch. There was no point in being awake when ale was not an option.

When Nadi awoke, the sun was setting. Zec laughed at something the vampire had said. He shook himself awake and yawned. Jumping down, Nadi shifted back into his human form and stretched. Zec threw his clothes at him. Picking them up, he noticed that, for once, Zec's eyes were not red but blue. This woman had taken the anger out of him.

"We should set up camp here." She stopped the camel and looked back at Nadi, who had managed to pull his pants up. "The sun is almost down, and the desert will finally cool off. It's the best time to drink dwarven ale."

Nadi couldn't agree more. She dismounted, pulling a few logs off her camel and tossing them to the ground. A sack hit the sand, causing dust to rise. Zec grabbed the wood and started the fire.

Slipping his shirt back on, Nadi remembered they didn't introduce themselves. "Miss Vampire, do we get to know your name?"

She laughed as she unraveled her tent. "You slept through the introductions. My name is Terika. I decided to visit the desert after traveling through the land of Vadnera.

Coming from the main tower in Lu'Bela, I was tired of being around my kind. Too many vampires for my taste."

Nadi grabbed the other side of the tent. "Can't stand your kind?"

Terika shook her head. "There is no room to feed in a hall full of leeches. They lust for power, while I wish for knowledge. I want to explore the world, learn all I can, and ignore the constant battles to rule over all vampires. Who will drink the blood of the first? Who will be worthy?" She shook her head. None of that matters. The ancient one will never wake, but all fight to rule in his place."

"Ancient one?" Nadi grew curious; he'd never heard the term.

"The ancient one is the very first vampire. Forever he sleeps and lets his children roam the earth." She smoothed the tent flap. "It is said the ancient one lost his name to time. Legend says if he were ever to awaken, then humanity would perish. It makes no sense to me, though: why destroy what you feed upon?"

What a good question. Nadi would not destroy every animal he sees for food or pick every plant that could bear fruit. Why would someone choose to destroy all that they need to live?

"Thus, why I search for knowledge," her tone seemed happy. "I travel the desert and study the empty dragon keeps. It's a shame the silver keep cannot be found, and only the golden dragons of the desert are left."

"Are there dragons where you come from?" Nadi asked curiously.

"Several," she said, securing one side of the tent. "We mostly have wild dragons on the mainland. Forest, swamp, and water are quite common. They come in many shapes and sizes. One water dragon seems able to communicate with people at harbors in exchange for food."

Nadi was intrigued by the information but didn't want to bother her with any more questions, so he quietly went back to work.

Once they had set up the tent and started the fire, Zec pulled a cloth out of his shirt and unfolded it to reveal some dried meat pieces. Nadi snatched a bit and had it in his mouth before Zec could protest.

"Hey, you should have thought to bring your own!" His brother yelled at him.

The sound of a bottle being uncorked stopped Nadi in his tracks. He swallowed the meat and spun around to see the most beautiful thing he had ever laid eyes on. Dark amber liquid filled a small glass with the sound of a trickle. Terika held it out for him. It had been an entire day without any drink that he desired, but it felt like an eternity.

Without hesitating, Nadi grabbed the drink and brought it to his mouth. It was bitter and sweet at the same time. He swore he tasted a hint of honey and berries, but the flavor was gone too soon. Nadi returned the glass to ask for more but was suddenly moving backward. He hit the sand, causing a cloud of dust to rise. His mind imagined he was the tent from earlier, being unraveled and pushed, even though he wasn't moving. He heard Zec say something, but he couldn't make it out. Terika let out a laugh before the darkness took him.

Chapter 2

Zec stared at Nadi after he had hit the ground, a pinch of panic gripping him. "Will he be alright?" As much as he didn't feel sorry for him, he certainly didn't want to be dragging around a dead body.

Terika laughed. "He'll have a headache when he wakes up, but he should be fine."

Zec watched her hands as she removed the cloth from her face. Her plump pink lips and pale skin almost glowed in the light from the fire. Pulling back the hood of the garment, she revealed her dark brown hair piled in a loose bun. Zec didn't realize he was staring until their eyes met.

"Sorry," he looked away, embarrassed. "I've never told anyone about our relationship. Usually, most expect us to be with our kind." It also had to do with children—no one was sure what kind of children would be sired if certain races were mixed. He wasn't even sure if they could have children.

"I feel that is not why you were staring?" She mused.

Zec gained the courage to look at her again.

"Well…"

He hadn't seen her in almost a month as she chose to wander the desert, sending traders in their direction. His father had enlisted her to watch out for slave traders and ensure they did not find the caravan. Nadi had been left out of the loop and was usually too busy stealing to notice when their father would slip away with her to discuss any concerns that had arisen.

"Vampires are pretty by nature. They are designed to lure in prey and lull them into feeling secure. Then, when the prey least expect it, vampires strike with a killing blow. Like spiders to flies caught in the web sprinkled with dew. The promise of water only to see the truth of death once it's too late."

He shifted uncomfortably, unsure what to make of her darkened tone. "Is that how you see yourself?"

She met his gaze before poking at the fire, causing sparks to rise into the night air. "I often wonder if anyone truly loves someone for who they are and not by their looks. A mind full of knowledge should be worth more than a beautiful face."

"I stopped wanting girls to like me when I realized most of them only liked me because I am the chief's son. They want to lead the caravan but don't understand what it takes. Most expect my brother here to fail on his journey. I am not expecting to return alive from this. I started leading us towards the dragons' keep when he fell asleep."

"What do you want to come of this, Zec?" She scooted closer to him. "Do you not want us to be together? Or to return to me after this journey? Do you not want to tell your father we are in love and that you no longer wish to follow tradition?" Her eyes held concern. "Zec, I don't want this to end our story."

"I want to kill Grumloc for taking my mother's life," Zec burst out, letting her ice-cold hand touch his face. A sudden sadness filled him as he realized this might be the last time he sees her. "My father knew my plan; that's why he chained us together. The only problem is that I believe my brother should have died that day. There is no reason for him to live now other than to follow me in death."

Her face was so close to his. "Your brother is smart for one who worships a drink and steals. I doubt he will let you die or allow himself to be killed. He is very trusting and naive, but I bet he is quick on his feet when trouble arises."

Zec's curiosity was getting the better of him. He did not want to think about his brother or stay on that topic. Her face was so close to his. The wild red in her eyes, yet also so relaxed, seemed to pull him in more. He wondered how her lips would feel against his after being parted for so long. "We shouldn't be this close with Nadi around." He pulled away.

Terika laughed, exposing her fangs. "He is out cold." Their eyes met again. "I love you, and even though I seek payment for the drink, I also hope that if you live through the dragons' keep, we'll meet again." She undid one of his sandals and pulled it off his foot. "Promise me—if you live, you'll come looking for this other sandal."

"You're not taking both?" He laughed as she returned her hand to his face, dropping the sandal beside them.

"When people lose things, they usually search until they find it. I am lost and have been for many years. So, now your sandal will be lost with me. Maybe you can search and find us both." She pulled his face towards hers and kissed him with soft, icy lips.

Slowly, her mouth left kisses along his jawline, and she made it to his neck. There, she pushed the collar aside and kissed his throat. Zec didn't know if he wanted to push her away or keep going. He struggled to think clearly since he had grown to love her even more over the past few months.

Before he could protest, he felt a sharp pain in his neck as her fangs pierced the skin. The entire area became cold, and for a brief moment, he realized he was a fly trapped in the spider's web. His body went limp, and slowly, he lowered onto the sand. With hands clasped and fingers intertwined, Zec questioned whether he wanted to lose this.

Pulling away from his neck, he could see the blood on her lips, but what caught his attention was the tear that rolled off her cheek. "What's wrong?" he whispered.

She wiped it away. "Your life is a sorrowful story. From your blood come memories, and they show me everything. You have not changed into another form, ever. All this was because of the death of your mother. Do you honestly believe your kind will all perish?"

Zec looked away from her, staying silent. It's true; he had yet to find any form to take. At first, he wanted to find something special, but now it was because there was no point since his mother could not be proud of him. Why learn something when your kind will be extinct before the end of a one-sided war? There was no point in learning to change forms when you plan on walking into a room full of dragons with no escape.

She forced him to look at her. "Live for me, if not for yourself or the end of your kind. Just live so one day... we can meet again." With that, she lowered her face back to his throat, and the ice-cold pain retook hold of him. Everything began to blur. Pulling back once more, she kissed him with her blood-stained lips. "Find me, my prince," her voice echoed in his mind as darkness found him.

◆ ◆ ◆

The sun was high in the afternoon sky when Zec awoke. His head was pounding as he sat up, sand rolling off his body, skin red and hurt to the touch. *I definitely should not have slept in the sun,* he thought. Looking around, he saw no sign of Terika or her camel. He remembered the cold feeling of her lips against his and of her fangs at his throat. Zec was going to miss her.

"Come on, Nadi. We should get going." He followed the red rope to his brother, who lay in the sand not far from him. He was also red from the sun. "We should have been gone hours ago. Come on. Get up!" He shoved at Nadi.

"What are you yelling for?" Nadi whined, slowly rising from the sand as he groggily put his head in his hands.

"You need to stop drinking! It's wasting our time, and I lost more than a sandal over this." Zec saw Nadi reaching up to grab his shoulder, but pulled back.

"No need to help me up?" He got to his feet and stumbled, weak in his knees. Nadi met his brother's glare, but then his eyes widened. "Are you hurt? Is that your blood? What happened?"

Stepping away as Nadi attempted to grab his shoulder again, Zec became impatient with his brother's lack of knowledge. "She took her payment for your ale, which was my blood and one of my sandals."

Nadi grabbed Zec's arm, trying to stop him, but he shook him off. "So you let her drink your blood? It was supposed to be my blood that was payment. I drank so that it would be easier for her to take my blood."

"You're so selfish! You drank! She didn't want to get drunk on your blood. I paid for your drink. When are you going to wake up and get your life together? I won't be around forever, and neither will Father! Stop making others pay for your mistakes—like Mother!"

As he clenched his fists, Nadi's face reddened, even more prominent than the sunburn. "I know Mother died for me, but who would *you* blame if I had died that day?" He swung, his fist catching Zec's jaw, causing him to fall back into the sand. "I blame myself every day for what happened to her. Why do you think I want to forget?"

Managing to get his footing, Zec let out a growl and tackled Nadi, sending both of them to the ground. He raised his fist and brought it back down, missing Nadi's face as it plunged into the sand. Years of anger had built up into this moment, and he missed.

Nadi grabbed him by the throat and rolled on top of him, pinning him. With his other hand curled into a fist, he smashed it against Zec's left eye.

Reeling from the blow, Zec worked his feet onto Nadi's chest and launched him before he could hit him a second time. Watching Nadi hit the sand a few feet away, he rolled off the ground and lunged at him with his balled fist. Nadi scrambled to get up, but with the momentum from his lunge, Zec's fist made contact with Nadi's cheek, sending him back into the sand.

Anger, like fuel to a fire, Zec kept going. He felt like he couldn't hit his brother hard enough. Putting a knee at the center of Nadi's chest, he kept hitting him repeatedly. "I hate you!" He screamed as tears began streaming down his cheeks. The sand picked up on the wind and stuck to his face.

Grains managed to find their way into Zec's eye, momentarily blinding him and allowing Nadi to shove him off. Unable to see, Zec rubbed the sand from his eyes as he shielded himself from the next blow.

Yet, the next hit never came.

Nadi cursed, "We're in a dust storm! We need to find shelter!"

Blinking away the sand, Zec saw that all around them, in every direction, was reddish-brown fog. In the desert, dust storms were common, but they knew to seek shelter because the high winds could cause the sand to tear their skin.

"There is no sense in fighting when we need to continue." Zec dusted himself off. "We should not waste our energy."

Nadi pulled himself up and looked around. "We cannot even see where we need to go. Where is a safe spot to wait it out?"

Shrugging it off, Zec shook the sand out of his hair. "We have no food or water. There is no surviving this unless we get to the oasis. I know which direction to go. You need to trust me."

Still looking around, Nadi said sarcastically, "Sure, scream how you hate me as you beat my face in and then ask me to trust you."

Zec looked over his shoulder at him, realizing they needed to work together, or Zec's plan wouldn't work. "One of us should remain human, and the other should be a small animal to conserve energy. You took more damage than I did, so you should be the one to change, and I'll carry you. Doing things this way will allow you to regain energy, and we can go straight to the oasis. Hopefully, before sundown."

Taking longer to answer, Nadi eventually heaved a frustrated sigh. "You're right. Lead on then." Nadi began shifting until the clothes piled onto the ground. With the collar still around his neck, he popped out of the pile as a little brown mouse.

Scooping him up, Zec gently placed him inside his shirt. He grabbed his clothes from the ground and wrapped the shirt around his face to prevent him from breathing in the dust. "You need a bath. Your clothes smell worse than the traveling drunkards."

Nadi squeaked at him, but it was nothing he could understand. Throwing his pants over his shoulder, Zec turned in the direction he was sure was east before the fight and began walking that way.

Zec had been walking for hours. Dust clouded the sky, hiding the sun. Nothing could be seen more than five feet in front of them. While he wished the storm to end, he knew the dust was hiding their true course. So there was no reason to complain. His bare feet were finding more rocks in the sand, so he knew they were getting closer to his destination. There was sand near the mountains, dotted with rocks, and patches of dirt with plants. Zec remembered how he wanted to learn how to change into the one white squirrel he had seen on the mountain before the accident. He thought it would have been amazing to be the only one with that form, but no animal was worth having now that his mother could no longer see him succeed at shifting forms. He would get revenge and then meet her on the other side.

His neck tingled as he touched the dried blood. Terika's words ran through his head: "Find me, my prince." Moving his fingers to his lips, he remembered how cold and soft her lips had felt. He stopped in his tracks, and Nadi poked his head out, looking up at him. Zec wanted to see her again.

Nadi squeaked, and Zec came back to reality. Ahead of him was a palm tree. As he got closer, he saw water. Zec had somehow made it to an oasis. He almost felt defeated. Looking behind him, he could only see the wall of dust. Zec was sure he had been heading towards the keep. They should have reached the steps of the fortress by now, not an oasis.

Nadi jumped out and transformed into a naked man, "Great job, and there is still daylight left! Once the dust settles, we can camp and ride out the month here."

Zec noted that the wind was no longer blowing; the dust should settle soon. He rifled through every excuse in his book, trying to find any reason not to go into the oasis, but it was too late. He must have gotten lost in the storm, even though he was pretty sure his path was straight.

Walking toward the water, Zec watched the dust land on the surface and eventually drift to the bottom. The water still reflected, and the settled dust did not disrupt it. He studied his dirty face in the reflection. One of his eyes seemed to be swollen and bruised from the fight. His neck looked far worse. Cupping water into his hands, he rinsed off the blood to reveal a bruise in its place.

Nadi stared at him, "Woah, vampire bites heal quickly. I always heard stories, but never thought I would see it."

"I'm not your experiment, so stop using me." Zec looked back at the water and saw the sun was beginning to show through the dust. Just as he got up, he realized the sun was in the wrong place. It should have been further down in the sky.

As he watched, he noticed it was getting closer—it was not the sun. Turning toward Nadi, he lunged and tackled him to the ground. The fireball hit the dirt where Nadi had just stood, flinging rocks into the air.

"What was that?" Nadi almost sounded panicked as he pushed Zec off him.

Zec got to his feet and looked at where the fireball had come from. The blast had cleared the dust around them, revealing Grumloc on the keep's edge. His rage-filled golden eyes were staring down at them. Light from the fading dusk shined off his scales. Zec knew this was his final fight.

"Grumloc! I, Zec, have come to snuff out your life for killing my mother!" His words did not affect the steadfast dragon, even though he had practiced that line a thousand times.

Nadi grabbed his brother by the shoulder. "Are you mad? We are no match for the Dragon King himself!"

"He must pay!" Zec pushed Nadi away. "I don't care if I die!"

Nadi looked to Grumloc, "Forgive him! A vampire bit him, and he has been a little off since then! We'll go into the desert and never come back!"

"I will not retreat!" Zec almost hissed at him. "I am making sure that our mother did not die for nothing."

"Killing the Dragon King does not make up for Mother's death!" Nadi's eyes were a dark blue as he pulled him into his arms. "Killing someone who took the life of someone you love will only cause a vicious cycle. This war will never end!"

Zec shoved him away. "Killing him is the only thing that can make me feel better and will stop our people from vanishing. Avenging Mother's death is what I must do!" He looked at Grumloc, then roared, "Come fight me!" He threw Nadi's clothes to the ground.

Smoke billowed out of the sides of the gold dragon's mouth. He leaped off the keep and ascended towards them. Zec stood his ground, ready to face him with everything he had. Pulling a hunting knife from his belt, he readied himself.

Unleashing a torrent of fire as he flew over, Grumloc left a trail of flames coming towards them. Zec began his battle cry as he started moving away from the oasis. Nothing could stop him.

Chapter 3

Nadi was at a loss. His brother started to move away from the water, and Grumloc, with his fiery dragon's breath, was getting closer. There was only one thing he could do to stop this.

His arms tingled as his skin became scaly. Fingers grew into claws, and his nose became a long snout. His teeth sharpened to razor points in his mouth, and a large tail thudded on the dirt behind him as he came down on all fours as an alligator.

Few roamed the desert, but he managed to gain the trust of one and its form. He needed the right mixture of brawn and swiftness to get him and his brother to safety.

Grabbing his clothes in his mouth, Nadi turned back to the oasis and dove into the cold water, jerking Zec out of the blast's range.

Losing hold of his knife, Zec scrambled to get to shore. He cursed, "I can do this! Don't stop me!" As he tried to swim to land, Grumloc was circling back.

Nadi knew he had no other choice but to dive into the depths. He hoped his brother had some form able to survive under the water for long periods. Diving toward the bottom, he began to anticipate that he was not the only alligator in the water while his brother thrashed around, trying to swim up.

Grumloc blanketed the surface in a fiery blaze, burning the vegetation surrounding the oasis. Nadi understood they needed to wait, but he could do nothing. Since Zec was not using his ability to adapt, things became more difficult. He didn't want to drown him.

Letting Zec up for air, Nadi realized that this oasis had not been here when he had visited several years ago. It was to the keep's right at the mountain's foot. Something had to be feeding it. He pulled Zec back down just as the fire lit the surface again. With his tail, he felt for any current.

Moving water brushed against him, and he hoped that the source was big enough to escape. Diving down, Nadi pressed his snout into the current of a cave system from the mountain that seemed to feed the flow.

Nadi let Zec surface for one last breath before diving into the darkness. There did not seem to be any fish or plants in the water, which was strange for a water source that had been there for years. Quickly, he pushed against the current and into the tunnel, pressing on until it opened into a dark cave. He pulled both of them out of the flow. It was utterly black, which did not help him with any sense of direction.

Panic gripped him as he realized that Zec was no longer moving. He pulled the line and still felt his weight. Cursing in his mind, Nadi transformed back, dropping his clothes and drawing the rope toward him, soon grabbing hold of Zec's limp body. Forcing his head above the water and struggling to keep himself afloat, Nadi urged him to live. "Stay with me, Zec!" His voice echoed into the darkness.

A thundering boom sounded, and he felt the water around him shake. He could not see what had happened or where it had come from. Fear gripped him as he held Zec tighter.

Nadi felt another pull from behind and realized he'd been sucked into an undertow. Barely able to catch his breath, Nadi clung to his brother as they were forced further into the dark waters. He tried to find something to grab onto, anything, but the darkness gave him the fear that nothing was there, that he was alone. He couldn't transform without air to suit his environment. *Here in this cave is the end*, he thought as the current dragged him farther. This would be the end of their journey, where they both die in the dark underwater den. No one was there to help them, no one knew they were ever in danger.

Shutting his eyes, Nadi struggled to hold his breath. With his lungs burning, he felt the loss of everything: his mother, brother, father, and tribe. Now, if he lost his breath, he would lose his life. Right then, he longed to return to his childhood, where there were no worries. Where his mother still lived, and his brother looked up to him.

With lungs begging for air, Nadi could no longer stop himself from taking a breath. Just as the air began to fill his lungs, he hit the hard ground and forced it back out.

More water poured down on top of him as he struggled to breathe.

Rolling over, he dragged Zec from under a waterfall and laid him on the grass. As his eyes adjusted, he realized they were no longer in the desert. Trees covered the land for miles, purple flowers dotting the space between trunks. Pulling his eyes from the world around them, he looked at Zec. To his dismay, he was not breathing. "No, don't do this to me!" He pleaded as he pushed against his chest. "You need to survive. You can't die now!"

"I don't think it's your choice if he lives or dies," a woman's voice came from behind him.

Nadi spun around to see a dark-skinned woman standing next to the waterfall. Her eyes were green, her hair a mass of black curls. Her silk dress was a darker shade than the trees around them.

"Please," Nadi pleaded as he stood up from his brother's side. "Save him."

The woman heaved a sigh, approaching him. "Well, I guess I've been bored here for quite some time now. Might as well keep the company I have." She knelt next to Zec and laid her hand on his chest. Nadi could hear her mumbling, but he could not make out anything she was saying.

Water flowed from Zec's mouth, spilling onto the ground. Suddenly, he began coughing and gasping for air. Slowly, he turned over and vomited the rest of the water out.

Nadi could not believe his eyes. She had brought him back to life with magic. "Thank you," he said, opening his arms to hug her.

She stopped him with a finger on his chest, "I am not touching you while you are naked." Instead, she dragged her finger to the collar around his neck and whispered. Both collars popped open and fell to the ground. "And now I made it worse."

Looking down, Nadi did not think the collar would be coming off so soon. Also, he had just remembered dropping his clothes in the cave. He returned to the waterfall to see if the undertow had pulled them out, but they were nowhere. "I'm sorry . . . I guess I can change into an animal for the time being."

A bright smile crossed her face. "An animal? Are you, by chance, a shifter?"

Zec coughed. "We both are." He got to his knees before bringing his focus to her face. His eyes narrowed, flashing a few colors as he went still like a rabbit in the presence of a wolf.

"Why are you staring?" she asked, her smile fading.

Nadi laughed nervously, "My brother here doesn't know how to talk to beautiful women, so he just stares." Zec glared at Nadi, his eyes gaining a hint of red. It was probably only the second time he had stopped to stare at a woman.

It was her turn to laugh. "I know that I'm enchanting." Her hand caressed the side of her face. "What brings two shifters through a waterfall into my secret garden?"

Zec seemed to have enough energy to dismiss his brother's lie. "Knock it off, Nadi. I can speak just fine." He turned his attention back to the woman. "Grumloc the Dragon King. He tried to kill us."

"Only after you screamed at him that you would kill him first," Nadi interjected. "What were you thinking? Are you invincible? You would have ended up like Mother."

"Better her than a thief like you!" Zec turned away as he stood up, bracing against the tree for support. "We should get going."

The woman stepped in front of Zec. "Because you want to kill the Dragon King?" They stared at each other silently, but then she grinned. "I have a similar goal."

As a smile crossed his brother's face, Nadi almost felt his heart sink. The Dragon Kings had practically been like family to them. Even though Grumloc had killed his mother, Nadi knew that neither he nor his Mother deserved to die. Mother had chosen to save her child just like most living creatures would, but if Nadi had stayed on Grumloc's back, then she would still be alive.

Zec happily talked with the woman as he leaned against a tree for support. "Why do you want to kill Grumloc?" He asked as though they had known each other forever.

Since they were kids, Zec had been open to conversing and making decisions. He should be the next chief of the tribe, but their father had stuck with the tradition of making the eldest the leader. But Zec was always quick to decide how to help out the villagers and tend to their needs. Most of his tribe preferred Zec over Nadi, and he couldn't blame them. Yet, Nadi couldn't help but feel that Zec was making the worst decision this time.

Sadness washed over her face. "There was a legend about the Ten Elders, those who created all elements on this land and then vanished from the sight of the world, making their home here. One had even become mortal and left the other Elders, so there were only nine." She looked both of them in the eye. "Gentlemen, I had discovered the Elders, but the dragons have them fast asleep with leech vines. The only way to save them is with a fertile dragon egg."

Zec glanced back at Nadi, but he already heard enough to know this was far too big for either of them. Sure—the adventuring wizard, sorcerer, or mage would wander the desert searching for rare ingredients. They would even pay a hefty price for a lock of their hair, but magic was something he had yet to wrap his mind around. Magic was not something that was needed in their tribe. There was magic in almost every living thing; it was even how he transformed. However, that was something nomads like them didn't dabble in for recreation. It was used in ceremonies or rituals, mainly by the chieftain.

"A fertile egg?" Zec put his head in his hands, trying to get his senses. "Those are well hidden from the light of day far into the mountain. The only ones who can get there are dragons."

The woman grinned at both of them. "Or...shifters who could change into dragons."

"Pass," Nadi said as he walked over to Zec. "Becoming a dragon means losing your humanity and the ability to shift. That is how wild dragons came to exist. Shifters get greedy and don't heed the warnings."

"Ah, 'Elias the Dragon'!" she exclaimed. "That was a good story. But what if I told you we could reverse the effect with magic so that you'd lose the dragon form and be able to shift again?"

Zec's eyes widened, and Nadi knew she had him hooked like a fish on a line.

"Hold on—have you even tested that magic on a shapeshifter? How do you even know it works?" Nadi wanted to find any flaw that would make Zec give up on this quest.

"I have used this magic several times to keep myself young and heal wounds. My age is nearing 100, yet

I look to be in my twenties. I am very proud of it! In essence, it's magic that can bend time." She waved her hands above her head. "The ability to manipulate time itself is hard to harness, but even we have found a detour. Bring back the dead, cure the sick, and never age. It is glorious magic that can help us in this situation." She eyed them both. "All we need is a shifter to change into a dragon."

"How do you know there is even a fertile egg in the keep?" Nadi had many questions, and he would keep them coming.

"The Dragon King is not letting visitors into or near the keep. His egg is the one that he is protecting until it hatches. He sits on the mountain above the keep to ensure no trouble is lurking." The woman seemed satisfied to answer him.

"How do you expect us to change into a dragon when—"

"Enough!" Zec boomed, glaring at his brother, his eyes almost as red as blood. "Stop trying to shoot down every possible chance we have to avenge Mother! You can do as you like, but they will feel my wrath when I become the dragon." He went into a coughing fit.

"Maybe you two need some rest before we continue," she said, helping him stand. "What do I call you, if you don't mind me asking?"

He smiled at her as he held onto her for support. "I am Zec, and the naked maniac who almost killed me is my brother, Nadi."

"Says the one who screamed at a dragon that he would kill him," Nadi mumbled as he followed them. Shivering from the cold, he didn't have much energy left in him to transform. This ordeal had been tiring enough.

"I am Icarri." She did not seem used to helping anyone as she stumbled while attempting to walk with Zec. "A sorceress from Vadnera."

As she led them through the woods, the last light of day vanished over the mountain, casting the entire area in shadow. Nadi began to see lights flashing in the bushes and trees. They seemed to fly sometimes, but he couldn't see what they were.

"Are those fairies?" He pointed to the lights. The traders would tell stories of them, and even his mother had sung a song about them. They were said to appear at the changing of seasons, but it was the middle of summer.

She laughed. "Those are fireflies. Bugs with butts that glow. Haven't you seen one?"

"The desert does not have much life in it." Zec struggled to get a better grip on her arm, but even in wet clothes, he was starting to shiver. "We don't see many creatures unless they can survive in the desert or come with travelers."

"You guys will get a kick out of how much life is in this little space."

The trees opened to a field. Purple flowers with white centers were growing everywhere. Nadi bent down and picked one, studying it. "What are these?" he had asked more to himself.

"Those little flowers are columbines. They mean something different depending on where you go. Here, they mean 'to repent.'" Icarri kept walking.

A towering structure stood off to the right with large stained-glass windows depicting winged people of different races. Each one also had a weapon: a sword, an ax, a hammer, a whip, and a bow. There were more weapons, but he was distracted by the wings, a variety of colors that almost looked like they should be on birds. *Are these dark angels?* he wondered. It had been years since he had heard about the winged heroes. Instead of asking about them, Nadi kept quiet, not wanting to make a fool of himself.

She led them to a massive structure that seemed smaller than the one with the stained-glass windows, with quite large wooden doors. A few more buildings in the clearing looked to be living quarters. One had a garden next to it, but the food there did not look edible. Flies clung to what looked to have been various vegetables and fruits. Something told Nadi she had never even had a garden before.

His attention turned to the large wooden doors with carved winged figures. They almost looked happy as they held books. Icarri pushed open the doors and stepped inside. Nadi slowly followed.

Shelves of books lined the walls, and tables sat in front of every window with wooden chairs. In the center of the first floor was an area with cushions and a fireplace. Looking up, Nadi noticed the glass ceiling, but as the lights inside lit themselves, Nadi could not see the sky.

Icarri helped Zec into a seat and, with a few mumbled words, dried his clothes. His dirty blonde hair still looked damp. Nadi's eyes trailed around the room in wonder. Above him was a second floor with more books and designated sitting areas with cushions.

"Never seen a library before?" Icarri began to rummage through a pile of clothes on the ground.

"No," Nadi kept looking around and even saw paintings of different places. "We only had stories of word of mouth, but our mother had a book she always loved and sang the poem from it." He noticed that despite Zec being exhausted, he also stared at his surroundings in wonder.

She pulled out a white shirt and black pants, tossing them at Nadi. "Sounds like an interesting book. Are you fond of reading, oh naked one?"

He wouldn't be naked for long. As he pulled the pants up, he struggled to keep his balance. "Didn't like it much. I liked hearing stories, not reading them. I was quite a restless child."

"Every child is restless until you can find something to satisfy their interests." Icarri pulled a blanket off the back of a chair and dropped it onto the pile of cushions. She did not know how to tidy up for a woman of such fine clothes. "You can sleep here, and then we'll get you situated in the living quarters tomorrow. I'll get us a feast going."

"How did you come to be at the waterfall?" Zec asked as he rested his elbows against the table.

She stood there for a moment in silence before meeting his gaze. "I had lost my temper and struck out at the cliff. I'm sacrificing a lot of time and energy just to be here. While my comrades are on the mainland seeking help, I'm stuck here watching this place. There is no one else to talk to; I wait to hear from them. I await them to bring supplies and answers about when I can return to my manor with all my servants. I've never thought I would miss my pampered life until now." She clenched her fists, "I struck the cliff with my power out of rage. It wasn't like I was expecting there to be water or you two to come out."

Nadi piped in, "It does seem a little too convenient that you just happened to blow a hole in a spot near where we were."

"Stop being rude, Nadi!" Zec sat up a little straighter, but he still looked exhausted. "I just wanted to know why she was there." Turning his attention to her, he said, "Sorry about that. How did you come to be here anyway?"

Giving a small smile, she stated, "By ship. We ventured along the cliff edge until we found the beach. We realized there were a temple and living quarters, but I wouldn't say I liked that there seemed to be no one there until we entered the temple. That is where the Elders are being held, but it is far too dangerous for either of you to go there. We don't need anyone else tangled in the vine." She paused momentarily as Zec's stomach growled, "Guess we shouldn't waste any more time. Seems you are famished."

"Yes, please," Zec winced as he smiled. "Food would probably be good about now."

Nadi thought back to the garden and wanted to find a reason to decline. A woman who lived like this could not cook or make a *feast*. Before speaking, he watched her slip out the doors and waited until she was almost to one of the living quarters. "Something seems off. The garden has nothing edible from what I could see; this place is a mess, and these clothes are high quality. Where is the food? What about these Elders she spoke about? What of—"

"Can't you be happy with anything that someone does for you? Why do you have to question everything?" Zec was irritated.

"Because it's my job to keep you safe!" Nadi knew his eyes were red as he let his anger slip. "I promised Father to bring you home safe, and here we are! Running towards dragons, playing with magic, and now you are trying to throw your life away to get revenge!" Nadi could see Icarri coming back carrying something in her arms. "Mother would not want you to throw away your life."

Zec sat there in silence for a moment before answering him, "Mother is dead. The dead cannot feel, hear, or see. They do not care if I decide to be a dragon and kill other dragons. The dead would not cry if I die seeking revenge, so quit trying to stop me."

The doors opened, and Icarri dropped a sack onto the floor. There were salted meats of many sorts, all in need of cooking. A few pieces of dried meat hit the floor, but Nadi noticed no vegetables. Grabbing a large portion of meat, she tossed it into the fire.

"What are you doing?" Nadi grabbed a poker and fished it out of the ashes. "Have you never cooked before?"

"Back home, I had servants to do everything for me. Cooking was not something I needed to do." She huffed and turned away from him. "Plus, I have magic to make things edible."

"How have you survived here?" Nadi pried as she turned away, embarrassed.

"I can duplicate food items. Plus, I have a pocket space to store certain items like food, which will not go bad. This meat came in when my comrades checked in last." Looking down at her hands, she seemed hesitant to go on. "I just wanted to make something special without magic for my guests."

Nadi could feel Zec glaring at him some more. He knew he would hear it if he turned around. Gently, he touched her hand, "I'll show you how to cook so that even when we part ways, you can have that knowledge."

Getting up from the fire, he left the library and headed toward the garden. The smell reached him as he was halfway across the field, and he knew finding something from that garden might be a lost cause. He searched for herbs and anything edible. The carrots were wooded, the cabbage was covered in worms, and the corn seemed to have the same problem. Herbs seemed to flourish like sage and rosemary, but others looked to have been eaten by animals. A raccoon watched him from the bushes as he searched. Picking a few almost ripe strawberries, he tossed them to the raccoon. He might gain some new forms while he was at it.

In the distance, he could hear howling. The sound seemed different from the coyotes in the desert. He went inside a cabin where he had seen Icarri venture; the room was dark and filled with rodents scurrying to hide. Barrels were open, exposing the food to the elements. Recently opened was the barrel with the salted meats. Closing the barrel, he knew the other ones had begun to rot. Rats had made their home at the bottom of the dried meat barrel. Another barrel, filled with fruit, was far past fermenting.

Searching the shelves, he found a hanging pan, pot, and cooking utensils. Cleaning supplies sat on a shelf above them. There was going to be a lot to teach her. Even tending to a garden was going to be a challenge. They had to clear the vegetation and replant new items. Filling the stores with meat was another thing. The caravan had stored food as they traveled across the desert. It allowed them to go for long periods without hunting. Here, he was going to have to hunt.

His fingers came across a glass bottle. Nadi plucked it from the shelf as quickly as he could and brought it into the dim light. The label was in a language he could not read. Uncorking it, he smelled its liquid contents. With his luck, he had found wine. He took a swig and held onto its bittersweet taste before swallowing it. He would have to ration it since he was still unsure when he would come across any more. It wouldn't hurt to cook with, but he had to make it last.

As he walked back, he looked at the building with the winged figures on the windows. Something felt off about this place. His eyes trailed up the tower above, and he could almost make out a giant bell. There were so many questions still burning in his mind. What was this place? How did the oasis from the dragons' keep lead them here? How close was the keep?

Suddenly, he saw the curtains move. Nadi stared a moment longer to see if they would move again. He wanted to know what was in there.

"Hey—what's the hold-up?" Icarri yelled from the door. "Are we going to eat?"

Nadi followed her back in, not saying a word. Feeling like someone was watching, he tried not to look over his shoulder as he set everything down. Out of the corner of his eye, he could see the curtain move again. Icarri closed the door just as he turned to look.

"Ready to cook?" She smiled at him, but to him, it looked forced.

"Yes, let's get onto the first lesson." He picked up the hanging pan and headed towards the fireplace. Nadi knew that if he was going to find the truth, he had to snoop around. He had to keep his distrust to himself; even Zec could not be trusted.

Chapter 4

Covered in sweat, Nadi sat up on the pile of cushions. It was the same dream that plagued him again and again. He wanted to forget, but still, he couldn't. It was his fault that his mother was gone, and his brother hated him. These things he could not change. Looking up at the skylight, he could see the blue sky and hear the birds chirping outside. In his head, he kept telling himself that it wasn't real. He was safe, but his heart still raced.

There was no telling when it would stop.

Zec was asleep in a chair in front of the fireplace. He didn't seem tormented by his dreams. Snoring, he looked so peaceful. Nadi envied him for that.

Outside, he could hear Icarri's voice but could not tell what she was saying. Getting up, he went to the door and opened it. She spun around to face him with her eyes wide.

"Good morning," he said, studying the scene but not seeing anyone. He eyed the porcelain cup in her hand, which held a brown liquid. "Are you talking to someone?"

"Just to myself," she gave a sheepish grin. "I've been alone for so long that it's just something I do now. I have conversations with myself to pass the time. Usually, angry ones."

Nadi thought about how similar it was to his situation, although he felt alone with all his thoughts. He didn't have anyone to share them with. Everyone in the village just thought of him as a troublemaker. Even his father seemed to treat him as such. Maybe Icarri just needed to talk about it. "I do that when I have a lot on my mind. Anything you want to share?"

She seemed to be taken aback by the question. "Share?" Taking a sip of her drink, she looked toward the sun peeking over the trees. "Have you ever felt like you were placed somewhere because no one likes you?" She closed her eyes and deeply breathed, "I feel like my comrades may not have wanted me around. Like I was a burden to them. The only thing I had to keep them around was gold...and so they'd do everything for me, see me when it was convenient so that I could sign off on funds for their quests."

"I have felt similar to that," Nadi watched how the light caught her green gaze and thought of how beautiful it seemed. "I remember when my father was proud of me. Gaining my first form, learning how to fly. After Mother died, he was no longer fun. Just serious. It's like all the happiness went out of the world, and he became a different person." He paused, running a hand through his hair. "We all became different people. My brother constantly hates me. No more looking up to me. His eyes are just constantly red."

"What about you?" Icarri looked at him over the lip of her cup. "What do you do to cope with this?"

"I wanted to forget everything, but it just haunts me." He heaved a sigh as he felt the grass beneath his feet. "I feel like my mother's death was my fault, and everyone else knows it. Before coming here, I was hoping to steal something worth losing a life over or drink enough to make the world forget that I exist."

The sorceress laughed, "How does your drinking make the world forget?"

He gave a sad smile. "I've heard that drinking too much can poison a man. I haven't been able to drink that much, though."

"Oh," she stopped smiling and traced the rim of her cup with a finger. "I see." Taking another sip, she seemed flustered. "I guess we all have to choose our poison at some point."

He decided to change the subject. "Do you ever wish you could be a kid again?"

"Not really," Icarri laughed again. "I'm happy staying in my twenties forever. I'm done with growth spurts and forced lessons."

"Why do you want to be young forever?" The question had slipped out before he could think twice about it.

Pouring the rest of her drink onto the ground, her gaze seemed distant. "I grew up the battered child of a nobleman. If I did one thing wrong, I was beaten for it. I was lucky to have survived. Then, when I was old enough, my father married me off to a man who was proud of my beauty. 'Women don't need brains,' he had told me when I asked for books instead of clothes. Until his death, I was nothing more than a child-bearing wallflower. So much for the fairytale most girls dream of." She threw the cup into the field. "By the time I was free of all the men who had put me down, my life was already over. Now that I have a second chance, I will live it to the fullest." Icarri turned to him with a grin, "Maybe I can even have my fairytale."

He laughed nervously as he sought to change the subject again, "Did you take that cup out of your magical pocket?"

She blinked a few times before looking toward where the cup had landed. "Yes, I did."

"Can I see how it works?" Some things he could only believe with his eyes. Since he wasn't with the caravan, he could be as curious as he wanted with magic. "Back home, it was tradition never to use any magical items. We would only see it in passing with travelers or when my father held certain ceremonies."

Pulling a brown pouch out of her sleeve, she opened it. To him, it looked empty. "Let's see, I think I put a sweet bun in here in case I felt like having something sweet for breakfast." Reaching her hand in, she seemed to search for something. As she pulled her hand out, a bun covered in icing came with it. "Here," she handed it to Nadi.

Taking it, his fingers stuck to the gooey glaze. He brought it to his mouth and bit into it. He had never tasted anything that sweet before. All the foods he had with the tribe were things they had hunted, grown, traded, or foraged for. Even baked bread had never tasted so sweet.

As he swallowed the mouthful, he offered her a bite.

"No, thank you." She pulled a hunting knife from the bag. The handle looked to be made of bone, and the blade was dark metal. "I have no use for this either; you can have it." She held the tip and extended the handle to him.

"Thank you! This is great." Taking it from her, he remembered that Zec had lost his knife while attempting to fight Grumloc. "This can replace the one Zec dropped," he said, primarily to himself.

"I guess that is very generous of me, isn't it?" She headed for the library doors.

"What would you do if you needed protection then? I don't want to take away your weapon," Nadi watched the light shine off the metal as he tried to return it.

Icarri smirked. "I have more where that came from —but magic is my first weapon. If I run out of magic, I use a blade."

"You can run out of magic?" His curiosity was piqued at the possibility of learning more about magic.

Heaving a frustrated sigh, the sorceress turned back to him. "Yes, each magic wielder has their limits. It's not an infinite well. It's more like…a flask that refills over time. The more you use it, the larger it becomes.

"To lessen the amount used, one must simply use the forces around them. It's like a warrior using their opponent's momentum against them. When I saved Zec, I used the water in his chest and pulled it out. I can sometimes manipulate the wind and use it with great force to push something. I can cause the ground to rise higher or lower. I can control even the tiniest pebble to a large boulder. With fire, I can make it a roaring blaze or sizzle out of existence." She played with one of her curls. "I really am a great sorceress."

"That all sounds amazing." He thought about how the torches lit when they entered the hall. "So, the torches, how do you light them?"

"I don't," her smile vanished. "That is simply a motion charm. When the doors open at night, they cause the torches to light. Charms can be placed on many things. Then there are enchantments, which are similar—but they can do more than light up a room. Placed on weapons, they can strengthen them to deal more damage."

He wanted to know all he could about magic. There were so many questions bubbling up in his mind. As he opened his mouth to spew another, Icarri held her hand up.

"I would love more than anything to answer your questions on how magic works, but if this continues, we will not get anything done." She turned and walked back into the library.

Nadi followed, still determining what needed to be done. The state of the place looked as though nothing had been done in ages. Certainly, there was something she had planned. As he entered, Zec sat up groggily in the chair. His hair was in disarray as he spotted Nadi. His eyes flashed red.

Setting the knife on his lap, Nadi watched as Zec became confused. "Icarri gave us a knife."

"You shouldn't take things from her. She may need it," Zec admonished, taking the blade as he turned back to Icarri. "We can't accept this."

"Where I come from, it is rude not to accept a gift." She walked between two of the tall shelves. A moment later, her dress was tossed over near the table. Both Nadi and Zec turned their backs on her. Nadi could feel his face turn red.

"I'm not trying to be rude," Zec said as he studied the blade. "We normally make trades for items. We cannot accept gifts. It's part of our traditions."

"Oh," Nadi could hear her footsteps as she walked towards the table. "In that case, I think we made a trade. I can have you two complete tasks for me in exchange for letting you stay here. Since this place is supposed to remain a secret from the rest of the world, I can have you work here. Gather supplies, cook, clean—and, of course, one of you can become a dragon for our cause."

Nadi peeked over his shoulder and saw she had changed to a blue gown. "That's not how the trading system works. We are not your servants. Even though I'm afraid I have to disagree with it, in exchange for you allowing us to stay here, one of us becomes a dragon." He looked at Zec, who also peered over his shoulder, "In exchange for the knife and breakfast, we have traded stories."

As he turned to face Icarri, she was standing right behind him. "Wrong, in exchange for saving your brother's life, he will become the dragon. In exchange for you living here, I expect you to assist me with cooking, cleaning, and anything I ask."

"Can't you just use your magic to do those things?" Nadi asked, matching her scowl.

"No," she turned toward the dress she had tossed on the floor. As her hand shot out, the dress moved with a gust of wind. The yellow fabric became nothing more than tattered pieces of cloth. "Magic is powerful, and if so much as a thought is not concentrated on the entire task, then things can break, threads can snap, and a life can be extinguished." She faced him with a look of rage. "Do I make myself clear?"

Nadi watched as the last few pieces settled on the floor. "Yes."

She turned to walk out of the library. "Make sure you pick up this mess."

"Actually," Nadi watched her turn around slowly. "You had said assist. So, I will assist you with those tasks; you can think of it as trading knowledge. I get to learn about how you like your food and where everything goes, and you get to learn how to do it yourself once we're gone." He grinned. "You can think of this as the happy ending you had never gotten; the only difference is we are not married."

Icarri seemed to turn red as she swept out of the library, slamming the doors behind her. He watched as she headed for the trees in a fury. He couldn't help but laugh as she vanished into the brush.

Zec shook his head, "You're digging yourself a grave if you think she's going to like you."

"Like me," Nadi scoffed. "I just wanted to make it clear that we're not her slaves."

"That was a lover's quarrel," he didn't seem amused. "You'll understand soon enough."

Nadi shook his head. "She's too vain for my taste. Not a fine wine or a dwarven ale. Definitely not a shiny trinket begging to be stolen. As common as they come, she is not rare. Icarri can't compete with my true love's sweet embrace, which I hope to succumb to later today." He picked up a piece of her yellow dress. "Come on, might as well get this picked up."

"Me," Zec grinned as he headed for the door. "You heard what she said. 'You' get to do the chores in exchange for your stay. I've traded enough."

As the door clicked shut behind him, Nadi grumbled, "I don't like her, and she most certainly doesn't like me." He picked up more of the yellow cloth. "Such a waste. I guess sewing is not something she knows either." Rolling one of the strips between his fingers, he had an idea of what he should make with it. Piling the fabric on the table, he began to work.

Chapter 5

Zec followed Icarri's footprints through the brush along what seemed to be a small trail, but it was hard to see with all the plants growing over it. Living in the desert had trained him to follow the tracks of animals and people. Travelers would get lost in the sea of sand and accompany their tribe until they met up with their group. For animals, it was to hunt for food or new forms. Here, he was trying to fix his brother's mistakes.

Some things never change.

As he broke through the tree line, the sunlight off the water blinded him. He blinked a few times as he stepped, his foot sinking into sand instead of dirt. Letting his eyes focus, he could see that a vast body of water lay before him, with no land in sight for miles as waves crashed against the surface. It was beautiful. He knew this was the ocean from the way travelers had described it.

Looking over the beach, he focused on Icarri sitting on the shore, staring over the horizon. Relieved to have found her, he made his way over before finding a good spot to sit. Keeping his eyes on the waves, he said, "You know, he did have a point."

"That's not why I stormed off," she responded, still not looking at him.

He felt as though he were talking to a child. "Then what was the reason?"

She did not respond. The sound of the waves and the call of a few seagulls helped fill the silence.

"Nadi can be rude sometimes, but I can tell he likes you. He wouldn't have bothered to inform you about our customs if he didn't like you. Hell, he would have ignored you and done as he pleased. I've seen it so many times at home."

"It was the fact that he twisted my words," she kept her gaze away. "I told him how I wanted the fairytale that every girl dreamed of, since my marriage placed me as an object of one man's possession. And he twisted that in a hurtful way."

"I see," he picked at the sand, pulling up a beautiful purple shell. He tossed it into the water. "He can be that way sometimes. I thought he would be dumber than a bag of rocks, but he is a quick thinker. Yet, he doesn't think about his words before he says things sometimes." Zec decided he didn't want to anger himself with talks about Nadi. "I disagree with your marriage, though. Speaking from personal experience, a woman is not a possession and should have her freedom. It hurts to be apart, but that makes it all the more fulfilling when we see each other again." Touching the sandal on his belt, he felt a pang of guilt in his chest. "I may have made a dumb choice, but I hope she'll forgive me."

"She must be lucky," Icarri's green eyes seemed sad as she closed them and lay back in the sand.

He shook his head. "It's not so lucky. Nadi's going to face exile from the tribe at some point. That means I'll have to take over as chief, which designates our relationship as forbidden. Our relationship would have no choice but to end because we cannot be with another race. I have to set an example for the tribe."

"So, do you think Nadi would not be interested in me because I'm a human?" Her expression was curious.

"It's more complicated than that." Rubbing the back of his neck, he realized he might have somehow offended Icarri. "Nadi has no love for anyone except his thievery and maybe the drink. Since our mother had passed, he had shut everyone out. He knows that he is to blame for her death, and so he loves the only thing that can make him feel better." Shaking his head, he wanted to be off the subject, but felt he should explain more. "There was a night when I had to help him back to his tent, and he mumbled about how he just wanted to forget. So, I believe that he wants to forget about the past, about what happened to our mother." Looking out of the corner of his eye, he saw her expression change to a gentler one. "But I don't think he is the right choice for anyone. Maybe if he stopped stealing, he might make a good husband."

Icarri laughed as she sat up, "It's a relief that I may still be attractive to someone. I was worried that my age might be catching up with me."

"Don't get me wrong; you are beautiful." He paused as their eyes met, "But I love someone, and Nadi…well, he loves whatever he can steal. Maybe if you pursue him, he can change his mind." He felt that pushing her towards Nadi might be the best thing. Zec only wanted one thing here, and that was to kill Grumloc.

"Thank you. I feel that is not said enough," the sorceress grinned.

Changing the subject, he decided to ask a question that was weighing on his mind. "There is more to this vine than you're telling us. I say this because you have time magic, yet you have not reversed time to rid the Elders of the vine. Why is that?"

She let out a frustrated sigh as she searched for the right words. "The magic is not that powerful. So, we need to harness the magic and then reverse time to set everything straight. Make it as though this never happened in the first place. Sacrifice one dragon to give more power to the orb of time."

Zec's mind began plotting. "In that case, can I go back and kill the Dragon King to prevent our mother's death?"

Her grin resurfaced. "We can do more than that. We can stop the dark angels from ever existing and prevent the death of many others. The orb can give us the power to correct every mistake and to stay the same age forever. We can watch history in the making and take any risk we want with no consequences."

Everything she said made him realize he could have the life he wanted with Terika. "When can I transform into a dragon?" He was ready to do all he could to undo the past. Thinking of how he might be able to see his mother again made his heart soar. It didn't matter what he had to sacrifice; he just had to make it happen.

Tugging at a curl, she turned away from him. "We have to wait for my comrades to arrive. They have the orb of time, but their journey is taking slightly longer than expected."

Zec stared at the horizon, hoping to see any signs of a ship. Travelers often spoke of them since they would pass over the ocean. They would compare the ones by sea and explain that the ones by air moved faster. Airships had balloons filled with hot air instead of sails. The stories of pirates were the best. He enjoyed the ones with a naga who went by Captain Cobra.

Nagas looked like humans from the waist up but were snakes from the waist down. They came in many different kinds and had two cities in the desert. To the west was San Helios, which had rattlers and vipers. Toward the south was La Dajia, the town of cobras. Captain Cobra faced exile for not following their strict customs. He had gone to the port and taken an airship to the mainland when he spotted a water ship that could rise into the skies. He jumped for it. After battling the entire crew, they succumbed to his will and became pirates. He waited for a new story to resurface every time travelers came to the caravan. Looking at the horizon, he hoped to see the flag that carried the serpent wrapped around a skull.

Yet, he wanted to see a different ship, one with Icarri's comrades. He was impatient to exact his revenge, but if he managed to return in time, he could stop everything from happening. With that power, he could be with Terika forever instead of dying before her. There was no telling what a vampire's blood would do to a shapeshifter. He wasn't sure if he wanted to drink his poison just yet.

Icarri tapped his shoulder.

"What are you staring at?"

He shook his head, "Sorry, I was deep in thought."

"The benefits of the orb can be tempting," she agreed, her grin devious.

He wanted to use the orb, just like they were going to—but he wondered if they failed, would the cost be too great? He had to try to help them succeed so that everyone could get what they desired.

As he opened his mouth to respond, the sound of someone stumbling out of the forest caught their attention. Nadi fell onto the sand with something yellow in his arms. He lifted himself onto his knees and seemed to stare out over the ocean in amazement.

Sighing, Zec called, "We're over here!"

Nadi's head turned toward them, but his gaze remained on the horizon. Getting up, he stumbled towards them with what looked to be yellow roses in his arms. Zec wasn't sure where he would have found them. As he got closer, he could see the flowers were cloth.

Pulling his gaze away from the horizon, Nadi held out the flowers to Icarri. "I'm sorry about what I said. I know it wasn't right for me to say those things. It's just that when someone makes a mess, the person who made it needs to clean it up. That's how we grew up. I know it may have been different for you, but we should come to a compromise. At the least, let me show you our ways."

She gave a small smile. "Fair enough. I accept your apology." Taking the roses, she leaned in and kissed his cheek. "It was very thoughtful of you to use the dress to make these. It was also swift."

Nadi rubbed the back of his neck and blushed. "Our mother used to make those and trade them to travelers. She taught us that we do not waste anything. Instead, we make use of it and leave only our footprints behind."

Zec's heart ached as he realized he had almost forgotten where he'd learned that. His mother hated for anything to go to waste. He remembered one of the mornings she said that. Picking up a bottle from the sand, she had turned with her long braid whipping behind her. She stated, like always, "Leave nothing to the sand, only your footprints."

Both Icarri and Nadi looked at Zec as he realized he had said those words aloud. Nadi smiled at him and nodded. "That is exactly what she used to tell us, word for word," he patted his brother on the back.

With the memory fresh in his mind, Zec could feel his eyes go red. He shook off Nadi's praise and stood. Zec was going to leave those two to their conversation, but he didn't want to sit with the man who caused this pain. Nadi was never going to understand why he was to blame.

Chapter 6

Five days have passed since arriving in what Icarri calls Crescent Cove. She said she'd been sent to explore the cliffs near the ocean and see if there was another route into the desert, but had stumbled across the Temple of the Elders. Trying to stop the leech vine from ensnaring anyone else, she forbade either Zec or Nadi from entering. Nadi, however, kept seeing the curtain move and often wondered if going into the temple was worth the risk of answering all the questions that filled his head.

Instead, he busied himself trying to hide from Icarri's unwanted advancements. At first, he had entertained the idea of a woman liking him, but her constant complaints and demands wore thin on his temper. With her extravagant dresses and delicate makeup, she reminded him of a peacock. Most of what she wore seemed revealing and held no protection against the onslaught of summertime mosquitoes. Constantly, she would ignore Nadi's advice on what she should wear and create excuses to flaunt her beauty. Nadi decided it might be time to start snooping around to see if he could expedite their plan and hasten their departure.

The library was where he had wanted to start. Still, Icarri ensured he worked hard from dawn to dusk. She never seemed to touch any books in the library or explain how they would gain a dragon's form.

Today, however, Icarri did not wake him. Nadi went to the door of his cabin and looked at the temple. As usual, the curtain moved, but nothing was there. His attention went to the library where Icarri had taken up residence. His brother usually explored the woods or was locked away in his cabin.

Zec had the patience to wait for Icarri to come to him. Nadi, however, wanted to be rid of her. Today was a good start since she wasn't ordering him around yet.

Turning back into his room, he pulled his clothes off and stuffed straw into them. He then placed them on the bed and tossed a blanket on top. Fluffing it, he made sure it looked like he was still asleep. It was the decoy to buy him time while he researched the plant if she went to wake him first.

Transforming into a mouse, he squeezed under the cabin's door and took off across the field. He aimed for the library. The first step to finding another solution to that vine was to study magic. He hated reading, but if it meant he could save his brother from the fate he desired, Nadi would read the entire library if he had to.

Nadi crept under the large wooden doors and hugged the wall. Icarri was not there, but he did not know how she felt about rodents. It was a good thing that she never cleaned up after herself. A sheet hung down from the second floor and lay across the top of a shelf. He could start with the books on the second floor and work his way down. Climbing up the leather-bound spines, he used their height to get to grip on the edge of the next shelf. Then he pulled himself over with the bookbindings. Being this small meant he could die easily from losing his grip. Finally, he had climbed and slipped through the railing to the second floor.

As he headed for the shelf before him, he spotted a green book stuffed under the edge of a cushion next to Icarri's pink dress. It was the one thing that stood out to him because Icarri did not seem interested in any books in the library. He struggled to free it in his small form but managed to clench his teeth in the leather and slowly back up. Once out in the open, he stood atop the book and read the title: *Otherworldly Vegetation and Their Many Uses*.

Staring at the title, he knew it would be bothersome to read, but still, this book may hold clues to get rid of the leech vine. He stepped off the tome and pushed open the cover. Deciding to skip a few pages, he flipped until he started seeing pictures. He skimmed the pages, stopping now and then on words that caught his attention.

By the middle of the book, he was astonished to know that there were many carnivorous plants—even one that could control a person's mind, leading them to infect others. The thought made him shiver; to be eaten or hypnotized, he wished never to see any of them.

Turning the page, he found a section called "Hemovorous Plants." *What did that mean?* He didn't want to skip it and miss something vital, so he kept turning pages to see gory depictions of drained husks of creatures and plants draining the blood out of people. Was this what Icarri was talking about? It didn't sound the same; the way he thought she described it was that they were asleep, unconscious to the world, but unable to die.

Nadi turned the page and saw a plant that, finally, did not give off a deathly image. The chapter titled "Sleeping Leech Vines" held a picture of a woman with a vine wrapped around her as she slept. It is described as follows: "Once it takes hold of a person, it can slowly drain their life energy without leaving a mark." Nadi turned the page and saw another image, the seed, still attached to the plant's roots. He read, "Placing the pit into an item equal to the energy source can produce a portable energy container. That power can mimic the magic of the creature it was taken from or boost one's ability.

"To destroy the plant, the seed must first be broken. Breaking the pit ensures that the plant cannot store energy. It will then wither away. Anyone ensnared will be able to awaken within a few hours. Still, their magic, abilities, or energy may not return for a few days."

The door to the library opened, causing Nadi to jump. He was sure that Icarri was looking for him. He ran to the railing and peered over. The doors closed behind her, and with a swish of her hand, all the curtains shut. She dug through the pile of clothes on the floor and picked up a stone with strange markings. As she mumbled something, it began to glow.

"Thorn, are you there?" she whispered.

After a moment, he heard a man's voice emanate from the glowing rock. "I told you I would be in Firstenfeld this month. Magic is forbidden here! What do you want?"

"Are you somewhere safe?" Her tone seemed more excited than worried.

There was a pause. "I am now since Dane took out a guard that followed us. I'm in Firstenfeld waiting for a late princess. What is it?"

Fear gripped Nadi as he realized that someone had been killed. Neither one seemed surprised by the action of their companion. For him, though, it seemed like these people were used to death.

"I have shifters—so you can stop your quest for an exiled golden dragon." Icarri sat in a chair beside the window and peeked out the curtain.

The man seemed annoyed. "What are shifters going to do? They shift into animals, and I doubt they would be willing to shift into a dragon, knowing the cost."

A devilish smile crossed her face. "I have a willing subject bent on revenge."

Silence filled the room as though the man was taking a moment to process the information. "I'll get to the Bog Fairy Inn. Is the pathway ready for me?"

"Of course," her tone seemed pleased. "What do you think I've been doing this morning?"

"Good, I'll come through tonight then." The stone flickered.

"Oh, and if you can, I need supplies. Meat and soap, maybe some wine. I'm getting tired of having to follow one of them constantly. It's ruining my nails to keep up this hard labor." She studied her hand.

"Fine, but you need to start utilizing the materials around you. How do you expect to survive as a great sorceress if you depend on others to get everything?" Thorn questioned her in a hushed tone.

The stone stopped glowing. Icarri huffed as she tossed it back at the pile of clothes. Just as she was about to say something, a shadow seemed to pass over her.

"Mistress," an eerie voice called.

"What is it, Corbin?" She looked at the drapes as the shadow took the shape of a small dragon with red glowing eyes.

Nadi nearly squeaked at the sight of the mythical black dragon. They had traded their bodies to the creature of wishes to become nothing more than shadows; this was his first time laying eyes on one of them.

"I've searched every spot in the forest looking for the trickster, but I cannot find him." He seemed almost reluctant to state the next part. "I do not think he is in the Enclave anymore."

"The Cove," Icarri corrected him. "This place is now Crescent Cove—and you had better keep searching, Corbin. He attempted to enter the library on the shifters' first day here. The last thing we need is for any words to be whispered to those who might be gullible. We need him locked up so he does not ruin our plans."

"But, Mistress," he paused, then quivered slightly as she glared at him. "What should I do if I find him? I cannot capture anything…I'm just a mere shadow."

She picked up her cup and threw it at the curtain. "Figure it out!"

The shadow rushed to the door and vanished at the hinges. Nadi stood there wondering if he was truly gone. The last thing he needed was a shadow to rat on him for reading a book.

"Now, I gotta go grab that man out of bed and see if he'll ever notice me. Honestly, some men can be so fickle." Icarri's irritation was showing.

As she stood, Nadi pulled away from the ledge and dashed for the window. He noticed it was open a crack, but he had to attempt something more challenging to stay out of sight. Lying on the floor, he switched to his human form and hurried away from the railing. He usually didn't shift in this position, but he was dead if she saw him. Taking a breath to steady himself, he switched into the form of the burrowing owl. Getting up, he heard the door shut.

At this rate, she would see him when he entered the cabin. Panicked, he spotted the blue dress on the back of the chair where she was sitting—an idea formed as he hopped up on the railing and glided down to retrieve it. Turning back, he took the dress to the second floor and headed for the window.

Pushing it open, he spread his wings and soared. Icarri was almost halfway to his cabin. As soon as he was right over her, he released the dress. It hit the ground a few steps behind her, causing her to turn around. He did not stay to watch. Instead, Nadi landed behind his living quarters and hopped to the open window.

Going in, he jumped onto the bed and pushed himself under the blanket and into his clothes. He changed back into his human form, realizing that stuffing his clothes full of straw may not have been the best idea. It was everywhere and very uncomfortable. He pulled at the clumps poking out of the neck of his shirt and the waist of his pants.

The door burst open. Icarri was standing there, holding the blue dress. Her expression was almost furious until she saw his current state, and then it went to confusion. "What are you doing?" She stared at the straw sticking out of his pants.

"I…uh…missed the feeling of a woman," he blurted out. Nadi had never even been with a woman, but it was the only excuse he could think of for his current appearance.

He was loyal to his thievery, and most of the caravan despised that.

Concern washed over her features as she turned away from him. "I don't think a woman feels like straw in your pants. I'll begin knocking from now on."

"Were you going to put me in a dress today?" He asked, amused.

"No," she paused in the doorway, keeping her back to him. "I guess it got caught on my dress and made it halfway across the field before it detached."

"Oh—for today, we should hunt, and I'll show you how to skin and gut an animal. I'll give you these clothes, so you don't have to get your nice dresses dirty."

She almost sounded panicked as she answered, "There's no need for that. I have dirty clothes, plus I can…" Icarri trailed off, and he knew she could not find an excuse not to go hunting.

"Great," Nadi smiled. "I can't wait to sink my teeth into something. We can refill the food stores with salted meat, and that will last us a while. Oh, and I can make you some clothes out of the skins."

Looking as though she was going to vomit, Icarri forced a smile as she peered over her shoulder. "Can't wait," and she quickly left, nearly running across the field.

Nadi laughed as he pulled his shirt off and dumped the straw out. He removed a few pieces from his hair before putting it back on. Doing the same with his pants, he wondered about what he had read. Would a dragon egg be strong enough to hold the power of the Elders? Why would Icarri need it? Either way, he was running out of time.

Chapter 7

"When can we stop?" Icarri complained after ten minutes of walking through the woods. "My feet hurt."

Nadi had never killed anyone before, but he wanted to right now. "You have to be quiet, or you'll drive any animals away. The food stores would remain empty."

"How do you even expect to kill an animal with a knife?" she huffed as she pushed away a branch.

"You have magic that you can kill with, so you just need to take something out with it," he looked over and stopped her. Signaling for her to be quiet, he pointed to a crouched fowl next to a tree. He directed her to aim for it.

"What?" she whispered.

"Use your magic and hit the bird." He tried to be hushed.

Pointing a finger towards it, she mumbled something. The fowl exploded into a puff of feathers. Other birds took off from the nearby trees, and small animals scattered through the brush.

Nadi put his hand over his face as she gave him a sheepish grin. "You did that on purpose." Going to where the promised food had sat, there was only a pile of feathers in its place. Nadi gave a frustrated sigh. "Let us continue then."

"Further into the woods? We're going to get lost." She looked back at the forest behind her.

"For a great sorceress, you have a lot of complaints." He pulled out the knife and marked the tree next to her. "I've been cutting the trees to ensure that we can find our way back. It shows us where we have been."

"More stuff that I did not know," she said sarcastically.

Nadi still had many questions for her. "I thought sorceresses valued knowledge?"

Icarri was silent for a moment as they wandered through the woods. Nadi had stopped to mark another tree. "I was the Duchess of Vadnera. We had a manor smaller than the castle. I had never gotten everything I had wanted, but life went by so fast. My sons fought over who would inherit my riches when I ceased to exist. Knowing this, I could no longer stand it and had them join me on a journey. If I died, they would have to split the fortune evenly, but if one of them died, then the remaining son would get all of it."

Nadi began taking steps, avoiding tree roots. "What was the journey for?"

She gave him a sad smile, "I'm getting there." Following him, she kicked a rock that vanished into some bushes off their path. "My first son lost his life when we entered the ruins because he thought he was going to win if he beat us inside. A swinging blade struck him. My youngest made it to the end with me. He was very talented in removing traps.

"Once he realized my goal was a youthful fountain, he pushed me out of the way and wanted to drink it himself. Ignoring all the bones around the fountain, he drank its sweet waters only to fall prey to its trap. A magic mirror which, if you stare into it after drinking from the fountain, will lock you inside your mind."

The expression on her face almost scared Nadi. Those guys sounded so selfish. It was cruel to care about their mother's riches and not her. He did not know if he wanted to hear the rest of it, but he felt that she would tell him anyway.

Continuing her story, Icarri stopped and picked up a rock, studying its round shape. "I broke the mirror, but not to help my selfish son. Instead, I scooped up the pieces into a sack and then drank from the water. I became young and did not lose my mind. My son, I left to rot because he and his brother never truly loved or cared about me. After that, I became a sorceress, accomplishing more than I did in my life with my selfish children." She pointed the rock towards Nadi as he looked at her in horror. The rock flew past his head and through an elk's ribcage, ten feet away, before embedding itself into a tree.

Nadi, absorbed in her story, did not see the elk. Yet, he had to keep himself from hitting the ground, realizing that she could have killed him at any moment. He could hear the elk collapse to the ground behind him.

"I still had servants who would do everything else for me, but I also now had magic. I did not learn to survive without them." She passed Nadi. "Are you going to show me how to skin it?"

"Yes," Nadi breathed a sigh of relief that he was not dying today.

As he turned around, Icarri planted her hands on either side of his face, bringing her mouth closer to his. Wide-eyed, Nadi did not know how to respond. He froze, uncertain of what he should do.

The sorceress paused, and her eyes opened as she gave him an emotionless stare. "You ever sneak into the library to spy on me again, and I'll have your head."

Fear gripped him as he tried to think, "Icarri, I'm not sure what you're talking about."

"You know very well because the book under my pillow was moved." Her nails started to dig in. "And it was open to the vine. Did you find what you were looking for?"

"That the plant could be destroyed by breaking the seed?" He grabbed her wrists and tried to pull her hands away. "That you plan to use the egg to harness the magic."

Releasing him, she stated, "You think it is that simple? There is no telling what destroying a vine with *their* power can do to the world. We need to harness the energy before breaking the seed. That way, the power is not released all at once."

Awkwardly, he leaned against a tree, not sure how to respond. Icarri's green eyes looked up at him, expecting him to say anything. He heaved a frustrated sigh. "I still don't understand. The book said it would just disperse. Not to mention, you have a shadow dragon lurking around."

"With normal beings, the energy would just disperse, yes." Walking over to the elk, she pushed against one of its antlers. "This has never happened to a god—or nine of them for that matter. There is no telling the damage it could cause if just released. You can also thank Corbin for saving your life. He told me to hit that part of the wall to free you two from the water."

"Sorry, I guess I do not understand how magic works." Nadi laughed nervously.

"You're right," her tone was cold. "You obviously don't." She turned away from him. "You're punishment for questioning me is to be my date for dinner. I expect you to tell me how beautiful I am and praise me in front of our guest."

"Guest?" Nadi remembered that she had been talking with a man through the stone. Her companions, whom he wasn't sure he wanted to meet after hearing they killed a guard with no sense of remorse. "Oh, that's right," he said, understanding that their journey was going faster than he expected now. He only wished he had more than just wine to drown out his thoughts and give him an excuse for disobeying her expectations.

Chapter 8

Blood soaked the ground outside his cabin as he separated the different parts of the elk, and he managed to cure the skin before noon. Icarri was disgusted throughout the entire process. Nadi tried to explain how to use the tallow from the elk, but Icarri looked pained as she tried not to listen.

"With this, you can make candles or soap. It can be helpful since it lasts longer than most other animal fats. It can also be converted into an oil to cook with."

"Please stop," she cried out. "I can't listen to any more of this!"

"Any more of what?" Zec arrived, eyeing the hunting knife that Nadi was holding. "I see this is where my knife went."

She looked up at Zec, her hands covered in blood from helping. Holding them up for him to see, she wined, "My nails! I don't think this smell will ever come out."

Smiling, Nadi teased her some more. "But you didn't even bite into the heart of your first kill. Come on; that's tradition to all hunters."

Gagging, Icarri turned away from him.

Zec sighed. "I'll take it from here. You can go wash up."

Without looking back, she ran towards the waterfall. Not sure how Zec felt, Nadi continued to work on sectioning the meat. His brother began to assist by holding parts for him to cut.

"Why are you torturing her?" Zec asked, watching the knife cut through the flesh.

It was Nadi's turn to sigh. "She keeps making advances towards me, and I am not interested. I just want her to realize I'm not the right one for her."

There was silence before Zec responded. "You're hiding something. There was a hint of orange in your eyes, which happens when you lie. Still, you are telling the truth because even I told her to go for you."

"Why?" Nadi looked towards the trees where she had gone to be sure that she was out of sight. "I don't want to be with anyone, especially her. It just feels like she is lying to us. I went into the library this morning to read through the books. It was to see if there was another way to free the Elders without an egg. Instead, I found a hidden book about plants and learned that the sleeping leech vine could die by destroying the seed. The egg, I believe, is supposed to be a vessel to harness their power. Yet, the vessel needs to be of equal power to them. I don't think it is."

"Nine Gods, who created the world, having their power harnessed in a fertile dragon egg?" Zec thought about it. "What more suitable vessel can you get than a dragon egg to harness the power of creation? But...I suppose there might be a reason she needs a vessel first."

Nadi gave his brother a questioning look.

"I don't know anything about magic—but think about it. If a dam filled with water somehow broke, where would all that water go? Magic may be the same way, where it needs something of equal power to hold the flood back."

It all made sense now. Nadi hung his head down in disappointment.

"We all have to make sacrifices. Once we get the egg and the Elders freed, I can be changed back. Then, I can put it back as good as new. With that magic, I can go back to being a shifter again. We spent the month well."

"And Grumloc?" Nadi asked, noticing Zec forgot to mention him.

His brother jerked the bone away from the meat. "As dead as this animal."

As Nadi began to feel disappointed, a growl happened behind him. He spun around to see a large grey wolf hunched down in the grass. Looking back at himself, covered in blood, he knew he was a prime target. He heard Zec take a step back. "Don't run, or it'll chase you," Nadi warned without looking.

Scooting back, his hand found the meat he had just cut off. He had yet to salt it. Without a second thought, Nadi threw it to the wolf, who jumped back. It let out a warning snarl before catching the scent. Slowly, it approached the meat, grabbed it in its mouth, and ate it. Cautiously, it looked back at Nadi, now without growling.

"I'm feeding more than just the three of us," Nadi returned to the elk and began working. His brother stood there with a bewildered look on his face. "Do you want a new form?"

"What?" Zec looked down at Nadi, trying not to move.

He laughed as he grabbed the bone out of his hand and tossed it to the wolf. As the wolf began to tear at it, Nadi turned back to his brother. "It's a lone wolf, or it would have howled by now. We can gain its trust and its form, or at least one of us can. I already have a predator. So maybe you can have this one to show everyone when we come back."

Zec thought about it. "Nah, I'll pass," he went back to work, holding the leg Nadi was cutting.

Every once in a while, the wolf would let out a whine, and Nadi would throw it some meat or a bone. They soon stripped it down to the skeleton and had every part they needed submerged in a barrel of salt. Nadi turned back to the wolf, who had an expectant look on its face. Holding meat in one hand, he watched as the wolf slowly approached. As it attempted to take the flesh out of Nadi's hand, he brought his other hand up cautiously towards the wolf's head.

The wolf let out a warning growl, but Nadi did not pull back. He let his hand stay there. Turning to look at the hand, the wolf smelled it and then licked at the dried blood. As they locked eyes, he knew he had gained its trust.

With that, the world became dark except for the eyes of the wolf. Hairs spouted from Nadi's skin, covering him. He gained a snout with a wet nose as his teeth became sharp points. Dropping down on all fours, he shook off his clothes to reveal a long furry tail. As he straightened up, he looked exactly like the same wolf.

Seeing that Nadi transformed, the wolf jumped back. Taking a moment to observe the now transformed shifter, the wolf slowly approached and sniffed him. Nadi stepped to the side and let the wolf get to the food. Taking a moment to see what Nadi was doing, the wolf licked his cheek and then went for the remains of the elk. He would wait for his new friend to eat its fill before burying the bones.

Nadi pranced around his brother, getting used to the feeling of being a wolf. He yipped and barked, running in circles, trying to see his tail. With tail wagging, he pushed his wet nose against his brother's hand, hoping that he would change into something too. He noticed his brother smelled of sand and sweat. Zec needed a bath.

Another scent filled his nose, one of musty perfume and burnt herbs. He wondered if that was how Icarri smelled. Turning his attention towards the waterfall, Nadi realized she had yet to return. He almost felt bad for not trusting her judgment on this and wanted to apologize.

"Hey Nadi," Zec was staring at the wolf as it ate.

Switching back to his human form, Nadi picked up his clothes and started putting them back on. "Yes?"

"Do you think that Icarri can bring Mother back?"

Nadi stopped after slipping his pants on one leg. The thought had not occurred to him; Icarri talked about time magic, but Nadi doubted it even then. "I think the way it works is her body might have to be present to change her back—because if you think about it, you would be there, and the egg would be there. Mother's ashes and braid were left at the keep years ago."

Zec stared off for a moment. "You're right. There is no bringing back the dead when there is nothing left."

Trying to change things to a brighter note, Nadi looked at the barrel of salted meat. "I remember the good food you always managed to cook. You should teach me all your secrets." He managed to get his pants on and threw the shirt over his head.

Zec poked him in the ribs. "The question is, are you going to be sober enough to remember?"

Nadi realized he had almost gone the whole day without a drink. "Oh, I can hear my love calling me. I almost forgot to grab a kiss of that sweet wine."

"Talking of kissing wine? Maybe I should steal a kiss to taste this wine." Icarri was standing a few feet away.

The wolf stopped eating and ran back to the woods. Nadi wished he could do the same. Looking over his shoulder, he could see she had dressed in a more delicate yellow gown, with lace flowers across her midsection. She did look attractive, but Nadi only had one love, and it was not her. "I'm willing to share it with dinner tonight, so no need to steal kisses," he laughed uncomfortably.

Zec seemed to eye him questioningly, but Nadi did not want to upset Icarri and end up like the elk. Going inside, Nadi retrieved the bottle of wine. "Goodbye, my love," he said longingly, taking one last swig. Then he went out to face the music.

Chapter 9

After giving his bottle of wine to Icarri, Nadi busied himself with burying the elk's remains before walking to the waterfall to clean up. To his dismay, he still did not find his clothes. The waterfall was causing the ground to become a muddy mess.

An idea occurred that he could divert the water to cut through the field. It was nearing dusk as he gathered large rocks to wall off the waterfall. He knew he needed to join them for dinner, but hoped he wouldn't have to deal with Icarri's hungry eyes—and he didn't mean for the food. Worry for the guest Icarri had spoken of was bothering him as well. Nothing seemed right about her plan: No physical dragons around to aid her cause, withholding information about the sleeping leech vine, and she had yet to change time with magic. It seemed as though it was impossible magic. Reversing time, killing someone to bring them back

—Nadi was sure that the dead stayed dead. Even if you heal a body, the soul is bound to have passed on.

"Dinner will get cold with you standing there," Icarri's voice rang behind him.

Suddenly, he was very uncomfortable. "I wanted to start diverting the water to create a stream through the field so that we can have easy access to it."

"You can do that tomorrow." She grabbed his arm and started dragging him back towards the library. "Let us feast! And tomorrow we can start our plan on infiltrating the dragons' keep."

Nadi was not thrilled, but he couldn't let her see his worry that something was amiss. "Yeah, can't wait." Feeling defeated, he let her drag him through the woods as she rambled on about how she had done her hair differently and how she had not worn this dress in ages. He began wishing that she would stop talking. Even the fireflies did not appear as they walked.

There were many things that Nadi now wanted to do. Once his brother was back home safe, he was going to travel the world. He wanted to explore and maybe even find a meaningful job that suited him instead of trading. He thought about how he would stop stealing and live a better life than he had in the desert.

Icarri flung open the library doors and waltzed in. Nadi closed the doors behind him and then looked at his brother. Zec had set the table, and Icarri had cleaned her clothes off the floor. Either the guest was significant, or she had shoved everything into her magical pouch. Nadi didn't care about that. He just wanted to drink his wine and forget about everything.

Zec had placed the food on the table. "I managed to find some potatoes in the woods. We can extend the garden and fit them in. The wild berries grow like crazy around here. This place could fit the entire encampment." For a moment, he sounded excited, but then his expression became sad. "We couldn't bring them here; they wouldn't get past the dragons."

"Hey," Nadi said as he sat at the table and poured a cup of wine. "Most of them would want to stay in the desert anyway. It's tradition, and like father, they will always choose to keep tradition."

Watching him sip the wine, Zec proceeded to take a seat across from him. "Says the one that never follows tradition." He cut off a portion of meat, placing it on his plate with some potatoes. "Once I kill Grumloc, we can bring our tribe here."

Icarri let out a laugh, "This is the training ground for dark angels. Once the Elders are free, you and your people cannot live here. It will become a training ground for the executioners of kings and queens. To go free into the world and kill the innocent if ordered to."

When the travelers passed through, they had always spoken well of the dark angels. They were heroes in tales, but they had vanished from the earth ten years ago after going against a sorcerer. What Icarri said made Nadi feel even more uneasy.

She ran her fingers down Nadi's back. "It's a good thing that they're gone. No more innocent people to slaughter. Once we reverse time, hopefully we can convince the Elders to never create them." She took the cup of wine from Nadi and raised it to toast. "May they forever rot and never return."

Without thinking, Nadi shoved her away from the table. The goblet slipped out of her hand and clattered against the wooden floor, spilling its red contents everywhere. His heart was racing, as was his mind. Memories rushed like a torrent before his eyes of his mother's last moments.

The sorcerer had said those exact words when Daron had vanished.

"Hey, it's just a cup of wine! There isn't a need to start pushing." Zec helped Icarri off the floor.

Wide-eyed, Nadi stumbled over his seat and backed away towards the door. "I'm sorry," he muttered as he continued backing away. "I...think I'm going to be sick."

Both Icarri and Zec stared at him, bewildered. Nadi's mind was reeling; how could she have said those same words? Possibilities were rushing in as the walls seemed to close around him. He could barely breathe as the room felt immensely warmer, but he was sure that he needed to think. Slipping out the doors, Nadi ran toward his cabin. But when he got there, he did not go inside.

Instead, he turned toward the woods and decided that he would keep going. Tree branches lashed at him as he leaped over rocks and tripped over roots. Animals that had settled in for the evening became startled by his sudden appearance in their territory, causing them to flee. Tears streaked down his face as he rushed through the foliage.

Suddenly, the trees were no longer around him, and the solid earth under his feet became sand between his toes. Wiping away the tears as he stopped, he looked over the horizon of the ocean. The waves gently crashed against the shores. Nadi noticed that the coast lit up with every wave, sparkling blue. It was so beautiful, he stood there and watched in amazement. Then, he sat on the beach and looked at where the water met the sky.

"Mother..." he felt ridiculous talking to himself, but he knew no one was around. "All of this feels wrong, and I don't know why I can't trust Icarri. She said the same thing the sorcerer had said, and it set me off. I feel as though I'm failing to protect Zec, even though Icarri promised that everything would be fine."

Nadi listened to the sound of the waves for a moment, as though expecting to hear her voice remind him of something or give him advice like she used to. But only silence aside from the calming sounds of the sea met his statement.

Balling his fists, he hit the sand, jarring his wrist and almost making him feel like a child throwing a tantrum. That feeling gave way to another memory of when he was a mere child, getting jealous of his brother because his mother no longer had time for him. More tears came, and he wiped them away quickly. Nadi wished he could go back to these simpler times. Back to when his brother looked up to him, and he was his father's pride.

Movement caught his attention, and he looked down the beach to see a wolf running across the sand in the light of the full moon. He recognized it as the one from earlier. It slowed down to a walk, panting as it approached him.

"Nice night for a walk," Nadi laughed.

With tail wagging, the wolf began licking Nadi's face. He laughed again, pushing the wolf away. Lying back in the sand, he could see so many stars. Nadi recalled his childhood when his mother told them stories about how the Gods made the stars to light the way for all who were lost. She was often fond of those magical tales and legends of old. Always, his mother enjoyed the fantasy of how magic existed. Her favorites were tales of ghosts and spirits, but Father would get upset when her stories scared Nadi and his brother.

At that moment, he thought about what his mother would think. "Mother would say, *Icarri has her own opinion. Her words were her own, just as your thoughts are your own.*" Nadi lay there a moment longer.

The wolf let out a whine, watching him. "I'm fine, I just may have overreacted to something that Icarri said. I should apologize." Nadi rose and both began walking back towards the library. Nadi felt a little better that he thought it through. He was glad he put his mother's reasoning to use.

Chapter 10

Emerging through the trees, Nadi could see Zec and Icarri talking over dinner. Icarri laughed as Zec made a gesture with his hands. It was probably Zec's favorite story of how a tarantula was on a tent, and one of the tribe members thought it was a good idea to try and tame it. thinking he could transform. The tarantula won by jumping on his face, causing him to faint. The poor guy was afraid of spiders ever since. He laughed to himself as he started across the field.

It was then that he saw the curtain in the temple move again. This time, a pale white face peered out. It was a young woman with raven black hair and a black dress. The pale white hand that held the curtain seemed to fade, and the red fabric fell through her fingers.

Nadi stopped in his tracks, realizing that he had seen a ghost for the first time in his life. It was almost impossible, but even now, the curtain was still moving. He thought that maybe he'd just imagined the curtain passing through her fingers. Part of him knew he could not stand by with curiosity growing inside.

Changing his course, Nadi crept over to the temple doors, which he noticed also had angels carved into them. There were nine standing at ready with their weapons. Slowly, he opened the door and crept inside.

The entryway was dark and dusty as he let the doors click shut behind him, sealing off any light. To him, it seemed odd that Icarri had not locked the doors; she'd been adamant that it was dangerous to go inside the temple. It was as though she did not believe her own words. Like it was a lie.

Nine black stone pedestals lined the hallway, and lying next to each one was a weapon, adorned with silver wings or feathers. With Nadi's gaze wandering over the display, he felt as though he should not touch them. It was not a feeling of warning but one of worth, as though the air around them told him he was not worthy of laying a finger on any of these weapons.

Next to the first pedestal on his left was a silver bow. The top and bottom limbs were in the shape of wings, and the feathered tips were positioned to hold the string. Except the line was missing. Unlike the limbs, the grip was wooden.

Turning back to the first pedestal on the right, he saw an ax on the floor behind it. The blades, a set of wings connected to an angel whose hands pressed together before it as though it were praying. Carved into the wood were intricate designs. Two spots were bound by leather, leaving areas to grip along the handle.

Crouching down, he made his way around the ax and came to the next stone pedestal on the right. He wanted to be out of sight in case someone went through the doors. Passing over a whip handle, he noticed a single silver feather attached to the other end. Ordinarily, these weapons had strips of leather where the feather was.

Rolling across the floor to the next altar on the left, he almost touched a dagger he had barely seen. Its blade was a single feather, and there was a ring at the end of it. It was a knife he had never before seen.

Coming to the third pedestal on the left, he noticed there was no weapon on the ground. Bringing his gaze up, he nearly jumped back as he met his reflection on the silver surface of a sword, floating above the dark, smooth stone. It was something that shouldn't be, yet he knew what he was seeing. Slowly, he passed his hand under the pommel to find that nothing was holding it up. There were no hooks in the ceiling or strings on the walls. Only one explanation occurred to him: magic held this weapon in place.

Taking a moment, he admired the guard, a pair of wings facing down. A plaque on the pedestal read "Fallen," and it made sense. With the sword drawn, it would point the wings toward the ground. It occurred to him that there was no sheath for the blade. How would a dark angel carry the sword?

Still, he did not feel worthy, staring at such a magnificent weapon. It was something he would never use, even to decorate his tent. It was too flashy for any nomad. Nadi had seen many swords from travelers, but none like this. The blade was silver, which meant the metal was too weak to withstand a hard blow. Most of the weapons bore the same metal with feathers or wings, through the thick layer of dust. For creatures that were so revered, they seemed so forgotten. The dark angels were fearsome warriors who had been talked about highly in passing tales. He was sure that weapons like these could not hold up in a battle.

Looking around, he realized he did not see the woman. The window she had been looking out of was behind the sword. No footprints disturbed the dust between the pedestal and the window. There were a few sets of boot prints on the carpet; Icarri's and one other that looked to belong to a man. Yet, they were nowhere near the window. Nadi studied the floor behind the pedestal and took note of the trail through the dust from the curtain moving.

As he walked down the hall, making sure to place his footing in the same place as the broader set of prints, he noticed that there were only eight weapons. Stopping, he counted each to make sure: "A sword, bow, ax, and a whip." Leaning as he peered around the other pillars and looked over the rest, "A scythe." The long, curved blade was a wing connected to a hooded angel at the top of the pole. "A spear, a strange dagger," Nadi eyed the tip of the spear, which was a feather. He inspected a stick with a feather wrapped around the handle. "A fancy stick? How did they ever win a fight?" Looking over each of them, he remembered that the window had portrayed a warhammer. It was not here.

Gazing around the room, Nadi did not see even a hint of the handle hidden behind a curtain. Someone must have stolen the hammer. It was a shame that he could not see it.

Following the footprints to the end of the hall, Nadi slowly opened the door. The dimly lit room held nine beings of Light, pinned to the walls with large green vines and red thorns. Heavy red curtains blocked out the windows. There was not a speck of dust in this room. The room's center held a mass of vines and a single red seed protruding from the middle. He looked upon the gods in wonder. Each of them looked similar to many races he had seen.

"Dwarf, Elf, Halfling, Dragon, Human…" he trailed off, unsure what the others were, since the rest looked human. One of them had horns and a tail. The only race he believed was missing was an Abandreal. They had animal and human features.

Stories had stated that one of the gods had left to live as a mortal. Legend says it was because the Abandreals had angered one of the elders. Instead of immense power and dominance over the other races, they had become restricted when their god stepped down.

Nadi looked around the room, but the woman was not here either. Maybe he had imagined things? Thinking of his mother's old stories had probably set the image of a ghost in his mind. One of her favorites was about how the silver dragons had vanished. The tale was in the form of a song.

Their king exiled all the men from the kingdom and would steal women from their homes. He feared that he could not sire his one heir with dragons alone, since dusk dragon females had become so few. All the women he had captured, he hid in the maze of his keep. One dragon called Lady Mira gave up her egg to set them free of the king's madness, only to realize her mistake and end her own life too. Her ghost haunts the silver keep, begging for the return of her egg.

A shiver traced his spine. It was just a tale meant to scare children who wandered too far from the camp. They had often joked that Lady Mira would take them away to her keep if they were terrible. Now Nadi wished he had taken the wine with him. He began to miss his mother again, terribly.

Turning to leave, Nadi's eyes passed over some black and gold fabric spread out on the floor. His eyes traced the designs, causing him to freeze as he realized it was the same cloak that had burned when Daron had vanished from the keep. Looking at the floor, he realized that the same symbol was there.

His thoughts raced back to Icarri, speaking to the man, and how she was waiting for him to arrive. The cloth piled on the symbol is how he would get here. Not by airship or by sea. A cloak of teleportation. The voice he realized was the same one he had heard on that horrible day. This man was the reason their mother was dead, and Daron was missing.

Anger began to rise in him. It was all their fault. Icarri helped this man with his plan, and in return, it cost their mother her life. It was time he set the Elders free, and they would hopefully seek their revenge on these two.

Nadi kicked the cloak off the symbol and ran down the hall, ready to do all he could to end this war. He slowed down as he approached the floating sword. Throwing caution to the wind, he slowly reached out his hand and touched the leather-bound grip.

His entire body froze as a searing pain coursed through him. It felt as though his soul was tearing away from him. Nadi could not breathe or release his grip. It was as though he had touched a lightning toad and could not let go. The sword vanished as a warm feeling entered through his fingers, creeping down his arm before filling his chest.

A woman's voice entered his mind as he fell to his knees. "The sword has chosen you as a guide for my apprentice, so your life is spared. All who touch the sword perish, except for the dark angel and her guide."

Afraid of what he had done, Nadi hurried away from the pedestal until his back was against the wall. "Who are you?" he demanded as he looked around.

"I am Cynthia Heartford of the fallen Kingdom of Gavran, and was the dark angel of Vadnera until a sorcerer took my life." A woman began to materialize in front of him. Pale skin, honey eyes, black dress, and raven black hair and wings. "No one else will be able to see me, but my power is weak because the Elders sleep. We must free them and restore order before my apprentice perishes."

"A…a ghost!" He cried as he pressed himself against the wall.

"Shush!" She floated toward him. "We don't have time for you to be afraid of me. I can't harm anyone." Her hand passed through his wrist. "See, I can't touch you."

Covering his mouth, he muffled his scream. The dark angel stood back as he did it again. Nadi took in another deep breath and steadied himself.

"Are you done now?" She folded her arms and glared at him.

Nodding, he did not say a word as he stared up at her.

"Let me begin again. I am Cynthia Heartford of the fallen Kingdom of Gavran and was the dark angel of Vadnera—until a sorcerer took my life. You are lucky that the sword has chosen you as the guide for the dark angel. Since it has, only you can see me. We must hurry and correct things before my apprentice dies."

"Why would your apprentice die?" He asked, still nervous about seeing a floating woman.

"The chosen are random since royalty are usually chosen first, but most of the higher class have cleansing rituals which stop them from being chosen. Because our power has weakened, we cannot call upon the guides to take our place or choose an apprentice. If the chosen do not arrive by the next full moon, then they are killed by the Angel's Fever."

An image of bloodied wings sticking out of the back of a young girl passed through his mind. He winced, trying to make it go away. "Alright, alright. I get it. Fail to return in time, and a person dies."

"You'll also be haunted by their death every night."

"Geez, what did I get myself into now?" He stood up, "So, first step is freeing the Elders?"

"Correct, once freed, my power will return," she began walking down the hallway.

Nadi noticed as he followed her that her footsteps made no sound and left no trail in the dust. Her clothes and hair had a magical, slow-moving breeze to them. He reached out to touch a part of her floating dress, but his hand passed right through it.

"Focus," she said as she got to the doors. "Do you have a weapon?"

Stopping in his tracks, he stared at her in confusion. "Don't you have a sword?"

Her tone became frustrated. "The sword is the magic inside you that leads you to my apprentice. It will not appear until they come here or have died from the Angel's Fever. If we don't free the Elders, then the apprentice will die either way. No magic to stop the fever's effects, no dark angel to take my place, endless nightmares because you failed in my task."

Rummaging through his pockets and clothes, he looked at her, concerned. "Why do I suffer from this when I didn't even want to be the guide?"

"You grabbed the sword," she pointed a finger at his chest. "Would you have preferred the sword to steal your soul and darken an angel's wings before they even sprout, or would you choose to live and guide the next dark angel here?"

There was no need to answer as he walked into the room. Grabbing a torch off the wall, he swung it a few times for good measure. The seed was glowing with power, but the thought occurred to him that his brother might be right. "Where will the magic go that is stored?"

"The vine uses it to live. It will take a few days for the vine to fully die, and then the Elders to recover. You have to damage the seed. Removing it would be faster."

Glad to hear that magic would not explode the room, he adjusted his grip on the torch and approached the seed. Looking at the green vines, he saw that they slowly moved. "They used that time magic to defeat them?" he asked without looking back.

"This time magic," a man's voice echoed through the room—and everything froze. He recognized the voice, but was unable to turn around. "I thought that having two shifters roaming about might prove to be troublesome, especially since only one is willing to go along with the plan. You are obviously the troublesome one who is proving to be against us."

Nadi wanted to confront the real person behind his mother's murder, but he couldn't move. Forcing the torch from his hand, Nadi could move his fingers for a moment. Around his neck, the sorcerer clasped a cold metal collar. An icy feeling fell over him, causing a shiver.

Time began to move again, and Nadi spun around, almost losing his balance. He looked at the man's brown eyes that showed amusement. Balling his fist, he was ready to hit that smug smile off his face.

"Look out!" Cynthia yelled—but it was too late.

With a grin, the man put his finger on the center of Nadi's chest. With the utterance of a few words from the sorcerer, Nadi became paralyzed and slumped to the ground. He let out a growl as the man grabbed the back of his shirt and dragged him towards the other side of the room.

"As easy as that was, I do apologize that things must be this way, but the dark angels must never return. When I was younger, they killed my father, only because I was in love with a princess, and she loved me. A prince could not take her denial and had my father killed by these so-called heroes." He placed him against the wall and grabbed his hair, forcing Nadi to look him in the eye. "The Princess, realizing my pain, had the Orb of Time created for me so I could go back and save my father." Releasing his head, he pulled on the torch above, and the wall next to them opened. "Unfortunately, it was not powerful enough. I could only go back for a few hours."

Nadi could not meet his gaze, but now he knew what the man was after. He wanted to use the egg to capture the Elders' energy and power the orb. It would be an infinite supply of power to take him back far enough to save his father. Nadi knew how it felt to lose a parent, but this man had killed his mother to succeed.

Even if this could bring back his mother, this magic was something they should not be using.

Chapter 11

The sorcerer dragged Nadi down the stairs, letting his heels hit every step. It got darker and darker as they descended further down. The man's orb gave off a faint light, yet Nadi was facing back where they had come. His eyes could no longer see the door. The sorcerer's echoing footsteps were the only sound, other than Nadi's body dragging into the darkness.

As they reached the bottom, Nadi heard a growl. He held his breath, hoping that this wasn't going to be the last thing he experienced on earth. The man pulled Nadi closer to the sound. He could also hear running water, almost like a stream or river. Pushing him against the wall, the sorcerer connected a chain to Nadi's collar before whispering a few more words he couldn't understand.

Nadi could feel his body again, but he was also hurting now. His heels felt the impact of every stone step. He rubbed his sore feet.

Finally able to look around, he could see he was in a cave. Dark and damp, the rough stone under him was cold to the touch. Certain parts of the cave were too dark to see.

"To what do I owe the pleasure of this visit, Thorn," a familiar voice echoed, stopping the growl.

Nadi looked across from him to see the golden eyes of Daron. Years of filth coated the Dragon King. His once fine clothing was soiled and tattered. A scruffy beard protruded from his once smooth chin, making him almost unrecognizable. For a second, a look of shock passed over his face before turning back to the sorcerer in rage.

"I have brought you a friend to keep you company. You can eat him if you like, since we already have one that suits our needs." The sorcerer smiled at him as he stepped back, getting out of arm's reach of both of them.

"How kind of you to leave him more than an arm's length away. Why did you bring me a shifter?" He asked as he waved his golden-clawed hand at Nadi.

The sorcerer tilted his head as he eyed them both.

"He was meddling in our affairs and had almost succeeded in destroying the sleeping leech vine. No need to wake the gods or bring the dark angels back. Once I get that dragon egg, the dark angels will never have existed."

With that, he took the cloak off and folded it over his arm before taking his leave.

Silence filled the air between them as they listened to his footsteps echo through the stairwell. Daron did not take his eyes off Nadi, and Nadi almost felt guilty, as though he were at fault for this. As he'd been enjoying freedom above, Daron had been under the temple. Here he was, suffering in darkness all along. The grinding sound of the stone wall filled the cave.

Once silence fell again, Daron spoke. "Young Nadi is not so young anymore."

Nadi looked down at his feet but said nothing.

"I know I probably look and smell bad, but so would anyone else who has spent many years locked in a cave. Thank goodness there are no bugs or animals down here, or I would have been picked apart by now." He waited, expecting a response.

Nadi began to feel the crushing weight of hopelessness. He moved the cloak, hoping that it would stop him from coming through, but it did not. He could have stopped Thorn from coming here had he simply destroyed the cloak. Yet, he realized he would not have been able to stop Icarri.

"What happened after I had vanished?" Daron interrupted his thoughts.

"I try to forget," Nadi said as he finally met the dragon's gaze. "The Sorcerer appeared and froze time. Made it look like we were working with him. Grumloc killed my mother, and a war started. It's mostly one-sided because we are not as powerful as the dragons. We just run and hide."

"Grumloc is not one to kill. It is shocking to hear you say he killed Modra. Was there anything left of her?"

"Just ash and her braid," he sighed as the memory hit him.

Daron was silent for a moment. "So, how did you get here?"

"It's more like How are we going to get out? These chains stop us from moving far," Nadi attempted to shift, but pain shocked his body. As the pain subsided, he seemed lost. All these terrible things were piling up.

"Nadi, you're looking at the problem." Daron's tone became stern, "We need to get out of here, and I do agree with that, but we need to look for a solution. This place is sealed off from the rest of the world, or should have been. Magic stopped anyone from seeing this place, but this place is visible with the Elders sleeping."

Cynthia appeared, leaning against the stalagmite that Daron was chained to. "Sure, there are plenty of ways out of this with magic. The cave, the ocean, teleportation cloak, magic circles—and hey, there is always death." After the last sarcastic comment, she stopped and gave him a puzzled look. "How *did* you get here?"

Nadi thought things over for a moment. "How do you know about this place?"

"The Dawn Dragons were once entrusted with their location. It was the secret that was given to the wish creature by my ancestors." He tugged at the collar. "What better way to protect them than to forget their location?"

"Zec and I came through an oasis." Nadi suddenly tried to get up. "I have to warn Zec! They are using him!"

"Calm down. We need to figure this out." Daron tried to get Nadi to sit, but he was too far away from him. "You went into the Oasis, and where did it lead?"

"To a cave," Nadi looked towards the sound of rushing water. "A water cave that fed into the mountain and flowed into the oasis. The waterfall! If we leave out through here, this will come out at the waterfall, but if we could make it past the undertow, we should be able to make it to the oasis."

"There we go," Daron went from his perched position to sitting cross-legged. "Now, we just need to get out of these collars and escape."

"We need to wait for Zec," Nadi stated. "I need to make sure my brother is safe and knows the truth. I need him to leave with us, and we can end this war."

"And start the one with the sorcerer," Daron let out a low growl.

Nadi stared in the direction of the water. His brother's near-death by drowning experience crossed his mind. As much as he wished that he could make the sorcerer disappear and find another way, he knew that the only way back home was either over the mountains or through the cave. Still, he wasn't entirely sure if it was the way out.

But it was their only chance at escaping. Nadi hoped that he could see Zec and warn him.

"Rest now, Nadi. I have a feeling that you won't get much from here on out," Daron leaned back against the pillar. "I believe that we have the advantage since Thorn does not know that we know each other. We need to keep it that way. The sooner he figures it out, the sooner he will separate us. We need to work together."

It made sense; Thorn wouldn't have put him here otherwise. He traced the collar at his neck, mulling over any thoughts of getting out of here. Yet his thoughts turned to Daron, who looked skinny and frail. He used to be strong and muscular, but Thorn seemed to have taken that from him as well.

"How do we get out?" Nadi asked. Daron, being a dragon, could not hold his breath long enough in the water to survive getting to the other side. Climbing over the mountains would take too long.

"We will think of a way," the Dragon King reassured him. "Once we correct everything, we can have a big feast to commemorate our return. For tonight—rest. We'll think of something tomorrow.

Yet, Nadi could not sleep knowing the truth. He knew he had to get free and find a way out. For his brother's sake, he was going to do all he could to foil their plans.

Chapter 12

The light of dawn came in through the open window, a little disorienting to Zec. He sat up, noticing that he had slept in a little later than usual. After dinner, he had spent some time looking for Nadi, but could not find him. He gave up after scaring off the wolf who stood outside the temple.

For a moment, Zec debated closing the window and going back to bed. His brother had acted so strangely last night that he couldn't help but wonder what had gotten into him. The wine was not that important to him. He could understand ale—but to push Icarri, like she had done the vilest thing to him, had gone too far.

Zec finally forced himself off the bed and adjusted his grey shirt. He should try to find him and see what had bothered him so. "What has gotten into him?" he muttered, running his hand through his hair.

As he left the room, his other hand brushed against the sandal still connected to his belt, and he stopped. His neck and lips tingled as the memory resurfaced. Even though he knew there was a possibility he would not live through this, he wanted to see Terika again. Touching two fingers to his lips, he took a moment to remember her red eyes and soft kisses.

As he walked to Nadi's cabin, he found the door open and a blond man emerging from the entrance. Zec stopped as he met his brown eyes. He reached for his hunting knife, but it was not on his side. Frustration toward his brother arose, but he kept his attention on the man.

"Oh—you're awake," the man smiled at him. "I was hoping to introduce myself."

Zec did not want to be rude, but the man had just come out of his brother's cabin. "I was hoping to see my brother since he seemed a little upset last night." Leaning to the side, he tried to get a good look around him. The cabin looked as though a storm had turned it upside down.

"Sorry to say this, but he is not in there," the man said with a grave expression. "Your brother had almost destroyed the world."

His eyes became wide. "What? How would he have done that?"

"I teleported into the temple to see what I could do with the vine, and he was about to strike the seed with this knife." He pulled out the hunting knife he was missing, "With no place for that energy to go, it would have taken out a great portion of the world—if not everything."

Zec was furious that his brother had still tried to destroy the vine after they had spoken. He didn't know what could have set him off. Nadi was usually one to listen to reason, so it made no sense that he would go off and do something so reckless after they had talked about it. Then again, he realized that, here in this garden, was the most that they had spoken since their mother passed away.

"I'm sorry," he managed to get out. "I don't know why he would do that."

"My boy, there are lots of things that we cannot explain." The man pulled a pipe out of a pouch on his belt. "Let me introduce myself." He reached into his pockets, searching for something to light it. Then he stopped and brought the wooden lip of the pipe towards his mouth. "I am the Great Sorcerer Thorn."

"I am Zec, and you already know Nadi. By the way, where is he?"

"Currently, he will be staying with the dragon for a while, but he is on his way to the library." Smoke started rising from the pipe.

Zec watched the wisps of smoke dance in the breeze, not sure how it had been lit. "With the dragon? Where is that?"

"All in good time," he took a puff from the pipe. "We first need to discuss your ability to transform and the plan to infiltrate the keep. Come—the tea must be ready."

The doors to the temple opened, and Icarri emerged with Nadi in tow. He stumbled after her, glaring at the back of her head, his eyes a bright red. Zec knew his eyes matched since he couldn't believe that his brother would blatantly disregard his warning and disobey Icarri's trust. The moment Zec thought he could change was the moment he only seemed to get worse. He could no longer depend on Nadi.

As Zec followed them through the library doors, Icarri sat down in a chair, holding a chain that was connected to Nadi's collar. She pulled on it, causing his brother to fall to his knees.

Nadi looked up at him with an exhausted expression. It seemed as though he had not gotten any sleep. Zec was furious, but also concerned about his brother's well-being. His feet carried him until he was standing in front of Nadi.

"Why, after our conversation, would you go in there and try to destroy the vine anyway?" He looked at Icarri and Thorn, who acted as though a chained shifter was the typical morning tea entertainment. "You know that magic is dangerous, and we don't know anything about it."

He lifted his head. "A dark angel told me that nothing would happen if we destroyed the seed."

"Lies!" Thorn poured the hot tea into his cup. "All the dark angels are dead!"

"Their bodies are only dead; their spirits are still alive!" Nadi looked up at Zec, his eyes turning yellowish-orange.

Zec knew that shade of orange could mean dishonesty, but that color also meant fear. It was the same color his eyes had changed to the moment he had realized Mother was gone. He didn't know what to believe.

"Then get this spirit to show itself," Thorn taunted.

Nadi looked as though he were listening to something before he spoke. "Why, so you could trap her as you did me? You want the power to reverse time and prevent all angels from existing. Even bringing your father back is not your true end goal."

Thorn laughed. "The dark angels killed my father and have no reason to exist. It was the dragons who trapped the Elders so they would be the strongest out of all creatures. They wanted to be the richest as well. They needed to be on top and would do anything for it, even kill the leaders of tribes."

The scene of their mother's death passed through his mind, causing his heart to ache. The dragons had killed their mother, a leader, without so much as thinking their actions through. None of this would have happened if the dragons had not laid claim to the desert. It was all their fault that he had to suffer.

"You need to trust me, Zec, we need—"

"Enough!" Zec yelled. "You dare ask me to trust you? When you ignore my advice? I no longer care about you. Nor do I care about this dark angel. I will become a dragon, take the egg, and correct the mistakes of the past. You can stay chained for all I care since you never listen to me!"

Nadi hung his head. Zec could see the tears streaming down his face as he began to sob. Nothing he did now could change his mind.

He was going to get Mother back.

The sorcerer finished his tea before leading Nadi out of the library, dragging him by his chain. Icarri went about acting as though nothing had happened. Zec, however, just stood there, not sure if he had done the right thing. All he knew was that these people took them in and asked for their help, and instead of helping them, Nadi tried to ruin their hard work.

A dark angel told me, rang through his mind. Nadi was one to hide the truth—but never really lie. He would admit when he had done wrong, even before getting caught.

"So how is it that he could speak to a dark angel when they are all dead?" he asked himself.

Icarri piped up, "It was probably a lie, or maybe he was going mad." She picked at the books on the shelf next to the table. "Heck, you can't even touch their weapons without having your soul ripped out."

Shaking his head, Zec took his leave. He needed to think alone without the influence of others. Their opinions did not need to push his thoughts further. Even then, all he wanted to do now was kill Grumloc. He was growing impatient.

◆ ◆ ◆

"No need to cry," Daron said gently, after the sound of grinding stone subsided.

Nadi curled up as best he could, hiding his face from him. The last thing he needed was to feel weaker than he already was. Powerless, hopeless, and afraid were all the emotions that filled him. He just wanted to slip away and not exist anymore.

"Come now—I could tell you something that would cheer you up!" He tried to persuade Nadi.

He finally looked up so that Daron would stop bugging him. Wiping away the tears, he waited for Daron to say something, but he looked as though he were deep in thought. He was exhausted from having to sit up all night. The chain was just long enough to allow him to lean forward.

"What would cheer me up?" Nadi figured that asking might get it out quicker.

"What would you say if I told you that your mother was still alive?" Daron gave a small smile.

Nadi just felt even more down than he did before. The last thing he needed was for his hopes to be up, wishing for a miracle. "I wouldn't believe you. She could never have lived through that?"

"Are you sure?" He stretched his legs out.

"Come on," Nadi was getting frustrated. "I just dealt with Zec, thinking that I almost destroyed the world and that I'm a liar. The last thing I need is false hope."

"Ok then." Fiddling with a ring, Daron looked around the cave. "I was only going to say that if we make it to the keep, then you're probably going to want to save those tears for when you finally see your mother again."

Nadi shot him a warning glare, but said nothing.

"Did you know that dragon's fire can do lots of things, even teleport something?" he gave a mischievous smile. "I would show you, but my human form cannot breathe fire that well."

Nadi let the information sit for a moment, "Are you trying to tell me that the fire teleported my mother? Ashes and a braid were all that remained in her place."

"Teleporting with fire is tricky magic for dragons. We know that it will not burn a living creature...but hair is not a living thing."

Suddenly, everything made sense to Nadi. He had always thought that there should have been more left by the blaze. Yet, he always pushed that thought aside. Only her hair and clothes had burned. He attempted to stand, but the chain was too short.

"Slow down there. You don't want to be a fish jumping into the bear's mouth, practically taking your head off. Take a moment to—"

"Zec needs to know!" Nadi almost shouted. "If I had known earlier, then I could have told him, and there would be no reason to do this. I need out!"

Daron gave him a concerned look. "Nadi, if I did, then those two would have muzzled me, and I wouldn't even be speaking right now. They would have used magic to kill one of you and force the other to do everything they want. Finding help is the top priority. If you can make it to the dragons and warn them about everything, then they will arrive, and their time magic would be useless."

Nadi finally sat back down and looked at him. So many thoughts were racing through his mind. A memory of his mother's smile flashed before his eyes, and all he could think about was what he would say to her if he did see her.

"Zec is safe for now, so all that is needed is to ensure that they can't follow through with their plan. But Nadi—I need you to do something for me." Daron sat on his knees, looking him in the eye. "I need you to take my form."

His eyes locked onto Daron. "I can't do that. If I do, I'll never be able to change back."

The Dragon King nodded in acknowledgment, his expression becoming solemn. "I know, but I can't risk them getting it. If you leave here and don't make it back in time, they could still have Zec take it and use him to carry out their plans. We need to cover all of our tracks here. The collar will stop you from changing into a dragon so you can warn the other dragons."

With his back against the wall, Nadi looked up at the cave ceiling. "So I become Elias just like everyone warned me about." He tried to look at it from every angle, but Daron was right. They had to take away every chance Thorn had at infiltrating the keep, even if he was sacrificing his favorite thing in the process. "You're right," he reluctantly agreed.

"I trust you, Nadi," he said as their eyes locked.

The world faded to black around those eyes, golden yellow standing out against the black. All the stars vanished as though a flame had flickered out of existence. Around the golden eyes, Nadi could see the metallic shine of matching scales. A growl slowly rose in pitch through the darkness, and the fire lit inside its mouth. Ready to release the flames, Nadi wanted to look away, but couldn't.

As though far away, Nadi heard Daron calling to him. "Hey, snap out of it. Show me that you're all right, kid."

Gasping for breath, Nadi pulled himself from the darkness. His head began to hurt with a throbbing pain. Suddenly, he felt nauseous and dry heaved. It occurred to him that Daron had not disclosed how he was getting out of here.

"Lean to the side," Daron instructed. Pulling off the ring he was wearing, he stated, "If I miss, this is going to hurt like getting too close to a volcano, so try not to move." Smoke started to rise from the corners of his mouth as he put the ring between his teeth. The metal circle vanished as he closed his lips around it.

Nadi cradled his head as he pulled the chain as far as it would go. Eyeing the metal links, Daron moved the metal around in his mouth. Readying his aim, the dragon spat the now liquid metal, launching it onto the chain. The molten metal made contact with the cold chain link and began to sizzle. Coughing, he told Nadi, "Keep pulling."

Feeling the chain give, Nadi jerked the chain harder. With a loud pop, a link on the chain broke. A piece of hot metal made contact with the white shirt, causing it to ignite. Burning hot metal and fire on his back, Nadi yelled out in pain and rolled to put it out. Daron instinctively tried to reach for him to help, but fell short due to the chain.

"Quiet, we don't want them checking on us, boy. Let's hurry, quick." He gestured for Nadi to get closer. "Come—let me check those wounds."

With the fire out, he took a moment to catch his breath. Getting off the ground, Nadi still felt as though his entire back was on fire. He crawled over to Daron. "Is my back burned?"

Inspecting the burns, Daron stated, "The chain managed to land on your spine, and the fire seems to have spread across your shoulders. That shirt is almost useless now, and you might have a scar after it heals." Daron took a few deep breaths, and smoke began to flood out of his mouth. "We need to send a message to the keep for your arrival."

"But you said you couldn't breathe fire?" Nadi recalled their conversation from earlier.

"I should rephrase, I cannot muster a flame that can teleport a person, but I can teleport items. They will pass through fire so the message might burn before someone finds it."

Peeling off the shirt, Nadi looked around. "I don't see anything that we can write with."

Daron smiled, "Your blood. I thought of the idea years ago, but my blood is hot enough to catch everything on fire. Rocks were an idea, except this place, even being a cave, has no loose rocks. All I had were the jewels I had been wearing, and even then, it only tells people that I am alive."

Laying his shirt on the ground in front of Daron, Nadi held out his hand. Using one of his golden claws, Daron gently cut the tip of Nadi's index finger. "Waste not, write something," Daron instructed as a red drop hit the white cloth.

Nadi placed his finger down and wrote. "Found Daron, Need Help, Nadi."

Lifting the fabric, Daron blew hot air on it to dry faster. Nadi had gotten an idea. He rolled the cloth up and took it towards the sound of rushing water. It was a stream that seemed to flow into a cavern. Dipping the fabric into the water, he dampened the outside of the cloth. As he brought it back to Daron, he stated, "There, now it should survive your flame."

"Good," he took a deep breath as he grabbed the damp fabric. Breathing out, a stream of fire engulfed the material. It lasted for a moment, but Nadi saw that the fabric had vanished instead of disintegrating into ash. Daron smiled, "Now we hope that it makes it to Grumloc before you get there. Make haste."

"Thank you, Daron," Nadi smiled even with the burning pain on his back. He looked at the stream and approached it. The image of Zec not breathing passed through his mind, bringing fear into him. Remembering the darkness that had surrounded him, Nadi took a step back. There had to be another way.

Pain shot through his head, and he knelt by the stream. The dragon was there in his mind, trying to force its way out, but with the collar, shifting was impossible. Anger rose in him, along with the desire to be free. Nadi tried to force it back, but it took him a moment to gain control.

As soon as he could breathe, he thought about what would happen if they figured out Nadi had the dragon's form. They would try to lure him back. He needed to be sure that they could not use Zec against him. Turning around, Nadi went for the stairs.

"Where are you going? You need to go that way," Daron called as he passed him.

"I need to make sure they can't use Zec against me," he replied, dashing up the steps until he reached the wall.

Cynthia appeared behind him, "What are you doing? You need to escape through the cave."

"I'm not even sure we can get out that way. We could drown before reaching the other side. If I leave through here, I can take Zec and make it to the waterfall—"

"And then what?" Cynthia floated until she was beside him. "Defy gravity? As a human, you cannot swim against a current, and you obviously cannot transform into anything else. You can't use magic to reverse the waterfall."

"Maybe I can use the orb." Nadi was looking for anything that could trigger the door to open.

"Not possible." She pointed at a torch. "You have to have Thorn's blood running through your veins. That item was designed especially for him by another item called the *Book of Creation*. It was created by the Princess of Vadnera to help Thadius Thorn rescue his father."

"How do you know that?" Nadi asked, halting his search.

Daron yelled from below, "Who are you talking to?"

"A dark angel," he responded, staring at Cynthia for an answer.

"Because I was present in Vadnera when Princess Lillian gifted it to him. She used a drop of his blood and a crystal ball to make it so that only he could use it. After Thorn's father died over a false crime, the King forbade her from seeing him again. She said her goodbyes in person, and after that, Thorn killed us all with the Queen's gift."

"So…no on the orb?" He ran a hand through his hair.

She shook her head.

"But—the dark angels are dead!" Daron called out from below.

"Only in body. I grabbed the sword, and the spirit of one has latched onto me. She said this makes me a guide," Nadi explained as he eyed the torch.

"What? That's impossible!" His voice echoed.

"I'm grabbing Zec and will be right back." He grabbed the torch and pushed it back up. The wall slid out and moved to the side.

"This is the dumbest thing I've seen you do," she stated as he entered the room with the vines.

Nadi wished he had a weapon to deal with the vine, but it was something he could deal with on his way back. He avoided the tendrils as he rushed out the doors and down the hall. Just as he made it to the first pedestal, the front door began to creak open.

Diving behind the stone pillar, he watched as light filled the room and then darkened as the door shut. He heard the sound of feet on the rug walking down the aisle. Nadi tried to hold his breath, but the pain in his head came back, causing him to wince. The sound came closer, and Nadi tried to scoot around the stone obstruction.

Cynthia hovered in the doorway with an amused look. "So, playing hide and seek from your brother, whom you were trying to save."

Peeking around the corner, he saw the bare feet, grey pants, and short sun-bleached hair as he entered the hallway, passing right through Cynthia. Nadi slowly got up and followed him. They made it to the area with the sleeping leech vine.

Zec huffed. "There is no dark angel in here."

"You can't see them when they have no magic," Nadi stated.

His brother spun around, drawing the knife. With the point facing his chest, Nadi backed up. He felt the magical circle under his feet as he realized Zec was not putting the knife down.

"I think you have lost your mind," Zec said as he moved closer. "Seeing ghosts, thinking that you can stop magic! The next thing you're going to say is that mother is alive."

"But Zec," Nadi felt the fabric from the teleportation cloak under his foot and avoided stepping on it. "Mother is alive."

"Stop this! You are delusional. Can't you see that you are making all this up because you want Mother back so badly?"

"No, Zec, I think that's why *you're* doing this. You hope to bring our mother back by falling blindly into a trap. You're willing to remove me from the picture so that you can succeed in what you think is correct." Nadi was surprised that those words even escaped his lips. He took one last look at the red in his eyes, as Zec drew his arm back.

Nadi caught a glimpse of Thorn as he entered the room. His breath caught as he realized he was out of time. There was only one route for escape now.

"Move, Nadi, move!" Cynthia yelled

With pain in his head and on his back, Nadi did the only thing he could and grabbed the cloak. Throwing it around himself, he spun once and lost his footing. His hands hit the wooden floor, and to his surprise, there was no echo of the temple.

As he got up, he noticed that he was in a small room with a table and a bed. There was a wooden chest next to the window. Acting quickly, Nadi stuffed the cloak into the compartment, just in case someone followed him.

Cynthia looked out the window, "Oh no. We're in Firstenfeld."

"What is wrong with that?" Nadi opened up a small closet and pulled out a long black coat and an odd-shaped turban with a cylinder. "What is this?"

"That is a top hat, which means that someone will be coming back for their stuff, and we need to move. Also, if anyone sees your eyes, we will have a witch hunter on your trail. If they catch you, then I'll have a ghost companion of my very own." She looked at the items around the room. "Great idea. We need a disguise, and please try to keep calm because orange and yellow are not normal eye colors. Blue, green, and brown are all normal. Just don't look at people's faces."

The pain grew in his head as darkness covered him and drowned out every noise. The feeling of anger rose again and made him feel so small. It wanted control, and he fought it back once again. He could feel that it wished to be free to do as it pleased, but Nadi was afraid because he wasn't sure how long he could keep battling it.

The room came back, and Cynthia was staring at him with a disappointed look. "That," she circled him with her finger. "Needs to stop."

A thud came from the chest, and both jumped. Eying a bucket of water, Nadi quickly grabbed it and placed it on top of the lid to weigh it down. Turning around, he spotted a blue velvet bag on the table. Retrieving the pouch, he put it into his pocket. Throwing the coat on and placing the hat on his head, he flung the door open. A woman in a brown dress gave him an odd look as she headed for the stairs.

Taking one last look over his shoulder, he saw the top of the chest fly open and the bucket tip, drenching the floor. A hand grabbed the edge, but Nadi did not wait to see who emerged.

Leaving the room, he dashed down the stairs and out the front door of the Inn. People seemed to be moving in both directions. Horses pulled carts of many different shapes and sizes. For a moment, Nadi was overwhelmed by the sights, sounds, and unfamiliar smell of this city. It was too loud, too crowded, and smelled foul of sweat, perfumes, and manure.

"Keep going!" Cynthia yelled as he stood there. "Head right to leave the city."

Not looking back, Nadi rushed into the street and kept going. He began trying to keep pace with people as he avoided looking up and stepping in horse droppings. Blending into the crowd, the only thing that separated him from all other people was his lack of shoes and orange eyes.

As they hurried along, Nadi began feeling a pull on his heart like a leash tugging him to follow. He wanted to ask Cynthia if this was him being a guide, but there were too many people around to start talking to himself. Hoping that it led him to freedom, he carried on in silence.

Chapter 13

Roaring filled the halls of the keep. Grumlock could hear Gillian's pain and wanted to stop it, but she was trying to birth their egg. He lay behind the empty throne on the dais while watching the desert. His mind was dwelling on so many things.

While his brother was missing, he had no choice but to continue with the duties of running the keep, which were not going well. Daron usually ran it, and Grumlock would simply act as a guard and patrol.

Now he was beginning to worry why it was taking her so long to birth their egg. There were no doctors in the keep. He tried to focus on memories of Gillian to pass the time.

Part of his duties had been choosing a mate, but he held no interest in anyone in the keep. As much as he wanted to wait for Daron to choose, he was not certain if he would return. Both he and Daron are considered the same dragon in their culture, even though they were two separate beings. Grumlock had to choose a mate for them both.

Gillian had been found in Vadnera in the slave trade. When he went to meet with the Elven settlement in Arvaria Woods. They rescued Gillian from the slave traders and contacted Grumlock to retrieve her.

Once there, he noticed that she was not a full dragon. Gillian was a half-dragon with a fiery rage. Her human mother had been killed, and her dragon father never returned. She lacked all the features of a dragon except for the eyes. Immediately, he chose her, but it wasn't so simple to win her over. He brought her to the keep, and even though she was greeted warmly, Gillian attempted to run away. He would always bring her back since the desert was unfamiliar to her, and she had a lot to learn about being a dragon.

Night and day, he would teach her how to hunt, shift, trade, and negotiate with humans for their goods, but no person dared to argue with a dragon. Eventually, Gillian accepted him, and now, their egg is being born.

Another roar shook the keep, causing him to worry more. Thoughts were coursing through his head, leading him down a darker path.

A guard rushed in, interrupting his thoughts. Gage held a rolled-up piece of fabric in his hands. He knelt before standing at attention. "Grumlock," he addressed informally. "This came through the fire that burns in Daron's room." He opened it to reveal the message, *Found Daron, Need Help, Nadi.*

This time, he roared. Grumlock was excited and furious. The message held no information on their whereabouts. He had no idea where he should look. Yet,

Zec was at the keep, and so Nadi must have been with him. The oasis next to the keep was his only answer on finding them, but they were not water dragons.

"Visit Vadnera and request the water dragon for assistance. We need her help to find Nadi," he stated as he rose and began to pace. "I cannot leave the keep since Gillian is in labor, but have a search party go out and scour every part of this desert. Don't take anymore shifters, just approach them for questions if found. We need to know where Nadi is."

"Understood," Gage rushed to the entrance and shifted into his dragon form before taking flight.

Another thought occurred to him. He had their mother. She may know something.

Chapter 14

Modra pulled at the silver collar around her neck as she stared through the bars. The collar stopped her from shifting, but on top of that, it was also an irritation. She was not sure how much time had passed since she'd arrived here, and while in the caves, there was no point in trying to count the days either; there was no telling day from night. Instead, she began to count the times that the guards scrambled to a cell. She had lost track of the countless marks on her wall, making her lose hope for her people. Her once fine robes were now nothing more than tattered rags. The boots that had covered her feet had fallen apart ages ago. Rats nibbled at her food in the corner of her cell —not like she felt like eating anyway.

A fire burned in the cell across from hers. It was how they teleported people into the cells. Thinking they are dying by fire, only to open their eyes to their new life behind bars. It had been a few days since she had witnessed burnt palm tree fronds and debris come out of the fire. The guards complained when they had to clean the cell because Grumloc had missed hitting two shifters near the keep. They had gone into the Oasis and never emerged from the water. She often wondered if they had drowned. Living here for so long, she had run into a few of her people in the cells around her. All had tales to tell of her sons and how Nadi had fallen from grace the moment she vanished. It let her know how much her boys needed her. At this moment, she could not change her fate, and she wouldn't, knowing that her sons would be free to grow up out there. Never once did she regret her decision.

Everyone who ended up here was assumed, by those on the outside, to be dead, burned to ashes. But in reality, the *victims* would only show up in the dungeon with slight burns that were immediately treated. It *was* magic— but not a perfected art. She lost her braid the day she arrived and, since then, kept her hair short.

A roar rang through the cells, and she covered her ears. It wasn't the first time she heard this cry. For the past few days, the guards seemed uneasy as they patrolled. Murmurs were going around that a dragon was in pain.

"From what I hear, Gillian's egg is stuck. She may not survive long," a passing guard said to another.

The other guard nodded solemnly.

Egg binding was a serious condition that could happen to birds or reptiles; it made sense that a dragon would have the same problem. When a shifter stayed in a form for long enough, the same thing could happen. She could help her people if she saw the signs, but few had died because she did not recognize it in time.

Holding the bars of the cage, she yelled out, "I can help!"

The two guards turned back. She almost wanted to shrink away from their gold serpent eyes, but stood her ground. "How do you possibly know how to help a dragon?" the other, a more masculine guard, asked with a grin.

"Because a dragon is a reptile—or have you forgotten that you're a reptile?—And my people can also change into reptiles." The guards looked at one another. "I can help. Please—tell Grumloc that it's not too late."

"How can we be sure that you are telling the truth?" the first guard demanded.

She huffed a frustrated sigh. "Are my eyes orange?"

Both of them answered in unison, "No."

"My eyes turn orange when I'm lying. I can teach you all the color meanings, but you need to tell Grumloc how I can help. Even if he says 'no' and allows her to die, I'll still teach you the meanings."

The guards stared for a moment before one took off out of the cells, and the other went back on patrol. A moment later, Grumloc's head was outside her cell, and a low rumble came from him. "I was just on my way to see you."

"Great, we can talk when I am in decent clothes and not smothering in filth."

He began pulling his head back when another painful roar rattled the walls. Grumloc paused before looking at her again. "I need answers and help, but if that is your only demand to help and speak with me, then let me oblige. Can I trust you?"

"I trusted both you and your brother for years. I just wanted my boys to grow up together and not forget what

it's like to be children. That's why I'm here and not Nadi."
Her heart ached at the thought of her sons. She missed them
both dearly.

"Fine, the collar stays on, though. No leaving the
keep. I'll prepare clothes for you, so hurry."

He moved back from the cells so the guard could
open the gate. She walked beyond the metal bars for the
first time, knowing that she might return right after she did
her good deed. Looking at Grumloc, who perched outside
of the dungeon, she stated, "I would like to discuss
arrangements for myself and my people after this."

"If both Gillian and the egg survive, then we'll
discuss arrangements." He went back out to his roost, the
guard escorting her further into the caves.

Another painful roar shook the stone around them,
and she knew she was closer. The cave she entered was
massive, with bright spots on the ceiling that almost looked
like stars. Steaming pools of water glowed all around,
helping to light the cave.

Turning to the guard, she asked, "Which one is the
coldest?"

"Um…" the guard looked around. "These are hot
springs."

"Yes, and if you're a dragon, then they are boiling.
Which is the coolest?"

Seeming to understand her, he pointed to the right.
"The dark area in the corner."

"Good," she peeled off he torn-up robes and tossed
them aside. The guard turned his back to her to give her
some privacy. "When I'm clean, we need to move Gillian
to one of these pools. It will help with the egg." She
stopped and looked over her shoulder. "On second thought,

I'll do a quick rinse since time is important here. Go ahead and bring her in."

"But that would mean that you are left alone," his voice seemed concerned.

"Yes, but I have no plans on leaving here. I have things to discuss with an old friend, even if his rampage has gone on for many years. Bring her here quickly. Hopefully, there is not too much pressure, or she might feel paralyzed from the waist down and will need more help."

She heard him step away as she climbed into the warm pool. A few bubbles rose to the top. Her main priority was getting rid of the top layer of dirt. The water turned a muddy color as she rinsed most of the stench off.

A gold dragon drug herself in, growling in pain as another female dragon in human form followed. She stepped out from the bath, receiving a silk robe from the guard who returned as he averted his gaze. Going from pool to pool, she found one that was not scalding hot, but would still seem warm to a dragon. Modra motioned for them to come, and Gillian slid herself into the pool, almost in tears.

"Breathe," Modra instructed. "If you breathe like this," she demonstrated by taking slow, deep breaths. "It will lessen the pain."

Gillian did, and her tears began to stop.

"Now, I need to rub your belly to ensure that the egg is coming out correctly." She stretched out over the dragon's belly, letting her fingers glide over the scales. They were softer than she expected. After all, this was her first time touching a dragon. Usually, it was Nadi and Zec who were climbing all over Grumloc. His scales looked as hard as stone. When she touched the sides, only those scales seemed solid. The egg felt as though it was more to the left than to the center. She gently put pressure on the egg, causing it to slightly shift.

The dragon let out a growl of pain; something was still wrong. She felt around toward the right, and was surprised to feel another round bump.

"Keep breathing," she instructed as she gently pushed the egg back up. "Looks like you have two eggs." Gently, she shifted the second one over toward the middle of her belly.

Gillian shut her eyes, keeping up the breathing. Slowly, she raised herself out of the water and placed her tail just above the stone. The other dragon woman readied herself to grab the egg. One egg came out, and the woman caught it, cushioning its descent onto the stone floor.

Modra slowly shifted the first egg back into position, and the woman at the tail end waited for the second egg to come out. After a moment, the gold and black egg slid into her arms and was gently set onto the ground. The woman behind Gillian cheered.

The exhausted-looking Gillian lay down in the pool. Modra knew that she needed rest after having to push two eggs out. She watched as the dragon wrapped her tail around the two eggs and blew a puff of fire onto each of them. Even dragon eggs had to be kept warm.

Now that Modra had finished, she retreated to the pool where she could scrub the signs of dungeon life out of her hair and skin. She had more pressing matters to discuss with Grumloc. While working the knots out of her hair, she watched the dragon as she left the baths. Both eggs were gently held in her mouth. She could learn a lot from the dragons—but the dragons could learn a lot from her as well.

Chapter 15

Modra wore a red dress with golden embroidery down the front and on the edges. It was tight around her waist with a golden belt. A matching scarf covered her hair. It was the expected attire for dragon women. Gold embroidery, stitched in the dress, was infused with magic that allowed the wearer to shift forms and not lose their clothes. The change would trigger a magical effect, which would cause the clothes to change with the wearer.

When her family was one, Daron had offered to give them clothes to allow them to shift. Still, Sova would always deny such a delicate material. They were nomadic people and did not need such fine things. Frilly dresses and silken robes did not belong in a traveling caravan. Yet, if she was going to be demanding things, then she might as well accept the things she could not change.

Claws on the marble floor caused her to look to the entryway. Grumloc entered the room, looking almost exhausted, but relieved. He took his seat on the raised area in the great hall behind the empty throne and looked down upon her.

"I am grateful that you saved Gillian and her eggs. It is rare for our people to sire more than one offspring in a lifetime. We live for hundreds of years, and only ever produce one living heir. My brother and I had been an exception, and now Gillian has given me two heirs to the throne. Unlike my brother and me, who shared the same egg, these two will be able to shift as they please.

"Now, what is it that you would like to discuss?" A little smoke rose from his nostrils.

She was startled to learn that Gillian was his mate and she had saved his offspring. Still, she forced her mind onto the most important things. "I do not wish for you to keep attacking my people. Keep me as your prisoner, but I ask that you release the others." She could feel her legs shaking as the urge to run filled her.

"Why?" His eyes seemed sad. "If I allow this war to end, then what punishment should your people face?"

"Your brother may not return because our people did not take him. We should be trying to find him together and figure out who the kidnapper is. We've been punished enough, having to live in filthy cells and being treated like criminals. I want peace."

"Sova handed Daron the cloak that teleported him." Grumloc's tone showed irritation. "He was responsible for my brother's disappearance and must reap the consequences of his actions."

Gaining a little confidence in knowing the truth, Modra held her head up high. "Even you do not wish for war. You keep taking our people, making it look like you are killing them, but you keep them alive in those cells. War has death, and so far, no one has died."

"Your son Zec was by the oasis and had threatened to kill me. Are you to say that a threat is not motive enough for death in war?" His growl deepened.

Her heart began to race as she remembered her young boy; she was uncertain of how he would even look now. "How do you know it was my son?"

"He yelled out his name," he stated, a stream of smoke coming out of his mouth. "He vanished into the oasis and did not come back up. I'm certain he did not die, though, since I received notice from Nadi that he found Daron."

Modra fell to her knees. Her sons were the ones at the oasis, and now Nadi had found Daron. "Are they alright? Are they safe?"

"I don't know," he lowered his head toward her. He didn't leave me with any information, just that he had found Daron and that they needed help. A search party is already looking for them." His tone was gentle as he asked, "Do you happen to know where they might have gone from there? I know it is a long shot asking you this question, since this oasis formed near the keep not long after we took you prisoner."

Shaking her head, Modra's mind was on her sons. Zec is making threats, and Nadi is with Daron. They should have more clues to go on. Then, she realized something.

"If he found Daron, then that sorcerer must be with them. Both of my sons are in danger! We must do all we can to find them!"

With a huff of smoke, Grumlock sounded disappointed. "It would have been faster if you knew. I guess we have to wait for Gage to return from Vadnera. We are recruiting all the help we can get."

Relieved that her sons were alive but worried they were in danger, Modra did not want to get off track: "I want to exchange the release of five prisoners for every good deed I do."

Taking a moment to think about it, Grumloc tapped his claws on the marble. "I will still capture all who come too close to the keep."

"And my living arrangements will change," she added. "If I am to stay here and learn from your kind as they learn from me, then I'll not stay in a cell." Trying to keep her tone as demanding as possible, she went on. "I will not settle for the scraps of bread and water you chose to feed all the prisoners. My people need a meal and baths."

A growl erupted from him. "You can have a bed, warm meals, and even baths. The prisoners, however, do not get those items. Depending on how many deeds you can accomplish will determine how many are released—and how long their stay will be." Standing back up, he began to leave. "I will release fifteen of your people today for saving the eggs and Gillian. You will be shown to your room by Ronja. She will also be your personal guard if you should need to wander the keep."

Modra silently watched him leave, feeling a bit triumphant in her demands. A guard approached her drawing her attention. At first glance it was obvious to see that Ronja did not look like the others. She had a strand of black hair sticking out from under her helmet. One eye was blue and the other gold, but her skin was still as pale as the rest of the dragons.

"Are you a Dawn Dragon?" Modra surprised herself with the bluntness of her question.

Ronja smiled, "Actually, I am mixed. I am a Dawn, but I also am a Dusk."

"A silver," Modra exclaimed. "But they have been missing for several years."

With a sad look, the guard began to walk, and Modra followed. "Yes, my father vanished as well, but since I am mixed, it seems that wherever they went, a mixed dawn dragon was not welcome. Enough about me, though. I can show you around the keep."

They walked, Ronja rattling on about the keep and dragon history. Modra's mind was elsewhere, though. Zec had been next to the keep, and Nadi had been with Daron. This meant that her sons might be in danger. She prayed that they were doing well and that they would soon be reunited.

Chapter 16

Princess Kiran Blackmoor peered out of the carriage window as they slowly made their way down the busy street. She pushed a strand of her blonde hair behind her ear. Her grey eyes studied the city in disappointment. Every year, her father forced her to come to Firstenfeld for a purification ceremony. An entire birthday parade to ensure she was purified, so that the dark angels never chose her.

Folding her hands in the lap of her purple silken dress, she looked at her mother. "The dark angels have been gone for several years. Why do I have to go through with this?"

Her mother, with white hair pinned back, looked out the window with her identical grey eyes. One hand still rested in her lap, standing out against the light blue she had chosen. Without looking at her, she said, "Precautions. Since you haven't chosen to wed or made yourself unable to be chosen by choosing a suitor, tradition binds us to this road. But I will not stop you if you choose not to go. You can leave this carriage...but your father would be furious if he heard that you did not show at the temple."

Giving a frustrated sigh, Kiran sat back in her seat and looked out at the bustling street. A city of only humans, no creatures or magic. It was a dull city for her.

On this trip, she had accidentally left a book at their last camp and was without entertainment on the ride. Her mother had often scolded her that she would never find love if she always had her nose in a book.

"Lord Keol said he would be waiting for you at the castle to give you a gift for your birthday," her mother said as she began sorting through the pile of papers that had been sitting beside her for the past hour. Queen Lillian Blackmoor of Vadnera was always a master procrastinator in getting to her paperwork or duties. Even though she would submit things late, she continually stated that everyone was expecting it early. She had her schedule and time; that's why they were a week late getting into Firstenfeld for the purification ceremony. Kiran should have been back at the castle by now. Yet, her mother delayed the trip with a detour to a lake and a village with the best sweets. She liked that her mother was funny that way, but still, her duties should come first.

"I wonder what my favorite vampire lord is bringing me this time?" she said sarcastically.

"You two were best friends as kids, so it makes sense that he should be a suitor. What would you do if he proposed to you?" She placed a paper on the seat next to her.

Her heart jumped at the idea, and her face flushed. "I don't think he would do that?" She lied. Keol spent every moment he could with her reading, talking, strolling through the garden, and sitting in on her studies. She did not doubt that he would propose, but she hadn't been outside the castle walls with him yet. Kiran only knew what Keol was showing her while he was there.

"You're avoiding the question," her mother did not look up from her work.

Kiran tried to avoid it. "I'm not ready for that. I haven't had an adventure yet. It's too soon to settle down." Yet, she would probably graciously accept since she would become an immortal and never have to worry about being so fragile and helpless.

"An adventure," her mother laughed. "You honestly think that you can be adventurous? My child, you always have your nose in a book and rarely go outside. How would you have an adventure?"

The princess was quiet as she looked out the window. "I'm not sure. Maybe by catching a thief or rescuing someone in danger."

Her mother sighed, "Don't be ridiculous. Princesses do not catch thieves or save people. We have guards to do those things for us."

"I know, but I could do those things too," she gripped her dress. "If I just had a chance."

"I highly doubt it." The Queen put her paperwork down. "If I witnessed you doing something so daring, then I would never take you to one of these ceremonies again."

A tall hat in the crowd caught her attention. The man who wore it walked faster than the rest. His gait was not as dignified as most of the other men walking. She felt as though her heart was pulling her to him. Watching closely, she could see the young man trying to hide his face. He seemed injured as he bumped into a passing woman with a wince. It was a miracle he could move through a crowd of people while looking down. His feet, she noted, were bare, even though he wore acceptable pants and a good jacket.

Yet, what made her almost press her face against the window was the dark angel next to him. She recognized her from the painting of the woman in her mother's room. It was Cynthia, the one dark angel that her mother spoke fondly of. "Mother, do you see that?" She was afraid to even blink.

Her mother glanced out the window, showing little interest. "What?"

"There is a dark angel! I can see her next to the man with the top hat." Just then, he looked in their direction.

"Honestly, child. I do not see a dark angel. Your eyes must be playing tricks on you." The Queen went back to her papers.

Kiran concluded that the man was a thief and had stolen the clothes, and maybe the dark angel was giving him a chance to return the stolen items. Looking far behind him, a blonde man with a brown vest was walking quickly, making her more suspicious. The man in the top hat stopped and looked around for a moment, seeming lost.

She was ready to do something daring. Every book of adventure had her wishing to experience a quest. This time, she would be bold like the heroes and capture the thief who dared to steal a hat and hide his face. She could prove to her mother that the dark angel was real. Then her mother would have no choice but to accept that she could be those things.

The Princess flung the door open, causing the carriage to come to a halt; Kiran ignored the protest from the driver. Multiple people stopped as they watched her emerge, a few bowed in recognition, one cursed, and many gazed in wonder.

"What are you doing?" her mother asked as she left the carriage.

Not saying a word, she rushed toward the man with the top hat and grabbed his wrist while staring the dark angel in the face. Just as she went to announce that she had caught him, a warm feeling slipped through her fingertips. It traveled up her arm to her chest and flooded into her back.

The young man looked into her eyes as his gaze flashed a yellowish-orange. Around his neck was a silver collar. She had always heard of shapeshifters, but never had she seen one. They spent most of their life moving around a desert. She couldn't fathom why one would be here!

"We need to move. Thorn is gaining on us," the dark angel's voice was almost frantic. "Can you shake her off and run? The Queen of Vadnera is here, and we don't need that much attention!"

"You're a dark angel!" Kiran said as she backed up, letting him go. "Why are you helping him? Isn't he a thief?"

The dark angel looked shocked. "You can see me?"

Kiran nodded but wasn't sure what she should do. It had been years since dark angels were around, and yet, here was one. She looked toward the blonde man standing at the edge of the crowd, his eyes locked onto her. A chill went down her spine as she took a step back.

The young man grabbed her wrist. "If you can see her, then you are in danger." They started running away from the crowd.

Kiran did not fight it, accepting that she was in danger. If a protector of their land was running from him, then that man was not someone she wanted to meet. She ignored her mother calling after her. For the first time in her life, she disobeyed the Queen and ran hand in hand with someone who would never be allowed inside her home. Just this once, Kiran did not regret that she would be in trouble with both of her parents. This was not how she had expected her ceremony to go.

Chapter 17

Nadi weaved through crowds of people as they ran for the bridge. Looking back, he could no longer see Thorn in the ocean of city folk. For the moment, he seemed to have stopped following them. They slowed to a walk as they caught their breath.

"Why is there a dark angel here—and how come no one else can see her?" The girl asked as she pushed one of her blonde curls out of her face, her purple gown now dirty from dragging on the ground.

Nadi did not understand how there seemed to be no color in those gray eyes. Remembering her question, Nadi said, "She is a spirit of one, and I had grabbed the sword, so I guess if I touch someone, then they can see her as well."

"That's not it at all. You didn't get to your ceremony on time, did you?" Cynthia asked the girl as she floated over his shoulder.

"No," she responded as she bit her thumb. "My mother had a detour on the trip."

"So I guess that makes you my apprentice now." The look she gave her was a grim one.

"That can't be. No, there have not been any new apprentices since you all had vanished." The girl was looking around, almost searching for something.

"You feel a pull in your chest, correct?"

Kiran nodded but said nothing.

"I want you to close your eyes and keep your finger pointed in the direction of that feeling. Only open your eyes when I tell you," Cynthia instructed.

Nadi watched as she closed her eyes as tightly as they would go and pointed toward him. Cynthia motioned for Nadi to walk around. He began walking to the right of her, and her hand followed. Then he stepped to the left, and her hand found him. An idea occurred, and he began walking backwards. Her hand stayed in one place, but she seemed confused.

"I can feel it getting further away," the girl's voice seemed concerned.

"Open your eyes," Cynthia told her.

Those grey eyes locked onto him, and he almost forgot to breathe.

Confusion washed over her face as she looked at the dark angel. "Why do I keep looking at him?"

"Because Nadi is your guide and you are now my apprentice," her tone bore no happiness for the situation. "You will always be able to find each other no matter where you are. Only the guide can find the path to the Temple of the Elders. Our only problem is that the path will not open for us. All we have to do is restore order before the next full moon or..." the dark angel trailed off as she pulled her thumb across her throat, signaling that Kiran would die.

"Oh no," she stepped back. "I'm going to lose my throne and be exiled from the kingdom. My father is going to do far worse than kill me. I can't become a dark angel!"

"You're a princess, right?" Cynthia leaned over and eyed the handkerchief that she had dangling out of her sleeve. It had a red V with a feather stitched above it. "Princess of Vadnera? I remember that Queen Lillian had a daughter . . . my, it has been quite a long time."

"My mother often spoke fondly of you," the Princess said as she took a step back. People were staring at Kiran as she talked to herself, not even looking at the ragged man standing next to her.

The pain hit Nadi again, and he gasped as darkness enveloped him. Before him, the dragon appeared as a terrifying force. Its mouth glowed with fire, and its eyes shone a bright golden yellow. The fire in its mouth dimly lit the golden scales. Nadi put up his arms, expecting to be hit by a blast of fire.

"Are you ok?" the Princess asked as she touched his arm.

And just like that, Nadi was back to reality. People stared and stopped to watch as he put his arms back down. "I'm sorry, I'm trying to control it."

"Control what?" she asked, studying him.

Cynthia piped in, "We will discuss that later. For now, we need to find shelter." Floating across the bridge, Nadi began to follow.

He noticed that the girl did not move. Turning back, he watched her fret with her dress; she twisted part of it in her hand, nervously. "I need to go back. Maybe if I purify myself, then I won't become a dark angel."

Floating back to her, Cynthia seemed distant. "Trust me, it won't do anything. I tried, and it did not help. If you go back, that sorcerer will kill you—if the angel's fever does not. He was the one who killed me, and he is out to destroy everything. That man is dangerous because he can control time."

Kiran looked up as though she had an idea. "Maybe I can—"

"No," the dark angel interrupted her. "You cannot seek his help. He is not powerful enough to reverse its effects. Plus, like all dark magic, you will eventually cause it to happen again. There is no stopping it. He will ensure that you never become one by killing you."

With that, the Princess followed the dark angel back to the shifter and grabbed his hand. As their fingers intertwined, Nadi suddenly felt nervous. It was the first time a girl had wanted to hold his hand. He looked her over, from her sad grey eyes that made her look so vulnerable, to her firm pose and strong stature, which showed her royal background. He knew that they were going to have to make her not stand out so much.

The Princess looked up at Nadi. "I'm sorry, I should introduce myself. I am Kiran Blackmoor, Princess of Vadnera."

Touching his head, Nadi felt the pain and winced, but the darkness did not come. Looking back at her, he said, "I am Nadi of the Púca Tribe."

"I am Cynthia Heartford of the fallen Kingdom of Gavran," the dark angel did not turn back.

"I guess I am not the only Princess to become an apprentice, then," Kiran stated. "If my mother had simply taken me to be purified instead of running off on all these side adventures, then I would have been home and not an apprentice."

Looking over her shoulder, Cynthia said, "I had felt the same way, but I found that my family was among those who trained me and taught me to survive as a dark angel. Honestly, I would have died long before the sorcerer if it had not been for them. Initially, I thought it was a curse, but I grew to understand that we are the key to order in this world, and it is a blessing.

"Yet, we must win a battle against the sorcerer if we are to ensure it is a blessing—because if we fail, then it truly will be a curse. At this point, however, the odds are heavily stacked against us. A shifter who can't shift, a spirit who can only be seen by the two of you, and now a princess. We need to get back there and free the Elders."

Kiran stopped in her tracks, letting go of Nadi's hand, "The Elders who created our world? Gods of untold power? Free them from what?"

Turning back, Cynthia gave her a stern look. "The sorcerer had used his magic to trap them. We almost had them freed, but he appeared right when we tried to free them and captured him," she pointed at Nadi, who was waiting on the side of the road. "Thorn stopped him from changing with that collar, but that right now is a blessing. Nadi here has sacrificed his ability to transform to ensure that his brother, who is working with them, does not transform into a dragon."

The Princess gave her a questioning look, "Why is it a blessing? He can transform into a dragon and destroy the sorcerer."

"It is not that simple," Nadi stated. "The dragon is a powerful form to take on. Once we shift into one, the person we are no longer exists, and the dragon has total control. It will not be able to discern who is a friend or an enemy. Instead, all will die who get too close. In the story of Elias the Dragon, Elias had killed his own family when he transformed. It was a warning to us that we cannot take on every form."

"Are you sure?" Kiran asked as she stepped closer to him. "Some stories are just stories, meant to scare people into believing that. If we remove the collar, then maybe—"

"No," Nadi backed away, clutching the silver ring. "We need to save it for when we get back to my homeland and face Thorn and Icarri. When this collar comes off, you'll need to get as far away from me as you can." He winced as pain shot through his head. "I know that, because I can feel it trying to escape. The collar is the only thing keeping it in."

Moving off the road, Nadi headed into the trees. "We need to make camp and figure out a way to get back to Crescent Cove."

"Please don't call it that," Cynthia said as she followed Nadi. "I knew that place as the Hidden Valley or the Elders' Enclave. That was what that witch started calling it because the mountains make a half-circle around the forest. Makes it sound like a good place for Pirates to find treasure."

Picking up sticks as he went, Nadi mumbled, "They certainly think that the world is theirs to control."

Kiran followed in silence as they went. Her eyes were on the ground as she stepped, trying to avoid mud, rocks, and bushes. Nadi understood why Cynthia had said that the Princess was on her list of hindrances for them. She didn't know how to survive on her own.

"We will find you some better clothes tomorrow that are more suitable for traveling. Right now, fancy dresses and shoes are not getting us where we need to go—plus you stand out in such fine clothing." He gave her a small smile as he looked for wood to make a fire.

"Says the boy wearing no shoes," Kiran interjected, but her tone was not playful.

"With no shoes, I can feel the earth under my feet and know whether or not I am on solid ground. Wearing shoes all the time makes your feet soft and unable to handle it when you step on even a rock. Your feet need to have calluses to protect them from the ground and hidden things under leaves. You can step on a thorn, and it will still hurt, but it will not go as deep."

"Ew," she gave him a disgusted look. "I prefer shoes to not step on those things."

Pointing to a branch as a hint for Nadi to grab it, Cynthia said, "Princesses don't leave the castle, know nothing of poverty, and other unsightly things. Also, they do not know the meaning of a royal mess until the servants do not clean for a day."

Grabbing the stick, he looked at both of them. "Well, it is going to have to change because we are trying to save the world. Getting dirty is something everyone is going to have to be familiar with. We need to stop caring about how we look or how others see us." He winced as he fought back the darkness and heard the growl of the dragon. Taking a moment, he looked around, ensuring he was still in the woods. "We need to be ready."

Walking farther in, Nadi knew that it would be a miracle to survive through this in his current state. He could not do a night watch or move too fast due to his headache. Right now, he wished he had ale to drown out everything and sleep away all his problems. Yet, he could not risk entering the city with the princess to find even a sip of the cheapest kind.

He pulled out the velvet pouch, hoping it was some gold. Tugging at the yellow drawstrings, he opened it to reveal a shard from a mirror. His thoughts trailed back to Icarri, and her talk of the mirror she had shattered. "I guess they do not trust her either," he said to himself as he put it back in his pocket.

Chapter 18

Thorn came back into the library, his shirt and vest still soaked, and his curly blonde hair was a mess. He strode over to the chair by the fireplace and plopped himself down on the red padded seat. As he snapped his fingers, flames rose in the fireplace.

"Aw, did you let him get away?" Icarri leaned over the railing while pushing her bottom lip out to mimic a pouting face.

"I am not in the mood, Icarri." Thorn pulled a sealed envelope from his vest pocket. His rough fingertips smoothed the edges of the fine parchment. Staring at the red wax seal of Vadnera on the lip of the envelope, he slowly put it back in his pocket, not wanting any prying eyes. "Privacy would be nice," he mumbled as Icarri came down the stairs.

"You could have had the decency to bring me back my pet. I would love to tame that mutt and keep him around to put on a show. A nice exotic creature to make others want one. So many things we can do with a shifter." She draped herself over the back of the chair and ran her fingers through his hair.

"He cannot shift while wearing the collar, and only a magic wielder can remove it." Thorn pulled away and glared at her hand. "It did not help that he also took the Princess with him, and has the entire kingdom searching for them."

"Which princess?" Icarri seemed amused.

"You know which princess!" He was getting aggravated with her constant nosing around in his affairs. "The Princess of Vadnera! The same princess I was due to kidnap at the temple this morning! She was to be a major part of my plans, and that bloody shifter ruined everything! All I had to do was wait for the purification ceremony to end and bring her here, but she grabbed his hand and took off with him. I don't understand why she would do that. Did she know?" he got up and looked at Icarri. "Did *he* know? Did you tell him about my plan?"

"I rambled on about my sons, but never once spoke your name or mentioned your plans. You are the last thing on my mind." Her fingers traced the wood at the top of the chair. "Only Nadi knew you were showing up here."

Going to the table near the window, he slammed his fist down, causing the cup of wine to jump. "I needed the Princess here! Everything is not going according to plan!"

"When does anything go according to plan?" A sly smile slid across her face. "It was a miracle that you took down nine elders without any help." Looking at the orb that was floating above the mantle, she said with an amused voice, "Oh...wait, you had the Queen's help."

"She does not know what I have planned, and she will not find out," his tone was threatening. A few times, he found reason to trust Icarri, but mostly he knew that she was dangerous. She had taught him what he knew now, and what he learned about her sons was that he could never let his guard down. Both may have died from their selfish actions, but she did not stop either of them from their demise.

"I wish to be alone," he said, turning his back to her.

"When have you not been alone?" Icarri laughed at her joke before going to the doors of the library and letting them slam shut behind her.

Going back to the chair, Thorn slumped into the red, cushioned seat and watched the fire burn. Pulling the letter out, he rubbed his fingers across the worn edges of the paper. The wax seal was still in place after all those years. Even looking at it now, his heart ached as he remembered that his queen left him this letter as she went to wed the man responsible for murdering his father.

Thinking back to the Princess, he wanted to grab her by the hair and drag her away. Yet, both of those shifters had ruined his plans. He was lucky the younger one did not destroy the teleportation cloak. Nadi, on the other hand, got away with his prize, and he was not sure when they would return. He needed the Princess, though. She was to watch her father's crimes as he reversed time, and then vanish once he had undone what her father had caused. The Princess would no longer exist. He would be with his queen, and her father would hang for his crimes.

Thorn held no resentment toward his love. It was an arranged marriage because he was not of royal blood. Her mother was going to allow her to choose her husband, but she had fallen ill. She did not live to witness her words get tossed aside for meaningless alliances.

Not too long ago, he had snuck into the palace garden to see if she would come. He saw that the guards did not patrol the area of the weeping willow. Standing under that tree had brought back so many memories. One of her smiles and how they would dance to the songs of the night. The way her eyes would light up when she would cross the bridge and see him under the tree. Her lips were always so soft when they would kiss, and her hair was silky smooth. Thorn missed how her fingers would intertwine with his as they held hands. It had felt as though nothing could come between their love.

While he was in Firstenfeld, their eyes had met for a brief moment before he had turned back the way he had come and vanished into the crowd as the Princess escaped with Nadi. Her eyes did not look the same. Full of fear and recognition. He wished she could give him that loving look again instead of one of regret.

Placing the sealed letter back in his pocket, Thorn knew he needed to continue with other plans. "Where is that shifter?" he mumbled to himself as he rose from the chair and turned to the door. "We need him to get the dragon's form for this to work."

Chapter 19

The night was loud, filled with the calls of cicadas. The sound of the stream would have been soothing, but it was blocked out by the buzzing of insects, the creaking of trees, and the feeling of being watched. Nadi could not sleep with all these unfamiliar things around him.

His back, now blistered, caused him immense pain, which also did not help. He tried soaking in the ice-cold water, but it did not seem to have any effect. He wished he could steal a healing potion or a scroll so he could use it, but it would have to wait until he was alone so that the princess would not get caught with him.

It also bothered him that the air was so humid even after it became dark. The desert was hot during the day and freezing at night. It also lacked trees, which Nadi had thought would make it colder, but instead they trapped the heat in. He was sweating worse than he did in the desert.

By the time he made it back to camp, Kiran was staring at the fire with worry on her face. He could tell a million questions were on her mind. "Can't sleep?" Nadi asked, poking at the fire.

The princess shook her head. "I have never really slept out in the open with strangers or disobeyed my parents. This is the first time I have spent without guards or my mother. I'm lost without them, or my books for that matter?"

"Ah, why books?" The heat from the fire was also irritating.

"Have you ever found a spot where you felt so safe that nothing would bother you there?" Her eyes stayed on the fire.

The memory of his mother came flooding back when she would tuck him in and read him stories. "Yes."

"Mine was the library at home. It was stressful learning how to be a princess. Dealing with diplomats and courting men. Even the ladies of the court were tiring and cruel, taking jabs at anyone to lift their ego. So, I escaped into books where I felt safest. It's only words on a page, but there were countless adventures."

Nadi winced as pain filled his mind, but it passed faster than expected. "Our tribe normally trades items for stories. My father tries to keep a record of all the stories that we hear so that they may never be lost. We only hear stories from travelers, though. My mother, on the other hand, had a few books that she used to read to us. Ghost stories and fables."

"Any interesting ones?" Kiran almost looked eager to hear a story.

It made him smile even through his pain. "How about my favorite story? I bet you never heard the one about how the dragons fought over the desert."

"I heard a little of it, but not much. My father thought it best that I mostly learn the stories of our human culture." She fiddled with a leaf by her shoe.

"That's not the smartest thing in the world. You are missing out on learning about cultures and how to communicate with those that are not human. You can't relate to those without understanding how they work."

She seemed annoyed. "My father is not dumb. He knows that I have classes to teach me about speaking with the abandreals, demon-kin, elves, and whatever other creature sets foot in the castle. Usually, my father is the one to speak with them."

Nadi looked around. "Where is Cynthia?"

"She is patrolling the woods, making sure we are notified if any guards or beasts appear."

"Beasts?" He stared at the dark forest.

"Yes, we have creatures of wild magic that roam the woods. They mostly hang around areas with livestock."

"You failed to mention this, why?"

"Because I figured you knew." She glared at him. "What idiot walks into a forest not knowing what may lie in wait. I just assumed you knew how to protect us."

Her insults were getting to him worse than the heat was. "Well, excuse me, Princess. I'm new here and have no other option but to sleep in the woods as the filthy desert rat that I am. You could have flashed some coin and offered an Inn for the night."

It was her turn to look insulted. "I'm not a walking chest of gold, you flea bag. I don't leave the castle with gold on me. My mother had the money, but we rushed off so fast that I couldn't explain anything to her."

"Flea bag?" He eyed her and decided to stoop a little lower than he normally would. "You're right, you don't have a chest at all."

Her mouth dropped open as she grabbed a fistful of dirt and threw it at him. "You mongrel! How dare you—"

"How dare I? If it wasn't for me, you would have been killed by the sorcerer! You wouldn't even know how to survive out here, let alone make a fire. If you even succeeded at setting a fire, you probably would have set the entire forest ablaze."

"Enough!" Cynthia floated by the fire. "I leave, and you are yelling so that the entire forest can hear your bickering. "What if a golem were nearby, or even a troll. You two are both idiots! Only I am allowed to yell because NO ONE CAN HEAR ME!" She looked them both in the eye. "Lie down and get some rest. If I hear another peep from both of you, I'll make sure to lead you into a harpy nest."

"Wait, there are harpies nearby?" Kiran asked.

Cynthia only gave her a warning glance before she slowly retreated into the woods.

Both of them sat silently by the fire before listening as the sound of the cicadas picked back up again. They were arguing so loudly that the bugs quieted down. He was being stupid and irrational.

Before he could apologize, Kiran asked, "What about your story?"

He had nearly forgotten about it. "Oh, back when the Elders had made the earth, they first created the dragons. Each one was brought forth into the desert. The gold dragons were made from the light of the sun, and the silver dragons were made from the light of the moon. Red dragons were birthed from the fires of Mount Aldjaalgor, while the black dragons rose from the shadows it cast.

"They each claimed a small part of the desert as their own. Yes, there was not enough food in their parts of the desert to survive, so they would often fight over territory. Eventually, the red dragons thought it best to have one ruler of the desert and demanded a fight to ensure that only the worthy remain. The black dragons tricked the silver into leaving the fight by disrupting their nests. The red dragons took advantage of the distracted blacks and beat them back into their corner of the desert. The gold dragons faced the reds with the help of the sun and won.

"Yet, they did not wish to rule the desert alone and asked instead for a bargain. They wished only to share the desert and what it had to offer with their fellow dragons, and so they did, until the humans came and challenged them. Then they tried to bargain instead and give their trash in exchange for gold and food."

The princess was already asleep. Nadi looked at her, so calm and beautiful in the light of the waning moon. She was completely different from the women in his village. Her blonde curls and grey eyes drew him in. Something so colorless was not a thing he thought would have been enchanting, and yet, he seemed to forget about his pain and worries when he looked into those eyes. She was nothing like Icarri either. Kiran was gentile, fragile, and didn't seem to fear speaking her mind to defend what she cared about. He almost wanted to protect her…almost.

Sucking in a sharp breath the darkness enveloped him and he found himself under the claws of the dragon. Hot breath against his skin made him squirm as he stared into its angry golden eyes. It opened its mouth and clamped it shut around his head.

He opened his eyes and patted his head to be sure it was still attached before breathing a sigh of relief. His heart would not settle, though. It beat a mile a minute and seemed to drag him further into staying awake.

Looking at the sky, he noticed the stars seemed so few and dimmer, unlike in the desert. It was almost like he traveled to another world. Nothing here reminded him of the comforts of home.

Chapter 20

Sweat beaded down Nadi's brow by the time he awoke. Dawn had already crept higher in the sky than he had wanted. The birds seemed to be deftly loud, and his mouth was extremely dry. His head ached worse than he had ever felt it. His dream was not of his mother, but of the dragon and the darkness. It was constantly seeking to take control.

Looking around, he noticed that he was alone. Kiran was nowhere to be seen. Cynthia wasn't either. He got up and stumbled around, knowing that he couldn't yell their names without drawing attention to himself. Searching the ground, Nadi found her footprints leaving camp.

Tracking them, he studied the small shape of her foot. Her feet were so small compared to anyone he knew. The heel of the shoe looked slightly lifted. It was not suitable for roaming the forest at all and could cause her to hurt herself. Since her feet may have never touched the dirt, they were probably too soft to even stand stepping on pebbles.

"Trying to sneak a peek at the Princess?" Cynthia asked, blocking his path.

"What?" He asked, unsure of her question.

"She's rinsing herself in the stream. Poor girl woke with a spider on her and was too frightened to even scream. She decided to wash away her worries."

Nadi spotted the dress and chemise on top of a bush and the shoes below it. "Oh…No, I wasn't attempting to peek. I didn't know where either of you had gone. Since she needs clothes, I might as well slip out of here with the dress and shoes and find her something at the closest town…which is?"

"You plan to leave her in the nude?" Her gaze made him feel smaller.

"No, I'll take the dress, not the chemise. I have no interest in someone as cowardly as her. I just wish I could just hand her over to the guards and have them take her back—"

"But you know what may happen if she returns before becoming a dark angel."

Nadi huffed in frustration. He was stuck with an unwanted hindrance, and if he couldn't follow through with his responsibility as a guide, he was going to face the gruesome consequences. He began feeling all of his responsibilities piling on him. Protecting his brother was beginning to look like he might be facing exile for being unable to stop his brother's desire for revenge. Being limited as Kiran's guide was also a problem. Without his forms and with the dragon trying to get out, there was no telling what might happen. He had never been so unsure about what the future might hold for him.

Grabbing the dress and the shoes, Nadi stated, "I understand. I touched the sword, and this was the best option. Where is the next town?"

She was silent a moment with frustration, "Go back to the road and head east for about 2 miles. When you reach the fork, keep left and you should arrive in Roden. It's a town filled with adandreals and other creatures. The royal guard should be there so you may be questioned as a slave. You will need to spout out a well-known name as your master. The problem is, I don't know what names are still in power."

Suddenly, he felt anger because he knew whose name he had to choose. Not because he wanted to, but because it was the only name he knew. "Icarri still has power here. We would have to use her name."

Cynthia cursed, "You're right. That is our only chance. Her last name is Vale. If you're asked, you will have to tell them that you hail from Vale Manor."

Nadi pulled off the jacket and placed the dress inside. "It's best to hide the dress with the guards on the lookout."

"Is your back doing all right?" There was a hint of concern in her voice.

"It doesn't hurt anymore," he lied.

"What about the dragon?"

"Quiet this morning." Nadi could still feel it in his mind. "I'm not getting my hopes up that it will stay that way. It could force its way to the surface at any time. I'm hoping to not draw attention if it does."

"Are you sure you want to go alone right now?" Cynthia looked back toward the stream, but he chose not to follow her gaze. "We could always go together?"

"No, the princess may be easily recognized." The pain from his blisters was bothering him, and he was growing impatient. Turning away, he left with his haul. "I'll be back shortly with new clothes."

"Be safe," Cynthia called out to him.

He made it about ten feet before he heard Kiran shout, "He did what?"

A mischievous smile broke, and he picked up his pace. "Serves her right." Nadi knew he was going to get an earful when he returned, but he was happy to get away from that one responsibility at the moment. She was a pain unless she was sleeping."

Going through the brush closer to the road, Nadi's thoughts trailed to his father. He wished he were home so he could ask him for help or plead his case, but he already knew that it would end in exile. He had failed. If he hadn't been adamant about getting spirits, he probably would have noticed the direction they were heading. It was all his fault and could have been prevented had he not taken advantage of the moment.

Yet, because he chose this path, Daron was found. If they had gone to the oasis, he would never have had that hope of freedom. It bothered Nadi to leave him behind, but as long as Thorn didn't know their secret, he should be safe.

Hiding behind a tree, he watched a group of guards pass on the road. Three humans, by the looks of them. One stopped his horse around a boy who was walking along the road and brandished a sword.

"There is a fee to travel this road, boy." He bent down, "Pay up."

"Sir, I only have three copper coins from my mother for some bread. We can't afford much since my father died."

The other two guards stopped but didn't say anything.

"Well, it looks like you'll have to pay with that, and I'll be generous and let it slide." He waited for the boy to give him the coppers and then joined the other two before laughing and carrying on their way."

The boy slumped down and began to cry.

Nadi waited for the guards to get out of sight before breaking his cover. He made it to the boy who stared at him, startled. "Are you alright?"

"No," the boy sniffled. "My momma is going to be upset if she finds out that the guards took the money she gave me. That was supposed to be for dinner."

"Bread isn't dinner. Maybe a snack or a quick breakfast." Nadi helped the boy up. "Here, let's go to town together, and I'll help you get things for dinner."

Together, they avoided the road and stayed hidden in the trees as they made their way to the town. After almost half an hour, they made it to the fork in the road. Nadi read the sign. South to Vadnera, West to Firstenfeld, North to Roden, and East to Lu'Bela. They stuck to the road leading north.

The road went through the middle of town. It was crowded with abandreals, findeli, goblins, dwarves, and a few elves. He was nervous about the elves since his thievery could never get passed them. He would have to do things the right way.

"Do you know where the clothing shop is? My… *mistress* wanted me to trade some items in," he said the word with distaste.

"Yes, follow me," the boy weaved through the crowd and ended up at a shop with a blue dress in the window.

As he took a step, an abandreal bumped against his back. Pain filled him, and he forced back a cry. The boy noticed immediately.

"Are you alright?" He peeked at his back. "Your mistress must be really strict."

"Oh no, that was the slave traders," he lied. "I attempted to escape, and they burned my back."

"Oh, I hate those guys. When my friend Tilly's parents couldn't pay their taxes, they rounded them up and sold her off. I wish I could get my friend back."

"That is cruel and unfair." Nadi stood up and headed for the door with the boy following.

Inside was an elderly goblin hemming a dress. She peered over her spectacles at them before gently placing the needle in the skirt. "How may I help you boys?" It didn't sound like a pleasant greeting as she stood.

Even though goblins were feared for their unfriendly manner, some were more pleasant. He had met some in passing in the desert. They often had a colorful vocabulary and were ill-tempered.

"My mistress sent me to trade in these items and get new clothing. The slave traders had burned my shirt off my back." Nadi resorted to the same lie for the boy's sake.

She eyed his collar suspiciously. "Why are you still wearing that?"

"I'm a shapeshifter who could only turn into a mouse. My mistress hates mice," he tried not to look her in the eye since his were orange.

She was silent a moment before asking, "Who is your mistress?"

This was the question he was dreading, he clenched his fist behind his back. "I hail from Vale Manor. My mistress is Icarri Vale."

"Oh, I'm surprised she didn't force you to go all the way to Vadnera to get clothing from Ramana Auryn. That seems to be the nobles' favorite shop. Bah!" She grabbed the clothes from his hands and picked up the violet dress and shoes. Rifling through it, she found what she was looking for. "Bloody Ramana Auryn! I called it! She probably spent ten gold on it with the shoes." Picking up the coat, she again found what she was looking for. "The late Eoin Paolini. Odd that it is so well kept. Not a hole in the fabric." She was silent for a moment before huffing a frustrated sigh. "Bah! I wish I weren't an honest shopkeeper, but this is worth two hundred gold due to its rarity. I honestly can't give you the entire worth of these items and would have to send you to Vadnera." She began to hand it back.

Nadi pushed it back toward her. "I don't mind getting less for this, I'll accept ten gold on two conditions." She stared at him, awaiting his response. "First, that I be allowed to choose two outfits from your shop. And second, that you give this boy a job to help him put food on his family's table."

She eyed the boy, considering the deal. "He looks to be about six."

"I'm nine," the boy pouted.

"What's your name?" She squinted at him through her spectacles.

"It's William. William North." He looked nervous as though he were expecting disappointment.

"Do you know how to sew?"

William nodded, "I can sew buttons and patch holes."

"Bah! Good enough, I guess. I want you here at dawn. Make sure to tell your mother that you work for Baba Gest. I want you to pick out something nice as well, since I don't want you showing up in tattered, patchy clothes. Doesn't do good for my business."

The boy grinned, "Thank you!" He began rummaging through her racks.

Just as Nadi went to thank her, she passed him a bottle of green liquid. "To thank you for giving me something valuable. I can't wait to tear apart this dress and discover why Ramana Auryn is so popular and make changes to my own work. That potion should heal your burns."

Nadi smiled, "Glad to be of assistance."

"Once you have your clothes, I'll give you your gold." She took the clothes to the back.

Nadi drank the potion, and his back tingled. He looked over his shoulder at a mirror and could see that the blisters were vanishing. He was glad he had made this trip. Picking out a green tunic with brown pants before skipping on boots and choosing a green cloak. He found a brown dress and a white apron for the princess. He realized that Baba had left the shoes and picked one up to match Kiran's size. He picked out a brown set for her.

Placing the items on the counter, Baba came back out and took Kiran's old shoes. She grabbed two bags from both of them and filled them with the clothes, only hesitating on the female clothing. She bid them farewell and told William. "If it doesn't fit, I'll adjust it for you tomorrow."

They made their way to the food stands and picked out vegetables and fruits. Stopping by the butcher, Nadi showed him how to choose the right meats. The butcher wasn't pleased to hear that he had undersold meat that was worth more. Nadi grabbed dried meats for the road.

Then the two made their way to the baker. The boy was pleased to get the bread his mother had requested. Nadi found a round with a wheel of cheese baked inside that would be good for the road. He eyed the sweet buns but passed on them when he thought back to Icarri. He regretted ever trusting her enough to take food from her.

With their bags full, Nadi asked the shops about ale, but no one seemed to have any. He couldn't try to forget what might happen when he returns to camp. Nadi decided to delay his return to walk William home so they both could avoid the guards. They stayed off the roads and only ventured to the edge of the woods. The beasts rarely roamed close to the roads, from what travelers told him. It was past noon by the time they made it to William's house.

The boy opened the door, "Mother! I am home!" He set down his bag on the table and invited Nadi in. The woman was facing a nearly empty cupboard, eyeing a few jars of spices. She was really thin to the point where her bones were starting to show. It was obvious that she was doing all she could to take care of William. Nadi knew he had to delay his trip a little longer than expected.

She turned around and cautiously eyed Nadi before looking at the bags on the table. "What's all this?"

"Hello, I'm Nadi, and I witnessed the guards taking the copper you gave to William. I couldn't stand by and do nothing."

She went to the boiling water holding one of the spice jars. "So you bought us food?"

"Not exactly." He studied the cookware, "William was helping me shop, and the items I traded were worth a lot. So I showed him how to bargain and even helped him get a job with Baba Gest."

"The goblin?" She wavered a little. "Are you sure. That woman doesn't like anyone."

"I gave her something rare that she could not pay me for," Nadi pulled out a chair. "Please, sit. You look like you haven't eaten in days."

"It doesn't matter, we cannot afford to pay you back for this," She began to sway.

"Hey, William and I will cook for you. Just rest for now."

She continued to protest, "I can't accept this. This is too much. Please leave and take all this with you."

Nadi moved the pot of water off the heat, switching it for a pan with butter, and began cutting vegetables. He had William checking spices. "I can't because if I leave you in this state, then who will take care of your son? You are the most important thing in your child's life, so how will he survive if you don't take care of yourself? It was something that my mother had told our villagers during a drought when we were lacking food and water. Parents were forfeiting their meals to feed their young." He threw the vegetables in the pan. Taking the spices from William, he instructed him to make sure they didn't burn. Nadi started cutting the meat. "I grew up without my mother, but I hope to see her soon."

William's mother began crying. "I didn't realize how hard it was going to be when Gerald passed. No one seemed to want to offer a woman a job. Men wanted me to marry immediately when he passed, but I couldn't do that. I loved my husband, and I don't want anyone else."

Nadi stopped a moment to hug her. He wondered if this was how it would be to hug his mother again. *Would she cry like this?* He held back his own tears at the thought and got back to work.

Before long, a meal was sitting before the two, and Nadi wrapped up a portion for the road. He stood at the door watching William and his mother eating. "Promise me that you will always eat before William. And William, you better wake up and be at that shop by dawn."

"I promise," she said, giving him a thankful smile.

William mumbled an agreement with a full mouth.

Nadi said goodbye and rushed into the woods. He knew there would be hell to pay. He left Kiran alone with Cynthia for over half a day. They were going to be furious. Feeling the pull in his chest, he rushed through the woods, praying he wouldn't come across a harpy nest or bump into a troll. Worry overcame him as he followed the stream back up to their camp. He found Kiran sitting on the shore, crying. Slowly, he approached her.

Chapter 21

Kiran had woken up to the feeling of something in her hair. At first, she attempted to brush at it, but her locks still moved. She lay still with her eyes shut tightly as the feeling persisted. The princess figured it was Nadi, bothering her while she slept. He might be making a game out of it. Eventually, she could take no more of it and sat up.

Looking over at him, he was lying on the grass, still sleeping. She wondered if he was faking it. It annoyed her that she even had to sleep under a tree near him. Her bed was better suited to her liking than sleeping on the ground like some vagrant. Kiran decided she would pester him awake.

Just as she stood, something fell out of her hair and onto the edge of her dress. Her eyes caught the movement and followed it as it went onto the ground. A large hairy spider camouflaged with the leaves and grass. Kiran backed up until she was against the trees. It would be too loud for her to scream. She did not want anyone nearby to come running. Silently, she stared at the spot where the unwanted guest had blended in.

Then Cynthia caught her attention as she approached the camp. She was hoping the spirit would somehow be able to deal with the vermin, but upon looking back, she realized that she had lost sight of it. The world was suddenly not safe. How was she going to be able to move when she didn't know where it had gone?

"What's wrong?" Cynthia asked as she glided toward her.

She was frantically searching the ground for the arachnid while remaining glued to the trunk of the tree. Kiran couldn't possibly live in a world with that nightmare. This situation made her wish to go back home and be locked in her library. Never were there larger spiders in her home. She never wanted to leave her castle again.

Movement on the ground caught her eye, and she watched it vanish into the bushes. That was her sign. Rushing toward the stream in a panic to leave the camp, Kiran wanted to be as far from that thing as possible. She didn't stop until she had found the water's edge.

"What's wrong?" Cynthia asked again, following her.

Catching her breath, she looked to the dark angel, almost in tears, "I—I had a—a sp—spider in—my hair." She could barely say the words.

"A spider was in your hair?"

Kiran nodded, trying to hold back the tears. "I was so scared."

"Well, maybe a wash in the stream will calm your nerves. You have been in a stressful situation since you left

Firstenfeld." Cynthia looked back toward camp. "I'll keep a lookout so Nadi doesn't see you."

Turning her attention towards the water, Kiran reluctantly agreed. She brought her focus to the woods around her. It was so open that she was nervous that Nadi might not be the only person to see her. Slowly, she removed her dress and chemise along with her shoes and set them on a bush. Her shoes tumbled off, but she didn't bother to pick them back up before returning to the water's edge.

Touching her toes in the stream, she could feel that it was cold. Her baths at the castle were always warm. She loved soaking while Ashlee smoothed her hair and worked out all the tangles. Ashlee was one of her only friends at the castle as well as an adandreal mix and her lady in waiting. Her father was a vampire noble but her feline mother had already passed away. From what Kiran had heard Ashlee was unable to be controlled by her father and her hunger could not be sated. It took several years before a she was able to be treated with a collar, but she seemed to only disappoint her father with her lack of noble knowledge. She was sent to Vadnera to learn alongside Kiran.

It was a rough start since Kiran had more ladies in waiting who had bullied Ashlee. After hearing about it, Kiran sent all of them away and only kept Ashlee by her side. Her father would try to send them back and she would refuse each time. Their actions had upset her.

Kiran thought, *Right now, Ashlee is probably worried about me*. Slowly she stepped into the water trying to get used to the temperature. The small stones shifted under her feet. Wading into a deeper area she submerged herself before returning to the shallows. She wondered how long she should sit there. A few minutes, an hour…maybe a lifetime.

The water seemed different then what she would receive at the castle when she bathed. Her's always had flower petals on top to give it a floral scent. This water smelled of the earth. Tiny fish danced around her legs and shot out of reach when she would move. Further down stream a doe and her fawn drank from the water and birds bathed in the shallows.

She felt peaceful shivering near the shore. This was a new feeling for her just being cold. No responsibilities or unpleasant meetings. No classes on poses and history. Kiran, wasn't a princess here, and the world only thought of her as a leaf on this journey, shaking in the breeze.

Just as she stood up, she heard Cynthia speaking, but not loud enough for her to make out the words. Turning away from them she treaded back into the deeper part of the stream and embraced the cold. She might be there a while.

Watching a fish jump out of the stream for a passing dragonfly, she listened to the birds call from the trees and the cicadas buzzing. She dunked herself and listened to the water running around her. It gurgled calm, whispering promises of a fresh drink and a cool bath.

When she came back up, Cynthia was waiting for her. "Nadi left to get you some clothes that would be more suitable for traveling."

"With what money?"

The dark angel seemed reluctant to answer, "He took your dress and shoes to trade them."

"He Did What?!" Kiran Stood from the stream raced toward the shore. She didn't want him to see her but she also didn't want to lose her favorite dress. At the bush, only her chemise was left and Nadi was already out of sight and the pull toward him was getting further away. "What am I supposed to wear now?"

"The chemise. He left it so you wouldn't be completely nude."

The princess huffed as she picked it up and threw it on, without drying off. She went to a patch of sunlit grass to wait for him as she dried off. Nadi was the one thing she didn't want to think about. He upset her because he didn't even bother to ask and just took her things to sell them. To her, he was nothing more than a pig headed jerk.

Cynthia sat beside her and looked over the woods. "So what has changed in Vadnera since I left?"

Kiran was silent a moment remembering that the dark angel had vanished before the shapeshifter dragon war started in the desert. She never got to meet them since the dark angels because they were being used in the armies that were searching for the sorcerer. "My mother married King Lucin Blackmore and had me." Then she went into the family history like she had been taught. "When King Lucin took the throne he decided to seek punishment on those who could not pay their taxes by establishing the slave trade. More people ended up paying for fear that they would end up there, but the abandreals suffered the worst due to the lack of their Elder. They were the first to join the slave trades and soon followed other creatures. The tax was used to better the city by using guards to patrol the roads and keep them free of monsters and beasts. Then several towns lost their nobles due to a history of embezzling. Now the towns are run by guards who collect the tax and keep the peace. Certain creatures that are not useful are hunted and captured alive to be given a purpose by the slave traders. An example is the changeling. They are captured and forced into human forms that fit the needs of workers. There are also—"

"Kiran, I don't need to know about the lies you were fed. I wanted to know what changed with the world. An increase in crime or monsters? Maybe even the surface of something rare." The dark angel seemed a little angry. "You don't need to tell me every last thing your father told to a scribe."

Kiran was confused, "I'm telling you about the history of Vadnera since before and after you passed. These aren't lies."

Cynthia shook her head, "You really think that magical creatures want to be enslaved? Do you think that guards should run towns and take taxes? Does any of this really make sense?"

Not wanting to be wrong Kiran simply agreed with her father's thinking, "I think that my father has done a good thing."

"Ha!" The dark angel got up and began pacing before her. "You're father! A good man? You obviously have never left the castle unless it is on a planned path and have only been shown what he wants you to see."

"I've gone to towns with my mother," Kiran argued the point. "She stopped at a village for some sweets."

"You mean the cluster of houses just outside of Vadnera? That can't be called a town and that's the houses of former staff from the castle's kitchen. She often went there to get things that her cooks didn't know how to make. You really haven't been anywhere other than Vadnera and Firstenfeld."

Kiran knew she hadn't. Everyone usually came to her. All her wants and needs were within the castle walls. She never really had a reason to leave.

"You want to know why I don't like your father?" Cynthia had stopped before her. "King Lucin threatened my kingdom demanding my hand in marriage in order to up his ranks. I couldn't even get a messenger out to request help because he would order them killed. I couldn't make it to my ceremony because we were trapped inside the city. I had to try a priest that was in the town and it didn't work. A barrier fell over my city to prevent the use of magic. I thought that being called to be a dark angel may have been my saving grace. I was able to slip out with the help of Dart and my guide, but my guide sacrificed himself to let me escape. Making it to the Elders' Enclave I became a dark angel and completed my training. I spent months there but only days had passed. By the time I had returned, my kingdom had already fallen. Dart was not there to greet me either. In the end, your father took everything from me."

Silently, Kiran tried to run through the history of what happened. Her father was not mentioned in the failure of Gavran. She wasn't sure if he was involved. Thoughts began muddling her mind.

"You're mother was actually supposed to marry someone else."

Looking at her, Kiran remained silent.

"Thaddeus Thorn who was a carpenter worked at the castle with his father had caught your mother's eye. She had been planning to announce her engagement when Lucin weaseled his way in. Your grandmother fell ill and your grandfather decided it best to meet Lucin's demands. Princess Lillian was forced into an arranged marriage with your father, but not before ordering the death of Charles Thorn for murder. Claimed he was the one to poison the Queen.

"I killed him, and regretted it almost instantly because Thaddeus had witnessed everything." Her voice held an unsteadiness of sadness and rage, "I paid the price when Thorn killed us all with your mother's gift. I don't think that Lucin is a very good man. I believe he is after something and he has yet to find it."

Anger was brimming in Kiran, "My Father isn't as vile as you make him out to be."

"Really?" Cynthia looked around, keeping watch. "What affections have your parents displayed in front of you? When have you seen them do more than dance at a gala or be present in the face of their country? Are they ever in the same room for more than meals? Did Lillian ever tell you that she never wanted to marry him?"

Thinking back to all that she remembered, her mother rarely got within arms reach of her father. Birthdays, they sat on opposite sides of the table and never knew what the other was getting for her. Her mother made it a point to always be late for dinner if the king was on time, otherwise she would eat very little and excuse herself the moment he arrived with some reason about having to talk to the cook. Kiran had assumed that's how their family worked.

Her father was always busy with speaking to other diplomats that Kiran rarely ever spent time with him and even when she was in his presence, she felt small and out of her element. He was constantly surrounded by people and it was almost unbearable trying to keep up appearances. It was why she liked the library. It was rare that anyone ventured there. That was her safe space. If only she could be there now.

"Well?" Cynthia asked.

"I don't want to talk about this anymore," Kiran hid her face wishing that she could just vanish from sight.

Silence filled the air between them, but it was still tense. Cynthia wanted answers on what had changed, but Kiran was not even sure herself. She had been within the castle for a majority of her eighteen years, whatever was outside the walls were a mystery.

"Look," Cynthia's tone was sympathetic. "I didn't mean to upset you, but I'm still sore on the subject of your father. He took everything from me. It was Vadnera that took me in and even then, he stepped into the picture and it was as though he were plotting to take that from me as well."

"He may be different than what you remember though," Kiran kept her face hidden muffling her words.

"He may have changed. People don't really change unless they have a reason to. I would hope that if he did change that you were that reason."

Kiran lifted her head to witness Cynthia float off into the forest. On the shore, she picked up a stick and moved it around drawing images in the sand. *Is my father a bad person?* Kiran asked herself. She recalled speaking with the children of other nobles and they had fear for the King. Kiran never really feared him or had a reason to until now. He was going to be upset that she ran away with a man she barely knew. No one could see Cynthia except the two of them so her explanation would be thrown out.

What is father going to say when he finds out that I am a dark angel? The thought scared her. She didn't want to lose her throne or become an executioner. She had never killed anything more than a fly. Killing people was the last thing she wanted to be doing.

Dark angels were contracted to kingdoms to become guards or executioners. They killed prisoners on the King's command and once their wings were blackened they were forced to create an item from the collected souls that would benefit the ruler's needs. Kiran did not want to be used.

She sat on that shore until the sun became too hot and moved into the shade of a nearby tree. Trying to focus on the pull she felt toward Nadi she could tell that He was further away almost enough that she could barely feel his presence. It made her wonder what the limit would be to this feeling. Would she not be able to feel him if he was across the ocean?

There were questions she wanted to ask, but Cynthia was probably still upset at her and currently patrolling. Kiran wondered if she could figure out how some of her abilities worked on her own. She tried to remember things that the court wizard had done. Grabbing a nearby stick, she tore it from a tree and waved it at a stone hoping to make it float. Nothing happened.

"Maybe warming water is easier?" She said to herself.

Going back to the stream she dug a hole in the sand before filling it with water. Pointing the stick at it, she thought about making it warmer. She gave the stick a swish. Her anticipation of steam was met with nothing. She dipped her finger in the water. It was still cool.

Maybe her abilities didn't work like a wizard's. She thought about things she had read from her books that were about warlocks. One story, *The Hapless Tale of Quilkey Rven* was of a really unlucky findeli who was an adventuring warlock. He wasn't the brightest bird and had set an entire priceless collection of artifacts ablaze by reading a spell aloud from a book. She tried to recall the spell. "Let these words light the flame to burn my enemies," she whispered the words feeling a little embarrassed.

Nothing happened.

Kiran gave a frustrated sigh and tossed the stick at the ground. "Why can't I use magic?"

"Oh, is that what you were doing?" Cynthia said amused from behind her.

The Princess jumped and spun to face the dark angel. "I was trying to see if I could use magic since I am able to feel Nadi's presence."

Raising an eyebrow, Cynthia observed, "So saying a warlock incantation you thought you could just use magic?"

Kiran felt like a child in her presence. "Well, it worked in stories."

The dark angel laughed, "Where do you think a warlock gets their magic?"

"I'm not sure."

"Warlocks get their magic by making a deal with a demon or some higher being that is not on this plane of existence. Both sorcerers and Wizards are born with magic but the way they use them is different. Wizards use objects to project their magic while sorcerers cast using magical incantations from their own hands. As a dark angel, the magic is usually bestowed tends to act like a sorcerer's but you get a few more spells that a sorcerer is unable to use that would normally belong to a cleric."

"A cleric?" Kiran was interested in learning now and had nearly forgotten that they were upset with each other.

"Clerics are the only ones allowed to use magic in the temples and Firstenfeld, aside from the witch hunters. They get their magic similar to warlocks but they get their contracts are from more positive beings. Blessings, purging, cures, and other similar magics are used, but they go through a stage of sickness when they gain a new magical ability. The only others to get sick from the inheritance of magic are dark angels. Since the magic that fills them is so great, they need the help from the Elders to survive the sickness. That's why the journey to the Elders' Enclave is so important. It will save your life."

The princess was silent a moment. She realized that there was a lot that she didn't know about the world she lived in and Cynthia may only be concerned for her. "I'm sorry for earlier. I admit, I don't know a lot about my parents or anything outside of the castle. Now that I am here, maybe we can—"

Cynthia shushed her, as she stared intently at the woods. Kiran, followed her gaze but saw nothing. "Get out of sight," she kept her voice low.

Kiran complied and crouched behind the bush that had held her clothes. Peering through the leaves she watched the now quiet forest. She had not even noticed that most of the birds had fallen silent. A few still made calls but they sounded like they were announcing the presence of something. Kiran had read in her books that birds will do that when a predator is near. The deer had already sprinted off into the woods and the animals had gone into hiding. Kiran sat there waiting to see what would happen.

After a moment, she noticed that Cynthia was not looking just at the trees, but up in the canopy. Kiran tried again to follow her gaze and this time, she froze. *It couldn't be*, her mind nearly yelled as she tried to keep from moving.

A harpy was caught in a large web that stretched out over the branches. It wasn't alone. Large hairy legs worked at encasing the creature that was making the alert calls in its web. It was not a sound that Kiran had expected to come from a Harpy and it became muffled when the arachnid wove its thread around the head. It bit into the cocoon and drank its fill. The princess paled as she realized cocoons of various sizes dotted the web.

Covering her eyes, Kiran felt sick. She waited for the sound of the birds and for the animals to come back. Silently, she waited for the spider to go away. She really wished she was home now, protected from any such creatures. The only place she would ever find such monsters was in her books and even then, she wasn't the one to face them. If only this were all a nightmare, then she would wake from it and be home again.

She peaked again to see it looking in her direction. She wasn't ready for this. There was no way she would ever have been ready to face that monstrosity. Spinning a web masterfully with its hind legs, Kiran watched in horror as it lowered itself to the ground and began coming towards her.

"Don't move or make any noise," Cynthia said without looking at her.

Any noise? Kiran covered her mouth and nose to try and lessen the noise of her breathing. Her heart was pounding in her ears causing all other sounds to fade from existence. She could not hear the sound of the spider approaching the stream.

The spider stopped and drank from the water, and then stood there. As still as possible. Just by looking at it,

Kiran could see how it could blend in with the canopy. Even now, it looked like an oddly shaped tree. She could not unsee the large arachnid though.

So much time had passed as Kiran sat there watching the creature as it proceeded to clean itself. She felt her feet going numb from her crouched position. Wishing she could move, she decided to feel for Nadi's position as a distraction. He was closer than she expected. She almost turned her head towards the direction.

He must have been on the road heading back towards them. She didn't know if she should be happy or afraid. Nadi could find a way for them out of this mess but if he didn't then the spider would eat him and she would have no protector or guide. She would have no choice but to return to the castle and tell the truth.

Then she was startled to find that Nadi had walked further than expected. *Maybe he had become lost?* Kiran thought, fighting the urge to turn toward him. She knew better than that though, because Nadi could feel her as well. Panic was gripping her because she knew he was getting further and further away.

Tears started streaming down her face and it did not go unnoticed. The arachnid stopped moving and seemed to be staring right at her again. Cynthia looked over and cursed. She knew she had messed everything up. This spider was going to eat her and she could either run or stay put.

Cynthia shot forward and touched the spider's leg, whispering something. The arachnid burst into flames screeching as it dashed into the water and up the stream. The fire did not seem to go out with water. Kiran could smell the awful stench of it burning as it eventually crumpled and stopped moving. The fire slowly fizzled out.

Looking to Cynthia, Kiran tried to stand but fell over from the price of being crouched for so long. The spirit was fading. Kiran wanted to rush to her but she couldn't get up. Faster than she had expected, Cynthia vanished from her sight.

The princess began sobbing. It was all her fault. If she didn't start crying, Cynthia would have been fine. All because Nadi kept walking and she had no way of defending herself, Cynthia sacrificed herself to keep Kiran safe. Now, she was all alone.

Once the feeling came back to her legs, Kiran sat on the shore with her face pressed against her knees. She had a choice to make; find Nadi or return to the castle. Her problem was she could not go wandering around in her state. If someone saw her in such an indecent state it would be very embarrassing. The Princess wandering the roads in nothing but her chemise. Questions would be raised on if she were still pure. Worse is if she ran into the wrong person they may get the wrong idea. She laid on the ground and sobbed.

Kiran had to stay put. She had to wait even if Nadi had abandoned her and wasn't returning. She could hope that a knight might find her and take her home before anyone saw the state she was in. Roaming the roads in her condition would bring shame to her family. She cried until she fell asleep.

Waking with the sunlight in her face, the summer heat caused her to sweat. Her nose was stuffy from crying. Slowly she sat up and assessed the state she was in. Cynthia was gone and she was alone. Even though the birds sang in the trees around her, she no longer felt safe.

Sensing for Nadi, to her surprise he was approaching from down steam. Tears flooded her eyes again, but this time it was relief. A pang or guilt was there because she had thought he had abandoned her. Her thoughts had been ill of him and now she was ashamed because she was going to have to explain that Cynthia was gone and that it was all her fault. Patiently, she waited for him to come into view.

Chapter 22

Approaching the princess, he noticed the large heap of smoldering arachnid further along the river. He quickened his pace dropping the bag as he looked for any possible danger near her. There was none, but he realized Cynthia was nowhere to be seen.

As he reached Kiran, the headache started again. He looked her over as he grabber her shoulders. "What happened?" Nadi asked trying to not shake her.

Her voice was almost a whisper, "A large spider was in the trees. Cynthia tried to protect me when it came down but she vanished when she cast a spell. I don't know what happened." She began pouring tears again.

Frustrated at the outcome of leaving, he turned back and retrieved the bag. Fetching out her new clothes, he dropped them on the grass before her. "Let's get you dressed so we can keep moving. We need to make it to the next camp site."

"We can't leave. What if Cynthia comes back," she took the clothes but only held them close to her chest. "She won't be able to find us."

Cursing, Nadi snatched the clothes back and pull the dress over her head. "We can't sit around and wait. The longer we wait, the more likely a guard will find us. If we keep moving we can get to a dock and board a ship. We just need to return to the desert and then we can make it back to the dragons' keep." Forcing her arms into the sleeves, Nadi had successfully dressed her, but her curly hair was in disarray. He didn't have time to help her sort that out. Pulling out the shoes, he placed them before her.

Kiran, only turned away from him. It seemed she was determined to stay.

This didn't leave Nadi any choice. Placing the shoes back in the bag, he did the only thing he could to win the silent argument. Ignoring the headache, he picked Kiran up and placed her over his shoulder. She struck at his back and cried, then just silently allowed him to carry her.

Following the path up stream, Nadi looked over the spider. There were parts he might have been able to salvage off the creature if he had time, but most of the day had already been wasted. He hoped some deserving soul found it and was able to profit from its corpse.

As they made it around the bend, Kiran said, "Enough, I'll walk. I don't need to be carried in such an undignified manner."

Gently, Nadi set her on the ground and brought her shoes out again. Crouching down, he slipped the shoes onto her feet and then met her gaze. Her face was red and she looked away from him. The response from the princess made him realize his actions may have been seen as intimate, causing his face to flush.

Quietly, he stood, grabbing her hand and leading her up the stream. Nadi's mind suddenly had a million questions about his actions. The shapeshifter understood that his reasoning was rushed by the dilemma of his tardiness. Yet, his actions had indeed been too intimate. He dressed the princess. Nadi had never been that way with any woman in his village, yet he bought clothes and dressed her. This made him question if she was going to get the wrong idea.

Bringing his focus back to their surroundings, he watched each tree they passed, listening for any small movement. Without Cynthia, it was going to be harder to keep from finding trouble. From his experience in the desert, he understood that most waterways were void of any trouble. They were the spots where prey and predator usually put aside their differences to quench their thirst. The only exception was the creatures that hunt in water. Being in a foreign land, Nadi was uncertain of any dangers that lurked here. Only Kiran would know if she knew anything.

"Are there any creatures that lurk near water?" Nadi asked.

Kiran took a moment to answer as she stumbled behind him, "Only those that lurk in deep water. Sirens and mermaids in the ocean, kelpies and nymphs in lakes or ponds."

Through the trees, Nadi spotted a lake. Just his luck that the river came from such a large water source. He hissed in frustration, eyeing the calm liquid surface. Crossing the river, he hoped that they weren't present during the day.

Wishing he could enjoy the new experience, Nadi emerged out of the trees and into the open, pulling the princess behind him. A few men were fishing together with an abandreal slave holding their bait. The poor girl gave a disgusted look at the bucket as they passed.

One man with a scruffy beard called out, "Isn't the owner supposed to be doing the leading, not the slave?"

The rest of the men laughed.

Nadi gritted his teeth as he wanted to hit the man. He was no slave, even if he was collared. Heat filled his face and ears. Revenge for that comment would be dealt with later. He planned to follow that man after the sun went down, back to his home, and steal something. He was hoping for ale to dull this headache of his.

"Yes, but he must lead the way so that I may not break my ankle traversing this terrain," Kiran said, releasing his hand and shoving him. "Come on, get going."

The men laughed again, but the fight went out of Nadi with the pounding of his head. He was tired and needed a rest, but was also surprised by her sudden confidence.

Looking back at her, he noticed that she was looking at the ground and still fighting to hold back tears. Cynthia's disappearance weighed heavily on her, and Nadi was hoping it was only he who noticed. A wave of nausea hit him, and he knew they were going to have to rest sooner than he wanted to.

Grabbing Kiran's hand again, he pulled her into the cover of the trees and far enough from the lake that the men could not see them. Nadi didn't stop until he found a nice flat area where he could easily set a fire. There was tall grass everywhere, which made it easy for them to hide but also harder for them to spot any enemies. He had to hope they were safe because he couldn't go on any further.

Pulling off the pack, he rummaged through it, planning a meal. "Princess, can you grab some wood for the fire?"

She turned to walk into the forest before pausing. Without looking back, she said, "Please, just call me Kiran. It's my name, and my title would be useless here."

Nadi ran his fingers through his hair, thinking she had gotten the wrong idea. It could simply be that she considered him a friend. Maybe it was just him throwing things out of proportion. Watching her walk away, he was glad to have her as a friend.

Chapter 23

Kiran lay sleeping on the makeshift bed with some of the tall grass. She was so well hidden that when Nadi stepped away, even he could not see her. He was losing sleep guarding her, which made him want to take a risk. Those fishermen must live nearby, and Nadi would have time to steal from them.

As he doused the fire and began walking out of the woods, his headache seemed to lighten. It was a relief that it was not a constant problem. Maybe the dragon inside him had finally fallen asleep. He could now complete his ill deeds without consequence.

Breaking from the trees, Nadi thought he heard a whisper but could not make out what was being said or where it came from. Shaking it off, he continued around the lake. A splash caught his attention, and he looked toward the water, but saw nothing. *It was probably a fish.*

Just as he turned toward his destination, he saw a white horse. He had no idea where it had come from, but was curious as it snorted. Thoughts of gaining its form entered his mind. He had no food on him at the moment, but maybe he could find some other means of taming it.

Taking a step toward it, his foot plunged into the lake, startling him to his senses. Wheeling back onto the grass, he was bewildered to find the horse walking on the water. He pushed himself back further from the edge to put distance between them. He did not bother to ask Kiran about the creatures that lurked here, which was now a mistake. As he stood, he looked toward the spot the men had been and tried to focus on his revenge.

The surface of the water broke where his foot had plunged in, and his attention was caught by a woman with dark hair. She folded her arms on the grass by the lake and gave him a playful smile. He could tell by her bare shoulders that she was naked. It was as though she were trying to tell him the water was safe. Her beauty seemed to hold him, and he thought about how her lips might feel on his. The revenge plot was forgotten at that moment. Everything was gone from his mind, and he wanted to hold her against him. His feet began taking steps on their own as he edged toward the water.

The woman moved further back into the lake and reached out her hand, beckoning for Nadi to join her. He wanted to jump in after her. Nadi wondered how her hair would feel tangled in his hands or what passions lay beneath the surface. Thoughts of lust began to form as his foot left the ground and crept toward the lake.

A body slammed into him from the side, knocking him off his path. They tumbled to the ground, and his presence of mind returned. He had almost died, and someone had saved him. Looking up, he found Kiran on top of him, her open hand making contact with his face.

Tears were raining on him as she nearly screamed, "Don't leave me all alone! Don't go to them!" Her fists were pounding against his chest.

Nadi rolled on top of Kiran, distancing himself from the water. The princess had suddenly become silent as he looked down at her in his arms. So small and frail like a fawn. Her mess of curls and her breath quickening as her wide eyes stared at him, startled by the sudden turn of events. Her bare legs were exposed as he realized where his hips were. His face got closer to hers as he brushed a stray curl out of the way. The thoughts of the creature were still fresh in his mind, but now, Kiran was the target, and a hunger he did not know was ravenously waiting to be filled. His hand trailed to her chin, lifting it.

Another slap from the princess jarred him back to reality. He pushed himself off of her and turned away. "I'm so sorry. I don't know what came over me."

She pushed her skirt back down and stood, raising her nose away from him as a sign of disgust or disapproval. He could not tell. Either way, it was a sign that she was not going to forgive him so easily. "Don't look back. I don't want you to fall under her power again."

They both silently returned to camp, and Cynthia stood in the spot where the fire had been. She looked amused with no hint of concern. "Not the brightest idea, I take it?"

"You're back, I see," Nadi said, sitting down, feeling his headache return as his face stung from the princess's wake-up call.

Kiran sat across from him as though there was still a fire burning, but did not seem to be excited at the spirit's return. She stared at her lap, and Nadi knew her mind was burdened with questions he needed to answer.

"Why would you leave me?" It was the first question she asked to break the silence.

Cynthia retreated to a branch to give them space.

Nadi knew that lying was not an option. "I left to steal from the men who insulted us earlier. I'm not a slave, and they probably had things that we needed."

"And what had you done if you were caught?" Kiran finally met his gaze, but it was only briefly as her face flushed and she turned away.

"I wouldn't have been caught."

"You can't say that!" Her voice rose. "You don't know the future, and what would have happened. If I hadn't been there, that nymph would have stolen your breath, and the kelpie would be feasting on your flesh! I would have been alone and not known you were dead! Your actions were purely selfish."

Kiran was right. He was in no position to take those risks, and it was selfish that he wanted to steal out of revenge and cost them everything that he was working toward. "You're right, I'm sorry. I shouldn't have left like that. Protecting you is one of my top priorities."

"If protecting me is one of your top priorities, then you shouldn't have been trying to get into my skirt in the middle of a field after such a dangerous experience." She couldn't look at him.

Nadi didn't know what to say to her or if it might offend her. He wanted to explain the power that creature held over him, but he wasn't certain of how he should word it. "When that creature—"

"The nymph," the princess corrected.

"When the nymph had me under her power, it was as though my thoughts were being filled with lust. I never wanted any woman that way, but she made me want to experience that. I don't know why I wanted to go to her, but when you put yourself before me after everything was fresh in my mind, I wanted you that way." He got on his knees and bowed his head, touching his forehead to the ground. "Please forgive me. I would not have attempted that had I been in my right mind. My job is to keep you safe until we reach the Elders' Enclave."

Kiran sniffled, and he raised his head to see her wiping tears from her eyes again. He tried to apologize, but he knew his words might still hurt in one way. Nadi had not told her that she was attractive; that if there weren't lives at stake that he would have been interested in pursuing her. She may be a snobby princess who didn't know about survival, but she held common sense better than most of the women in his village. He shook his head, thinking that maybe it was the nymph's effect still whispering lewd thoughts into his mind.

"Ok, children," Cynthia floated between them. "An adult has returned from a lack of energy. Time for sleep, or none of you will rise with the dawn."

Both Kiran and Nadi complied and went to the grass area to hide and sleep. Kiran lay with her back to Nadi, and for a moment, he thought of closing the gap to apologize again. His mind still held the image of her beneath him. Again, he tried to shake that vulnerable idea from his mind. Nadi had to focus on saving Zec.

He tossed and turned with the thoughts, bringing more questions. Nadi feared the outcome of losing his brother. He wouldn't have minded exile had his brother been safe to lead the tribe, but if Zec died, being exiled would cause his father to be challenged by other members of the tribe. Not all of them were fit to lead.

Hearing Kiran turn in her sleep, he rolled to check on her and froze. Above her was almost a reflection of Nadi himself, but half of his face was covered in gold scales along with one arm. With a sly smile, it placed one claw under her chin and moved her mouth closer to the creature's.

Rage and fear filled Nadi at once, and his hand shot out to grab the creature, but it vanished. He looked around and didn't see it anywhere. With his head throbbing, the world darkened around him, and the creature was there in the shadows of his mind. It grabbed him by the throat and held him with immense power. "Mine," it said with Nadi's voice. "The princess will be mine!"

In that moment, Nadi understood this was the dragon. He clawed at the arm for release. "Never," he choked. "I'll never…let you…touch her!"

The sharp-toothed grin deepened as fire backed his words, "She'll come to me willingly, you'll see." With that, he was tossed out of his mind, and panic filled him. The world where his forms were stored was completely taken over by the dragon. As Kiran slept soundly, Nadi was now unable to sleep because the enemy in his own mind was getting stronger.

Chapter 24

A hand pressed over Kiran's mouth, waking her from her sleep. She nearly screamed in panic until she saw Nadi's face right next to hers. He placed one finger over his lips to indicate her silence. She wondered if asking a question would be too much. Cynthia looked worried as she floated above.

"Guards are everywhere. They discovered the fire, but they are searching the grass for clues. There is an elf looking at your footsteps right now and an abandreal tracking your scent. It is only a matter of time." The spirit was eyeing the other guards who were heading out of the woods towards the lake.

A guard spoke, "It smells similar to her highness, but it is more earthy. It is hard to determine if it is the same scent we are searching for."

Looking at Cynthia, Kiran began making hand signals. She held up two fingers, then three, and shrugged her shoulders.

"You want to know how many?"

Kiran nodded, trying not to rustle the grass too much.

"Two now, that are near the campfire. The others wandered toward the lake, following the path leading out of the woods. They fear you may have succumbed to the lake creatures."

Kiran picked up a rock and aimed out of the woods. Throwing the rock, it hit a tree, landing on the ground among the grass. "What was that?" The elf's accent betrayed him as he moved toward the noise.

"Oh, brilliant. I'll lead them away." Cynthia headed toward the noise.

The sound of the grass moving had the guards' pace quicken. "Something is moving here!" The abandreal nearly shouted as he ran after it.

The elf followed, though his footsteps were silent. Kiran waited until she was sure they were far enough away. She began crawling through the grass. Nadi instead stood, pulling her to her feet, and running north. She ran with branches lashing at her face and pulling at her hair and dress.

They stopped near some tall grass just as Kiran was beginning to tire. Nadi had her crouch down and take her shoes off. They didn't dare speak yet for fear that a guard might be near. Nadi backed out of the grass, careful of where he stepped and swept at their footsteps before using the shoes and his own feet to head east. He walked backwards again and leaped into the grass, handing her back her shoes. He was covering their tracks and creating false ones. It was brilliant.

Again, they rushed north and broke from the trees. Past the field was a town, and Kiran could only hope for two things—a bath and a bed. Nadi took the hood off his shoulders and placed it on Kiran. His collar glinted in the sunlight, but the redness of his neck was the reason she stared. He had bags under his eyes, showing his exhaustion. Kiran was becoming worried that he might be ill.

"We should rest at an inn for the night," she expressed.

"There are too many people, you could be—"

"You're neck is becoming red. That collar and the dragon are both taxing on you. We need to rest while we think of the next part of the journey. We need to obtain a map and orient ourselves."

Cynthia popped out of the trees, nearly startling them. "She is right, rest is well needed."

"I didn't think you would be joining us so soon," Nadi stated as he began walking toward town.

"Well, I gave them a run for their money and had to fly above the trees to spot you. The good news is that they have not contracted the help of any findeli to assist with the search. We can only hope the findeli are refusing to cooperate," Cynthia followed.

"The findeli refuse to work with Vadnera due to the disappearance of their long-tailed diplomat shortly before I was born," Kiran stated, covering her face with the hood. "I hear his feathers were darker than the night sky, except the red patches on the shoulders. The findeli have refused to participate in any event Vadnera has until he returns, but father said that he may make peace by having me court the findeli prince."

Nadi spun on her, "Is that all your life is? To be tossed at any man in the hope of creating a connection for the kingdom?" His face was becoming as red as his neck.

Cynthia was the one to join in, "The duty of a princess is to strengthen the kingdom—however the King sees fit. This stunt may put her in a darker light."

The group became quiet as they entered the town. Kiran thought about Nadi's reaction and wondered why he would be upset. It was her life, and she couldn't change her father's decisions. She could try to argue the point, but if it helped Vadnera, it was a sacrifice she was willing to make.

Entering the inn, she looked at the table with a drunken man passed out. The woman behind the counter looked unpleasant with her hair in a bun and stains on her dress. Kiran cringed as the woman gave a loud snort at her approach.

Kiran waited for the woman to greet her, but she only narrowed her eyes at the young princess. Kiran spoke first, "Do you have two beds that we can occupy for the night along with a map?"

"Only a room with two beds is available," her response was very nasally.

"How much?" This interaction was making Kiran uncomfortable.

"Three gold," she gave a grin, exposing her yellowed teeth.

Nadi pulled the coins out and put them on the counter.

The woman eyed him before saying, "Slaves sleep in the barn."

"I beg your pardon?" Kiran nearly let her high status show.

"Your filthy slave must sleep in the barn. I don't need my customers thinking I appreciate slave owners," The woman glared down at Kiran as she took her money back.

"How much to sleep in the barn then?"

A snort came from the woman again, "I don't give the barn to slave owners, only to the slaves."

Kiran dug through her internal library, trying to come up with anything that might suit this situation. What book should she use if someone despises slave owners? She could be honest, but there needed to be a lie in her words. Some story she concocted for this very reason. *The Creation from Ingall* was the only book that fit this moment. The character had to lie to get their creation onto an airship. She remembered the lines from the book and twisted them to fit her need.

"He is not a slave, and I shouldn't be telling you this, but he was experimented on in Ingall before I rescued him from the market. Yet, he is dying, and if I take that collar off, it will only quicken his death. Do you see the inflamed area around his collar? He'll fall to pieces without it." Kiran watched the woman's guard drop and knew she had this sealed now. "I have to take him to Lu'Bela so their researchers can somehow stop this from happening."

Silently, the woman thought for a moment before tossing the key on the counter along with a map, "One gold. A discount for a good woman. I'll bring food up to you because I prefer him to stay hidden from prying eyes, and you leave at dawn, you hear me?"

Kiran nodded, "Understood, thank you."

"Door at the end of the hall up the stairs," She went back to staring at the door, waiting for the next customer.

The group went up the stairs and entered the room. Kiran dropped onto the bed and looked at the sky through the window. It was almost noon, and they were going to have to stay in the room until dawn. She knew this was a waste of time, but she also felt the reasons may have been selfish as well. A tub sat off to one corner, but her reasoning shattered as she remembered that Nadi could not leave the room. Her face sank into the pillow with disappointment. A bath was out of the question.

"How do you do that?" Nadi asked as he sat down on the other bed. "How do you tell lies out of nowhere and make them sound like the truth?"

The princess lifted her head to look at him. "I read a lot of books, and sometimes I have to wear a mask to deal with problems in the court. The people demand so much, and my father sometimes pawns his duties off on me, so I simply place the mask on and use a character I read about to fill my shoes instead. Same problem, just the twisted truth as an answer. It's not a lie as long as they get the desired results. As long as we leave before dawn, it will remain the truth in their eyes."

"But we are not heading to Lu'Bela, are we?" Nadi seemed concerned.

Kiran sat up and opened the map. Placing a finger on Typhen, she stated, "We are here. And as long as we continue east, Lu'Bela will be south, and North Shore Port will be north. We simply head in a different direction when out of sight."

The shifter nodded in understanding, "But if we could just go that way now, wouldn't we be able to make it to the port within a day or two?"

The princess once again went back to her internal library to find a story that might have been worth telling to match this situation. A children's story came to mind of a goose that lost its feathers. "You are like a mother goose, meant to protect her young. If you lose your feathers over stress, how will you teach your young to fly?" She saw the moment things registered and knew he was on the hook. Kiran simply needed to end it with no argument. "Without you to guide me, I am alone and lost. Even with a map, I have no idea what troubles lie in your land or how we would reach the Enclave. You must take care of yourself first."

"I understand," Nadi lay on the bed. "So tell me, Prin—Kiran, how did you grow up?"

"I normally played around the castle with other noble children, and eventually stopped seeing them because they were always so cruel to my staff at the castle. They would threaten to have them beheaded just to show off, so I stopped inviting them over. I at least have that much power. It's either Lord Keol or my lady-in-waiting who are my friends. And now you." She hadn't thought of Keol in a while. Her thoughts of him did not hold their usual spark that made her excited. If she were to see him now, he would surely be cross with her.

"Sounds like most nobles are royal jerks," He gaze was focused on the ceiling.

Kiran felt her face flush as she remembered that she had been on top of him, hitting him. That was embarrassing to lose her composure in such a vulgar way. All she could do was hope that no one had seen her that way, even Cynthia. She realized their spirit companion had not entered the room with them but poked her head through the door every once in a while. Kiran had been woken by her return, and Cynthia had sent her to chase after Nadi. She did not want to think of last night's events, though. "How was your childhood?"

Nadi stared at the ceiling for a long moment. Kiran almost gave up when he answered, "I used to be looked up to by my younger brother and the proud child of my family. I was a quick learner, and the dragon kings were like uncles to me. When the sorcerer showed up and drank from my father's cup, that's when everything ended. The sorcerer appeared when Daron went missing, and Grumlock took it out on my tribe. My mother saved me, but she vanished into the dragon's flames. From there, I got into fights, stole from anyone who had something I wanted, and began drinking. My brother hated me, I became a burden to my father, and my tribe despised me.

"This trial I was on could mean exile for me if Zec is harmed in any way. My only task is to bring him back safe and sound, and I'll redeem myself. But Zec is working for the sorcerer, and Daron is locked under the temple of the Elders. Getting him back to the dragons could end the war, but it would be pointless if my brother doesn't come out of this unscathed."

"That's why this is so important," Kiran met Nadi's eyes that were now orange. She wondered why his eyes had been red last night and looked away from him. "We should rest until we need to leave." She hoped that she could at least sleep until then, but it was going to be hard to find in the middle of the day.

Letting her thoughts wander, Kiran tried not to think of Nadi and how he had looked at her last night. Her heart raced with his apology, but also stung. She was supposed to love Keol, but Nadi seemed to hold her attention more now. The princess questioned if it was just the fact that he was a new man in her life or if she started to have feelings for him. Everything was so much simpler at the castle, where she hid in her books, and decisions were made for her. The only decision she hated now was becoming a dark angel, but it made her question if she really wanted everything decided for her.

She rolled toward the wall and hoped that she wouldn't be trapped in these thoughts for long.

Chapter 25

The guards huddled around the charred corpse of an arachnid. Keol even stared, unsure of what had transpired. He knew that Kiran was here, and she had been around the area alone for some time. He could not fathom how the girl would have been saved from the arachnid. There was no other scent of magic. The scene did not make sense.

"What is the verdict, Keol?" The King sat on his black steed, awaiting an answer.

The vampire followed Kiran's tracks around the camp once more. "From what I can tell, Kiran had woken and gone over to this bush where I presume she had removed her clothing to bathe in the river. The man with her stirred later and left her alone for hours."

"And she stayed put?" The King questioned.

Keol nodded, but stared at the spot she had sat. "It seems as though she dried off in the sun, but…" he trailed off as anger filled him. The imprint of where she sat held a thin strand from a piece of fabric. Plucking it from the ground, he stared at it. "She was only in her chemise."

Most of the guards were watching them now, waiting to hear more. Lucin broke the silence as he bellowed, "Keep searching, you fools!" The men rushed to busy themselves.

"So she was kept here only by her lack of clothing," he closed the fabric in his fist and stood. "Kiran then saw the spider and backed behind a bush, but there were no other footprints around. She didn't use magic because the bush would have been burnt, so I'm not sure how that spider met its end."

"And that man?" The King was looking at the bare footprints that came from downstream.

Keol shook his head, "If he is indeed wearing a collar like the witnesses state, then he would be unable to use magic. Maybe the death of the arachnid came after they left, but then Kiran's actions would not make sense. She came out from behind the bush, wept, and seemed to have fallen asleep. Then he returns, picks her up, and carries her further upstream." He followed the path and then saw the shoe prints, "Placed shoes on her feet." He made a note of the knee imprint on the ground, and he wanted to punch the man. He put himself in a position of one who may be proposing. To be so informal to her was an offense Keol was not willing to stand for. He almost stormed off the path until the king stopped him.

"Keol, we are going to wait and harvest parts from the spider. Your help is progressing this faster than expected, but by the looks of it, no harm is coming to the princess, and she may be needed alive. For now, we can waste a little time before catching up with them."

"But, sire, Kiran could be in danger. We need to—"

"Are you objecting to my decision, Lord Keol?" The King dismounted and approached the vampire, stroking his black beard as his dark gaze threatened him.

Status was the only power the king held over him, and that is why Keol was left to do his bidding. When Lillian was the princess, the kingdom flourished. It was more peaceful than when Lucin took over. Being forced to replace the dark angels in their work by slaughtering the condemned at his command left the vampire with a sense of hopelessness. Keol despised Lucin and was biding his time for when he would ascend the throne with Kiran by his side and bring peace once again.

"No, sire. I will await your command," Keol sat down, staring at her footprints. Her feet changed from small bare feet to shoes in an instant. He hoped she was safe and that the man who stole her away had no ill intentions with his bride-to-be.

Night fell, and Keol watched the tents go up. The king retreated for the night, but still the vampire sat in the same spot. It wasn't until the waning moon was directly above him that he decided to slip away from the camp and venture up the stream a little further.

A wood wolf crossed his path, and he shattered the beast in a fit of rage. He was uncertain if it would have done any harm, but he was upset with what he had become since the rulers had changed. From a trusted friend to nothing more than a royal lap dog. Keol to change the look of the vampiric people for the better, and now they were mere executioners. He tossed the limp, splintered body of the wood wolf into the brush and proceeded on his way.

Following their footsteps up the path, he crossed the river and made it to the open area with a lake. A white mare walked around the water, creating the illusion that the lake was a solid flat surface. Keol knew better than to believe it. It was simply a kelpie waiting for its next prey.

As he tore his eyes from the water, he noticed a spot next to the lake where the grass was flattened. He approached it and took in the scent. Kiran's smell was a little different, but he knew it was hers, along with the smell of the man, sand, and fur. It was an odd scent for this area. His eyes focused on the spot where the grass was flattened, and he froze. The imprint of her back and his knees. If his heart could beat, it would be for fear and anger. He was a little taller than the man, but he placed himself in the same position her captor would have been. It was as though he could see her beneath him, tears in her eyes, he towered over her. He was bombarded by mixed emotions as his imagination went wild.

The surface of the water broke near him, and he saw a nymph with dark hair come to the surface. Instinctively, he grabbed her by the throat and dragged her to the surface. She hissed and flailed, trying to get out of his grasp.

"What happened with these two by the Lake?" He was going to get an answer no matter what. "Tell me and I'll set you free."

She froze with her dark eyes staring at his red piercing gaze. It was his power to influence those to do his bidding. The nymph knew she had no choice but to comply. "My prey was stolen by a girl. She knocked him to the ground and hit him several times before he moved away from the water."

"And then? What happened when he was on top of her?" He squeezed her throat.

She sputtered, "The girl slapped him again and they retreated into the woods."

"You're lying! Why would she willingly save her captor and boss him around," thrusting her back into the water, he pulled her back out again and waited for a reply.

"They looked more like lovers to me. She was crying about not wanting to be left alone. I took pity on the girl and let them get away." She grimaced, squirming under his grasp.

Keol felt betrayed. If he pursued her and brought her back, the king would seek to punish him, but if he waited too long, Kiran would no longer be his. Releasing the nymph, she wasted no time returning to the lake. Her head bobbed a little further from the shore, watching him cautiously. "Make yourself scarce tomorrow when the king arrives. He is off your menu, and this conversation stays between us."

She blew a few bubbles and then questioned, "Why doesn't my ability work on you?"

He held up his right hand to show his ring, "I wear a charm that dispels any mind control. It was passed down to me from the last leader of the tower. A keepsake sake so if the first one were to ever awaken, I would not be held under his control." Keol turned his attention to the ground and pulled at the grass, making it harder for anyone to see what had transpired there. He would not tell the king what he had found and instead remove the evidence for a different story. No one needed to think that Kiran would willingly run off with some vagrant. The story will still be that she is kidnapped, and maybe he can talk some sense into her before they return. He has to succeed the throne, and Kiran is the only way he can do that. He has to protect her image even if it means lying to her father.

Chapter 26

The sky was still dark when Kiran and Nadi left the inn. Instinctively, they went for the cover of trees but found that a cliff blocked their path from cutting through. They wandered back to the road, but it was becoming crowded with carts, carriages, and people. Hiding on the edge of the woods near the road, they continued on their way, stopping only when patrolling officers came into view. At one point, they were stuck for a few hours as the guards questioned every individual who passed if they had seen the Princess. It was apparent that only trouble lay ahead.

When the road quieted down, they moved further toward their destination. People banded together as a group of guards held up the road. Everyone was on edge as the guards checked carts, cajoling for tolls to pass. She cringed as they rummaged through a decent-looking carriage with purple curtains and pure white horses. The guard let out a laugh as the wealthy family tried to stop them.

"Relax," he said, brandishing his sword. "We have to make sure these valuables look nothing like the ones our dear Princess Kiran carried. We might have to confiscate a few to check with the King. You can't be too cautious."

"This is all wrong," Kiran whispered as she hid behind a tree. "Vadneran guards stealing from the people."

Nadi stood behind her and took her hair out of the braid. "Our main concern right now is trying to get past them. Those people are a distraction right now. We need to take advantage of this."

Cynthia hovered out in the open. "How? This delicate girl still looks like royalty, and they will recognize her on the spot."

Nadi was silent for a moment as he ran his fingers through her hair, "Maybe she just needs to find the right mask to wear from one of her book characters." He pulled the hood she was wearing around her face and inspected her. "No one needs to see her face, but maybe she can pull off an act." His eyes locked onto something near the edge of the woods. "Got it! Stay right here."

Kiran spun around to ask, but he was already gone. Cynthia seemed to be watching him but said nothing. After a moment, Nadi returned with some rope.

"Tie my hands," he checked towards the guards as they seemed to find a small box with coins in the carriage.

"I can't," Kiran held out her hands. "I don't know how."

Nadi began looping the rope. "I'll teach you."

"I doubt that you know how to do that," Cynthia said. "Create two loops at one end of the rope."

He placed the rope on the ground and followed her instructions.

"Now, overlap the edges." She eyed his work as she floated above him. "Take these edges and pull them through this loop and that other loop. Then tighten it."

As Nadi did that, Kiran saw how it worked. "Oh, so he puts his hands in the holes, and the ends of the rope tighten?"

"Exactly," the dark angel smiled at her pupil.

Kiran put the rope around Nadi's hands and tightened it, but her gaze stared at the rash around the collar. He was getting worse. They could only hide it for so long. She could only hope that continuing on this path would help him.

"You need to act like I am your slave," Nadi said as he looked back at the guards. "You are their Princess, bring out that authority without revealing who you are."

Walking out into the open, Kiran started on the path. She tried to remember some of the adventure books she had read that were similar to this situation. Kiran recalled her favorite pirate, Captain Cobra, who was a Cecrops, and how he had faked being a guard to break out one of his comrades from a dungeon. This moment was almost the same. She was living that character now, and all she had to do was play the part.

"Halt, there is a fee to pass." A guard smiled down at her. She could see her reflection in his steel armor. As she looked him over, she realized he was one of the new guards from the court. With a spear in one hand, he held out the other, waiting for compensation.

She kept one eye covered by the hood as she met his green gaze. Kiran didn't want to reveal that she had any money because they needed it to board the airship. "You're telling me that I have to pay a toll on the same road I just walked down a few days ago to spend the last of my savings on a slave, only to come back now to return it because he is diseased!" Tugging on the rope angrily, she kept glaring at the man. "The rest of my coin went to this! I'll pay you when I get my gold back from the slave market!"

The guard took a few steps back. "Maybe you don't have to pay with coins?"

Turning back, she reached into Nadi's bag and grabbed the thin white cloth that held some of their food. "How about my meat?"

The guard bit his lip, but Kiran wasn't sure what he wanted. "Don't you have anything else to give?"

Cynthia shook her head at the guy. "Disgusting pig. Can't even decently court a woman."

Kiran's nearly lost her composure as she realized what he wanted. "If I wanted any of that, I would have gotten my slave to do it!" She went back to her one-eyed glare from under the hood. "How about you let me through, or I'll let you have what he's got."

Nadi started scratching the inside of his leg and then around the collar. "Mistress, I need you to hit me again. My whole body itches."

With a grimace, the guard backed off the road. "You can pay us later. I'll even discount you for your troubles, miss."

"That's better," she tugged for Nadi to follow. "You'll get your beating soon."

Smiling at her victory, they continued down the road. As soon as they turned the bend and were out of sight, Kiran could no longer contain herself. She began laughing, and Cynthia followed as well as Nadi. They looked at each other, and another burst came.

Taking the rope off of Nadi, they carried on. Cynthia was guiding the way along the road as Kiran brought up the rear. Looking around, she realized that it was so quiet. Birds did not sound, and the wind had died down.

Nadi stopped in his tracks, holding his head with both hands.

"Are you ok?" Kiran placed her hands over his.

In an instant, Nadi pinned her to the ground. He sniffed her hair and then brought his face close to her. She stared in horror at the one wild golden eye as he let out a low growl.

Kiran, filled with fear, knew she could not scream or the guards would come running. His grip tightened on her wrists, and she tried not to cry out. Tears began streaming down her face, hoping that he would come back to his senses.

Cynthia realized that something was amiss and turned back. "What's going on?"

Nadi snarled at her, causing the spirit to back away. He turned his attention back to Kiran and seemed to smell her again. As their eyes met, a grin passed over his face, causing her to whimper. "My princess," he growled before falling limp on top of her.

Panicked, Kiran pushed his limp body off and scooted away. Unable to hold back, she began to sob as Cynthia came to her side. The way Nadi had acted was the scariest thing she had ever experienced.

"It seems that the dragon is corrupting him," Cynthia said as she reached for Kiran but stopped. Looking along the road ahead, she went on, "We need to get him out of the open and make camp for the night."

"How?" Kiran wiped at the tears that were still coming. "I could barely get out from under him."

The dark angel thought for a moment, "Remember how you wanted to practice magic in the middle of the woods and it wasn't working?"

Kiran nodded, wiping the tears away.

"I'm not sure your magic will be strong enough yet without the Elders…but we should try to make it easier to get him back into the woods if it works."

Standing up, Kiran looked at Nadi, "What do I need to do?"

"Imagine that energy is flowing from your hand and surrounding him. Once you feel that he is surrounded by it, you say 'Elevo,' and he should begin to float. Be mindful because if you don't keep your concentration on it, you could drop him or throw him into the sky." Cynthia gave her a worried look.

"This sounds dangerous." But the princess knew she had to try, since if she attempted to depend on Cynthia for everything, she would vanish.

"It's either this or dragging him into the woods tied up," the spirit jested, but seemed worried.

Reaching out a hand, she imagined blue magic flowing from her fingertips and surrounding Nadi. "Elevo," she said, and the magic faded.

"You need to steady your breathing," Cynthia instructed. "Never hold your breath; keep a steady flow. In through your nose, out through your mouth. Try again."

Kiran tried the breathing technique as she imagined her magic flowing out of her and around Nadi. As she breathed out, she whispered, "Elevo." Nadi began to float two feet off the ground. "I did it," she smiled, and the shifter hit the ground.

"Well, I think he deserved it," the dark angel gave her a sheepish grin. "This is why we practice on objects."

Giving a frustrated sigh, Kiran put the ropes on Nadi's wrists and tightened them. "I give up. I need to gain more strength, anyway." She looked at Cynthia, who shook her head.

Pushing Nadi over, she grabbed the other end of the rope and proceeded to drag him into the woods. Kiran tried to avoid prickly bushes and ant hills, but there were no promises that he would wake unscathed. The ground was rough under his back, and it was hard to maneuver around the trees. Kiran only stopped when the road was out of view and unraveled a sleeping mat. With much effort, she rolled him onto the mat and made sure he was lying on his back.

"Maybe we should seek a doctor," Kiran thought aloud.

Cynthia shook her head again, "A doctor would want to remove that collar, and that would endanger not only you, but the entire kingdom."

That only made Kiran feel worse. It was hopeless. She wandered and gathered sticks for the fire. She listened to the woods and enjoyed the peaceful sounds. Yet, the world ignored that she needed help or that Nadi was becoming something she feared. More than anything, she felt hopeless and wished that she could be of more use to him.

◆ ◆ ◆

After making camp, Kiran watched Nadi as he slept. Sweat beaded his brow as he tossed and turned. The rash was spreading around the silver collar, causing his neck to become red and blistered. The woods darkened as she made the fire with a little more trouble than expected. As the flames came to life, it did not ease her mind that she might lose the man guiding her to her destiny.

Even though Kiran did not want to face her destiny and become a dark angel, she also didn't want Nadi or herself to perish. Hiding the truth from her family would prove difficult. Often, she wished to return to the castle and never come out of the library. There was so much that was new to her: Being dirty, working hard, knowing what hunger is. All of these things she would never have known had she stayed within the safety of her books. Even the way some of the guards acted, she would never have known had she stayed with her mother.

Nadi had tried to take care of her, but he became corrupted, and it scared her more. She often worried about the changes he had been going through. From fatigue, rashes, and headaches, Kiran was not sure if he would survive. Her fear of being left alone to complete this journey scared her. She was one woman against the world and that task was far too big for her to carry on her shoulders.

"Maybe we should find him a doctor?" Kiran said again as she watched Cynthia pace around the camp. "He may not live long in this state?"

Cynthia stopped. "That won't help him. He is fighting against himself and has to win this fight on his own, or we could lose him. The doctor would only make it worse by releasing the dragon." Even the spirit sounded near tears. "Nadi sacrificed his ability to transform to ensure that Thorn did not get the power he needed to reverse time."

"Could we nudge him in the right direction?" Kiran was hopeful. "Maybe we can use magic to guide him?"

"Every mind is different, like a maze of its own design. You could end up lost in a memory or trapped in a dream. It's not a risk we should take."

"What about me?" Kiran asked as she stood up. "Since I am to be a dark angel, I can use magic. There has to be something that I can do."

Cynthia thought for a moment. "I feel that your magic might not be from a dark angel. It could be something you were born with." Taking a moment to think, she sat beside Nadi. "But we can try to heal his wounds. You did manage to scrape him a bit."

"Born with it?" Kiran thought about her lineage that she had memorized. "I'm descended from a bunch of nearly magicless humans. There is no way I should have it then."

The dark angel looked at her in deep thought and then gasped.

"What?" Kiran sat on her knees.

Turning away, Cynthia said, "I realized that I never told the other spirits I was leaving, but I guess they figured that out." Clearing her throat, she looked at her apprentice. "Let's try our hand at healing."

Hesitating for a moment, Kiran recalled the corruption and how one of his eyes had changed. She shifted towards Nadi and placed his head on her lap. "What should I do?"

Placing her hands on the side of his head, Cynthia guided Kiran. "Put your hands like this. Imagine that you are pulling the darkness from him and pushing the light into him. With each breath you take in, you pull out the darkness. Every breath out, you push in that light."

She took a deep breath. "Now, let's begin."

Her hands passed through Cynthia's as she placed her palms on the side of his head. Kiran felt a little self-conscious as she began. Breathing in, she put the image of his body in her mind, covered in black dust, and slowly she began pulling it off, revealing the light underneath.

After repeating the process, she realized that she was starting to feel off, as though the darkness weighed her down. "Something is wrong with this," Kiran said as she retraced her steps. "The way that I am doing this, there is already light under the darkness. Yet, I am pulling the darkness into myself. Shouldn't I be breathing the darkness out to release it?"

"You just passed the first test." Smiling at her, Cynthia explained, "You pull the darkness into yourself instead of releasing it. It is not something you want to hang onto, and yes, it should be released. As a dark angel, your wings are your vessel for holding that darkness, but since you do not have those wings, you must release it. This process is called cleansing. You remove the build-up of darkness from a person. It is time-consuming—but helps with healing."

Kiran wiped the sweat from Nadi's brow with her sleeve. It made her feel guilty that he had been risking so much for her. She felt as though she was burdening him because he was doing most of the work. He took care of her, prepared the camp, and kept watch. Nadi made sure she was fed and clothed. She had not held any coins with her when she parted ways with her mother, so she could not be more useful. The shifter could be locked up or lose his life for his crimes, and Kiran would still be helpless. She did not want to be useless.

Focusing again, Kiran pulled the darkness from him, revealing the light beneath, and breathed the sickness out. With every breath, she began to feel lighter, and his body seemed to glow. Opening her eyes, she could see that the rash around the collar was starting to fade, as did the blisters. Soon, the last of the darkness vanished, and his sleep seemed a bit calmer.

"When every piece of darkness is gone, release your hold. Nadi should be able to sleep soundly tonight. Just remember: keep breathing and do not break your hold instantly." Cynthia glided behind her. "Go slow, and I'll let you know if something is amiss."

Listening to Cynthia's words, Kiran closed her eyes again and followed the blue energy from her heart into his head; she couldn't sit by and let him fight alone. Disobeying Cynthia, she ventured into his mind. The princess now found herself in a black desert. Instantly, she became uncomfortable as she looked up at a black sky with no stars.

Turning around, she called out, "Nadi? Where are you?"

Hot air hit her back, and she spun to see large golden eyes staring down at her. Embers floated into the air from between pointed teeth, lighting up the gold scales around its mouth. As the dragon lifted its head, she could see Nadi pinned under its claws.

"Please, let him go," Kiran pleaded as she began to tremble. Taking a step back, she noticed that the dragon almost blended in with the surroundings, its eyes like lonely stars in the sky.

The dragon let out a growl. "Mine!"

A small flash of light caught her attention as it vanished behind a mound of sand. Kiran wanted to see what it was, but she was too afraid to move. The dragon lowered its head back down to stare at her. Backing up, she said, "Please, I need him to restore balance to the world and free the elders."

"He is mine, and you shall be mine," the dragon snarled. "I will have my freedom."

Behind the dragon, she saw more of the lights that almost looked like stars, floating downward and ducking behind mounds of sand. Kiran began to wonder why this reminded her of a song her mother always sang. Staring at the lights, she began to see different creatures outlined and realized what she was seeing was their eyes: they were hiding from the dragon. Even they were afraid of such a fierce beast.

Slowly, Kiran knelt into the sand and wondered if she could convince the dragon to let him go. What story would she pull from, what tale would she weave? Nothing was coming to mind.

"But I need him for my freedom, too."

The dragon cocked its head to the side, "You are free."

"I am not free from my destiny. Trapped, unable to go where I please or do what I desire."

Giving a frustrated huff, he grumbled. "You mock me! I desire the world, and the world shall be mine! Once he gives me control of his body, then I shall roam the earth and be free."

Kiran watched the eyes of other creatures peering over the dunes. She began to realize how the power of a shifter worked. "You have an entire mind to make your own. Create a world with it's imagination, and travel to places you can only see in dreams. Be anything you desire."

Watching the dragon look around, Kiran noticed that the other animals were moving closer around them, their eyes showing like stars in the night. Slowly, the dragon lifted its claws, releasing Nadi. Fading into smoke, the shapeshifter vanished from his spot in the black sand.

The dragon turned into smoke as well, the dark mass quickly filling the area. Kiran could not see around her. She knew she needed to find her way out—and fast.

A figure appeared in front of her, and she recognized Nadi's silhouette. Rushing toward it, she began sinking into the sand. Only a few feet away from him, she reached out. "Nadi, please help me."

His hand came out of the fog and grabbed her wrist. Kiran took in a sharp breath as she realized golden scales and claws replaced the skin and nails that should have been there. He pulled her close, wrapping a scaled arm around her waist. His golden eyes seemed to burn into her soul. Nadi looked like he should have been a dragon, only with sandy brown hair and tan skin.

"You shall free me, Princess," he said, with Nadi's voice. "With you, I shall feast upon armies and decimate kingdoms for their gold. Once I am finished with those goals, you will be of no use to me. Just a snack before the next kingdom falls."

Kiran tried to get away, but he was too strong. She began to scream and cry as he laughed. Smelling her hair, he put his face in the crook of her neck. Kiran stiffened as he growled, dragging his teeth across her skin. Tears streamed down her face as she realized she had made a horrible mistake.

He brushed his nose against her cheek. "What's wrong, Princess? Can want the man, but not the beast?"

She was quiet as she played those words over in her mind. Steadying her breathing, she placed a mask that she usually wore for the court. She pushed back the thoughts of meeting Nadi and the events over the past few days. Looking him in the eye, she whispered, "I don't even know him. I love Lord Keol, but Nadi is my friend, and I care for him."

The dragon laughed. "Foolish girl, your actions tell the truth. Just remember: I'll always be a part of him. You will be the one to set me free." With that, he shoved her out of his reach and back into the fog. She fell through the ground and woke up in the world.

Blinking a few times, she realized that she was back at the campfire, Nadi placing his hands over hers. Gently, their fingers intertwined, and he opened his eyes. No longer did he look as though he was in pain or fighting to keep control. Instead, his eyes seemed to widen as he realized that she was sitting over him with tears streaming down her face.

Letting go of her hands, he sat up to face her. "What are you doing?"

Cynthia floated towards him. "She healed you, but was dumb enough not to listen to me. Kiran disobeyed me and went into your mind."

"How?" Looking at both of them, he touched the collar around his neck, seeming to make sure it was still there. "She isn't a dark angel yet."

"You don't have to be a dark angel to use magic. It could be that she has the magic to the elders would provide her to open a gate to the Enclave, or she may be born with it." Just as Nadi went to say something, Cynthia interjected.

"It is not that simple. We cannot have her use teleportation magic in an open area. As a guide, you need to lead her to the area where she can teleport to the temple. It is a fixed area where there is a gate. Without the Elders, it will not work."

"Nothing is ever easy," he grumbled as he stood up and turned toward the woods.

"Where are you going?" Kiran asked as he stormed off.

"To get your food, your Highness," he said over his shoulder as he vanished into the brush and out of the light of the campfire.

"The least he could have done was say thank you." Cynthia glared after him.

"He has every right to be mad. I'm useless to your cause. I nearly got trapped in there, fooled by the dragon." Kiran felt a pang of guilt. "If I could learn more magic, then maybe I could be of better use. Nadi would not be so upset with me if I could be better."

"Stop." The dark angel looked into her eyes. "You are not the problem. His fears are getting in the way of what he needs to do. Nadi is afraid that we will not make it in time. Yet, he has delayed their plans because he took on the dragon's form. There is a lot of weight on his shoulders, but you also have a lot on yours.

"Your throne is threatened by you becoming a dark angel. Soon, you'll see the true nature of your 'allies' and 'friends.'" She emphasized those two words as though they had sickened her. "Nations will ask for your contract, and you will no longer get special treatment as royalty. You should start training as a knight and gain your defensive skills. I can teach both of you to wield a weapon and defend yourselves."

"Nadi wouldn't want to learn," Kiran stated, craning her neck to look at the spot where he had disappeared into the woods.

"I would be surprised if he didn't. Nadi, like all shifters—he depends on using his skills for everything. It is part of his culture to become an animal to hunt or fight. They trade what they have for other materials and are Nomads. So trees and forests must be new to him."

"I heard they were at war with the dragons," Kiran inquired as she wrapped her arms around herself. "How did he come to possess a form?"

Cynthia gave a sad smile. "The Dragon King who had gone missing is the form he has taken. He was captured and imprisoned by Thorn and Icarri. It was easy for them to get the dragon lord since they had the teleportation cloak. When Nadi and his brother stumbled upon the Temple of the Elders, Thorn thought he had won. His brother Zec, desperate to avenge his mother's death, attempted to kill Nadi so that he could gain the dragon form and bring her back. Little does he know that she is still alive. Nadi escaped with Daron's form, but there is no telling how long before they realize that the dragon's form was stolen from them. When that happens, they will come looking for Nadi."

"That's horrible," Kiran said, sitting there a moment. "I have no siblings, but I would hate it if someone I loved and trusted tried to kill me. The closest person I have to a sister is my guard, Ashlee. She is a mixed Abandreal. Her father was a vampire, and her mother was an Abandreal. I miss seeing her unique form with her human features and her feline nature. I was glad to grow up with her—plus because she is half-vampire, she can walk in daylight without a stone."

"Mixed, huh?" Cynthia seemed deep in thought for a moment. "I remember when I loved an Abandreal. Dart was always so playful and energetic. There would be moments when I felt as though nothing could ever separate us. Yet, I became a dark angel, and he vanished along with the destruction of my kingdom. The last thing he promised was to find a way for me to no longer be a dark angel, and to keep my kingdom."

Leaning herself against a tree, Kiran thought about it. "I think I know what it means to be in love like you were. I miss Lord Keol. He is the vampire lord of Lu'Bela. He is so handsome, and smart…I can't wait to be immortal with him."

The dark angel shook her head. "Why would you want to live forever?"

"To stay young with Lord Keol," she smiled.

"But then you wake up one morning and realize that your Lord Keol never changes. All your family and friends die before you. Then you want children, and you cannot bear any. Your home is always dark and empty of all the things you once desired. Blood begins to taste bland, however, no other food will satisfy your hunger. That is when you realize that being immortal is not the best choice for loving someone." Cynthia looked up at the waning moon. "A vampire had all those complaints when I once asked them about living forever."

Kiran had never thought about that before. Silently, she tried to think of the real reason she loved Keol. She realized then she did not truly even know him. He showered her with gifts, but what was his favorite color, clothing, or thing? Did he like to do anything in his free time? Does he like anything the way she does?

Cynthia stared at her. "I don't think you know what love is. It's hard to figure that out when you are limited on who you can see. I can honestly say, though, the way you and Nadi have been acting, I wouldn't be surprised if you two start courting each other."

The princess could feel her face grow bright red as she remembered his red eyes staring down at her. "I'm tired," Kiran laid on the ground trying to avoid talking about him. "I think I need some sleep."

"Alright," Cynthia floated towards the fire. "Rest up, we should hopefully be off this continent tomorrow."

As she shut her eyes, her thoughts were haunted by the face of that dragon. She could still feel its grip on her arm and hear its voice. Kiran shivered as she remembered his teeth at her throat. Distancing herself from Nadi was her priority for tomorrow. She could not allow herself to release the dragon. Going into anyone's mind was not something she was ever going to do again.

Chapter 27

Thorn slowly dragged Zec into the cave, huffing as he tugged at the rope around his wrists to ensure it was secure. Zec thought of fighting back but decided against it. The silver collar sat loosely around his neck as Thorn connected the ring to the chain on the wall.

"A new friend?" Daron said, eyeing him.

Zec almost didn't recognize him with the beard. He observed the dark, damp cave around them, listening to running water echo off its walls. He shivered at his memory of nearly drowning.

"Yes, he told me how he and his brother were the sons of the chief." Thorn pulled the rope off his hands. "I realized that both of them knew you, decided not to take any more risks, and locked him in here with you."

"Oh," Daron sounded amused. "That makes sense."

"I need to take my leave and figure out where that Princess has gotten off to." Thorn made his way back up the stairs.

They listened as Thorn's footsteps reached the top and the wall started grinding shut. Daron grinned at Zec, and laughter erupted from him. The shifter stared at him, not sure what was so amusing.

As soon as the sound of the wall stopped, Daron asked, "Tell me—what has become of your brother?"

He narrowed his eyes at the dragon. Of course, he would want to talk about Nadi since he helped him escape. Thorn had made sure Daron had no more metal on him to use in escaping. "He used the cloak and teleported to a city on the mainland," Zec responded, his eyes turning red.

"Good," the Dragon King nodded as he stroked his beard with a smile. "How have you been?"

Zec was skeptical and confused; why was Daron acting so relaxed with him?

"Honestly, not the best with my mother being dead," he said slowly. "And now, being sent into this cave because of my brother. I am miserable."

Daron began laughing hysterically. "Oh, sorry. I have an inside joke that is running through my mind."

"Do you care to share it?" He gritted his teeth; this situation was no laughing matter.

"Well, that depends." He leaned as far as the chain would allow and whispered. "Do you trust me?"

Zec's heart began to race. This was the moment he had been waiting for. Daron may give him the dragon's form. "Yes," he tried not to smile.

The grin on his face got bigger. "Your eyes are orange, Zec." He laughed, listening to it echo off the walls before going on. "I knew the moment he brought you in here that this was all a trap and you two were working together. You honestly believe I would have given you my form after listening to you betray your brother? He didn't close the door when he left the cave, and your jealous voice carried like sand on the breeze." He turned to the stairwell, calling upward. "Speaking of which, I can still hear you over there, Thorn. I have to compliment you. I know you are not dumb enough to fall for the same trick twice. You would not have trapped Zec in here with me like you had done with Nadi, knowing that we knew each other. So, the only other option left is to assume that you were working together."

Anger gripped him, realizing that Daron had made a mockery of both of them. Standing up, the collar fell off his neck and clattered against the ground. He could no longer stand the sound of Daron's laughter. Taking a step forward, Zec slammed his fist against the Dragon King's face. "Give me your form!" Frustration fueled the fire of his anger, particularly because he knew he was getting nowhere.

Spitting his steaming blood to the ground, Daron smiled at him. "You think that beating me is going to get you my form. Try again. Maybe hitting the other side of my face will make me become a shifter like you."

The mocking tone of his voice sent Zec into a fury. Multiple times, he struck him, hoping for something to give. Never had he changed into anything, but what if he was able to change into a dragon, so that he could be the first to return? He'd prove the story of Elias wrong as well as see his mother again; it would be an outstanding accomplishment. Nadi could never top his first transformation, and maybe his father would give the chieftain title to him instead.

Daron ducked as Zec's fist struck out again, causing it to hit the wall with a sickening crack. His hand went limp, and he yelled out in pain, cradling his wrist. He glared at the smiling dragon.

"You didn't expect to hit a moving target, so I think the wall is a more suitable opponent." He laughed. "Boy, if you were a dragon, you would be dead already. Of course, I choose not to kill you because I know your parents. Unfortunately, your parents and Nadi could not see you for the monster you truly are."

Zec went to hit him with his good hand, but time froze around them. "Enough," Thorn had emerged from the stairwell. "This is getting nowhere. I need to tend to both of you." Grabbing Zec's shirt collar, he unfroze time, and his fist only met air.

"I'm getting close, I can feel it!" Zec tried to pull away.

"I said enough. The orb can only heal you to a certain point. Once I have the dragon egg, I can go back farther, but right now, the damage could be permanent if not tended to." Thorn began reversing the effects on Zec's hand until it was no longer hanging limp at the wrist. He turned his attention to the dragon and healed him as well until there were no marks on his body.

"You're wasting your time, Sorcerer," Daron smirked at him. "Their power works on trust, and as long as I don't trust him, he will never get my form."

Thorn gritted his teeth and pushed Zec out of the room. Silently, he went back up the stairs and opened the wall. Out into the main hall with the Elders pinned above, Thorn silently scowled at Zec, but as soon as the stone door ground shut, Thorn slapped him, "Does hitting build trust?"

Stunned, Zec took a moment to answer. "No," he said, confused as he backed away.

"If your power works on trust, then you should have said so instead of beating him to the point where trust may not be an option!" Thorn began to storm out of the room. "We must find another way to get it now since it has been too long to wipe his memory."

"Can't Icarri just use her magic to get him to do as she wants?" Zec stated as he followed him out of the room.

"Magic doesn't work how you think it might. It's not that simple!"

"What about a potion?" Icarri appeared in the doorway. Both Thorn and Zec looked at her, leaning against the door frame. She smoothed her lilac gown as she started walking towards them. "Maybe like a love potion, only it makes them do everything you say. I'm sure I read that in one of the books they had in the library." Putting a finger under Zec's chin, Icarri leaned in, "There is always another way."

"Potions!" Thorn scoffed. "You did that before, remember? And we couldn't return to your manor for a month because all your staff were obsessed with you. Nothing got done."

"Let's not speak of such trivial things," Icarri stated with a grimace. "It won't be as potent and should only last a day or so. I just need a few ingredients." She handed Zec a piece of parchment. "Be a doll and get these for me?"

"Didn't Nadi teach you how to scavenge?" he blurted out.

Without warning, her hand wrapped around his throat, and her nails began to dig in. She brought his face closer to her own as she spat, "Never address me like that!

You will not remind me of what I am capable of, and instead do as I say."

"Why not use that tactic on our dragon friend? I'm sure it'll work out smoothly." Thorn had a sarcastic tone as he turned to walk out of the room.

Icarri let Zec go, and he scrambled to his feet. He could feel the marks on his neck where her nails dug in, still flaring with pain. As her expression went to a joyful smile, Zec understood that this was a dangerous game. If he made one false move, they would remove him from the picture altogether.

Slowly, he stood and backed towards the door, gripping the parchment in his hand, feeling like a rabbit stalked by a fox. While he knew that she couldn't kill him —they depended on him for success—Icarri might be crazy enough to kill him so that Thorn could bring him back. Zec did not want to tempt her, though.

Leaving the room, he rushed out of the temple and into the safety of the woods. He didn't stop until he could no longer see the building behind him. Coming to a large tree, Zec opened up the list. His heart sank at the ingredients. "A sparrow's wing, a snake's skin, the heart of a wolf, and the eye of a hawk," he read in a hushed tone. Their tribe only killed if they needed food, and even then, these were not animals that were considered food by the tribe's standards.

They had superstitions about needless bloodshed. Tales said that if you needlessly kill, you would change into a mix of several animals and become lost in the sands of the desert. Zec only heard them as stories, but even he had never been tempted to stray from the path before. This time, such things did not matter. His mother would come back and never know what he had done. All the dragons would pay for their treachery.

Zec had a sudden thought as he started to move silently through the woods. *What if, after I defeat Grumloc, I become king?* He smiled at the idea. Then his tribe could live like royalty as they made the keep their new home. He imagined all the fine things he would be able to have, such as silk robes, silver plates, and cold stone floors. The desert heat would no longer be a bother when they could hide inside the keep all day. He would be like a rabbit inside a burrow with many tunnels. Endless routes to explore and endless opportunities to hide when needed. Yes—when he took on Grumloc, the keep could be his tribe's reward.

A flutter of wings grabbed his attention. Watching, he saw a group of sparrows fretting around a bush. The group took off out of the brush and looped through the air, weaving between branches. They circled back and rushed into the same bush before dispersing again.

Grabbing a leafy branch from the ground, he tried to keep his eyes on one of the sparrows as it soared through the canopy. Other brightly colored birds tempted to distract his eyes from the one he needed. It zoomed toward the same bush as a few others followed.

Just as it reached the tree beside him, Zec lashed out with the branch and missed. He was not aiming to hit it, though. It was a thought he often had when thinking about Nadi in his owl form. Change the air current so that he would crash or fall. The breeze he created was just enough to shift its direction.

The bird's eyes locked onto Zec as it gave a startled cry before smacking against another tree with a crack. As it hit the ground and lay limp, all the sounds of the forest grew quiet, and the animals vanished.

Bending down to grab the bird, movement through the trees on his left caused him to look up. The wolf was looking at him as it trotted away. He recognized it as the one his brother befriended. It must have watched Nadi enter the temple and must be waiting for him to return. Zec was sure he would see it again and would take its heart.

Grabbing the lifeless sparrow, he began to say the prayer. "Shifting Gods of the Desert tribe of the Púca…" Zec trailed off, realizing that his gods were probably the same as in the temple. "I guess there is no point in these stupid prayers anymore."

From above, a shrill voice answered, "A prayer should always be said even if it is not to the gods."

Clutching the bird, Zec looked up at the sound and stumbled backward. He met the yellow eyes of a creature staring at him. It had large black ears like a rabbit, but hands almost like a person. A long tail wrapped around the branch it was sitting on, as did its long toes. Black fur covered most of its body, and what looked to be dragonfly wings protruded from its back.

Zec yelled out, not sure what to make of the creature. He scrambled backward, losing his grip on the sparrow. Sitting with his back against the tree, he stared up at the odd creature who was laughing at him.

"Way to fear the one thing your tribe is named after," it cackled. Turing around, it swung backward, hanging upside down on the branch. "You seem a little lost to me, Sonny."

Looking closely, Zec realized that it was the creature from his childhood tales. "You're a Púca? Mischievous demigod behind the shapeshifters' exile to the desert?" Zec was trying to recall the stories, but many of them had mixed views, from a harmless trickster to a bloodthirsty monster who desired the blood of children. He wasn't sure what to believe. But a demigod in this place did make sense.

"No one could take a joke back then." The creature fell from the tree, landing on its face, and got up, dusting itself off. "I've been watching you, young one. This magic you seek is not something you should trifle with. All life could change if they destroyed the wrong thing."

"Don't come any closer." Zec pulled the hunting knife out and pointed it at the creature.

"Calm down! I am not an eater of meats. I'm more like a cuddly rabbit who loves playing tricks." The creature hopped closer, but Zec did not put down the knife. "Zec, is it?"

The shifter nodded but stayed quiet.

"I am Skadi. Can you put the knife down now? I may be a demigod, but I prefer not to be holey."

After a moment of staring at each other, Zec sheathed the knife back into his belt. "I'm going through with their plans. I am going to bring my mother back."

"Is that it then?" Hopping closer, Skadi stared into his eyes. "I can bring forth your mother, but it would be nothing more than an image that you desire and not the real thing. That's kind of like some ghosts of the past. A repeating moment in time, they are there, but they're also not. Just an endless loop caught in the fabric of time itself." Taking a strand of tall grass, he began to chew on it. "Look, Sonny, I know that brother of yours is against it, and he was even heading towards the temple as a wolf as we speak. Maybe we should just let things flow the way they should and let this madness end."

Zec's eyes widened—if his brother makes it inside the temple, the plan could fail. Without another word, he grabbed the dead sparrow and began running back towards the temple. Icarri would kill him if he returned without her ingredients, but the punishment would be far worse if he let his brother get past him into the temple.

Branches whipped him in the face as he rushed past, twigs snapped underfoot, and leaves crunched with every step. Panic was digging in. Everything that he desired was at risk. He didn't want anything getting in the way of seeing his mother again.

The doors to the temple came into sight, and he rushed at them. He had to ensure that nothing got through them! As he reached for the handle, he stopped. Zec recalled that Thorn had stated that Nadi was teleported to the mainland and how it could take days, weeks, or months to make his way back by sea or air. Nadi was miles away, and he couldn't return so quickly—especially since Thorn ordered Dane to move the cloak.

"Brother," a familiar voice came from behind him. "We should go into the temple and talk this over. Quickly, before someone sees."

Zec slowly turned to see his brother standing there, dressed in the white shirt he had on before when returning to the cave. But for once, Zec was confident in his decision, knowing he couldn't fail. Releasing the handle, Zec took a few steps away from the door.

"Come now, *Brother*. Since when do we use such titles?" Putting a finger to his lips, he acted as though he were deep in thought. "Or should I say...Skadi? Nadi was too dumb to use such titles anyway. I'm going to guess that you can't enter the temple."

The apparition faded away, leaving Skadi standing in its place. "Prying Pixies," he cursed as he backed up towards the trees. "It was worth a shot—but heed my word,

Shapeless Shifter. Suppose you mess with magic and unravel time. In that case, your mother could be lost forever, along with everyone who dares to manipulate the stream." With that, the strange creature faded out of existence, leaving him standing there.

Zec knew better than to listen to a creature known for tricks and lies. When he goes back in time, he'll be sure to make that creature pay, too. *Everyone who ever wronged me would pay*, he thought as he looked at the lifeless bird in his hand.

Chapter 28

Modra waved to the next group of five as they made it over the first dune in the distance. She had ensured that they all had enough water and food to get them to camp. Knowing that they would spread the word of how they were alive would also make the others less fearful, but at the same time, she had wanted them to be cautious. Modra had asked that they carry messages about her sons and Daron with them.

Standing behind her, Ronja watched the desert closely. There were a lot of things she had learned from her. Even though Ronja was always happy and adventurous, she was one to follow the rules and commands. She was a very loyal guard and had taught her about their culture: meetings with the tribe were supposed to be formal. Daron was supposed to wear his most acceptable attire, or let Grumloc change and handle those affairs. Every year, the dragons treated them as though they were family and not another group. All this time, she had overdressed to meet for a simple event.

"Shall we head back?" Ronja said as she smiled at her.

"Yes." Modra began walking back into the main hall of the keep. "I wonder what other tasks I might be able to do?"

"Well, you had the medical knowledge that helped Lady Gillian. Maybe you can teach a few of us the same thing?" The guard suggested.

"Great idea—but how do we spread the word to others?" She pulled at a loose strand of hair by her ear.

"Through a meeting with Grumloc," she said as she waved to the massive dragon lying on the dais, opening an eye at the sound of their footsteps.

Modra was afraid she was going to say that. Looking to Grumloc, she said, "Good morning, my Lord. Do you have time to speak before your daily guarding duties?"

"You do not have to be formal, Modra." He yawned and stretched before sitting upright. "What is it that you wish to speak about?"

She still felt so tiny in comparison to him. "I wish to share my medical knowledge with your doctors."

"We do not have doctors," he stated as he stretched his wings. "We have kings and guards."

"Who cooks the food or cleans the keep? Who files the paperwork for treaties and keeps track of your coins?"

"The guards," he said, uninterested. Getting up, he began heading for the entryway.

"Wait—may I propose a plan that can make things easier for you? May I teach your guards different things which, if they choose, will give them another title?" Grumloc looked like he was going to disagree. "They will still be guards, so if a threat does somehow make it to them, they can still defend. It will also give them a permanent position in the keep."

Grumloc thought on it. "You may put up a flyer asking for those who wish to become something other than a guard to join. Yet, I want it to be a limited number so that not all my guards are missing from their posts."

Modra smiled. "Understood. I will—"

"Lord Grumloc!" A guard came running in, holding a rolled-up parchment.

"What is it, Namib?" Grumloc turned back to look at his guard.

He held up the poster for him to read. "This was found in Vadnera. Their princess was taken, but you can see who."

Moving to an angle where she could see it, she recognized the features of her son.

Before she could say anything else, Grumloc roared. Guards came rushing from every direction. It seemed as though he waited until they had stopped moving to speak. "I need most of you to search from the skies over Vadnera, see if we can locate Daron or the shifter Nadi. A few days ago, Nadi and Zec were outside the keep. We need to find them and locate Daron. For now, there is a truce between the shifters and the Dragons. Approach any shifter you see until you find them." He looked at Namib. "I need you to go to Firstenfeld and inform Gage of this finding. If Nadi is with the princess, then it is for a good reason, so we need someone who can locate them." His eyes found Modra, who wasn't sure how to take the news that her child was now a wanted criminal. "Also, a few positions are opening up around the keep. Please speak to Modra if you wish to have a title other than guard." Grumloc turned back to the opening and took flight.

The guards assigned to patrol took their leave, changing forms and taking to the skies, but a few ran up to Modra and started asking several questions.

"Are we no longer guards if we choose this position?"

"What kind of benefits would we get?"

"Can I bring my pet thunder toad with me?"

"One at a time," Modra was glad to have a distraction, but was a little overwhelmed. So many guards were gathering, and more questions started coming. She took a step back, trying to get enough space.

Ronja tapped her spear on the floor three times. The room fell silent. "There will be flyers hanging up on the positions that we need. You can put your name down for multiple, but a select number of applicants are required. Modra will meet with each of you for that position, and you can audition. If you apply for multiple positions and get accepted for those, you can only choose one.

"As a reminder, this does not mean you are no longer a guard, but it gives you a second title, which can strike fear into those who wish to sneak into the keep. You are the last line of defense if someone manages to get inside and into your area. Make any intruder fear you like the title that you hold.

"You are all dismissed."

They all went back to their duties, leaving Ronja and Modra in the front hall. As the last few guards left the room, she turned to Ronja, "Thank you. I wanted to bring order, but some chaos comes with it."

"Well, we have a lot of work to do. We should start on those flyers and hang them in the main hall. I'll bring another quill and ink so we can do this together. I want to see how well this works." They walked back to her room. "Not saying that you will fail, but this will be different for us dragons."

Modra laughed, "You have a dragon kingdom and no order other than guards and leaders. Some changes can be good."

"I wonder how Daron is going to take it when he returns and finds that everything has changed," she laughed.

Even with a smile, Modra could not help but worry that Nadi, or both her sons, might be in danger. She wished that she could leave to help him, but even she did not know which way to go. It was best that she remained here to assist the dragons and her people as best as she could. Still, she could not help but wonder how her sons were doing.

Chapter 29

Sova embraced the dawn as he looked over the golden dunes. He wasn't sure how much time had passed since his sons had left, but part of him was hoping for their safe return. He had good news to share with them, as each day more shifters returned to the camp with stories of his wife. He couldn't wait to rejoice as a family. Yet, he was also given the news that both of his sons may be in danger. Nadi had managed to send word that he had found Daron, but no update on whether they were safe.

The Chieftain had hoped that Nadi would lead his brother astray and keep him close to camp in his animal forms, but he knew that Zec had never changed before. He simply refused to comply with any lessons, stating he no longer saw a point. Still, Sova was hoping that the bond between them could change Zec's mind.

A figure appeared over the dunes, riding a camel. Traders often sought their camp to exchange goods, but even he had been wary of slave traders lately. Since their numbers began to dwindle, slave traders had been sneaking into the Gamada Desert, seeking to increase their lists with unwilling victims. Sova blew his horn as a call to ready their wares. The camp became alive as people bustled about preparing their goods for trade.

The Chieftain looked over everyone's sellable items. Trying to ignore the one villager who chose to be a goat as they dragged their cloth-covered materials through the sand, Sova focused on other campers. Collette with her stone jewels, Cooper with his wool clothing, and Harper with the furs and bone knives. These were the best sellers. Others had clothes, blankets, and pottery presented on quilts. The goat had items that looked to have been lost to the sands and found again: shells and odd-shaped stones, a wooden doll, and a walking stick. The edges of the mats had holes and smelled of dust."Hey, Chev," the chief tried to think of a better way to put it as the goat looked up, still chewing on a corner of the quilt. "There is a shaded spot next to that tent that might be a little more suitable. Don't want you roasting in the sun." Sova pointed at a tent further away from the other merchants.

Chev sat there, still chewing the fabric. Sova gave a frustrated sigh and turned back to the rest of his camp. With everyone lined up, it created a wall to stop anyone from entering their encampment.

The camel trotted up and came to a halt. Sova recognized the rider as Lady Terika. "You are back so soon. Usually, we don't see you for at least a month or two at a time."

"Sorry to get your hopes up for a trade," she held up a sandal. "I passed your sons on my way around the desert. They were heading for the dragons' keep. Zec wanted to challenge King Grumloc."

"So I've heard," he was worried for them.

"I tried to convince Zec not to do it, but he insisted. Nadi didn't realize where they were going." She seemed a little flustered as she pulled a flyer out of her robes. "I came across a slave trader who had this wanted poster from Vadnera. I guess Nadi is there, and he has the Princess with him."

Sova cursed as he snatched the paper and studied it. There was no doubt that it was Nadi. How he managed to get to Vadnera was a mystery. "And Zec?"

She shook her head, "No news since we parted. The dragons are on full search alert and have called a truce. They are sending dragons to Vadnera on short notice to the King. Hopefully it doesn't cause a panic."

Folding the flyer, she turned back to the camp and waved at them. "Pack it up! We're moving out!"

"What are you doing?" She slid off the camel.

"The only thing I can do," he gritted his teeth as he grabbed the walking stick from Chev's mat. "I'm going to meet with Grumloc and see if we can find my sons."

People slowly packed their tradable goods. Sova looked into her red eyes, his an uncertain yellow. He thought of asking a favor of her, but then turned to head back into the camp.

"Sova," she called as she pulled the reins of her camel along. "I am leaving the desert for the next few months and will be unable to keep the slave traders away. The battle of the Lords is going to start, and I must go; all vampires have to compete to keep their status if challenged."

Without turning around, he nodded, understanding her plight. "That's fine. My people are returning, so I think we'll be off that list." He walked into his camp, watching as some villagers prepared carts, emptying tents of items. They seemed to pick up the pace as he passed.

Frustrated, he stormed into Nadi's tent, half expecting to see him passed out with a skin full of ale. Only his angry memories and the scent of old spirits were there. Since the day Modra vanished from their lives, Nadi had been nothing but trouble. Picking fights with other kids, stealing from traders, and then becoming addicted to spirits. The next leader of the Púca tribe was a far cry from what they needed. If Nadi could not change, exile was the only option he had left. Now, he was wanted for kidnapping the Princess herself. If it wasn't for a good cause, then he was going to face worse than exile.

Yet, now that Zec had been dragging them towards the keep, both of them could be in danger—or worse. Maybe his youngest son was onto something. He thought that everything needed to change. Now that his people were slowly returning, this would be the optimal time to push to end the war.

The tribe had no experience with fighting or war other than running and hiding. The route near the dragons' keep was an unfriendly path. He felt like a coward to his people. Rules are supposed to keep them safe, yet their traditions led to the capture of most of their camp. He had no choice but to try and put an end to this.

Grabbing the cushions from the floor, he began tossing them aside to pack. He threw the blankets and clothes into the center of the room, and with each item, he began to throw harder. As he lifted another pillow, he spotted a small book that he recognized. The little green leather-bound cover held a fairy with a mischievous smile. He recognized it as the one that Modra used to read. "Dance of the Seasons," he whispered as he traced the imprinted design with his fingertips.

It was a poem, telling the story of how one could find a path to a creature of wishes. The beast would grant a wish in exchange for something precious to the wisher. It told of the silver dragons and how one silver dragon female had outsmarted their king. She had given up her egg to end his life, only to realize her mistake before killing herself.

"It's a lesson," Modra's voice rang in his head. "Nothing is more important than the lives of our children. I wish for nothing more than what I already have."

Tucking the book into his pocket, he let out a calming breath and went back to packing his son's tent.

Chapter 30

"My legs hurt," Kiran complained as they walked farther along the road. The thick woods had been proving difficult for her to navigate. Each time she looked away, Nadi would vanish, and she would have to stop in her tracks until he returned. It was a higher risk on the road, so Nadi had rubbed mud on her face.

"Sorry, Princess, we can't stop for anything." Nadi kept moving forward without looking back.

Cynthia frowned but kept silent as she floated along.

Pulling a strand of hair out of the dried mud, she gave a frustrated sigh. "It's been days since I bathed. We have to stop at some point."

"She does have a point," Cynthia chimed in. "Both of you smell worse than a barn."

Nadi shot her a glare. "You can't smell anything; you're dead."

"Well, that's just rude." She fell back to float along with Kiran.

They had been walking for miles, and there seemed to be no sign of another person on the road. Still, her feet were beginning to hurt. "Can't we take five minutes? A water break, maybe?"

"Uh!" He threw his hands into the air. "Can I wander upon the creature of wishes and fix all my problems? Return the Princess to her castle, foil the sorcerer's plans, and save my brother!"

"Creature of wishes?" Kiran became curious. "What is that?"

Nadi stopped in his tracks, caught off guard by the question. He spun around and began walking backwards to look at her. "It's a story meant to scare little kids, nothing you would be interested in." Facing forward, he continued.

"I'll have you know, my father would always tease me and call me the *Bookworm Princess*," she retorted. "My only way out of the castle was through books. All stories are good."

Silence filled the air between them as they continued. Cynthia stared at Nadi, then back at Kiran. As she looked about to say something, Nadi began the story. "Long ago, there were four main Dragon Keeps of the Gamada Desert. To the west, there were the fierce red dragons, whose rage was unmatched. To the south were the black dragons, secretive and wild. To the east, the golden dragons of the dawn. And to the north, the silver dragons of the moon. Each of them, the keepers of the Gamada Desert, was assigned to protecting its hidden secrets.

"There was a day when a creature covered in many items visited the dragons. The red dragons wished to be the strongest of their kind, and they became too large for their Keep. The black dragons hoped for the power to be like shadows. They cast their bodies away, and they became nothing more than ghosts. The gold dragons wished to be like the shapeshifters and were blessed with the ability to have a human form.

"The wish creature came to the Silver Dragon King, but he had everything he wanted. A harem of women he had stolen from villages and his people, a human form made by magic's design, and more gold than the humans could fathom. He was simply mad with the fear he was unable to sire an heir, and so he wished for that."

Nadi looked over his shoulder and gave her a stern look. "The wish creature wanted to take his gold for that wish, but the silver dragon became outraged and cast him into the desert. Still, the wish creature came back and found the harem. The Silver Dragon King's wife was among them and chose to make her wish. She took out the egg she had kept hidden and hoped for the ability to kill her captor. He took her egg and granted her wish.

"She marched to the King on his throne and tore out his throat. Looking at what she had done, the Queen realized she could have done that all along. As the harem fled the keep, she begged for the return of her egg, but the wish could not be undone. No longer able to live with her decision, she ended her own life."

"Oh, how terrible." Kiran bundled her shirt around her collar.

Nadi went on, "Legend says that before she took her life, she wrote down how to find the creature of wishes."

Cynthia slowly began to sing an eerie tune as both Nadi and Kiran stopped. "Out of the darkness and into the light, dances the fires in the night. Seasons will change as people do, too. How do I ask this of you?

"Go through the forest that rains down with leaves, far past the evergreen trees. Tread through the white snow that blankets the earth. Stay warm if not by a hearth. Stride through the waters that stay at your knees, be wary of all that you see. Follow the fairies that dance until spring, try not to fall as they sing. Walk through the desert with shadows that leap. There lies the dragon heir's Keep. Into the mountains there, you'll see what has been hiding from thee."

Both Kiran and Nadi looked surprised. Coming to his senses, Nadi started walking again, "That's not how I remember the song."

"There are a few versions of the story floating around over the years explaining why the other dragon clans had vanished. Each of them varies, but not all are true." Cynthia smiled as Kiran began walking again. "Either way, it was a great distraction from hurting legs."

"My version went into more details," Nadi seemed to quicken his pace. "Never mind, I don't want to talk about this story anymore."

But Kiran thought about the story still. If she could make a wish, she would wish not to become a dark angel. Keeping her throne was a better option. She could lose her entire kingdom if she were to become a dark angel the same way Cynthia lost hers. Kiran looked around and realized that Nadi was holding his head. Another headache seems to have struck him. "Maybe we should stop?" She suggested as she looked for a place to put up camp. "We need to keep that thing at bay."

"No, we have to keep moving." Nadi walked past her. "We need to get to the next port city so we can cross the ocean. They should have airships to get over the mountains. It would be easier if I could fly, but I may never be able to transform again."

She watched as Nadi turned his back on her to continue moving. Kiran didn't want Nadi to feel frustrated anymore. Running ahead of him, she put her arms out, stopping him from moving forward. "I believe in you, Nadi. I think that you will be able to change into whatever form you like for all its worth. Never give up on something that seems out of—"

"Enough!" Nadi looked upset. "I don't need your false hope or your dumb beliefs." His eyes were green when he faced her. "You can at least go back to your normal life with your servants and be a *princess*!"

A tear slid down her cheek as she looked at her feet. "I don't get to go back to a normal life. I gain a pair of wings that mark me as a monster, and I get to lose my throne. Sure, no more galas and treaties. Instead, I get arranged executions when I haven't even killed anything more than a fly!" She watched as his eyes changed to a dark blue. "You know nothing of what I'm losing—all because I met you!" Regret crossed her face as she realized she had said something more hurtful than she had intended.

"You know what, Princess?" Nadi grabbed her chin and forced her to look him in the eye as his gaze turned red. "You are like a beautiful gem stuck in the ground. Instead of picking yourself up and dusting yourself off, you are simply waiting for the world to erode around you. You can't do anything for yourself and are always depending upon others."

Pulling away, Kiran screamed in frustration and ran back the way they came. She didn't want anything to do with him. All she wanted to do was go back home and get lost in her books. Forget about being a dark angel and worry about what treaties to make. She wanted to go on her long walks with her lady-in-waiting in the garden to talk about her frustrations. Not on an endless journey with a ghost and a cursed creature.

Unexpectedly, in her distraction, she bumped into a woman along the path, nearly knocking her over. Eggs broke against the ground as her basket dropped. "Oh no, I just bought those from the market." But the woman didn't seem all too upset.

"I'm so sorry," Kiran said, wiping the tears away. "I wasn't looking where I was going."

"It's fine. It doesn't look like you have money to pay for it, either," she mused as she salvaged what she could.

Nadi came running up, "Why do you have to run off like that?"

"Because you yelled at her," Cynthia said.

Nadi looked as though he were about to respond to her, but stopped himself. "Forgive her—we argued, and she got upset."

"Ah, trouble in paradise for a new couple." She winked. "You can always come home with me and work off these eggs," laughing, she pushed her blonde hair out of her face.

Nadi huffed a frustrated sigh, "We have somewhere we need to—"

"No, I broke your eggs, so I need to repay you." Kiran interrupted.

"But we have to get on the airship to get across the sea," Nadi said. "We don't have time for this!"

"It's just one day. Then we'll be back on track, no more delays."

He looked at her, trying to be emotionless. "Fine."

"Good, I run an Inn with my husband, and we could always use an extra hand." She led the way down the path. "I am Nezra, and you are . . . ?"

"I am Ki-Kairi, and this is Nadix." Kiran nearly stumbled across her words as she realized that she shouldn't give her real name.

Nadi shot her a look at the poor names she had given them.

She realized that she would have to tell Nadi's lies because his eyes would change if he tried to.

All of them followed Nezra down the path. Kiran stood next to her, eyeing the tall blonde woman. Her clothes were all brown tones, from the dark brown dress to the tan apron.

"What brings you people to my neck of the woods?" she asked, peering at Kiran from the corner of her eye.

"We are trying to travel the world to find the creature of wishes," Kiran responded.

She could hear Nadi miss a step as she said it. There had to be a reason she would go to the desert, and the song led to a desert. It made sense to spout such nonsense.

"Oh? And what would you wish for?" Nezra asked, raising an eyebrow.

"That our love will last forever," she said, and Nadi tripped, hitting the ground. Both women looked back as he picked himself up. "Or maybe for my love to be less clumsy."

Both laughed as he dusted himself off. "I'm going to like you." Nezra patted her on the shoulder as they continued.

They soon came upon an Inn on the side of the road. Three horses hitched to the post outside were covered in armor. Vadneran guard horses. Kiran was ready to run back the way they had come.

"Maybe we should go in through the back. That collar your love is wearing may get their attention. Don't want anyone dragged back to the slave market."

Both Nadi and Kiran followed in silence. It bothered the Princess to know her kingdom would be so irrational. "Would the guards do that?"

"How long have you been in Vadnera? The King himself has outlined slave operations since he married the Queen. If something seems rare, he takes it upon himself to add a new name of creatures to the list. Shapeshifters have been on the list forever. I've seen changelings, but never shifters."

Tears began to well up as she realized that her family was to blame for this. "How cruel," she whispered.

"You're a shifter, aren't you?" She picked at her basket.

"I am a shifter, but this collar is on to protect everyone from me," he looked toward his feet.

She stared at him. "Do I dare ask what a shifter is?"

"We take on forms of animals at will, but I'm different. I have a dragon form, and I can't control it. It would be like having a wild dragon on the loose."

"Keep that collar on, then. I prefer my establishment all in one piece." She opened the back door and peered inside. "Clear."

Nezra ushered them through the wooden door and led them up the stairs. Entering the room, she gently closed the door and rushed to a painting of a mountain on the wall. Removing the picture, she revealed a small door behind it. She pulled it aside to show a vent. The sound of the hall was amplified into the room. "Can you believe they have me searching back roads to find the Princess? Boy, if I do find her, I'll let her know how man enough I am."

Kiran cringed at the way he talked about her.

The other guards laughed.

Another said, "How about you court her on the way back. Maybe the King will see that you get her hand and not Keol."

"I hate that snobby bloodsucker. He walks in like he owns the place, and the King keeps inviting him to court his fair daughter. You can tell who he favors. He has plans for a banquet when the Princess returns, and he wants to marry her off to that scum."

Nadi touched her shoulder, letting her know he was there. She was trying not to take it to heart, but these words bothered her.

The first one spoke again, "I will take her flower and make sure that Lord Keol knows his princess is a whore." He laughed as he swung his mug around, sloshing his ale.

Kiran did not realize she had approached the vent until she was craning to see one of these men.

"Maybe we shouldn't talk about the Princess like this," an abandreal guard said, holding his ale with two hands. His ears flattened as both of the men looked at him. "The King would have our heads if he ever heard this. We can't speak like this when so many ears are around."

"Look around, Keaton. We're the only ones at the Ravenous Splinter. No one to hear except the old man who runs the place, and if he so much as whispers a word of this, I'll run him through."

The door flew open, and Nezra stormed down the stairs and straight to their table. "If you make threats about my husband, I'll throw the lot of you out! You make a bad name for the Vadneran guards. I hear the King himself is wandering the woods looking for his daughter, too. If he sets foot in my Inn, I'll spill my guts about you lot. Only one good member of your group has the decency to know when enough is enough."

The guard pulled out his knife and shoved it into her ribs. Nadi wrapped his hand over Kiran's mouth to stifle her scream. Nezra toppled over onto the floor, clutching the knife. The guard stood over her and threw coins at her, "Keep the change, Wench." Looking at the old man, he said, "I did you a favor getting rid of this mouthy wench. Now you don't have to hear her yapping." He turned to Keaton, "Get my knife for me as you clean up this mess." The two guards walked out, leaving the abandreal to stare at the scene that unfolded.

"Are you ok?" he asked as he leaned over her.

Standing back up, she pulled the knife out of her side, "Not the first time a human has stabbed me. Too bad he ruined my dress. It was one of my favorites."

"Close the chimney and smoke the place until we are out of sight. I don't want them catching a water nymph and sending her to the slave trade."

"Oh, and if you find the Princess, keep her away from those guys. She needs someone to protect her from those creeps." She walked over and closed the chimney, placing more wood on the fire. The Inn quickly filled with smoke.

The Abandreal left through the doors and rushed off with the other two guards on horses. As soon as they could no longer see them from the window, she opened the chimney and windows to let out the smoke. "Well, Vadnera has one good guard, that's for certain."

Kiran had slumped onto the floor, her eyes welling up with tears. Her father let these people run amok all over their land, killing people, ruining homes and businesses. She felt hopeless.

"Maybe we should find the creature of wishes in the song so that I can keep my throne. Then this won't happen," she said, wiping away the one tear that escaped.

"You don't need magical wishes; you just have to stand up for what you believe in," Nadi said. His face was so close to hers.

She touched her forehead against his. "I hope you're right."

"Now that *that's* over, how about I show you two love birds, the place?" Nezra popped in out of nowhere.

"Way to ruin the Romance," Cynthia piped in from the corner of the room.

Kiran wanted to say something but stopped, remembering that Nezra couldn't see or hear Cynthia.

Getting up, they were led to the dining hall. Nezra grabbed a grey scarf that was hanging next to the door. "This was forgotten last winter and never claimed." She threw it around Nadi's neck, covering the collar. "Perfect—just make sure your eyes don't change?"

"You know my eyes change?" Nadi said as they flashed orange.

"Kinda hard to hide your emotions with a pretty girl around, huh? They turn pink every time you look at her?"

Kiran looked at Nadi, but had never seen that color come from his eyes before. Maybe it was red for anger, and she was mistaking it for pink. Kiran looped her arm through his. "Always so obvious with his love for me."

They were led over to the old man. "This is my husband, Harmond. He's not a talker, but he is a looker."

The wrinkled older man gave a gummy grin.

Kiran gave her a questioning look; Nezra seemed to be in her late twenties.

"Or 'was' I should say." She kissed him on the head. "He was a handsome man sixty years ago. Strong and smart. A water nymph trying to steal his breath instead became his bride. Unfortunately, I age more slowly than he does, and I don't have children. If I could have a wish come true, that would be one of them." A deep sadness pooled in Nezra's eyes, as though her world was falling apart in front of her, and it was taking all her strength to keep her life from shattering.

But in a flash, the sadness was gone. "Well, on to the kitchen." Whipping around, she walked back out the door.

Chapter 31

Nadi followed Nezra with Kiran in tow, while Cynthia floated off towards the window, mumbling something he could not hear. Walking through the doors, he saw a young boy working over the stove. His brown eyes looked over the group as they entered. He pushed his black hair out of his eyes and stared at the poster by the door. Speaking another language, he pointed from the sign of the missing Princess, then to Kiran.

"Yes, Pip. I'm quite aware of our guest, but she prefers to be called Kairi," Nezra gave a small smile as she looked over the pot. "It sure smells good. Now, if only I could teach you to cook meat and fish instead of soup."

"You knew," Kiran looked at her, surprised.

"The ways of royalty are hard to hide when most of us live in poverty. If you put rags on the rich, you can still smell their expensive oils and see their stance of power.

How well they keep their heads up when the rest of us look down. Not to mention—your face is plastered everywhere." She looked at Nadi, "I doubt that was your given name either."

"It's Nadi, and I can cook if you would like." He stepped forward but winced in pain as he touched his head.

"Maybe after meditating," Kiran said. "He keeps getting these headaches...some of them may be caused by the collar, but I think he may also be sick."

Nezra leaned in close and studied him. "Aye, he is sick. I have a cure for the sickness, though." Grabbing a tankard from the stack on the counter, she scooped water into it and then went to a barrel. Uncorking it, she caught some of the dark amber liquid in the cup as well. As she replaced the cork with a hard smack, she handed the tankard to Nadi. "Drink. It may not taste great, but sobriety is a hard road. You can't go cold turkey and not have repercussions. Watered down ale, once every other week, until your body stops needing it."

"Thanks," Nadi looked at the liquid that he had cherished so much, and for once, it was not the one thing he ultimately desired. Lifting the tankard, he sipped the bitter ale. Even watered, his body wanted more, but he realized that the water in the mug was much more important to him. He'd hardly drunk anything since arriving here.

With the mug empty, he handed it back to Nezra. "Water, please."

"That's it. You know now what is needed," Nezra encouraged. She ladled more water into the empty tankard. "Water can be life or death, but in this case, it is life."

Nadi downed the second one in no time and then wiped his lips dry. "I grew up in a desert. The closest I've ever come to death by water was with my brother recently, when we dove into the oasis, and he refused to transform."

"Hmm…" Nezra thought about it as she grabbed a seat. "Transforming into another creature should be instinct as well. His body should have shifted into anything, trying to cope with the new environment. Maybe he can't shift or lacked any form to shift into…"

"Well, that can't be true because…" Nadi thought about it, but he couldn't remember his brother ever changing. Not once could he recall a moment his brother had shifted or stated any form he could become. They were never close, but still, if his brother transformed in front of someone, he would have heard. "I can't recall him ever changing."

"Could it be possible that the gift skipped him? Was he a half?" referring to those known as half shifters.

"No, we are brothers by blood." He thought back to when they were kids, and he had shifted into a bird in front of his family. His brother had sworn to find something better to change into, something their mother would be proud of. "Zec wanted something special as his first form for Mother. He wants the dragon so that when Thorn reverses time, he can be changed back once he sees Mother again. The story of 'Elias the Dragon'…only there will be no loss of control, and Mother can watch as he shifts back, unlike the unlucky character."

"That was a good story," Nezra waved for Pip to bring some tea. "I am guessing that your brother is after the same dragon you have the form of, and that form can only be claimed once?"

Nadi stared at her, unsure if he should answer.

"Magic has limits, and all are usually simple, but reversing time is harder on a different scale. That magic is impossible." She tapped the ladle against the table.

"Remember the Sorcerer Thorn from the war?" Kiran piped in.

"Aye," the water nymph poured herself a glass of tea, as well as one for Kiran. "All the dark angels vanished from the earth the day he attacked. Like a one-person army. Soldiers fell, lives were lost, and only a horn from the Vadneran army was heard when many hit the ground without being touched. I was there, aiding the soldiers. I did not understand why they needed so many warriors for one man, but they retreated and left him up to the dark angels. They certainly thought the victor would be their prized peace-keepers."

"But we fell as well," Cynthia whispered from a corner of the table. Zec hadn't seen her come in.

"They vanished that day, even with their wings blackened for battle." Nezra lifted her cup to her lips. "No one expected to face defeat that day. The sorcerer vanished, and the dark angels had never returned. It was hard to forget."

"The reason I'm here is because of him," Nadi said with a solemn tone. "He can control time with a magic orb. I'm not sure of the limit it has, but he stopped me in my tracks with it. He also defeated the Elders and is trying to harness their power. Taking on the dragon's form prevents them from using it to get into the dragons' keep and using a dragon egg as their anchor to harness that power. I can no longer shift—but he can't reverse time like he wants to."

Setting the cup back down, Nezra seemed as though she was taking a moment to soak up all the information. "Such destructive power taken from the Elders to reverse time. There must be a lot of things he wishes to change. The power may not be enough to change things. It could only extend the time by a minute. Hard to go back and change the past. It could heal and reverse time by hours and minutes, but it could also be harmful."

"Harmful, how?" Kiran held her cup in both hands but had yet to take a drink.

"Say that he can go back months, years, or even decades. He kills one bird from so many years back, but that one bird now no longer exists. An entire flock cannot simply vanish since it had spawned from that one bird. So here in the present, they would all fall out of the sky, dead. It could make an entire species go extinct just from killing one."

Nadi mulled it over, thinking of everything he had just heard. "Thorn was gifted the orb by the Queen of Vadnera to prevent the death of his father. What if he loved the Queen, and being in Firstenfeld was more of a tactical move than trying to hide the fact he was using magic in a holy city?" Looking at Kiran, he could feel his eyes change to purple while in deep thought as he met her gaze. "What if he was after you? He did mention that he was there for a princess and that she was late."

"Me?" Kiran's grip on the glass tightened. "Why me?"

"Thorn's father was killed because Thorn was courting your mother. Suppose I were a madman with the ability to control time and lost the chance to sire a child with the woman I love. In that case, I would try to get revenge by taking their most prized possession from them."

Realization filled her eyes. "My purification ceremony…"

"There was no reason for him to come after me into the city since he still had my brother. He knew of your arrival and was on his way to steal you when he witnessed my fight with my brother and my escape."

"I was late, though," She began to look sick.

"Alright," Nezra set her cup down. "Let's get off this subject. It's obvious that you need to finish this journey of yours, but you also need to pay for the eggs you broke. One night here, working in the tavern, and then on your way. From the sound of it, you have a world to save." She paused. "We need to make the Princess unrecognizable, though."

Grabbing Kiran's arm, Nezra pulled her out of the room and back up the stairs. They went through a different door with a large bed and a wardrobe. Nezra opened the wooden doors of her armoire, revealing several dresses.

Chapter 32

A few hours later, Kiran was bathed and in a black sleeved dress that hung off her shoulders. A red bodice squeezed her ribs and pushed her breasts up. Make-up caked onto her face made her unrecognizable, but also uncomfortable. Her skirt was lifted on one side, revealing her leg. Nezra had pinned up her mass of curls in a loose bun.

There was a knock on the door. "Is everything ok in there?" It was Nadi; his voice seemed hesitant. "It's getting dark, and people are starting to fill the tables."

"Oh, that late?" Nezra opened the door and shoved Kiran into Nadi's arms. "I gotta find that bard before he starts playing." She was out of sight before either of them could say a word.

Kiran looked up at Nadi, but his eyes were a shade of pink. The expression on his face seemed to remind her of how Keol would look at her.

"You look beautiful," the words seemed genuine.

"Thank you," Kiran blushed, but doubted it showed under the make-up. Still, she smiled at the words that came from him unexpectedly.

His arms tightened around her as he pulled her in for a hug. Her breath seemed to catch, and her heart raced. Nadi buried his face in her neck, and fear suddenly gripped her at the memory of the monster.

Shoving him back, she looked into his eyes only to see that they went from pink to orange. The expression on his face was confusion mixed with fear. "I'm sorry, did I cross a line? I thought that—"

"No, sorry," Kiran stumbled backwards into the wall. "We should get to work."

"Shouldn't we talk about what just happened?" Nadi began to follow her.

"No." She realized that she feared the monster in him, but not knowing when it would take over was even scarier. It made her more hesitant when meeting his gaze. She needed to work on distracting herself from what had happened.

She went from table to table, taking orders and serving food as she had seen her servants do so many times before. Kiran tried to be swift and silent, but she was clumsy and slow. Her servants made it look so easy.

Nezra had to warn some of the men already not to touch her. "Don't go scaring away some good help," she said to a man who went to pinch her bottom.

Kiran was having fun talking to people, hearing stories of battle scars and travels. A bard sang of stories about dark angels and heroes of old. The place had become so lively after the sun went down.

Before she knew it, Nezra had closed the Kitchen and sent Pip to bed. "Take a break. You earned it," she said, passing her a cup of ale.

Taking a sip, she coughed at the bitter liquid. "Ugh, definitely not like wine."

"Of course not," the nymph laughed. "Bitter and nasty, but drowns out sorrows and makes you forget. That's why most drink."

"I usually do it because 'Royalty must have the finest tastes,'" she mocked her father's words. "I never cared for it. I usually choose juice or water instead."

"Oh, so you don't like my ale," Nezra lifted her brow.

"I think it is good, just not my taste," she laughed.

The bard struck a happy tune, and both of them watched Nadi jump on the table and dance with other men chanting to the beat. "Oh, a merry bard is he! One who washes in these sweet melodies!" Drunken men were practically shouting the song.

"You are lucky to have someone who looks at you the way he does," Nezra said, watching Nadi grab a guy by his shoulders and dance with him, laughing.

Kiran was surprised by the conversation. "I don't think he likes me. I must be burdening him by being here."

"My Harmond used to look at me that way," She looked back at the old man passed out in his chair. "His age makes him silent and weak, but I know he still loves me all the same."

"I love someone else," Kiran raised the tankard and grimaced at the taste before placing it back on the counter. "I question if he truly loves me back. Recently, I understood that neither of us knows each other." She watched as Nadi fell off the table onto a few drunken men, laughing with them all. "With Nadi, I don't think it would last even if he did love me. That monster inside him has to come out."

"Maybe, if you love him, that might help him conquer his inner beast. Or it will make it easier on him when he has to let it take over."

Kiran had not thought about it that way. "How do I know what love really is? How would I get someone to truly love me?"

Laughing, Nezra grabbed her face and forced her to look her in the eye. "Men are thirsty, so be like water."

Confused, the Princess pulled away from her hands, "Like water?"

Smiling, the nymph smoothed her hands down her dress. "Hot like fire."

Her hands moved up over her heart. "Cold like ice."

Then she lifted a hand in front of her face and balled it into a fist. "Hard like a stone." Lastly, she opened her hand and blew a kiss. "And light as air."

To Kiran, it almost looked like she was dancing, but she understood since water could be all those things. "Like water."

The song ended, but the bard struck up a tune she remembered. It was one of the happier songs from the castle that they played during special events. Both she and Nadi stared at each other for a moment as they heard it. She had only followed her father's rules on courting, but with her newfound freedom, the Princess was going to fall out of line.

Following the steps that she had remembered from court dances, she made her way to Nadi. Raising her hand up for the line dance as she recalled, Nadi did not mirror the pose as expected. Instead, he pulled her into his arms and spun her around. She didn't know what she was doing, and it seemed that Nadi was also at a loss. They tried their best to keep pace and have fun. Kiran's hair fell out of the bun as Nadi spun her around. By the end, they were face to face, trying to catch their breath. The whole room was silent as he closed his eyes, remembering to try and hide the color.

Her hand touched his chin, and she began moving his face towards hers. He opened his eyes, blazing pink color, causing her to freeze. Heart racing, she felt a flutter in her stomach, and her cheeks flushed bright red.

He blushed and looked away, the smile fading from his face. "Are you sure, Princess?" Nadi whispered.

Kiran's eyes opened wide as she finally looked around at all the expectant faces. In her heart, she realized she was not sure that she wanted this right now. She wasn't even sure if she truly loved Keol or Nadi.

Pulling away, she heard the room cry out in disappointment as she rushed up the stairs and back to the room with the painting. She began wiping off the makeup as tears streamed down her face. At the moment, she felt lost and alone.

"Kiran," Cynthia came through the door. "You looked so happy. What happened?"

"I realized that I don't even know what I want or who I love. I'm so lost out here. At the castle, I was told who I love and who I dislike. Are these feelings even my own?" Kiran wiped her eyes, black eye makeup streaming down her face.

Cynthia sighed. "That's something you have to figure out on your own."

"Really?" Kiran sniffled.

The dark angel nodded. "You eventually will figure it out, but you can't just go off of what other people tell you. Now wash up and get some rest; we have to leave at the first light of dawn."

Chapter 33

"Someone said my daughter was here!" The King's voice boomed through the Inn at the early hours, waking Kiran. Fear gripped her, knowing they needed to keep moving on their journey. Her heart raced, understanding that she did not want to face her father when he was angry.

Trying to get up, she realized there was an arm around her, pulling her in close. Their breath tickled her ear. Looking over, she saw Nadi, still asleep. Her father would have both of their heads if he so much as glimpsed them together right now. She wasn't even sure when he had ended up in the same bed.

"Sire, it is late, and I assure you I have not seen any princess enter my tavern." She could hear Nezra say. "I think some poor bloke was out for money."

"I can smell her," a familiar voice said.

"Keol," she whispered. Shaking off the blankets and Nadi's arm, she threw her boots on. She was lucky to have changed back into her traveling clothes before going to bed. "Nadi," she shook him until he awoke.

Just as he opened his mouth to say something, the King's voice interrupted, "I am going to ask again. Where is my daughter?"

"Look, there were lots of people out here last night. I don't know. She could have been any one of them."

"There were no other women in the Inn other than you and her." Keol's voice was cold.

"That's not true. I hired a barmaid yesterday. She should be back in the morning for work."

"The scent never left the Inn."

Nadi was up and at the door, but Kiran pulled Nadi to the window. A guard was waiting at the back door, as well as two near the front. The guard at the back looked to be falling asleep on his horse. If they made it to the trees, Kiran knew they could make a run for it.

Nadi nudged the window open, trying to make as little sound as possible. As soon as it was open far enough, he let Kiran climb onto the roof and followed. A cart of hay sat under the ledge of the roof. Kiran made sure that only the sleeping guard was in view before jumping into the pile. Rolling out, she hid under the edge of the cart. Nadi followed. From under the edge, she saw one of the guards at the front look around the side. Yet, he didn't seem to notice that Nadi was in the hay. Kiran held her breath until the guard went back to the front of the Inn. Nadi dusted the strands off and helped her out from under the cart.

They both ran for the cover of the woods just as she heard Nezra shout, "Excuse me! You can't just go flinging doors open. People do sleep here, and you'll give my fine establishment a bad name."

Holding Nadi's hand, she rushed through the forest, avoiding branches and trees. Crossing a stream, she looked back. A shadow stood at where they had entered, and she knew the chase would soon come to an end. Releasing Nadi's hand, she slowed her pace as the piercing red eyes of a vampire glowed in the dim light of the shaded wood. She recognized his maroon coat with embroidered trees and his black shirt, the blood red stone on a gold chain around his neck. Coming almost to a stop, she watched a victorious grin part his lips as a few strands of his black hair fell in front of his eyes.

"Nadi, I'm sorry." She panted, turning back to the shifter. "Keol would find us anywhere we go."

"Kiran, we need to keep running no matter what. We can't let them win!" He reached for her hand, just as a different hand grabbed Kiran and pulled her away from Nadi.

Keol wrapped his arms protectively around her. "You are going to be alright now."

Nadi stopped and looked around as Kiran began to cry, "I'm sorry." She watched as he attempted to run, but in every direction he turned, there was a crossbow pointed at him. Guards littered the forest, armed and ready to let loose their attack when presented.

The shifter backed himself against a tree, arms raised. The King looked at her and then at him. "What do you need with my daughter?"

Nadi stayed silent, glaring at the King dressed in black furs. His normally groomed dark brown hair was slightly astray from his recent travels. Stroking his beard, he studied him a moment. "It's obvious you are not human, nor from Vadnera. Where do you hail from, boy?"

Silence. Nadi's eyes, orange and red, almost looked like blood.

The King looked to Keol, "Is he a vampire?"

"No, Your Highness. He smells different. Like sand and fur. Plus, he has a pulse."

"Kiran," the king looked to his daughter. "Why did he take you?"

Nadi met her eyes and shook her head slowly. Still, she could not be silent. "He did not take me. I went willingly."

Almost shocked, the King walked up to her. "Why? This is not something you would normally do."

Kiran pulled away from Keol, "For once, I desired adventure and not to be cooped up in a castle, but here I was on my way to a ritual when I thought I saw a thief. Instead, I met *him*, trying to stop the sorcerer from destroying the world. He saved me from being kidnapped, and we need to help him get back home to warn the dragons of what is to come."

Keol stood staring at her before meeting the eyes of the King, "She speaks the truth."

"Or the lies he fed her. The sorcerer vanished with the dark angels. He has not been seen in years." The King turned back to Nadi, "What's your story, boy?"

"The Princess already told you, but both of us know you're not going to let me leave." Nadi put his arms down, and the archers raised their crossbows more intently at him.

"Are you dumb or trying to be brave?" Her father raised his hand, and some of the archers took a knee to steady themselves.

"No!" Kiran jumped in front of him. "Let me at least say goodbye."

Her father narrowed his eyes at her as he thought about it. "Fine," he signaled for the guards to lower their weapons.

Kiran approached Nadi, putting her arms around his neck. With her heart racing, she did the only thing she knew to do. Gaining her courage, she ran her fingers through the back of his hair and held him close for one final embrace. Tears streamed down her face as she pulled away. "I'm sorry," she whispered. "I have to give up the fight here."

"No, you don't. You are giving up, and it's not for a good reason. My life shouldn't matter to the rest of the world." He closed his eyes and gritted his teeth. "Forget about me and aim to stop them no matter what."

Kiran kissed his cheek and whispered, "I am making the right decision." Her hand slid down to the collar around his neck. She whispered the word she had read in a book to unlock the collar. An audible click sounded as she removed it from his neck and dropped it onto the leaf-covered ground. Backing away, Nadi's eyes opened, but one of them was gold and wild. A deep laugh erupted, and a wicked grin crossed his face. His hand reached for Kiran's throat.

Keol grabbed Kiran and retreated behind a tree. "What have you done?"

"I freed him," she said in a hushed tone. "I freed the monster."

Looking over her shoulder, she saw Nadi enveloped in golden light, and all the guards backed away slowly, some aiming their crossbows at him. The King stood his ground, watching the transformation unfold as the light grew bigger and bigger. Soon, the light dimmed, and a pair of golden wings unfolded to reveal a dawn dragon. It roared at everyone surrounding it.

"You ruined everything!" Cynthia was suddenly beside her. "You set free a wild dragon who will kill and not stop! The world may be doomed."

Kiran looked away from the dark angel, "I had no other choice. He would have been dead otherwise."

It took to the skies with its giant wings, causing all the birds in the trees to fly up with it. Another roar cut through the air as guards began to scramble for safety. The dragon looked down at the forest and let loose a torrent of fire. Guards screamed as they were caught ablaze. They began rushing for the Inn.

The King abruptly turned and yelled to his men, "Do not lead the dragon to the Inn! Head for the road!"

The dragon landed in its blaze and brought its gaze to Kiran. "The Princess, or your lives," his voice rumbled.

Keol gripped Kiran tighter against his chest. The King stepped in front of her. Soldiers shot a torrent of arrows that did not seem to affect the dragon. "The Princess, or your *liiiiiiives*," it was a deep growl this time.

"King Lucin," Keol called. "We do not stand a chance right now. We need to retreat."

"We need to stop him from going on a rampage." He looked back at his daughter, "Kiran—do you understand what you put at stake here?"

"I have a plan." Kiran looked to the vampire, "I need to speak with Keol in private."

The King spun around, livid, "You unleash this beast in my kingdom and tell me you have a plan? Why do you need to speak to him?"

"Because he is rational at this moment, and I can trust him!" Kiran looked at the Dragon. "I'll go with you, but I want to say goodbye first."

"The hell you will!" He strode towards his daughter, who was still staring at the beast. Without a word, he slapped her, causing her head to jerk to the side. Her cheek stung from the impact, and a few guards even stopped in their tracks. Kiran met her father's angry gaze with tears in her own.

Again, he raised his hand.

"King Lucin!" Keol caught his hand on its way to her face. "It's best not to mar such beauty. It can deter some from marrying her."

"Keol," he pulled his hand out of the vampire's grasp. "She freed her captor and unleashed a terror on this land." King Lucin looked to his scattered men, "There is only one region of gold dragons, and I am going to need a word with King Grumloc. Get me a messenger!"

"Sire, that is not a dragon," Keol said as the King strode towards one of his archers that were getting their bearings. "It is a Shapeshifter." Taking off his coat, Keol wrapped it around Kiran. "The Princess can probably tell us more about her captor."

"He was not my captor!" Kiran nearly shouted, "He is my friend!"

Glaring at her, the King turned his back and began pulling his men from the woods. "Your sacrifice better be worth it," he grumbled under his breath.

The rain began to pour, and she looked at the dragon again. "We should wait for the rain to stop so our journey will be safer. This will allow me to get my things together and be on our way."

"So be it," the beast growled. "But if you so much as leave this area without me, then I will burn everything to the ground until I find you."

Chapter 34

Keol did not let go of Kiran until they were back inside the Ravenous Splinter. They took their seats at a table near the center of the room. The King and his guards were posted outside, ready, even if they were going to lose their lives. Nezra looked uneasy as she placed the tea before Kiran and Keol before turning back and closing the curtains.

Moving some of the wet strands of her blonde hair from her face, she met Keol's gaze, acting as the Princess that she was. His red eyes, which always held a gentle look, were filled with concern. Her fingers traced the lip of the cup as she thought about her words carefully.

Keol spoke first. "What is your relationship with this creature?"

"He is my friend," Kiran wanted to start at the beginning.

"You kissed him, though," Keol started to sound angry. "Friends do not kiss other friends."

"Keol." The Princess could not find the words she wanted to say. She began to feel guilty for kissing Nadi in front of everyone, even though it was a peck on the cheek.

"I've been worried sick that you had been hurt—or worse." He stood up, leaning over the table. "Instead, you've been kissing some unstable creature who could kill you. I can't believe I wasted so much time and effort trying to find you."

She looked down at her cup with a sad expression before meeting his gaze. "If that creature were you, I would have done the same thing."

Silence filled the moment between them as he cocked his head to the side, seeming to want her to explain her reasoning.

"I love you, but Nadi would have died. I didn't want his last moments to be full of arrows and pain. Instead, I kissed him on the cheek so that he would feel loved before I betrayed him and unleashed the one thing he feared." Watching Keol slowly sit down, she went on. "He may not even remember that it happened. Right now, Nadi is lost to the black sands of his mind."

Looking uneasy, the vampire sipped the tea. "So you haven't chosen him as your husband?"

"Keol," she gave him a distasteful look. "I barely know him. I don't know his favorite food or if he likes the color blue. We're practically strangers, but I have realized these past few weeks that you and I are practically strangers as well, and I wish to know more about you. I love you, but it will take time for me to decide who I want to marry." Kiran reached across the table and laid her hand on his. "Please just trust me."

He touched her cheek, catching a tear that escaped. "Why do you always cry? After all these years, I thought you would understand that you have no reason to cry when I am here."

Kiran dried her eyes and smiled at him. "We should work on the plan."

Taking her hand, he nodded.

"To avoid casualties, I am leaving with him." She stiffened at her own words.

Cynthia floated between them. "You understand that dragon out there has not said why he wants you. Not once has he stated if you are to be his food."

"It's a chance I'm willing to take!" Kiran yelled at her.

She heard a cup drop behind her and clatter against the floor. Keol stood up and stepped back from the table. Kiran realized that she answered a ghost no one could see.

"Did I miss something?" Nezra picked up the mug off the floor. "You answered a question none of us asked."

Balling her fists, Kiran swallowed her fear and decided that the truth was needed. Averting her gaze, she said, "Maybe I should start at the beginning. Tell you the secret I've been bearing and part of the reasons for my travels." She didn't want to look at him and instead focused on the cup in her hands. "The day I stepped out of the carriage in Firstenfeld, I didn't know that I would be running for my life. I saw a dark angel."

"Impossible!" He slammed his hands against the table. "They're all dead."

"Her name is Cynthia, and she is the spirit of one." She gritted her teeth, "I am the apprentice of the dark angel. Next in line to be given wings and take up arms."

Slumping down into his seat, he whispered, "That is impossible. That can't be. Cynthia died with the other dark angels. If this is true, then you'll lose your throne."

"I know, and that's why I don't want you to tell Father. He'll not think twice about casting me out and adopting some child to be the heir to the throne." Shaking her head, she went on. "I took off that day after meeting the eyes of the sorcerer, Thorn. We think he might have been plotting to kidnap me."

"Kiran, this is all sounding absurd. Cynthia had died, and Thorn has not been seen in years. I knew that dark angel myself, and she would always tease me. I swear that woman hated me. If she were alive today, she would..." He trailed off, giving her a pained look.

"Call him a lecherous bug, take the pins from my hair and poke him with them." Cynthia hovered behind him and acted like she was slapping him on the back of the head, "Idiot, where is your pride. I died a noble death!"

Kiran decided to relay what she heard. "She would call you a lecherous bug and poke you with her hairpins."

Slowly, the vampire raised his head to stare across the table. "How do you know these things?"

"Because," Kiran began. "I answered her questions a moment ago. Even now, she is in this room. Yet, only I can see her." Keol went to say something, but she held up her hand to stop him. "Let me continue my story."

Nodding, the vampire took his seat, "Go on."

"I knew nothing about Nadi, but it seemed as though I was a burden at first. Helpless and weak, he had to fend for me. Slowly, we became friends, and he let me know what Thorn was planning. He needed a Shapeshifter to become a dragon so they could steal an egg from the golden dragons' keep. Thorn intends to use the Orb of Time to save his father, but it will sacrifice an unborn dragon's life in the process." She realized she was missing some details as she finally took a sip of her tea. "Nadi understood that Thorn and Icarri had trapped the Elders there and planned to siphon off their magic. To prevent one part of the plan, Nadi took the form of the dragon and escaped. This prevented his brother from transforming. It's only a matter of time before they figure that out."

Pinching the bridge of his nose, he took a deep breath. He seemed to give her words some thought before answering. "You mean to say that Lady Icarri, *a great sorceress*, is also involved in all of this? Not only that, but the Elders, creators of all life, are their victims?" Shaking his head, he stood up from the table. "We're done here."

"You don't believe me?" Kiran stood up as well.

"Do you hear yourself? This nonsense you're spouting. Did you ever consider that this creature lied to you to lure you away? He spun this web off of things he heard, and you are playing into his trap. That shapeshifter probably knows everything about you because he is behind this twisted tale!" He turned his back on her. "At this moment, I am ashamed that you can be so naive."

Before Kiran could respond, a familiar voice came from above. "If she is naive, then I am the one at fault for making her so." Looking up, Kiran saw her mother leaning against the railing. Her grey fur cloak was damp from the rain, but her white hair was dry, in a tight braid. With her cold, grey eyes locked on Keol as he bowed, she said, "So I must assume you are stating that I am also naive."

"No, your majesty," Keol lifted his head but stayed bowed. "I was expressing that the story she has spun is delusional."

"So when my eyes fell upon Thadius Thorn in the crowd after Kiran ran off with that boy, did that also make me delusional?"

Standing up straight, he met the Queen's cold gaze as she descended the stairs. There was silence as he seemed to be thinking of his words carefully. Letting out a sigh, he answered. "No, my Queen. I did not know you had seen him."

She held her head up proudly, with her unflinching gaze. The vampire looked away in defeat. "When has Kiran ever lied to you? When has she given you reason not to trust her?"

"It's not her that I don't trust," he offered the Queen a seat, but she shook her head. "I don't trust that creature."

"So, you don't trust someone who has kept Kiran safe? He has ensured she was fed, clothed, and taken care of to the fullest." She leaned in next to his ear and loudly whispered, "You mean to say that you are jealous that it was not *you* taking care of her?"

"He has no right!" Keol shouted, "I worked hard for her hand, and he steals her away!"

A smile curled at the edges of the Queen's lips. "Looks like the vampire lord can't take a little competition."

Keol clenched his fists as she turned away from him. "You find this amusing?"

"I find it amusing that you thought you already had her hand when she hasn't chosen anyone." The Queen looked down at Kiran, who was now tightly holding the empty cup. She had drained it as her mother spoke down to Lord Keol. It was her turn, and she knew her mother would make her aware of the trouble she was in. "Do you understand why dragons favored princesses in the tales of old?"

Startled by the question, Kiran met her mother's gaze. She was surprised to know that her mother had been listening to the entire conversation. In response, Kiran shook her head.

"Wild dragons of the past—before we had treaties and commissioned trade—would go and steal princesses from kingdoms. They were always kept alive, safe from harm." The Queen tugged at one of Kiran's curls, letting it bounce back into place. "Kingdoms would march on to find the dragon's lair, and many would attempt to slay it. Armies of men fed the dragon until their domain no longer had their reinforcements. It would then eat the princess and destroy the kingdom, taking its precious treasures."

Her heart raced at the thought of a destroyed Vadnera. Far worse than her losing it to gain a pair of wings. It made her think twice about her plan. She was hoping for Keol to rescue her, but what if he fed the dragon, too?

The Queen opened her cloak and planted a heavy book on the table. "I figured we might need to create an item to assist you with your plan."

Both Kiran and Keol stood up at the table, staring down at the book. It was a white leather-bound cover etched with a tree, but the branches and the roots intertwined to make it into a circle. It was the one thing her mother always kept hidden and had only told her stories of. The Book of Creation was said to have helped bring life into existence in their world.

"Are you mad?" Keol took his jacket from Kiran and tossed it over the book. "Your most prized possession, a one-of-a-kind treasure passed down through your family, and you leave the castle with it? You just tossed it on the table like a history book!"

Pushing the coat off, Queen Lillian opened the cover to a blank page. "It's just a book to me, but it may be the key to saving a life for Kiran." Pulling the quill out of the spine of the book, she handed it to Kiran. "This book will belong to you someday. Maybe it's time that you make an item with it."

Kiran looked at the white-feathered quill hesitantly. This was the first time her mother even showed her the book. Her mother had told stories about it when she was younger, but made it seem like she did not know where it was. She gripped the cold metal of the quill between her fingers, almost expecting some magical enlightenment to befall her. Nothing happened. "What should I make?" she asked, seeming to be at a loss.

"Think hard of the road laid before you. A dragon will take you from this place and attempt to lure many to their deaths. Maybe you can make an item to remove the dragon from him?" Queen Lillian tapped on the book. "Or you could make a way of escaping from him if your plan should fail."

Kiran suddenly thought about how she could use the book to stop herself from becoming a dark angel. A necklace to nullify the effects of the curse. She shook her head. Kiran thought about the dark place of Nadi's mind. If she had to face the dragon there, she was sure to lose. It was no place for her. Only Nadi belonged there.

A thought flickered in her mind like the flame on a candle. "Cynthia, you had once mentioned that the dark angel and her guide shared a bond. How does that work?"

Queen Lillian and Keol looked at each other. Nezra peered out the window, seeming to check on the rain. The dark angel hovered over Kiran's shoulder; a small smile parted her lips.

"You have a bond with your guide. It's as though you have a rope that connects your souls." Touching her chest, she seemed sad. "If you can focus on that connection, you two will always be able to find each other."

"That also means that the dragon can use it," Kiran said aloud. "I am not strong enough to fight yet. We need something to ensure that Thorn does not win, even if I fail at getting Nadi back to normal. I'm prepared to do what I must for the future of Vadnera."

"Kiran," her mother touched her hand. "Promise me that you'll live."

Touching quill to paper, Kiran tried to be strong in front of her mother as she made the first line.

"I'll try."

Chapter 35

Fog filled the woods as the rain became a drizzle. The dragon had let out a roar, signaling that it was time. Its golden eyes and scales shimmered through the fog.

Kiran could not sleep after making her item, worrying that the choices she made were incorrect. The book gave her a limit of three enchantments to place on her item and a time limit she wished she could expand. She gripped the piece of chalk before placing it back in its grey cloth pouch.

Guards lined up as she stepped out of the door of the Ravenous Splinter, fists over their hearts. They seemed to be saluting her as she walked to her death. Her father sat on horseback, watching her walk into the charred forest, as her mother took the opportunity to slip out the back unnoticed.

Keol grabbed her arm, pulling her against his chest. She could feel his breath against her cheek as his grip tightened. A warning growl came from the dragon. Slowly, Keol slipped another pouch into her hand before releasing her, "Take care of yourself, Princess."

Holding her head up high, Kiran continued her walk to the beast. She didn't stop until she could feel his hot breath on her face. Looking up into the golden eyes, she could not see any sign of Nadi there. He opened his hand and gently closed his claws around her. Feeling his scaled hand tighten, she shivered. Taking a deep breath to steady herself, Kiran knew this was going to be a long trip.

✦ ✦ ✦

Keol had waited for the dragon to be out of sight before turning to the King. "Your Majesty, I am going to bring your daughter back safely."

"Lord Keol," the King did not seem amused. "If you can bring her back alive, then you can marry my daughter."

A guard handed the vampire a bag filled with a few supplies he might need for the trip. A rope, rations, and a few metal items from what he could smell. "I could not accept her hand until I knew she wanted me..." his thoughts trailed. "I would instead ask to keep her for a week to tour Lu'Bela. After that, we should have a ball to celebrate her return."

The King laughed. "So be it. If she can return alive and by your hand, that is your reward."

Just as Keol went to thank him, the guards began yelling and scattering.

"Dragon!" one screamed as he dropped his crossbow and ran for a horse.

Keol looked behind him to see a golden dragon land a reasonable distance away and change into its human form. "Wait," he shouted at the men. "This one is not an enemy!"

A few of the men stopped and stood at attention, while others scrambled to ready weapons or flee.

Through the fog, blonde hair stuck out from under his golden helmet, and slitted eyes glowed brightly through the mist. Scales lined the sides of his face and jaw. He gave a salute and knelt a few feet away.

"King Lucin, I am Gage of the Dawn Dragons. King Grumloc sent me here to locate the water dragon and seek her assistance. She was not in Firstenfeld, but people had said she was aiding the search for your daughter." He lifted his bowed head to meet the King's tired gaze. "We are close to finding the location of King Daron. Do you know where I might find her?"

"Cecil was last on the western coast," King Lucin pulled his horse around and approached the dragon guard. "We no longer have use for her services. If you find her, please inform her that the search is off. Also, we'll pay her for her services once she returns to Firstenfeld."

Standing, the guard gave a frustrated sigh. "Understood."

"Wait," Keol walked to the guard. "May we have a word over a hot meal? I have a few questions, and it looks like your journey has been long enough."

Puzzled, he looked between the King and the vampire. "Uh, sure. Might I ask what business you have?"

"Forgive me," he gave a bow. "I am Lord Keol Dacus. I only have a few questions about your kind."

His eyes widened, and he knelt again. "I'm sorry for not recognizing you sooner. Lady Terika often speaks fondly of you when she visits the keep. Your sister is quite the scholar."

Both stood, and Keol gave a smile, "Yes, she is. I have not seen her in months, but with Lady Dane challenging her title, I feel that we might be seeing her sooner than expected."

"Keol," the King narrowed his eyes. "My daughter should be your first priority."

Nodding, the vampire met his gaze. "I assure you—she is always my first priority. I need information that will help me safely retrieve her."

Without another word, the King raised his hand, and his army lined up. Turning the horse around, they began moving east towards the castle. Only four men and a carriage stayed behind at the Inn to assist in bringing the Princess back. Moving to the middle, King Lucien marched with his troops back to their home.

Heading into the Ravenous Splinter, Keol and the guard sat at a table. Nezra gave a confused look at them both as she placed down the utensils. Her gaze wandered between the two.

"I thought you were leaving, and now we have someone new in here," she looked over the dragon guard nervously. "Been a long time since I had one of those wild-eyed creatures in my establishment." She placed a mug down in front of Gage. "I assume you want high-end dwarven ale?"

He smiled at her as he took off his helmet. "You certainly can read minds. Are you a psychic?"

"No, just someone with a good memory." She looked at Keol, "I don't suppose you want anything exotic?"

Shaking his head, he answered, "No, just a hot meal for our friend here."

Muttering something under her breath, Nezra hurried to the back. As the door slammed shut behind her, Keol watched the older man in the chair give a toothless smile. The vampire was glad he didn't age.

Gage jumped to the point, "I'm guessing that Nadi passed through here."

Keol eyed him suspiciously, "Your kind knew about this?"

"I told you that we were close to finding our king, and the last I heard was that Nadi had found him, before being updated that the shapeshifter was also spotted on the mainland by the wanted posters," leaning back in the chair, the dragon put his boots on the table. "Seeing the burnt forest, I'm betting that the form Nadi had was Daron's and it was unleashed at a most inopportune time."

Keol huffed, "You are correct."

"What do you wish to talk about?" Gage asked.

Trying to find the right words, Keol fiddled with a fork. "This might be blunt, but what is a dragon's weakness?"

The guard's eyes narrowed as he sat up. "What is the reason you would need this information?"

"The shapeshifter took the princess in his dragon form, and it will only bring ruin to our kingdom. If I have to end his life to save her, I will," the vampire's tone darkened.

Gage was silent a moment before he responded, "I can't tell you because that would be giving away the weakness of every dawn dragon." Eying the vampire wearily, he went on, "I can accompany you on your journey to find him so that I can take him back and you can retrieve your princess."

Keol nodded in agreement.

Nezra placed the food and ale down before retreating to the back.

"Tell me what you know of Nadi and the Princess," Gage began eating.

"Princess Kiran spoke of their journey together. She stated that Lady Icarri and the Sorcerer Thorn were behind your king's disappearance. They are keeping him beneath the Temple of the Elders." Keol wasn't even sure where that was.

The dragon guard slammed his fist against the table, splintering the wood. "What is their purpose for taking him?"

"Thorn wants to reverse time by harnessing the power of the Elders. He plans to steal an egg from the dragons' keep that will harness their power. She stated that Thorn had captured the Elders." He realized that he had gripped the fork too hard and bent it. Tossing it aside, he continued. "Thorn needs a power source to match the Elders. The egg he seeks must be fertile."

"Now it all makes sense," Gage said, sitting there trying to smooth out the table where he had hit it. "They must have thought we had a fertile egg, to begin with. They had to wait years, and now it is harder to get in unless they have a dragon on the inside. So, then Nadi..." he trailed off.

"Nadi took Daron's form to keep it from Zec, who is cooperating with those two." Running his hand through his hair, he looked over to the door, wondering when Nezra would return. "They had already poisoned his brother's mind, and Zec attacked him.

"Nadi escaped by teleporting to Firstenfeld. He ran into the Princess and kept running, trying to find his way back." He paused a moment as a flash of Kiran kissing Nadi entered his mind. Ignoring the feeling of betrayal, he continued. "When we caught up with her, she freed the dragon inside him to ensure he escaped unharmed. Now I must bring her back safely, even if it means killing Nadi. That's why I asked you about a dragon's weakness."

Gage was silent as he thought for a moment. "Have you ever gone against a dragon before?"

"No." Keol was confused as to why he would even ask that question.

"In the old days, we were filled with pride and greed until we gained a human form. Then we realized how civil we could become." He tossed two of his scales on the table. "Each one of these is worth ten gold each. That is enough to pay for the food, the table, and your mangled fork. I can't tell you a dragon's weakness—we need Nadi alive so he can tell us where Daron is. If you kill him, that gives more power to the magic wielders."

Keol knew he was right. Still, he wanted to end Nadi's life since he was coming between him and the throne. He needed to correct what Lucin was doing.

Gage finished and stood. "Shall we be off then?"

Standing, he followed the dragon outside. Gage walked toward the burnt woods and changed into his dragon form. "Get on," his voice was a deep growl.

Climbing on, Keol knew he could lead them in the right direction. He planned to follow that scent. It seemed to have changed a bit since he had last seen her. She no longer smelled of books and vanilla. Kiran now smelled of the woods and a hint of vanilla. He never thought that smell would have changed.

Chapter 36

Thorn watched as Zec struggled with Daron, trying to force his mouth open. As he had instructed, Icarri made one potion, and Thorn wanted to be sure that every last drop went into the dragon's mouth and not into his own cup. The sorcerer had no trust in her. After this was over, he hoped to sip wine with his queen. Until then, he was refusing to drink anything.

"Stop struggling!" Zec shouted as he put Daron in a headlock.

Icarri held the bottle as she approached them. "Come now. It's not going to hurt."

"You got tired of hitting me," Daron laughed as he pried Zec's arm away from his throat. "Face it, boy—I'm too strong for you." With that, he threw the shapeshifter onto the ground before him, almost hitting Icarri. Looking towards the sorceress, he spat blood at her feet. The stone started to melt where it hit. "Don't want you to ruin those shoes," he laughed.

Zec got onto his feet with a growl and swung at the dragon. Time froze before his fist could reach his face as Thorn activated the orb, filling the room with a grey light. Shaking his head with a frustrated sigh, he began to stroll around the scene.

"Ten years of work all set on the two of you to get one thing done. If I had Dane here, we would already have the egg, but she would have blown our cover. Instead, I have to go with a sorceress who's afraid of getting old, and a shapeless shifter who is quick to anger." He grabbed the back of Zec's shirt and pulled him back. "It is hard to find such reliable help. I depend upon the two of you to do tasks such as gain his form or make a potion. Instead, the shifter beats the dragon, and the sorceress can't get her nails dirty." He plucked the bottle from her hand. "Honestly, I have to do everything myself." Turning to Daron, Thorn took the opportunity to uncork the bottle and poured the contents into Daron's open mouth. Tossing the vile aside, it stopped in midair. Using his free hand, he quickly closed the dragon's mouth. As he went back to the place he was initially standing, time started again.

The glass shattered against the floor as Daron sputtered. Zec's fist only met air as he fell backward a few steps before catching himself. Icarri shot him a glare.

"If that leech Dane can do it faster, then why am I even here?" Magic crackled at her fingertips, giving him a warning.

He breathed another frustrated sigh. "Because, should we fail, I don't need the dragons hunting us down for kidnapping their king. We can make him forget our names and faces, but when it comes down to the entire dragon kingdom versus a noble vampire assassin, I doubt we can erase that many minds."

"What about Nadi?" Zec asked as he stared at Daron, who was seething.

Thorn smiled. "The voice of one is nothing but a conspiracy to the voice of many." He looked over Daron, "How long does the potion take?"

Letting the magic die, Icarri smoothed her dress. "It can take a few minutes to an hour, at most. Not all potions work instantly."

Daron growled, "What did you give me?"

Icarri pulled at one of her black curls as a grin crossed her face. "The same thing that I give to only the best servants, or soon-to-be servants. It makes you obedient to me in every way."

Daron looked around the room as he cursed, "I will never bow to the likes of you!"

"I don't think you have a choice," Thorn smiled.

Zec tapped the sorcerer on the shoulder. "If you could use a potion, why did you not use it on another dragon or Daron to begin with?"

Thorn looked at him, confused. "For one who lived around them for so long, you certainly do not know anything about them."

Daron lifted his head, "It's because we hunt for our food, and we mostly drink water. Only on our travels or for formal affairs do we eat cooked foods and drink wine. Harder to poison a dragon that eats fresh meat. He couldn't use me because we had no fertile eggs until now, and I am too weak to fly."

Suddenly, Daron winced. Shaking his head from side to side, he let out a low growl. Icarri came forward with a look of excitement as everyone else stepped back. The growl slowly turned into sobbing.

The Dragon King lifted his head again to show the tears streaking down his face, leaving trails of pale white skin beneath the dirt. He looked at Icarri, and the sobbing grew louder. "Mistress, please forgive me," he began to wail. "I had so many ill thoughts about you."

Shushing him, she ran her fingers over his matted blonde hair. "It's alright. You were not yourself."

"No, Mistress." He tried to wipe away the tears but managed to create more streaks of dirt. "I wanted to kill you, imagined my hands around your throat. It was joyful at that moment, but I find no joy in it now. Please, kill me, mistress. I deserve this punishment!"

"Now, now," she grabbed his chin. "I forgive you for your ill will, but I need you to do something for me."

His expression instantly turned into a joyful smile. "Anything, Mistress!"

"You see that young man there," she pointed to Zec. "I need you to give him your form."

Daron began to wail again. Every word that came out of his mouth was jumbled together with his sobbing. "I —sorry!"

"Hey Thorn," a buzzing call came from the sorcerer's pocket as a woman's voice echoed. "You're not going to like this."

Pulling out the glowing stone, he became annoyed at her untimely transmission. "What now?"

Daron became stuck on whatever he was trying to say. "I gave . . .I gave . . ."

The voice echoed, "I found that shifter boy and the Princess."

"And?" he watched as both Icarri and Zec turned towards him.

"Well, with the King, guards, and almost getting to watch an execution, it was hard to get close. That boy turned into—"

"I gave the form to Nadi!" Daron shouted as he caught his breath.

"Yeah, a dragon, and took the Princess away from the King," she finished.

Icarri grew pale as Thorn thought about smashing the sending stone against the ground. Zec became enraged, grabbing Daron by the collar.

"Stop!" Thorn yelled. "He is useless to us now." Thorn waited for Zec to let go of the collar. "Let us leave here and discuss our options."

Icarri looked at the crying mess of a dragon with an emotionless expression. "Go to sleep and don't wake up until someone comes for you."

Almost instantly, Daron was curled into a ball, sleeping. The sound of his snores filled the silence between them all. The whole situation, though, was far from peaceful.

Icarri stormed out of the room with Zec in tow. Thorn walked towards the stairs, his mind at a loss for what to do next. He thought about looking through the countless books in the library, but it would take another decade to even skim through most of them. Yet, he couldn't risk Zec finding out the truth of the sleeping leech vine. Killing Zec or Daron would get them nowhere.

Almost forgetting his one last task, he turned back and uttered an incantation. Floating wisps of light emanated from his hands and wrapped around Daron's head. Then it shattered like the breaking of glass before dissipating into thin air. When he awoke, he would not remember their names or faces.

Climbing up the staircase, he entered the hall. All nine Elders still clung to the ceiling, filling the room with dim light. Both Icarri and Zec seemed to be looking to him for the answers; unfortunately, they were all the same questions he had.

"What now?" Zec asked, fiddling with the sandal at his waist.

He thought about it for a moment. "Icarri, what materials do we have for dark magic?"

The sorceress cringed as she pulled a small book out from between her breasts. Flipping it open, she read: "One Phoenix feather, five unicorn hairs, ten large jars of black dragon bone dust, two mummified fairies—"

Thorn began leaving the room. "Keep reading. We need to find a book that can help us."

Icarri carried on as she followed, with Zec trailing behind. "Six changelings' spines, a vile of cursed gold flakes..." She began mumbling something about poison.

Thorn burst through the front doors of the temple. "I can't hear you."

"Wyvern Venom!" she shouted as she picked up her pace, "A case of vampire blood, and two harpy talons."

Thorn halted at the door to the library. "Why did you stop?"

"That's it," she turned the book towards him.

Rage filled him as he realized that many items on the list had a line through them. "You ask for food, wine, and dresses, but not for magical supplies?"

Icarri shrugged. "No need for magic supplies when an orb can keep me young forever."

Exasperated, Thorn ran his hand down his face. "Why did I not look elsewhere for assistance?"

"Because I'm the only sorceress within a hundred miles willing to team up with you." With a grin, she walked past him and into the library. "It was either me or the gallows. Plus, I have the finances you need to cover up any mistakes." Looking over her shoulder, she asked, "Do I need to remind you of the Wizard's Guild?"

Thorn did not respond. Instead, he strode into the library and began skimming the books. "Uses for Eye of Newt, Enchanting Your Undergarments, Tooth Fairy Trades." He was becoming flustered as he walked to a different shelf. "Illusory Manifestations?"

Icarri grabbed his arm, "Stop looking in the children's section and go to the areas that would be off-limits to anyone who can't see them." Dragging him up to the second floor, she stopped at a large painting of a dark angel. It was a male elf with long white hair, green robes, and enormous black wings. The sorceress released him and walked into the painting. To his surprise, the image of the elf faded as the room inside lit up. Cobwebs seemed to litter most of the open spaces around the room. A thick layer of dust clung to almost every book. Turning his attention to the lights, he noticed they were tiny white pillars with a magical flame. They almost looked like candles. "Here is the dark magic section of our library. Please make sure to tip your guide."

"Here is a tip," Thorn smirked. "If you don't want to get pushed off a balcony, you had better help me find what I'm looking for."

Without batting an eye, she plucked a book off the shelf and tossed it at him. He caught it and looked at the black leather cover with a skull on the front. "Summoning the Deceased," he shot her a confused glance. "How will this help us?"

"Black dragon bone dust," she replied as she took the book back and flipped through the pages. "We can summon one of the black dragons if we make it a host body."

Thorn began reading, "Summoning black dragons requires a host body made from the remnants of the bodies they cast aside. Only then will a soul be drawn to its newfound home. The black dragon can stay up to twenty minutes before returning to the shadows from whence it came." He snapped the book shut in frustration. "Twenty minutes is not enough time to retrieve a dragon egg."

The sorceress grabbed his chin and forced him to look towards the doorway. Zec stood with a nervous uncertainty about him. Slowly, he smiled as he looked at Icarri.

"Mixing magics!" he exclaimed. "This is why I chose you. We summon the black dragon, and Zec takes on the form—thus absorbing the dark magic. He would be an unstoppable force!"

Icarri lifted a large jar that was next to the bookshelf. Black dust filled the container to the brim. "You don't know how long I've been waiting to use this."

Thorn pulled out the sending stone and waited for it to glow. "Dane," he said happily.

The woman's voice crackled in response. "I was just enjoying a warm meal." As she calmly spoke, a woman's scream came through loudly, but was cut short. "And you thought my timing was awful."

Ignoring the sound of her killing, Thorn continued, "Get back to Icarri's manor and have the cloak set out. We all plan to return by the end of the day."

Chapter 37

The world had vanished around Nadi, and he found himself in the sands of his mind. Clouds of dust obscured the view of the sky. It swirled around him even though there was no breeze. Every once in a while, he could hear the thunder of a storm rumble. He seemed to be lost, but he could not remember how he had come to be here. The sand of this desert was black and familiar. Yet, he could smell the scent of something burning.

It seemed like hours he walked without seeing another soul. Looking behind him, his footprints had vanished as if they had never been there. He could hear a tune gruffly hummed as if by an enormous beast, but the storm seemed to hide it from him.

"Hello!" Nadi called out.

He heard a chuckle, "Only us two are here, boy." From the clouds of dust, a golden dragon emerged. "I'm here, finally alive and free. You can thank the Princess for that."

"The Princess?" He saw a flash of grey eyes in his mind. A tear-streaked face looking down at him as another image forced its way into his mind. "Kiran," he whispered as he began to remember. "Where is she?"

"Here," the dragon replied. With a flourish of a clawed hand, the clouds parted and revealed images in the sky. A damp cave with rain falling in front of the mouth came into focus. The vision moved to the Princess, huddled next to a dwarf with a large pack. Her dampened blonde hair stuck to the sides of her face and forehead.

The dwarf was dry, but he did not look amused. He wore simple traveling clothes but carried no weapons. A red braided beard protruded from his chin.

Around them were broken furniture and scattered firewood. Clothes and blankets littered the floor, no doubt due to the dragon's trespassing. The fire pit between the dragon and its captors was smoldering out. Kiran was shivering.

"You can't treat a human like that. She'll get sick or die." Nadi wanted to be there.

"So you want me to save the girl who betrayed you?" The vision stopped, and the dragon came off the dune to tower over him. "She could have left you to die a helpless shapeshifter, and yet she freed me."

Flashes of the soldiers surrounding him with crossbows ready blinded him. Seeing the vampire holding Kiran caused him to shake his head. The feeling of her hands around the collar, unclasping it, made him stiffen. Nadi reached for those hands, but they were never really there. His heart raced as he looked around, not sure what was real anymore. Looking toward the dragon, he began to sink into the sand.

"Face it—you're losing this battle," a grin slid across the dragon's sharp teeth. He walked back to where he had come.

From the edge of a dune, he saw black ears perk up. A rabbit slowly came out and folded them back as it eyed the dragon. Its body almost looked like the night sky. Closing the distance between them, Nadi could see that dark brown eyes practically blended in with the rest of its body. Edging its way to the shapeshifter, it began digging.

Nadi touched its head and it looked up at him with its big eyes. Even the rabbit seems to have a mind of its own and is not just a constellation.

The dragon huffed, and the rabbit made a mad dash for the highest dune. It leapt off the peak and found its place in the sky. It was then that Nadi remembered how his ability worked. He turned his attention to the sky, where all his stars were missing, and back to the rabbit constellation. He made his trade.

The world shifted, and Nadi was in control. He looked at the Dwarf and Kiran as he realized he was a rabbit. Hopping around joyfully, he knew he was free. He had to let Kiran understand he was in control.

It was gone in an instant. Back into the desert, Nadi was up to his waist in the sand. The rabbit dropped from its place in the sky and hid behind a dune. Pain flared in the center of his forehead, and it became stained with his blood.

The dragon reeled back and roared. It was almost like it had hit something, and then blood began trickling from the same spot as Nadi's forehead. It was then, Nadi realized how connected they really were.

He could see a part in the clouds. Kiran stood up and approached the dragon, with the dwarf reaching after her. "That must have been scary, but I can help you."

A growl came from the dragon that seemed to echo along with his voice, "Don't think I'm scared just because he gained control. I don't need your help."

"But you're bleeding." Kiran took another step towards him. "You hit the roof of the cave pretty hard. Please, let me heal you."

"No, I am fine on my own." He turned away from her, and the dragon focused on Nadi.

Before another word could be uttered, Kiran's voice caused the dust to settle. "If I don't heal it, you could get an infection. Lots of creatures can get sick or die from an infection."

The dragon huffed a frustrated sigh as he turned back, "Fine—if it pleases you."

Nadi caught a glimpse of Kiran grabbing onto the dragon's snout and closing her eyes. Suddenly, she was on the sand next to him. Grabbing onto his hand, she tried to pull him out, but he seemed to sink quicker.

Kiran stopped pulling and leaned in close. "Nadi, listen to me, this is your mind. You have control over everything here. You must believe in yourself to succeed."

"Kiran, I've only ever succeeded at disappointing the people around me. I failed at getting you to the Elders, failed at protecting Zec, and even failed to tame the dragon." The sand was now up to his chest as Kiran pulled harder. "I will never be able to face my father and my people. I have failed at being a leader and a guide."

"No, you haven't!" she whispered as she looked over her shoulder. "You led me away from the sorcerer, provided for me since I could not provide for myself, and have made me want to learn so much more about the world around me." Nadi started to rise from the ground, "I promise you—"

The dragon began thrashing around, and Kiran seemed to hold on tighter. The image from the sky showed Kiran hanging onto his snout for dear life as the dragon fought to shake her loose.

"I'm not going to let you go," she pulled harder. "Please, just believe in yourself!"

Suddenly, Kiran vanished, and Nadi jerked around. The dragon snarled and spun around. Nadi could hear Kiran scream, but it was cut short by the sound of her hitting the stone wall.

"NO!" Nadi cried out as he pushed against the sand.

"All humans are nothing more than traitorous, selfish creatures." The dragon glared down at him. "Stabbing each other in the back to get what they desire."

Worry filled the shifter as he listened, hoping to hear anything more from Kiran. But silence met his ears as he played back the dragon's words. Gritting his teeth, Nadi responded, "You're wrong." Rising out of the sand to his knees, he stared back at the golden-eyed glare. "Kiran just made a sacrifice for me. She put herself in danger just to try anything that might help me escape. That princess is human, and she already proved you wrong."

The beast chuckled, "She tried to deceive me to get to you."

Wiping the blood off his forehead, Nadi revealed that there was no wound. "Kiran still healed you." Pulling a leg free from the sand, he smiled with his newfound confidence.

The dragon looked disappointed. "I see you have risen from your losses. Rest assured, you'll sink again before reaching me."

"You know, I think I know what you are." Nadi managed to get his other leg free as he started towards him. "You're my failures. I've failed at so much, disappointing my father constantly. Yet, I know he'll never stop loving me, no matter how many times I fail his expectations. Sure, I face exile when I return home—but I'm going to achieve something great today. I'm going to change back into my human form. Unlike Elias, I am Nadi of the Púca Tribe, and I am good at disappointing those around me." He grinned as he came to a stop at the bottom of the hill. "Good thing you're the only one here to disappoint."

Flapping his wings, the dragon caused the air to become clouded with dust. "You are nothing but a nuisance."

"Really?" Raising both hands, he quickly moved them apart, and the fog cleared, revealing the dragon still standing in the same spot. "I never would have guessed."

Growling, the dragon's mouth began glowing, readying a blast to unleash. Suddenly, he sank into the sand, causing his head to lift towards the sky, and the blast was released into the air. Furiously, he flapped and jerked away from the sand, trying to free himself.

"Looks like the sand works both ways, but I'm afraid you're in my domain." Nadi began to slowly raise and lower his arms. The sand around him began to ripple. Soon, the dunes became waves crashing against one another.

The dragon struggled to get into the air as the ground began to bury him. Waves slammed against him, causing the dragon to work against the tide. Nadi watched as other animals started coming out of hiding. As the surf rose, an animal would find its place in the sky, forming a constellation. A rabbit, a mouse, and a squirrel almost seemed unnoticed. The owl flew in and found its perfect spot, along with the sparrow. One of the waves tossed the alligator into its place, just where it needed to fit in, and the small fox raced into its area. All was followed by the wolf, who trotted into its new home among the stars.

Nadi brought his hands together, and the sea of sand calmed. The dragon managed to pull itself from the dust and lifted itself into the air. "Enough of this!" He roared as he looked down at Nadi. "This body is mine now! All will fear me as a mighty beast, and I shall bring ruin to any kingdom that dares to rise against me!"

"No, this is my body, and I will not doubt myself any longer," Nadi smiled. "You just made a mistake."

Confused, the dragon looked around. "How?"

"I caused you to fear the ground, but what you should have been fearing was the sky." Just as he finished saying it, the dragon's wings turned black and became outlined with stars.

"No!" he thrashed, trying to get away. As his arms and legs also became one with the cosmos. "NO!" He wailed as his head joined the same fate as the rest of him.

Silence filled his mind as he stared up at his starry night that now held a moon as well. If someone else could witness this moment, they would not realize that Nadi had fought the hardest war of his life, and it happened to be against himself. He knew it was time to return to reality, even though he wanted to use the dragon's form himself. But Nadi understood it would have to wait.

Opening his eyes, he slowly picked himself off the cold, damp floor. A breeze blew through the cave and made him shiver. As he got to his knees, he saw Kiran lying motionless on the floor. The dwarf was standing over her, as though he were trying to protect her.

Scrambling to his feet, Nadi rushed to her side. He pulled her onto his lap, trying not to shout into her face. "Kiran! Please, Kiran, say something."

The dwarf shook his head, "Lad, that was a mighty blow you gave her. You may have broken something."

"But she's breathing," he looked to Cynthia, who had a worried look on her face. "Can we heal her?"

Cynthia closed her eyes and slowly shook her head. "You do not have magic, and neither do I at the moment. All we can do is wait and see if she pulls through, but I don't think the creature of wishes can help her now."

He pulled her closer to him and started to sob. Nadi realized that he might not get to see her smile or dance like they had at the Inn. The warmth of her healing touch wouldn't be there for him. His heart sank as he remembered how he had treated her. He regretted thinking of her as a burden. "I'm sorry. All I wanted to do was protect you and Zec. I don't want you to lose your life or your kingdom." Nadi pushed a few strands of hair off her forehead. "I like you more than I've liked anyone. Without this journey, I wouldn't have realized how much I needed you. Please, stay with me."

The dwarf laid a hand on his shoulder. "She told me how she wasn't going to give up on you; begged me not to hurt you." He picked a pipe off the floor and tapped it against the palm of his hand. "I have a trick I learned from a wizard during my travels." He picked up a small tin container and opened it. Nadi could smell the strong scent of tobacco as he pinched a small amount and packed his pipe. Taking a bit of smoldering wood from the floor, he lit it and took a few puffs. "That wizard was a heck of a fellow, but he was a dirty thief." He took out a small pouch and knelt beside Kiran and Nadi. As the dwarf opened it, all Nadi could see was ash, filled to the brim. Pouring some into his hand, he placed it under the center of Kiran's back.

Sparks rose from the dwarf's pipe as he hummed a tune. Kiran's body slowly became warmer as a glow lit her chest. Then it faded as Kiran gasped.

Sitting up, she coughed a few times and looked around. Then she met Nadi's tear-stained gaze. She began to cry as she wrapped her arms around him, "You won! You're really here."

Nadi couldn't be happier. He was glad to be able to hold her. "I thought I had lost you."

The sound of someone clearing their throat caused them to look towards the cave entrance. Keol stood there, glaring at Nadi.

A dragon guard next to him gave a warm smile, "I can see you're definitely not Elias, but maybe you need some clothes." He began rifling through a bag.

Keol snatched the bag and tossed it at the shapeshifter. "Here, Mutt. I'd appreciate it if you did not hold the Princess while you are nude."

Kiran looked at Nadi before shoving him away. Her face became bright red as she averted her gaze. Cynthia laughed as the dwarf shook his head.

Opening the pack, Nadi stared at the dragon clothing. "These are dragon clothes. Can I really wear them?"

The dragon nodded.

He quickly slipped on the pants, which were a little big on him.

"I'm Gage," the dragon said, seeming to be in a good mood. "I've come to take you to the keep to discuss the whereabouts of King Daron."

"So, are there any more of you showing up? Because this event is not an open invitation," the dwarf said unhappily.

Everyone looked at Keol, who let out a frustrated sigh. "No. I came to retrieve Kiran and go home."

"But Kiran needs to come with me," Nadi said as he eyed the open vest shirt. "We have to…" He trailed off as he watched the dwarf pick up an overturned table. "We have an errand to run back towards the docks."

"You have to run an errand," the dwarf repeated. "No! You have to clean up this mess you made and fix my home for me. I wasted the ashes of a Phoenix to bring back your female. The least you can do is stick around and help."

"Actually, I want to help you fix your home," Kiran curtsied to the dwarf. "As Princess Kiran Blackmore of Vadnera, I am at your service."

The dwarf bowed, "I am the hermit, Auric. You've had quite the ordeal. I can't request that you clean up the mess."

"I insist," she picked up a painting that had fallen off the wall and handed it to him.

Taking it, he stood and began walking towards a smaller room near the back of the cave. "I'll grab some cleaning supplies. It might take a moment since that dragon made a mess."

Chapter 38

Kiran watched Auric vanish into the room before turning to her companions. "I have to stay," she said, observing Nadi's eyes flash yellow as he looked confused.

"But you are needed at the temple." He reached for her hand, then stopped. A pained look crossed his face before he let out a frustrated sigh, and his arm dropped back to his side. "Why do you have to stay?"

"It's far too dangerous for me to go to the temple now. Thorn and Icarri are there, possibly anticipating your return." The Princess tucked a damp strand of hair behind her ear. "Nadi, if I go with you, it would only be putting me within Thorn's grasp."

Cynthia floated beside Kiran. "I have to agree. There is no telling if we would win this or not. Either way, we can't let Thorn get her."

"How am I going to do this alone?" Nadi seemed as though he were about to give up hope.

Gage put a hand on his shoulder, "You're not alone. I'm going with you. I need to bring you back to the keep."

"Then you can stay there and not come back," Keol eyed him with an amused expression. "That way, I can take credit for defeating a dragon and saving the princess."

"Don't listen to him," Cynthia put herself between them. "I'll be with you every step of the way, only in spirit though."

Kiran smiled as she pulled out a small pouch from her sleeve. Opening it, she retrieved a small piece of white chalk. Looking at Cynthia, she held it out for her. "Here, take this."

The dragon guard looked confused. "Who do you want to take it?"

"Cynthia," she said as she smiled at the spirit.

"Oh, real funny. Hand the spirit something to hold," Cynthia laughed as she reached for it, then gasped and quickly retracted her hand. The tips of her fingers shimmered as they started to become dense. "I touched it! I really touched it!"

Kiran's smile grew into a grin. "Now, you don't have to be alone." All of them watched as she began to appear before them physically.

"Is that an arm?" Keol asked as he gave a disgusted look.

"It is Cynthia," Kiran chided, turning back to Nadi. "I ended up creating an item from the Book of Creation. This one piece of chalk not only gave Cynthia the ability to become a living person until sundown, and will create a portal to the drawer's destination. To work, the drawing must closely resemble a doorway or archway in that area.

Once you pass through, it will also protect against time magic, as long as the sun is up. You can only use this chalk once."

Cynthia's feet touched the floor as her body materialized. Holding back tears of joy, she smiled at the vampire. "Hello, Keol. Nice of you to see me."

As her black feathered wings came into existence, Keol looked stunned. Slowly, she walked toward him. He grabbed her shoulders. "Is it really you?" he asked, watching her carefully.

"Who else would it be, you lecherous bug?" the dark angel laughed.

Gage stayed silent but seemed awestruck by the magic that was unfolding.

"Remember, that will only last for today," Kiran said, placing the chalk into Cynthia's hand. "I forgot to mention that you should also have all the same magic that you did when you were alive. That way, you can have a fair fight."

The dark angel waved her hands over herself, and her dress shifted into black armor. Turning back to Keol, she grabbed the sword at his hip and drew it. Swinging it around, she smiled. "This will have to do." With a wave of her hand, it changed into a different sword with wings as the guard. "Not the real thing, but...it will bring fear to Thorn."

Nadi stepped toward her. "What door are you going to draw?"

Giving it some thought, Cynthia put the chalk on the wall. "The portal all dark angels pass through before getting their wings." She began drawing a pattern with overlapping bands.

"I'll keep Auric busy," Keol said, walking towards the back of the cave.

Cynthia did not stop as she repeated the design on the other side. At the top was a circle with two smaller ones overlapping on either side. Just as she finished, the center began to glow. An image appeared of a wooded area with a tower in the background. Nadi seemed to stiffen at the scene.

"Times up," Cynthia said as she turned to Nadi. "Let's say our goodbyes."

The shifter looked down at his feet before turning around. Lifting his head, he met Kiran's gaze with dark blue eyes. "Thank you. You have been there for me every step of the way. Without you, I—I don't think I would have made it this far."

Kiran held back her tears. "Nadi, I know that you can't promise me that you'll live, but I hope that I'll get to see you again."

Smiling at her, he pulled her into his arms. "Remember, Princess. I am still your guide and have to return no matter what."

Cynthia was getting aggravated. "Just kiss and let's get going."

Both of them blushed as they released each other.

Gage walked through the portal and looked to be enjoying the change of scenery.

As Kiran clasped her hands nervously before her, the strings of the second pouch snared her fingers. She pulled it out, realizing it was the one that Nadi had always carried.

Handing it to him, she steered the conversation in a different direction. "Here—Keol found this after you transformed." As it left her hand, she thought to ask, "What is in there?"

Without opening it, Nadi responded, "A shard of a magic mirror." The shifter looked to the dark angel, and both walked into the portal.

Kiran could still see them on the other side. Her heart was racing as her mind filled with questions. The one that scared her the most was—what if he didn't return? She knew she had to tell him how she felt. "Nadi!"

Just as he turned, the portal closed, and the drawing vanished. Staring at the stone wall, Kiran touched her heart, which felt like it was going to burst. Taking a deep breath, she whispered, "I like you, too."

Nadi turned around, but he was only staring into a small cavern. A stone arch at the front of the cave, almost like the one that Cynthia drew. Nadi recalled that he had passed by it several times before, but it blended in with the foliage. Vines and moss coated its surface.

Turning to Cynthia, Nadi asked, "Do we have a plan?"

The dark angel smiled. "We currently have the element of surprise. The only problem is finding them before they realize we're here. We should—"

A blood-curdling scream cut her off, causing her to grab her sword. Nadi's blood ran cold as he realized that it was his brother he was hearing. "Zec!" The shifter yelled as he ran towards the sound. Jumping over a stump, he made his trade and landed on all fours as a wolf. As he got closer to the temple, the smell of something burning filled his nostrils, driving him to fear the worst. Reaching the stone walls of the building, Nadi shifted back and proceeded to round the corner.

Cynthia caught him and pressed him against the wall, covering his mouth with her hand. "What are you doing? We don't even know the danger that awaits us when we go out there. If we just run out into the open, we are nothing more than targets. We have to observe the scene without bringing attention to ourselves." She slowly released him. "Quietly—and without being seen!" She peered beyond the wall and cursed.

Gage planted himself behind Nadi, ready for anything.

Zec's screaming grew louder and almost had an unearthly echo to it. Leaning over, Nadi had to stop himself from crying out at the scene. Standing before Zec was a massive black dragon with red eyes. Its entire body appeared to be made of dust, moving and layered with shadows—and Zec was being covered in the dust as the darkness enveloped him. On the ground was a strange circular pattern with symbols that seemed to burn into the earth. Standing on either side of the circle were Thorn and Icarri. Both had their arms raised into the air, chanting something he couldn't understand. Green energy seemed to connect them as it encircled the dragon and the shapeshifter.

The dark angel pushed him back. "I'm sorry, Nadi. We have to wait until the spell is complete. If we interrupt them now, not only will Zec be killed, but it will scar this entire area with dark magic. It would take us out too, and nothing will ever grow here again."

"What about Zec?" Nadi wanted to cover his ears as the screaming turned into a roar.

Cynthia looked nervous as she slowly drew her sword. "Dark magic clings onto people who use it or are used upon. As a dark angel, I could normally expel it from my body by turning it into an item like the souls I would take. Yet, even by doing that, the victim of that magic loses something important to them. Sometimes it stains them by turning parts of their body black. Other times, they lose their voice or sight." She turned away as it started to quiet down, "There is no telling what he may lose—but he may never be the same again."

Clenching his fists, Nadi knew there was no way he could hide the truth from his father. He had failed at his one objective, and the only consequence he was going to face was exile. Even if he wasn't allowed to go home, Nadi had to try everything to save Zec no matter what.

"Go now," Thorn's voice rang out. "Get to the dragons' keep and return before nightfall with the egg so I can change you back."

A low growl came in response, and Zec took off. His black wings left a trail of an unearthly shadow with every flap. Nadi, Gage, and Cynthia watched as he soared over the mountain. The shifter hoped that no other harm would come to his brother, but he also prayed that Grumloc could hold him off long enough to get there.

Gage cursed, "Looks like I have no choice but to leave you here. I must warn Grumloc of the coming danger. Don't die, I'll wait to leave until the magic users are distracted."

Footsteps approached as Nadi crouched, and Cynthia readied her sword. Their enemies stopped a few feet away, and they heard Thorn chuckle. Leaning over, the shifter peered around the corner. Both Thorn and Icarri were smiling and conversing near the door to the temple.

"Once we get back, we should celebrate," Thorn said to the sorceress. "At *my* castle."

"Don't get ahead of yourself, Thadius. You still have to reverse time and make the Queen yours. You can save your father, but the competition will still be there." She sympathetically patted his shoulder. "Too bad the Princess got away."

"With the orb, I doubt my competition will even exist," he laughed. "I can't wait to be king."

"You're only going to be the King of Failure, Thorn." Cynthia stepped out and blocked their path to the temple.

A look of shock passed over both Icarri and Thorn. "Impossible—I killed you!" Thorn exclaimed as he took a step back. Quickly, he grabbed the orb from his vest and bathed everything in the grey light.

Nadi felt it come across him as a tingling sensation on his skin, but there was light emanating from both him and Cynthia. He stood up and strode to her side. "That won't work on us this time."

The light slowly faded, bringing the color back. "How?" Thorn put the orb away and pulled out his sword. "You should be a mindless dragon! This can't be real!"

Icarri raised her hands above her head, and a green wall surrounded all of them. It faded, and she cursed. "We're out of magic," she stated, bringing her arms back down.

Cynthia smiled. "Seems like you didn't count on us being here. Maybe we should make a bargain."

"What kind of bargain?" Thorn eyed them both suspiciously.

"We fight with our weapons only. No magic. If we draw blood on either of you, then you leave this place and never return." She looked at Nadi, making sure he understood. "If either of you can manage to draw blood on one of us, we have to let you succeed with your plan."

Icarri gave them a wicked grin as she reached for her boot. She drew out Zec's hunting knife and tossed it to Nadi, "I'm taking you on, my pet."

Thorn stared at the sword in Cynthia's hands. "Seems your cut may not be worth the challenge. I lose my soul even if you don't draw blood."

"I'll give you an advantage then," Cynthia put her right arm behind her back. "I'll fight you with one hand." The sword's form wavered.

His eyes narrowed. "No need, I was mistaken. That is not your sword." Looking at the temple, he became silent. "Where is your sword? I saw it was missing, but I just assumed the dust had covered it."

"Just one more thing to worry about if we win this." Cynthia took a swipe at him, and he brought his sword up to meet.

"You couldn't have found an apprentice!" He gritted his teeth as he pushed the blade away from himself. "The Elders are not able to give you magic."

Nadi was so absorbed in their fight that he almost didn't notice Icarri getting closer to him. "I had so many plans for you." Her grin was terrifying. "Too bad...because if I cut you, you're dead."

Dodging her, Nadi realized her blade was longer than his, and the sharp edges of the metal were curved and wavy. There was no guard on the handle, which left her fingers wide open. His only problem was that he had never fought with a knife. Drunken fistfights with other shifters, he had no problem with. Going against a crazed sorceress with a hunting knife, he was starting to feel cornered.

The clang of the swords hitting each other caught his attention again. "Are you sure you know how to use that?" Cynthia jabbed at Thorn. Missing his shoulder, she went on. "You're pretty slow for an old man, not like the kid that used to sneak into the castle garden."

"It was a shame I had to kill you," he retorted as he parried another blow. "You were always loyal to Lillian."

Suddenly, Nadi felt the tip of the knife against his chest. His head spun to meet Icarri's gaze, his eyes flashing orange with fear. Stumbling backward, the shifter tripped over his own feet and landed on his back. As he brought the knife up, Icarri kicked it out of his grasp. She planted her heel in the middle of his chest.

"Goodness, you are making this too easy." Leaning over him, she placed the dagger above his throat. "Looks like this is the end, my pet. Any last words?"

He saw a flash of gold as Gage flew over the mountain. He had hoped for one last distraction from the dragon, but it didn't come. He could only hope to get out of this mess.

"Nadi!" Cynthia called, but her attention was quickly grabbed back by Thorn attempting to slash at her.

Looking at the knife, it was too far out of his reach, along with any sticks or rocks. He brought his arms back to his sides as he felt the tip of the knife pressing against his throat. His fingers touched the small pouch that had slipped out of his pocket when he fell. Working his fingers inside the opening, he touched the smooth surface of the glass.

"Nadi!" Cynthia cried out again. Thorn was not giving her any room for movement as he swung wildly.

"Well?" The sorceress's face was inches from his. "How about a kiss?"

Pulling the shard into his hand, he met her gaze. "You're not my type." With that, he swung his hand, the fragment of the mirror catching against her cheek.

Jerking back, Icarri touched the bleeding scratch that stretched from her cheekbone almost to her nose. She opened her mouth as though trying to speak, just as black webs spread out from the wound. Letting out a scream, she fell backward and cupped her face. She dug her heels into the ground, looking around fearfully. Then she began crying hysterically.

"No!" Thorn dropped his sword and ran to her side. Pulling her into his arms as she fought, he removed the orb from his vest. Grey light bathed her, but the wound did not close. Cursing, he put the sphere back and touched her head as he whispered something. Icarri fell limp.

"Looks like you have lost," Cynthia said to the sorcerer as she helped Nadi to his feet.

Glaring at Nadi, Thorn responded, "You said no magic."

"So I did," she eyed Nadi. "But I did not say no magical items." Turning back to the sorcerer, she picked up his sword and held it out. "Either way, you have lost. Make your blood oath."

Letting out an exasperated hiss, he snatched it from her grasp. Thorn fumbled as he attempted to put it back on his waist. Then he pried the dagger from Icarri's fingers. Staring at Cynthia, he drew the blade across his palm, "I, Thadius Thorn, shall never return to the Elders' Enclave once I leave." His blood formed a red circlet around his wrist.

"Now leave and never return," Cynthia pointed her sword at Thorn, watching him stand with Icarri in his arms.

As they approached the doors, a strange creature appeared with long ears like a rabbit and big yellow eyes. It had long fingers and toes as well as a lengthy tail. It was familiar to Nadi. "Welcome back, Madam Cynthia," it said in a shrill voice. "I'm so happy you are bringing order to the Elders' Enclave. Might I ask if I can also help? I can assist in waking the Elders. Please, can I go inside?"

Cynthia drew her hand down her face. "Skadi, you know I can't invite you in. The Elders will have my head if I break the rules."

"But who will care for the Elders once you leave?!" It hopped forward, blocking her path. "Who will ensure that the vine does no lasting damage? Can I please come in just this once?"

"Are you a Púca?" Nadi asked, remembering the flags of his people bearing the same creature.

"Yes," Cynthia said, then her eyes widened. "No, no, no!"

"You said yes!" Skadi dashed to the temple doors and opened them. "I can finally enter the temple again!"

The dark angel glared at Nadi.

"Sorry," he said as he watched the creature happily hop inside.

Together, they all followed him in. Down the corridor, Nadi looked at the place where the sword, Fallen, once floated. It seemed like so long ago when Nadi had been in here, but only a week had passed since touching the sword. He wondered then what kind of dark angel Kiran would turn out to be.

Following the group into the chamber with the Elders, Nadi eyed every corner of the room for signs of movement, and the vines' slow coiling caught his gaze.

Thorn lifted the cloak as he looked around the room one last time. "Answer me this, Cynthia. Why did my father have to die?"

She gave him a solemn look. "It was a mistake. We didn't know it was your father. We were just told that a murderer was hiding in that home and...did as ordered."

"My father was a carpenter, not a murderer," he shook his head. Stomping one foot on the ground, he shouted, "Libero!"

Both Nadi and Cynthia looked at each other before looking back at Thorn. "What did—"

"I can't say the same for you, Cynthia. You are a murderer." With that, he spun around with the cloak on and vanished.

As the fabric hit the floor, the symbols ignited. Nadi watched as the cloth vanished from the circle before it died out. He almost wondered why it had not done that when he had taken it.

Skadi stood in front of the leech vine's seed. Cynthia raised her sword and, with a swift downward stroke, cracked it open. The vine began to slowly shrivel up as each Elder fell to the floor, one by one. Without missing a step, she strode to the torch on the wall and pulled it before vanishing into the hidden stairwell.

Nadi started to follow when Skadi grabbed his pant leg. "Young shapeshifter?" the Púca called. "Thank you for helping me get back in. To show my gratitude, I want to gift you with the ability to speak while in any animal form."

"What?" Nadi asked, but he felt the warmth of the magic seep into him and travel into his throat. He gave him a kind smile. "Anything for our tribe's patron." Just as he turned to leave, Nadi suddenly thought of a good question to ask. "Skadi, what trick did you play on the elders that was so horrible it caused the shapeshifters to be cast out into the desert?"

Tugging at one of his long ears, he took a moment to answer. "I'm not the best god, and back then, I thought it would be funny to impersonate an Elder and have one of your tribe members fall in love with them. I convinced the poor girl to stand before the Elders and pronounce her love for the one I impersonated. Yet, they did not take it so lightly. They could see she spoke the truth and stripped the accused Elder of his power. Then they banished him and the entire Shifter tribe from the enclave. I have felt horrible ever since—but please do not hold it against me."

Kneeling, he rubbed the head of the trickster god. "We all make mistakes, and sometimes we just need to live with them." Rising, Nadi turned around and slipped into the stairwell.

Chapter 39

Modra stood in the entryway to the keep, staring out over the desert. The last members of her tribe were released earlier that day, but still, it seemed too calm. She had been restless, wandering the halls and checking on the progress she had made. Ronja was always by her side as she tried to decipher what was bothering her.

The cooks in the kitchen were planning something exquisite with the rabbit meat they had brought back from the market near the airship port. Modra and the caravan had never gone near the port; they avoided it at all costs. It was not in their migration path. Plus, from the sounds of it, they would have a lot of competition in the market. Their route was always a circle, leading to three out of four dragon keeps.

The maids had discussed the dullness of dusting, but seemed to have been finding lost items. They almost had a mountain of things that needed owners. For some of the items, Modra would have suggested tossing. A bent ring, a dragon's tooth, and a handkerchief with the initials "IV" stitched onto it were among the debris. They gossiped over which princess it may have belonged to.

Guards seemed to greet her as though she were part of the family. When she passed them in the hall, they would wave or stop their conversation to share a few words. She thought it was amazing how she had managed to turn the keep around in a week. From doom and gloom, to almost the shining palace she remembered walking into.

The keep almost seemed empty with all the other dragons on patrol. She would have checked on the eggs, but the keep was a maze of passageways, and Ronja stated that she did not have permission to take her there. The eggs were off-limits.

Now, she was simply uneasy. It had been hours since her people had set out, but she felt as though something was wrong. She paced in the entryway to the keep, trying to remember if she had forgotten anything. Ronja stood at attention, watching as she walked back and forth.

Grumloc grumbled from the dais, "Stop that. You're making me nervous."

Stopping, she looked up at Grumloc. "I have a bad feeling, but I can't put my finger on it. Did I forget something?"

"No," Grumloc stood up and stretched his wings. "I, too, feel that something is amiss. The birds have grown silent, and the squirrels have gone into hiding." Walking to the entryway, he looked over the desert. "Something must be approaching."

Modra looked over the dunes again. It seemed so calm as she watched the sand shift with the breeze, covering up the footprints. Clouds dotted the sky and slowly moved, leaving their shadows across the sand. She almost wanted to stand in the sun and feel its warmth. Yet, the feeling kept nagging at her.

"Can you tell where—" Modra began, but was interrupted by a dragon landing on the steps to the keep.

Transforming back into their human form, Gage knelt in front of his king. "Grumloc, a dragon of shadow, approaches. I raced here as soon as I could. It is coming from the east."

"Of shadow?" Daron eyed his guard and then looked at the two guards and Ronja. "The black dragons have no physical form. They cannot do any harm here."

Standing, Gage looked worried. "This was made of dark magic." He eyed Modra. "It is Zec."

Modra nearly fell to her knees at the mention of her son's name.

"Magic," the Dragon King hissed as he planted himself at the entrance. "Why would they resort to magic? They have Daron."

Gage eyed everyone standing around him. "Nadi was given Daron's form. He managed to overcome the beast within, but he was facing off with the magic users when I parted ways." Concern washed over his face as he took in all that was around him. "Is this all we have?"

Growling, Grumloc did not say anything. He stared out, waiting for the monster to appear. But only sand moved before the keep.

"Maybe you should send Gage out to find the other dragons, and we can try to stall until they arrive?" Modra suggested out of fear for her son.

The dragon turned his head towards the chieftess. His stare was cold and calculating. Eventually, he nodded and whispered, "Libero."

The collar around her neck opened and hit the ground, leaving a ringing echo through the hall. She stared at him in confusion. "Grumloc, why are you freeing me.

"Because you are my greatest ally." He turned to Gage, "Go find the others and have them return immediately." Looking at Ronja, he smiled. "Protect her at all costs." He turned to the two guards, "If I fall, do not let it reach those eggs. Warn those in the keep of the danger."

Everyone left except Modra and Ronja. The shapeshifter picked up her collar and clicked it shut. She had no intention of leaving and planned to see this through to the end. "I'm not going anywhere."

"Then we fight to the end," he grinned.

An eerie roar filled the air, and the sky darkened. They watched as an enormous black dragon hit the sand, causing the dust to rise. Its red eyes locked onto Grumloc. As its gaze found Modra, she stiffened. Fighting the urge to run, she stood her ground, knowing that it was her son.

"Grumloc," the voice held an echo that caused the hairs on the back of her neck to rise. "I've come to avenge my mother!"

The Dragon King took a step back as his eyes widened. Modra focused on the monstrosity as she spoke to Grumloc, "Stand your ground. Do not show fear."

"Modra," he lowered his head. "That creature is Zec. I don't want to hurt him, but if I face him, I may not have a choice."

Her heart began to race as fear gripped her. He was right. They needed to find another way. Gaining her strength, she took her first step outside the keep in ten years. "Then I'll speak to him."

"You're not going alone." Ronja was by her side.

"No, it's too dangerous," Grumloc tried to argue.

"If we can solve this without conflict, it would be best." Modra began walking down the steps.

The black dragon's voice boomed, "Sending women to fight your battles! You are so weak compared to me now!"

"Enough," Modra discarded her shawl. "Zec, I am alive!"

The dragon's red eyes seemed to pierce her soul. "That is impossible. I watched you die."

"No," Modra stopped at the bottom of the steps. "You watched me vanish from the room. I was transported to a cell where I was kept. It was the same for everyone else who went missing. Please stop this. There is no need to fight. We can fix this."

There was a moment of silence as he lowered his head. "No, I need a fertile dragon egg to change back. I will reverse time so that none of this ever happened."

"Reverse time? Zec, please explain!" she pleaded.

"The sorcerer can return me to normal with a fertile egg. He promised to correct the wrongs that were committed against us once he stops the death of his father." Smoke began to rise from the corners of his mouth. "I'll fix everything."

"Run!" Ronja yelled as she jumped in front of her and transformed. Her golden form was different from what she had seen. Ronja's body slithered around the chieftess, and her wolflike head bared its fangs. Modra braced herself on the steps as a blast hit Ronja, leaving black flames across the sand. Ronja let out a roar as she gained her footing.

Before the mixed dragon could retaliate, a gold dragon landed between them. Modra stopped at the top of the steps and turned back. She was staring at the dragon, but she also saw Daron being held by a dark angel.

The dark angel looked at Ronja, "Take King Daron and get him to safety."

Looking up, the gold dragon met her eyes as his went from orange to blue.

"Nadi?" Modra whispered to herself.

Grumloc pulled her into the keep with his clawed hand. "We have more company than we were intending." He nodded towards the horizon, where the flags of the Púca tribe showed over the dunes. They marched toward the keep and only stopped once the black dragon was in view.

The dark angel stepped inside and bowed. "Lord Grumloc. We have returned King Daron, but he needs attention. He is in a weakened state, but is alive."

Ronja carried him in her jaws and gently set him down on the cold stone floor. He was almost bone-thin, covered in filth. A scraggly beard protruded from his jaw, and his once fine robes were nothing but dirty rags. His scales were not as shiny as they used to be.

The gold dragon backed into the keep as he kept his eyes on the black monstrosity. He stopped halfway in. "Any plans?" he asked in a gruff voice without turning back.

The dark angel rose and turned around. "Not yet. He is surrounded by dark magic and dust. We need to get to Zec so that I can do something. Can I count on you, Nadi?"

Modra reached out and touched the dragon's cold, smooth scales. His head turned, and she saw his eyes change to a lighter shade of blue. "Nadi? Is that you?"

He nodded, "Yes, Mother. It is I, but I'm fine. There is nothing to worry about."

"Young Nadi, a dragon?" Grumloc held his head up high as he mused. "Don't let your clan know. We don't need everyone trying to change into a dragon." He looked around the room. "And no one here is to breathe a word of it."

A roar sounded from the black dragon. "Are you afraid of me now? Cowering in your cave!"

"Time's up," the dark angel tapped the flat edge of her sword against Nadi's flank. "We need to fight now."

"Nadi," Modra called as he took a step. "Be safe and bring your brother back alive."

A sad look crossed Nadi's face, and he nodded, "I promise, I'll try." With that, he leaped off the steps of the keep and glided towards Zec. The dark angel spread her wings and followed.

Modra clasped her hands and prayed. "Oh gods of old and Elders, please protect my sons."

Chapter 40

Nadi landed in the sand before the black dragon. Its red eyes were burning with hatred. He did not want to fight his brother. If anything, he hoped to help him peacefully. "Brother, stop this. Mother is safe. You can return to the tribe. Thorn and Icarri retreated. They are no longer waiting for you." Cautiously, he took a step forward, "You don't have to do this anymore."

A haunting laugh emanated from the dark creature, "Do you know what it's like, living in your shadow?" Smoke rose from Zec's nostrils, "The thieving drunkard son of the chief, next to rule the tribe. I, who slaved every day to ensure our people did not see Father as an idiot for keeping you around, had to fix your messes constantly. The first shifter to almost face exile in a hundred years—but still, the tribe praised you. Nadi has a new form. Nadi is good with predators." Black flames began dropping from his mouth, causing the sand it touched to turn into black glass. "Father favored you, but you took away my chance to show Mother that I can be even better."

Nadi jumped to the side as Zec released a blast. The sand instantly turned into jagged black shards upon impact. He realized that this magic would ruin the desert.

Cynthia glided and landed on the back of his neck, holding herself there with one of his spines. "This is bad. Those shards are full of dark magic. It means the spell is not stable and could leak into the land." She took flight again. "Don't touch those shards!"

It was easier said than done. The ground under Zec's feet was also turning to glass with each step. Nadi wanted to prevent this. "Zec, stop! Look at what you are doing to the desert! If you continue, nothing will be able to live here!"

"The cost to reverse the mistakes of the past," Zec took a swipe at Nadi. His claws grazed his cheek.

"You can't reverse this," Nadi tried to keep the beast in the same place by circling him. "Thorn tried with Icarri, but nothing can fix dark magic. It clings to the darkness inside you and will not let go. There may be a way we can help you—but you need to stop!"

Zec lunged and dug his fangs into Nadi's throat. Letting out a cry of pain, he swiped at the beast with his claws, but they only passed through the black dust. For a moment, they briefly made contact with something before the dragon released him and backed away. On the tip of one of his golden claws, Nadi could see blood. He had made contact with Zec.

"Not as solid as you thought," Nadi said. Feeling the blood dripping down his neck, he shook it off. "Looks like you're really not a dragon after all." He watched as the glow in the red eyes seemed to deepen. "You pick on me for being a drunkard, but I am sober. I think you deserve a jab at your confidence." Zec fired another blast that missed and hit the sand behind him. "At least I'm real. You're just dust and magic!" Nadi moved back as Zec swatted at him. "Can you turn back into your human form? Because I can!"

The monstrosity laughed, "What game are you playing?" He took a step towards him. "You act as though having that form means something, but you underestimate the power I hold. The dragon within me explains how to use all of their abilities." He swung a paw at the ground, kicking up sand and shards of glass. Nadi covered his face.

Zec took advantage of the moment and shoved him backward. Falling onto the sand, Nadi watched the dust settle, realizing how close his brother was to winning. Beside him, in the sand, was a solid spike of glass. He couldn't take any more chances. Zec had to go down.

Getting back up, Nadi flapped his wings as he raised himself onto his hind legs. The sand lifted into the air and surrounded them both, a tactic he needed to use to stay hidden. Quickly, Nadi transformed back into a human. A blast of black fire roared above his head as he slid the knife out of his pocket and tossed it onto the ground; a risky decision. Then, shifting again, Nadi became an owl. Grabbing the handle with his taloned feet, he lifted himself into the air and out of the dust.

Cynthia met him as he glided over the scene. "Have you figured anything out?"

Black fireballs shot wildly out from the cloud of dirt below. One hit the steps of the keep. Another hit the mountainside, while a third exploded against the dunes, causing some of the tribe to run. A few of them shifted into birds and took to the sky. Out of the crowd, Nadi could see his father looking up at them.

"I think only certain parts of him can be solid at a time," he found his voice was slightly different as he spoke. In this form, it was a somewhat higher pitch. "I grazed Zec with a claw, but I think he is going to keep his distance or guard himself now. We need to figure out how to pull some of that darkness away from him."

"I might have something for that," she said, as they started gliding lower, doubling back. "A starlit blessing was said to drive away the darkest of shadows, but it will make any weapon glow as bright as a star for at least an hour." Whispering a few words, her sword and the hunting knife began to glow brightly.

Above the keep, several gold dragons now perched, watching the scene below. They eyed the two of them as more landed around the keep. Nadi saw that they were a terrifying force.

Focusing on the head that peered out from over the clouds of dirt, Nadi swooped in low. Coming across the back of the neck, he dragged the blade through the blackened dust. Cynthia used her sword and went across the chest. Zec roared in anger as light filled the wounds. Turning his head, he could see the beast using its wings to fan the dust away.

"We either need to finish him off now or get the dust to rise again," Cynthia called urgently as they began to come back towards the dunes.

Nadi parted and headed towards the tribe. He might need a little help that only they could provide. Quickly, he glided in and shifted, landing before his father. The knife hit the sand before his feet. He was sure he was facing exile for everything so far, but he had to try. "Father, I did my best to protect Zec."

"Nadi?" Sova looked shocked but quickly became serious. "What do you mean?"

"Zec was fooled by a sorceress into believing that he could bring his mother back. She pinned us against each other and convinced him to become a dragon by using dark magic." Nadi watched as his father's gaze flashed red, then orange. "I tried to stop him, but he's out there right now," pointing at the black dragon, he watched as the last dust clouds settled. "Cynthia is the dark angel that may be able to help him. We just need to keep him distracted long enough for her to reach him. This is the only time I'll ever ask for your help. Please—help me save Zec."

Sova's eyes slowly turned to a dark blue as he looked over his tribe. He plunged the staff into the sand. "Looks like the dragons need our help, even though they held some of you captive for years. Before this so-called war, they were our friends, even our family. Yet, there is no justice in this world if we let one of our own fall victim to revenge. There is a dark angel out there fighting to save him. She is the only one who can do it." Everyone looked towards the field where they watched as Cynthia, with her sword glowing brightly, dropped toward Zec like a shooting star, slashing at one of his wings. He retaliated by blasting the air with black flames. "We can distract him long enough for her to get in and save Zec. I do not ask you to fight, but to simply create a diversion. If you feel that it is too dangerous, you can watch it from a distance. We simply need to buy them time."

Zec smiled as his father looked him in the eye. "Thank you."

"No need to thank me yet." His father shifted into a horned owl, his clothes falling onto the sand. Letting his wings carry him, he flew towards the battlefield. Several others changed into different birds and followed. Their clothes littered the dune.

Happy to have their assistance, Nadi changed back into his burrowing owl form, grabbed the knife, and returned to the battle. As he closed the distance, Cynthia joined him again.

Eyeing the flock as they dove, swooped, and rose again, she said, "I don't know if this makes things better or worse."

Members of the tribe swarmed before Zec's face, and confusion ensued. They gave Cynthia the perfect cover for each of her slashes. Nadi aimed for a spot at the back of the creature's head. Dragging the blade through it, light erupted from the wound.

Dragons began to come off the mountain. They created a wall between the keep and the threat to their home. Soon, they encircled him, ensuring there was no way to escape.

Zec lowered his head and stretched out his wings. Black smoke came off his wings and began to cover the ground. A few of the shifters touched it as they flew by and instantly dropped back into the fog, and the rest scattered into the air. The dragons backed away; a few flew into the sky to escape it.

"Get back," Cynthia yelled from above.

Nadi cursed as he caught up to her. "Don't tell me that —"

"They're alive," she interrupted. "We have to finish him off, though. If he steps on them, there will be no bringing them back."

The fog began to fade. Nadi realized it was his only shot. Taking his chance, he dove, aiming for the eyes of the beast. Gripping the knife tightly in his talons, he pushed the shining blade towards his target.

A red glowing eye found him as he closed the distance. Zec lowered his head, and Nadi's blade dragged across his forehead. In one swift movement, the beast swung his head up, knocking the knife from his grasp and sending him tumbling towards the desert below. Quickly, he shifted back into his human form, hoping to change into anything that could take the impact.

Yet, as he slammed against the steps of the keep, he heard a sickening crack as pain flooded his leg and back. The air left his lungs, and he struggled to breathe. As soon as enough air seeped in, Nadi screamed. He'd been down and still for too long.

Leaning over him, the beast lowered his head. The light faded from the wound, and Nadi screamed in pain again. Zec, covered in the darkness and eyes glowing red like burning embers, laughed at his brother. "Looks like today the sun will set on your life and will rise only if I choose so." He began lifting a clawed hand.

Suddenly, Cynthia dropped in from above, landing on his snout. She placed her hand into the gap, cupped his face, and began to glow. The darkness latched onto her as it began to peel away from Zec. He seemed almost frozen as she pulled the dark magic into herself.

"No, Cynthia!" Nadi yelled, wincing from the pain. Stretching out his arm, he tried to reach her. It was no use. Her wings, if possible, grew darker than they already were. Shadows began to seep out of her feathers and cover her body. "Stop it!" Nadi screamed at her. "You'll die!"

Cynthia did not respond. She kept her hold as the darkness ate away at her. It fit her hand like a glove as the dragon began to deteriorate. Slowly, they both lowered onto the sand as the last of the shadow dragon dissipated. A small shadow broke off and dashed for a nearby rock. Zec collapsed onto the ground before the keep. The dark angel used her sword as a crutch. Turning, she revealed that the darkness covered half of her face and gave her one red eye.

Quickly, Nadi tried to back away. Pain flared through his left leg and back, stopping him from moving. The entrance of the keep was too far for him to escape. He turned back as a wicked grin crossed her face. Nadi knew he was dead.

The look vanished as she shook her head. "I…must remain…in control." She grabbed onto Nadi's leg, and he could feel warmth flood into him as the pain began to lessen. "Try…not to…move," she got out as she released him and wandered towards the desert.

"Where are you going?" he tried to shift his weight, but pain shot through his back.

Cynthia did not answer but seemed to be mumbling something to herself. Shifter birds began to awaken and flew off towards the rest of the tribe. Some stayed to watch from a safe distance as the dark angel hobbled towards the largest shard of black glass. It was smoothed from Zec turning in place. Walking onto it until she was in the center, she raised the sword, then stabbed it into the surface. The sand blew out in all directions. From her hands, the darkness began pouring into the blade. The black glass in the desert started to vanish. Nadi could almost see the shards break down into sparkling flecks and head towards Cynthia. Slowly, the blade became encased in the glass.

Just before all the dark magic left her, she released the sword's handle, and a bright light flooded the area.

Nadi shielded his eyes and called out to her, but he realized he could not hear his own voice. The wind picked up, even causing the dragons to grip onto the mountainside around the keep. He tried to force himself up, only to feel the pain of injury surge across his back.

Grumloc loomed over him, seeming to block the blast. "Are you alright, Nadi?" His voice was barely audible.

Tapping his chest twice, Nadi signaled that everything was fine. Peering around one of his legs, he could see the light fade, and a glass statue stood in before the dark angel. A black and gold dragon locked in battle was the gleaming result of her releasing the magic. Gently, she fell to her knees before collapsing onto the ground.

"Cynthia!" he yelled.

The tribe cheered from upon the dunes as two of the dragons glided towards the dark angel. Grumloc scooped up Nadi in his gold talons and whisked him into the keep. Once inside, Grumloc slowly lowered him onto the floor.

Nadi could see the four dragons of the land perched above him in stone. It was his favorite scene, and he missed how Daron would tell him the story of the battle and how they had made peace with one another. Knowing that he faced exile after this, he knew that even the dragons' keep would be off-limits to him.

A warm hand touched his cheek, and he found himself looking into his mother's dark blue eyes. "Oh, Nadi. I'm so glad you changed back. I was so afraid you had sacrificed everything for your brother." A tear landed on his forehead.

He reached up and touched her face. "I would do anything to protect him. I'm just sorry I didn't listen to you so many years ago."

"Let's move Zec into a room," Grumloc's voice boomed. "Take Nadi and the dark angel to the war room. Have Sova meet us there." Just as Modra stood to argue, Grumloc lowered his head to her. "Watch over Zec. He might be missing something with all that dark magic he was using."

One of the dragons shifted back to their human form and lifted Nadi over his shoulder. "I see my clothes did you some justice," Gage laughed as he walked down the hallway.

Nadi couldn't see his face. He watched another dragon carry Zec in and his mother look him over before they turned around a corner. "These clothes are nice. I like the fact that I don't lose them when I shift."

"Keep them, I have others to replace them." They made a few more turns through the corridors.

The guard strode into a room and gently placed Nadi on a pile of cushions before stating, "Wait here for the others to join you." He took his leave.

The room drew Nadi's attention. Crystals on the walls provided ample lighting, as there were no windows. Many different colors were carved into the floor as a map of the world, with cushions lining the map's outskirts. A painting of the war of the four dragons hung on the wall.

Daron, shaved, cleaned, and in new robes, sat at one side of the room. He smiled at Nadi as he sat up. "So, young one. How did you like being a dragon?" he asked, sipping from a steaming cup in his hand.

"It was different," Nadi said as the door opened again. Another dragon holding Cynthia entered and laid her down next to him. He touched her shoulder. "Are you alright?"

She gave him a weak smile and a short wave with her left hand.

Nadi's eyes locked onto the movement as he realized her hand was still black. It had claws and scales. She even stopped to look at it. "Dark magic has its price," she mumbled.

"I'm curious," Daron said from across the room. "You took in all that dark magic and released it. Yet, your wings are still black. I heard many tales of the magical items they create, but after they release the souls, their wings were no longer black."

"Call it a curse," Cynthia propped herself up to meet his gaze. "I was the first dark angel to come out with my wings as black as night. I lost my kingdom, and yet every kingdom wanted me in the hopes that I could grace them with an item. That's why I chose Vadnera to contract with."

"Because they already had the book?" Daron mused.

"Because the Queen was smart and did not greed for anything but adventure," she seemed deep in thought as she said that.

The door opened again, and Sova strode in. His gaze immediately locked onto Nadi.

"How much trouble did you cause the tribe now?"

"Calm down, old friend," Daron called, and Sova spun around. His jaw hung open as his walking stick hit the floor. "What, have you seen a ghost?"

"It can't be. I watched you vanish," the chieftain walked over to his friend. He seemed to have a million questions, but the right one would not surface.

"Nadi, here, managed to find me in the bleakest of moments," Daron smiled at him. "Your son is a hero."

"A hero?" Sova looked at him, confused. "But he's a thief."

"Not anymore," Nadi said as he grabbed the walking stick off the floor and pulled himself up. Ignoring the pain, he stood to face his father. "On my journey, I overcame my selfishness with the help of the Princess of Vadnera and Cynthia."

"The Princess of Vadnera?" Sova shook his head in disbelief. "I saw the wanted poster of your kidnapping her. A ship to the mainland can take at least a month. How did you return so quickly?"

Before Nadi could respond, Daron interjected, "That's why I want to talk to you—because there are a lot of things that will not make sense until you hear the entire story."

A guard pushed the door open, and Grumloc lay his head next to the opening. Sova took his seat next to Nadi as he sat back down, cringing in pain. The room became silent as everyone looked at Daron.

"Nadi, it's time for you to tell us the entire story, even the part about the Elders." He took another sip of his tea before placing it on the floor.

Looking at Cynthia, she nodded her approval to tell them the one thing he knew he should keep secret.

Chapter 41

Sova sat in silence as Nadi finished his tale. He took a few deep breaths, and it made the young shifter nervous. Seeming to study everyone in the room, the chieftain stroked his beard. "It's still hard to believe," he shook his head.

"Which part?" Daron asked as another guard brought in a platter of fruits.

"All of it!" He seemed to lose himself as his voice echoed through the room. "My son, a dragon? The Elders defeated by a pair of magic users? And a dark angel back from the dead?"

"Temporarily," Cynthia chimed in.

"Yes, because death is now a temporary thing?" Sova scoffed. "What about you, Daron? Do you honestly believe this?"

Smiling, he set down his plate. "Sova, if I did not live through it myself, I would not be here to say it is all true." He stood up and stretched. "Aside from that, there was something I had wanted to discuss with you before I was taken." Placing a hand on his shoulder, he seemed unsteady on his feet. "It seems that the King of Vadnera had married into the throne in the hopes of getting his hands on the Book of Creation. In the wrong hands, it could cause chaos to run free in this world. We do not know what his intention is with it, but so far our intel has stated that he has not gotten his fingers on it."

"What does this have to do with us?" Sova seemed confused.

A different guard came forward with a scroll and handed it to him. It was an older scroll and looked stained with time. The letter "V" on the red wax seal told Nadi it was from Vadnera.

"I received this many years ago, and hoped that I could share it with you," Daron opened the scroll and passed it to Sova. "The King of Vadnera, after taking the throne, had insisted upon the slavery of almost every kind of magical creature who held no fortune and were not in the higher class standing. We assume that the King has a secret hatred for almost anything that is not human. Yet, he keeps an alliance with the vampires. It does not make any sense." He gave him a sad look, "I don't want to keep any secrets from you. King Lucin is hiding something with these slave trades, and he's making a profit in the process."

Seeming defeated, he looked up at Daron, "What can we do?"

"Well, I have an idea, but I have to tell you one of the greatest secrets that only the leaders and those closest to them must know." Daron took the scroll out of his hand and rolled it up. "I want to create a shared kingdom with the shapeshifters, but if you agree, I must tell you our greatest secret, and when I do, you can never breathe a word of it, or I'll have to kill you."

Sova shot him a wary glance. "Do I want to know?"

The Dragon King nodded. "It follows along with Nadi's story."

Turning to stare at his son, Sova asked, "So, to hear this secret, I must agree to create a city with you for my people to thrive, or the slave traders will continue to hunt us down?"

"And if you tell my secret to anyone, I'll be forced to kill you," Daron gave a smile.

"I guess I don't have much of a choice," he glanced at Nadi one last time. "What is this secret?"

"The story of the four dragons who fought over the desert was a lie," The Dragon King turned to the picture on the wall. He pointed to the white star in the center. "The dragons had fought over who was going to protect the Elders' Enclave. When the creature of wishes had visited our ancestors, we traded our most kept secret to gain our human forms. The location of the Elders' Enclave was taken from us when we made our trade. They ones who made the deal knew that the dark angels trained there and were powerful enough to take out any creature just by touching them."

"So, you are the protectors of the Elders?" Sova turned to the dark angel, "And you have seen them and been there?"

Cynthia nodded. "Every dark angel gets to meet the Elders. If you pass the test, that's another story."

"Test?" Sova and Nadi asked at the same time.

"Another time," Daron said as he eyed Nadi. "We must keep these secrets from everyone. No one must ever know that we had once guarded the Elders, or that Nadi can change into a dragon."

"Or speak in any of my forms," Nadi stated. "I know."

"What will happen to Icarri or the Sorcerer Thorn?" Cynthia asked, observing Daron.

Nadi noticed that he didn't jump in at the mention of their names when he was relaying his tale.

"Ah…the Sorcerer Thorn," he mumbled, seeming to think hard.

Nadi was just about to ask something when his mind suddenly went blank. The name and face of the person escaped him. It was almost as though the conversation they were having just vanished from his mind.

Cynthia jumped up in a frantic state, "What were we just talking about?"

"I don't remember," Nadi mumbled.

Daron shrugged and looked to one of the guards, "Gage, what were we talking about?"

He shrugged as well. "I remember you told Nadi to keep a secret, and the dark angel said something about those who locked you up. Then everything became a fog in my mind. I can't remember exactly what was said."

Cynthia gripped her clawed hand. "They put a chain spell on Daron! When he repeated what we said, he immediately forgot it as well as us. Whatever we said must have been very important."

"So if we repeat it, will we forget it?" Nadi asked as he tapped the walking stick against the floor.

"No," Cynthia was lost in thought. "It only works once unless cast again."

The young shifter smiled," Then Kiran would know what was so important."

"Nadi!" Cynthia walked up to him and grabbed his shoulders. "You're a genius! Kiran would know!"

Nadi glanced at her blackened hand, and she released him with a look of embarrassment. He didn't want to make her feel bad for having dark magic in her hand. As he opened his mouth to say something, Daron stood beside Cynthia. He extended a hand to him, "Now that we have everything settled, why not celebrate with us by announcing a new city?"

"City?" Sova looked to his friend.

"Yes!" The Dragon King helped Nadi to his feet. "To protect your people, we must come together to form a city, and we shall be kings."

Cynthia wrapped an arm around Nadi to support him as they began leaving the room, "Sorry, you may feel better after the sun goes down. Broken bones take a little more time to heal."

"But don't you have until sunset?" Nadi asked, concerned.

Cynthia smiled at him, "Then I guess we make the last moments the best."

By the time Nadi limped to the great hall, several shifters stood in the keep's entryway. They eyed the dragon guards as though expecting a fight. The guards simply stood at attention. Modra entered from another hall and ran to Sova. They embraced as tears of joy streamed down their faces. The chieftain kissed his wife passionately.

Daron cleared his throat, causing them to part. He looked over the crowd that had gathered.

"Thank you all for helping us defend our home. I wanted to apologize for the years that we had spent apart.

My disappearance caused my brother to lash out and close off the keep to anyone. You were wrongly blamed for my disappearance." One of the shifters coughed in the moment of silence. "Today, I want to reward the bravery of your tribe. Nadi had found me and did not stop fighting until I had returned home. Most of you traveled here expecting to fight us, from the looks of it, but rescued us instead. The reward we came to terms with is to build a city, bringing our two kinds together to create Naga-Phooka."

The crowd began to murmur. One of the Oldens looked to Sova and asked, "What about our traditions? We keep the path to three of the four keeps."

Another spoke up. "Why should we trust them? They locked us up for years!"

Sova looked around for a moment, then grabbed the staff that Nadi was holding onto. Tapping the walking stick on the stone ground, the room was silenced. "I want this back," his father whispered as he released it. Turning to the crowd, his voice echoed through the hall. "Are those thoughts that our people should have? Look at where we came from. Cast out of the Elders' garden because we listened to the trickster god and ended up here. We were once servants to the Elders. Why can't we live like royalty or damn near it? Do we not deserve better?" Nadi watched as the people cheered and agreed. A few still looked unconvinced, including the Oldens. "We still honor the trickster in memory as we keep his name. For tomorrow, we shall build our home in this desert we were cast into, while hoping that someday we'll be able to return to our true home. Until then, we shall live among dragons and build a city meant for peace. And tonight we will learn what it means to celebrate among those who were once our enemies."

The room lit up with cheers. Even dragons joined; some of them had brought out platters of food and drinks.

Daron leaned towards Sova. "Maybe I should put you in charge of the speeches?"

They both laughed, and it made Nadi smile. Cynthia drew his attention by tapping his side. She forced a smile. "We should go for a walk."

As he took a step, his mother touched his shoulder and hugged him."I'm so proud of you."

"How is Zec?" he had been worried about him since the battle. He didn't know what would be missing or blackened by the magic.

His mother shook her head. "He is still sleeping. It might take a day or two for him to recover."

Cynthia tugged again, and he nodded, "I'm going to slip out for a moment to say goodbye."

"Oh, is she leaving?" She smoothed back a strand of her hair, and it reminded him of the last time they were together.

"Sort of," he replied. "You and Father have a lot to catch up on." He walked with the dark angel out of the keep.

The sun was just above the dunes on the horizon. Nadi felt terrible, slowing her down. She didn't have much time left.

"So, what is the plan to get the Princess back?" she asked as they took the steps of the keep, one at a time.

"I guess I can fly across the ocean and hunt down her scent from the Ravenous Splinter."

She laughed, "There is an easier way, young guide." Placing her hand in the center of his chest, she said, "You can feel a connection to her. It's almost like a pull, leading you in the right direction."

"Oh," Nadi thought for a moment. "How will I know the feeling?"

"You just will." She released him.

He tested his pace on the steps by himself. It didn't hurt as much. He still needed the staff, though.

"So, do you like the Princess?" she pried.

Nadi tested his ability to take the steps a little quicker. "Well, she was whiny and cried a lot when we met, but I sort of miss her now." In his mind, he could see the sun shining off her blonde hair and remember her sweet scent.

"Are you going to court her now?" Cynthia grinned.

"What?" He stopped at the last step. "Why would I do that?"

Her grin widened. "Because you are now a prince. How do you think you are going to get close enough to be her guide?"

"A prince?" Nadi missed a step. "But I'm to be exiled?"

Shaking her head, she looked towards the dune. "I don't think your father will exile a hero."

They walked towards the statue as he tried to think up a way to change the subject. "So...there were really ten Elders?"

"There were. The Abandreal Elder was exiled by the trickster god's misdeeds." Cynthia seemed sad as she thought about it. "Dart was an Abandreal. He was so rebellious against those who sought to enslave his kind. Always talking about how he knew their Elder would not wish that upon anyone. I wonder if he is still out there, somewhere."

Nadi noticed that the sun was almost gone and decided to ask about the object she created. "What does the statue do?"

She glanced at her glass creation, "It is a compass. If you touch it and ask it a question, it will guide you to finding the answer."

Nadi eyed it as they got close enough to touch it. "Not as convenient as having something pocket-sized."

"Says the Prince of the Sands," she laughed as she ran her fingers across it. "I can't use it, though." Cynthia watched as the last rays began to vanish over the horizon. "Looks like our time is up." She turned back to him. "Promise me one thing. That you'll get the Princess to the Temple before her time runs out."

Suddenly, fear gripped Nadi as he realized that Kiran could die. His blood seemed to run cold at the thought of never seeing her again. He didn't want to lose anyone. "I promise."

"Also, when you see her. You should tell her how you feel." She smiled as the last light of the sky faded. "Well, this is goodbye..." Her body became transparent. "Until we meet again."

"Until we meet again." Nadi watched as Cynthia shimmered.

And then she was gone.

For the first time since Nadi began his journey, he found himself alone. He touched the statue's smooth surface, happy that he was no longer on the run from anything. To be able to rest was a relief. He no longer cared for the ale he once drank, or for forgetting the past. Nadi accepted the past and knew that nothing could be changed.

He thought about what Cynthia had said about Dart. She couldn't use the statue, and his curiosity was nagging at him. He had to know, just in case he saw her again.

"Where is Dart?" he asked the statue.

Several voices talking at once replied to Nadi in his mind: *You'll find the one you seek with the creature of wishes.*

The creature of wishes was said to grant almost anything, but it did have its price. It could be that Dart had his wish granted. There was no telling what he had asked for, though. And there was no point in dwelling on it.

Walking towards the tribes' tents, Nadi relished in the feeling of the sand under his feet. Kicking some of it in the air, he was happy to be home and ready for the well-needed rest on his pallet. Locating his tent, he pushed the flap open, placing the walking stick against the wall, and lay down upon the pillows. It was good to be home.

Almost instantly, sleep seemed to find him as well as his dreams. For the first time in years, he didn't dream about being a child in the darkness. Instead, he was a man in the fog. Looking around, Nadi saw that water surrounded him.

Through the mist appeared a figure he recognized. Cynthia smiled at him. She wore the black dress that he had first seen her in. Her hair and clothing seemed to flow about her with a magical breeze of their own. Nadi smiled back, knowing that his next journey was about to begin.

To be continued.